ROB COUTEAU is a writer and visual artist from Brooklyn whose publications have been praised in *Midwest Book Review*, *Publishers Weekly*, *Evergreen Review*, *Witty Partition*, and the *New Art Examiner*. His work is cited in books such as *Ghetto Images in Twentieth-Century American Literature* by Tyrone Simpson, *Gabriel Garcia Marquez's 'Love in the Time of Cholera'* by Thomas Fahy, *Conversations with Ray Bradbury* edited by Steven Aggelis, and David Cohen's *Forgotten Millions*, a book about the homeless. His interviews include conversations with Pulitzer Prize-winning author Justin Kaplan, *Last Exit to Brooklyn* novelist Hubert Selby, Simon & Schuster editor Michael Korda, LSD discoverer Albert Hofmann, Picasso's model and muse Sylvette David, sci-fi author Ray Bradbury, film star and bibliophile Neil Pearson, and historian Philip Willan, author *Puppetmasters: The Political Use of Terrorism in Italy*. In 1985 he won the North American Essay Award, sponsored by the American Humanist Association. He has appeared as a guest on Bob Barrett's The Best of Our Knowledge (WAMC), Len Osanic's Black Op Radio, and on Monocle 24 in Europe.

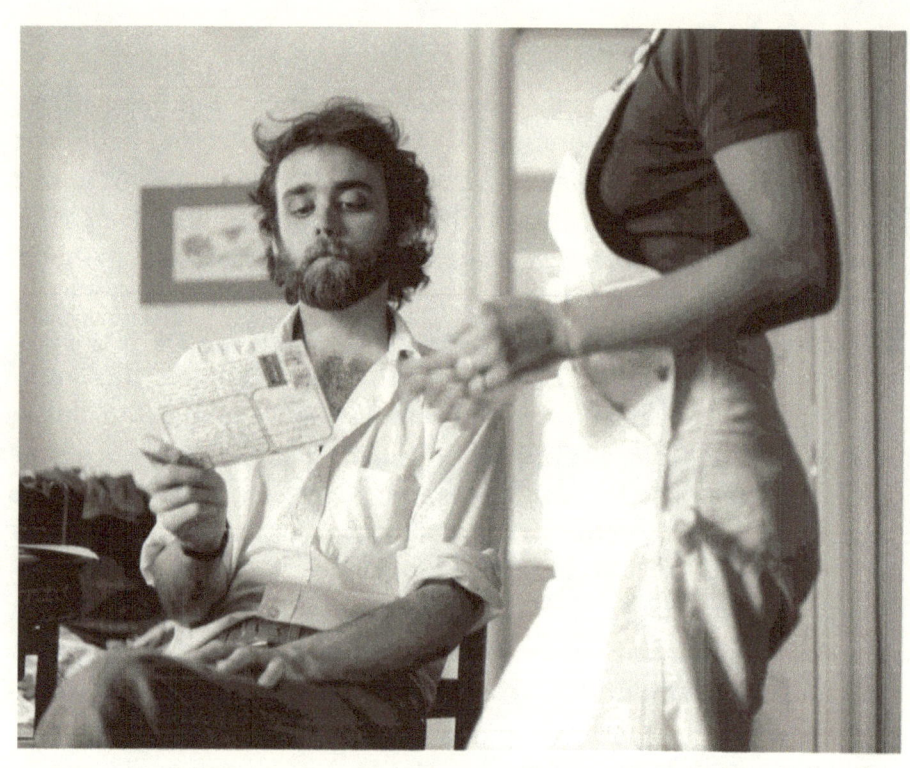

Rob Couteau in Gravesend, Brooklyn circa 1979

Intimate Souvenirs

Intimate Souvenirs

Rob Couteau

Introduction by
Robert Roper

Afterword by
Christopher Sawyer-Lauçanno

DOMINANTSTAR

ISBN 978-1-7360049-5-1

This book is a memoir composed from personal experience. Although it reflects the author's best recollection, "Memory is a fickle muse." Events have been compressed, and some dialogue has been recreated. To protect the privacy of certain individuals, names and identifying details have been changed.

Thanks to Sylvette David, Ed Foster, Tanya Gaitanis, Jim Lampos, Jessica Manley, Bobbie Marks, Robert Roper, Christopher Sawyer-Lauçanno, Scott Sublett, and Yongzhen Zhang.

Excerpts have appeared in the following publications.
– *Talisman: A Journal of Contemporary Poetry and Poetics* (2023): "Rosebud," *"La Belle Noiseuse,"* "Teaching Little Dybbuks in the Lion's Den."
– *Talisman* (2020): "The Cantankerous Krishnamurti."
– *Talisman* (2019): "Crawling King Snake."
– *From Somewhere to Nowhere: The End of the American Dream.* (Anthology). New York: Autonomedia (2017): An excerpt from the chapter, "Freddie and the Mobsters."
– *Talisman* (2017): Excerpts from various chapters.

Cover photo: Frances Boyle Couteau, circa 1916.

RobCouteau.com

10 9 8 7 6 5 4 3 2 4

Contents

Sylvette David. "Mont Ventoux Still Life – Bowl of Cherries."
Watercolor on Langton watercolor paper. 16 x 20 inches.
(Collection of Rob Couteau.)

Introduction by Robert Roper

Here we have a new, possibly classic memoir of New York. It begins in Gravesend, Brooklyn, and moves outward, to Manhattan and Paris. Its central character, the writer who has done this creating, starts at the beginning (not the "moocow that was coming down along the road" of *Portrait of the Artist*, but on Day 1 of kindergarten at St. Anne's, the local site of Catholic youth imprisonment). Soon we are deep in the family drama as well, Rob Couteau's parents and uncle Byron and grandmother Mammie and others arranging themselves according to psychic forces that the future writer labors to understand. The first thing to say about this family is that it is not horrifically screwed up and soul-murdering, but only moderately, intriguingly screwy; it is a human unit rich with love and indifference and insight and misunderstanding, the young hero taking life anew as all children must, working to figure it out by way of these totemic figures.

Being right up close to his loved ones – never really alienated from them, in the sense of feeling superior – Couteau is free to judge robustly. In particular he judges his father, Arthur, a social worker who doesn't seem to have had much fun, who, according to Couteau, was "annoyed by life." Every evening he checked out behind a copy of the *Times*, pretty much missing out on his growing son. This is not the birth of a "wound" in that son, but rather the start of a long struggle to comprehend, to resist, to work out a counter-philosophy.

The aforementioned Byron, a New York cop who lived in their basement, is a charismatic alternative. Sensing artistic tendencies in his nephew and not inclined to make fun of them, Byron brings the six year-old a fascinating gift on a snowy day, a paint-by-the-numbers kit. It includes "a sable-haired brush, numbered tins of pigment, a small vial of linseed oil, and a canvas board" with the outline of Emmett Kelly on it. They spread out some newspaper and young Picasso goes to it, magically transforming the outline into a colorful clown as the fragrances from the pigments get up his nose. We have here, incidentally, not just a sudden bloom of fun and love, but the introduction of an unfussy attitude toward art. Couteau goes on to paint for the rest of his life, ever at home in art, transformed by its study and practice.

His portrait of Bridget, his mother, is equally radiant. James McBride's mother in *The Color of Water* comes to mind – both Couteau and McBride write of mother-love *with* love, their mothers' force of personality a tremendous gift to them, not a worrying diminishment, and Couteau's mother, like McBride's, is quietly heroic (if not so sorely beset as McBride's, the Jewish mother of twelve children by a black minister in Red Hook). Couteau's Bridget is warm and ever on the same wavelength as her son, whose life in consequence is rich in comfortable encounters with girls and women, frank fascination with them, and later, many love affairs.

Reading this book in 2022, one keeps thinking, though, "He can't be writing that, can he? Oh, my god, they're going to hand him his head for this," so out of favor are straightforward accounts of heterosexual experience from a male perspective. Just a few short decades since the heyday of Mailer, Updike, and Roth, the Great Male Narcissists, as David Foster Wallace called them, have been not only dethroned but largely expunged, and the salted earth of their once-vast literary realm has given rise to … practically nothing. The leading male novelists of an ensuing generation – think of Wallace himself, or Jonathan Franzen, or Michael Chabon – do many things well, but they are not to any degree sexual buccaneers, or even very sexy.

Which is all to the good! We are so much the better for it, aren't we! Feminist scholar Katie Roiphe, in her famous essay "The Naked and the Conflicted," registers serious regret, however, daring to re-read the dead masters and falling again under the spell of their outrageousness. Yes, there was misogyny, yes there was solipsism and a gleeful going too far – but for Roiphe there is something messily exciting about the now-dishonored works, which reminds her of the mess and thrill of sex itself. The post-1960 *Lady Chatterley* decision books exhibited a juicy joy in sex, something she finds sadly missing now – indeed, the latest generation of novelists with big reputations is prissily ambivalent about sex, she argues: "Rather than an interest in ... consummation, there is an obsessive fascination with [their own] trepidation, and with a convoluted, post-feminist second-guessing."

I have no idea whether Couteau has read or even heard of Roiphe. This whole arena of concern, sex as neurotic minefield or honeyed meadow of visionary orgasms, seems not to be on his screen. That doesn't mean he isn't well-read. On the evidence of this memoir, I would not bet against his having read any book of worth of the last five hundred years. He adduces a large literary culture on almost every page, and to an unusual degree seems to have found his way in literature on his own, by a kind of instinct. Possibly his dry relationship with his father led him to Whitman, moist father-figure extraordinaire, or it might only have been that Walt was also from Brooklyn, as was Henry Miller, Couteau's other principal progenitor, a sort of rogue uncle.

From Miller he got elements of his characteristic tone, a comic tone bubbling with amused outrage; St. Anne's gave him an early dose of oppressive absurdities to kick back at, but a reader notices the precise characterizations of the teaching sisters who year after year abused, terrified, bored, and enlightened his class of Irish and Italian kids. The kids come in for character sketching as transformative, as colorful, as that of the paint-by-the-numbers clown. I hesitate to quote because the verve of Couteau's writing is not usually in short phrases, but rather in the cadence of whole scenes, but here's one from the Cuban Missile Crisis, when Couteau and his fellow first-graders have been marched into the basement cafeteria, recently declared a bomb shelter:

> We were instructed to chant Hail Marys ... At first, we were seated at the sagging masonite folding tables, which always smelled of sour milk. Then we were lined up beside the cinderblock walls, beneath the louvered windows ... Crouching with my classmates ... I recalled how, during our first day at school, Mike Arena had cracked a joke, and Nicky Panatela had laughed so hard that the milk he was drinking from a cardboard carton ran through his nostrils ... Meanwhile a boy named George Costello had grown so terrified of St. Anne's ... that he refused to even nibble on his liverwurst sandwich ... Then he burst out crying. The nuns belted him a few times ...

Another quick scene, from Robert Kennedy's 1964 Senatorial campaign:

> Bridget volunteered to bring us to see "Bobby," and the three of us took off, with much excitement ... soon the crowd – which wasn't entirely sympathetic to the Democratic Civil Rights agenda – began to swell. The audience was also growing restless because Bobby was stuck somewhere in traffic

... Finally Paul O'Dwyer, a platinum-haired pol who'd emigrated from Ireland, took to the stage and wove his magic over the surging mass of Brooklynites ... Bridget and I were only a few feet to O'Dwyer's left ... when a rotten egg sailed over the swarming mass, headed directly toward O'Dwyer. At the last possible moment he calmly shifted a few inches to the side, and it smashed against a wall ...

It's that shift, and the sound, a few seconds later, when "the klieg lights were turned on with a soft *pop*," that bring everything into focus.

Also from Henry Miller comes the overall plot of Couteau's life. Early years in Brooklyn, not Miller's Williamsburg but that "rearguard Sicilian ghetto," Gravesend, a "grimy hellhole," according to Couteau, down whose "mean, racist pavements" Couteau's liberal family sometimes walked as if in enemy territory (but that Couteau depicts as a kind of paradise for an adventurous boy); birth of an artistic temperament, a writerly vocation; determination – because no other way was viable for him – to take on the sackcloth of the aspirant writer, head for Paris if he could ever get a few bucks together. In his pre-Paris years he was part of a crew of charming hustlers filming interviews for public-access TV; a substitute teacher with a scary black beard; a construction worker; a linoleum installer in the East Village, working for his landlord, a made guy named Freddie; and a psychiatric caseworker at the Walt Whitman Asylum, where psychopathic schizophrenics were housed.

With no training to speak of, Couteau undertakes to minister to these gravely ill people. He applies for the job out of economic necessity, "carrying an empty briefcase as a prop" and feeling "strangely at home" the first time he arrives at the "seven-story building [with] gray brick facade" and "leafless, skeletal trees that stood gaunt and Edgar Allen Poe-like ... gripping a fluttering pair of pink bloomers ... and a faded orange hat."

He has read most of Jung's collected works. But it was "perhaps for the best" that during his interview with the professional staff he "avoided any discussion of their more esoteric contents," and for reasons of equally dire need on the part of the institution, perhaps, is quickly given the job. In the extraordinary pages that follow, Couteau the youth and Couteau the author come into surprising maturity, his quickness to see into people and to judge situations by his own lights serving him well, inoculating him against hopelessness, and making him a game interlocutor for these patients, whose disordered self-presentations often move him.

Not quite thirty, he is well-equipped to make sense of such a situation; it isn't his reading of Jung so much as his whole enterprise of self-creation, his long readings whither-he-may, in a spirit of hunger for useful knowledge. This is what has prepared him to sit patiently while picking out traces of meaning from madly disordered stories. Jung and the Buddhist sages, plus assorted novelists and poets and philosophers, attend him as he works; when a fellow caseworker, a Franciscan brother, approaches him because of a disturbing dream full of sexual images, Couteau's well-stocked, cross-indexed mind gives him a tale from *Report to Greco*, in which another man of the cloth is tormented by an encounter with a half-clothed woman. Kazantzakis is a major source for Couteau. The Greek author's pursuit of "seers, saints, and sages" models an essential activity for Couteau, a sort of intellectual pilgrimaging, although he draws the line at Kazantzakis' enthusiasm for Nietzsche: "Nikos is moved by the ramblings of Friedrich Nietzsche ... whereas I myself prefer to read Nietzsche simply to absorb his mad passion: his exultant, overblown enthusiasm and vituperative contempt … if you scan through a work such as *Ecce Homo*, even if you only read the chapter headings, Nietzsche is always good for a few vivifying laughs: *Why I am the greatest philosopher; Why I am the wisest sage; Why all men are mere shitpiles as compared to Nietzsche* … and so on."

Here are a few other talismans / reference points / possible influences: Brendan Behan's *Borstal Boy*, from 1958; Frank Conroy's *Stop-Time*, 1967; Tobias Wolff's *This Boy's Life*, 2007; *My Life and Loves*, by Frank Harris; *Just Kids*, by Patti Smith; *Bronx Boy*, by Jerome Charyn; plus various works of Rimbaud, Basho, Blake, Céline, and Hubert Selby, Jr. A writer's memoir little known to Americans, but for my money one of the most powerful of the 20th century, Xavier Herbert's *Disturbing Element* (1958), shadows Couteau's work, seeming almost to predict it; early in his book, Herbert writes:

> My very first memory is of being on a beach, watching my father and my half-brother and half-sister sporting in the sea. That's all there is to it, except a feeling of detachment … Such perception in a tiny child (I could have been no more than three) might be thought incredible. But without allowing for it in any child, how account for life-long memory of seemingly trivial things? My theory is that preoccupation with the puzzle of all puzzles, the riddle of the reality of one's own existence, begins with the very dawning of awareness, and that lasting memory is always concerned with it.

Whether or not he read Herbert, Couteau, too, builds his memoir from such indelible memory printouts, his own puzzle of puzzles becoming to some extent our own.

At thirty, Couteau is ready to play out the next act of his life-schema, launching himself, à la Miller, Paris-ward, without money or connections or French. To see how he overcomes stern prohibitions against non-EU citizens working in France, and how he turns a few book reviews written stateside into bankable French literary credentials, read on. The story is amusing and richly rendered. That there still exists a path to a writer's life that is not a dutiful march through creative writing academies, with perhaps the apotheosis of becoming a teacher of yet more academy-shaped writers, is heartening to learn. Couteau does not make fun of that approach nor of any other, but he does model something much different, and to see him continuing to write books like this one, which well deserves a place on his already considerable shelf of valued books, is excellent news.

A widely published novelist and former professor at John Hopkins University, Robert Roper is the author of *Nabokov in America: On the Road to Lolita*. The recipient of several awards for works of fiction and nonfiction, Roper's *Fatal Mountaineer*, a biography of the climber-philosopher Willi Unsoeld, won the 2002 Boardman Tasker Prize; and his *Now the Drum of War: Walt Whitman and His Brothers in the Civil War* was an Editor's Choice pick in the *New York Times Book Review*. Roper's journalism has appeared in the *New York Times*, *Los Angeles Times*, *National Geographic*, *Outside*, and numerous other publications.

For Marge Couteau

"The gods who love, at the same time they hate."
– Pier Paolo Pasolini, *Medea*

"If, when you get to be a man, you know these two things, poetry and the science of extinguishing wounds, then you *will* be a man."
– Jean Giono, *Blue Boy*

"It's when you think you're least free that you're sometimes the most completely so. And you aren't at all free when you feel you have giant's wings which stop you from walking."
– Picasso

Gravesend

I wash my hands at a sink in the boys' bathroom, then turn to a kid next to me and ask: "Do you realize that we have *eight more years of this?*" I was only five years old, but already I was counting the days of imprisonment at St. Anne's Elementary School.

As with any other prison, the occupants were expected to wear matching uniforms, for individuality was not to be tolerated. Donning red crisscross neckties, white button-down blouses, and ultramarine plaid skirts, the girls provoked many an idle daydream among their male counterparts in the years ahead. Of course, hemlines were supposed to remain below the knee; and any girl foolish enough to disobey would be walloped by one of the nuns bearing a long wooden pointer, which hung from a hook at the front of the room, next to an American flag.

Seated beside the girls in alternating rows, the boys were stuffed into navy-blue trousers and starched white shirts with clip-on ties. As soon as the final bell rang, we were marched in single file down the stairs and out into the street, where we tore off our ties in a triumphant gesture of surviving yet another torturous day under the icy glare of those pathological Roman Catholic "sisters."

How I survived so many cheerless mornings and afternoons I'll never know. *Eight more years!* I envisioned each grade as a rung on a ladder that was stationed at the hub of a Dantesque circle of hell. One had to mount each rung before escaping over a wall, but it required a full year to ascend to each respective level.

The first was lorded over by Sister Anastasia, a broad-shouldered wraith whose temperament alternated between the beatific and demonic. Since I was a year younger than most of my classmates (having been born in November, I was only four years old when I was first enrolled), I remained that much more gullible. Thus, I quickly fell prey to one of her threats.

We'd just completed a long, tedious, insufferable math lesson, and now we were growing restless – as boys and girls often do when trapped like beasts in a cage. Perhaps fearing that her control over the class was about to slip away, Anastasia's benign regard quickly transformed into an ugly grimace, and she screeched: "If you don't calm down, you'll spend *the rest of your life in here!*"

In other words, we'd have to remain there for an extra hour after school. But due to my overactive imagination I took her literally, and now I was convinced that I'd be stuck in this dreary dungeon for all eternity – so I burst out crying.

Anastasia suddenly stopped screaming and approached my desk. And along with my classmates, who began to circle round my chair, she did her best to reassure me that we'd eventually return home! But it took a while to convince me that it was all, indeed, a hoax.

* * *

On October 23, 1962, our penmanship lesson was cut short when President John F. Kennedy became embroiled in the Cuban Missile Crisis. The TV broadcasters said that a historic "tipping point" had been reached after the president ordered the navy to enter the Caribbean and "draw a line in the sand" by refusing to allow Russian ships to pass, stocked as they were with nuclear warheads for their Cuban ally.

So now we were told to put away our fountain pens since the end of the world might be imminent. The stalemate in the Atlantic seemed to be escalating into a full-scale nuclear confrontation between the Super Powers, with their brilliant policy of "mutually assured destruction," or "MAD." While the Joint Chiefs of Staff – those rabidly hawkish leaders of the U.S. military – continued to pressure the president into launching a "preemptive nuclear strike," Kennedy held firm to his conviction that such an idea was insane.

Unbeknownst to anyone in the U.S. government, there were already 162 fully operational nuclear warheads in Cuba. If Kennedy had listened to the "brass hats" and attacked, the result would have been an apocalypse. What the Joint Chiefs also didn't realize was that JFK had opened a secret channel of communication with Soviet Premier Khrushchev, via Russian Ambassador Anatoly Dobrynin.

"The president is in a grave situation," the president's brother Robert told Dobrynin, "and he does not know how to get out of it…. In fact, we are under pressure from our military to use force against Cuba…. Even though the president himself is very much against starting a war over Cuba, an irreversible chain of events could occur against his will. That is why the president is appealing directly to Chairman Khrushchev for his help in liquidating this conflict. If the situation continues much longer, the president is not sure that the military will not overthrow him and seize power."

Prescient words, especially considering what would come to pass on November 22, 1963.

Fortunately, Khrushchev had begun his secret correspondence with President Kennedy the year before, thus skirting round JFK's military advisers. It was due to this discreet thawing of personal relations that the Soviet leader now made a startling remark to his Foreign Minister, Andrei Gromyko: "We have to let Kennedy know that we want to help him. Yes, *help*. We now have a common cause, to save the world from those pushing us toward war."

Although the American media liked to portray Khrushchev as a raving maniac, he played a pivotal role in saving the world from its most dangerous moment. As Khrushchev later told Norman Cousins (an American journalist and peace activist, who had served as an intermediary between the two world leaders):

> The Chinese say I was scared. Of course I was scared. It would have been insane not to have been scared. I was frightened about what could happen to my country – or your country and all the other countries that would have been devastated by a nuclear war. If being frightened meant that I helped avert such insanity, then I'm glad I was frightened. One of the problems in the world today is that not enough people are sufficiently frightened by the danger of nuclear war.

But before the crisis was resolved, one by one, our classrooms were emptied, and we were marched along the corridors while the nuns fingered their rosary beads or clutched the iron crosses that dangled on chains from their spooky, crow-black habits. As we descended the musty stairwells and headed to a basement cafeteria that was now designated as a fallout shelter, we were instructed to chant Hail Marys with a mechanical precision.

At first, we were seated at the sagging masonite folding tables, which always smelled of sour milk. Then we were lined up beside the cinderblock walls, beneath the louvered windows that faced the schoolyard. As Khrushchev had phrased it so eloquently: "The smell of burning hung in the air."

Crouching with my classmates at the base of a wall, I recalled how, during our first day at school, Mike Arena had cracked a joke, and Nicky Panatela had laughed so hard that the milk he was drinking from a cardboard carton ran through his nostrils and down his chin. Meanwhile, a boy named George Costello had grown so terrified of St. Anne's military regimen that he refused to even nibble on his liverwurst sandwich in this loveless concentration camp of a cafeteria. Then he burst out crying. The nuns belted him a few times, but for some reason this didn't help to calm him. Instead, he grew even more hysterical, so his mother finally came and carted him away.

It was the last we ever saw of the poor devil. But who knows, maybe *we* were the unlucky ones and Georgie was blessed, for he was the only prisoner who'd managed to escape. I vividly recalled his oily black hair, swarthy skin, and the terrified look in his tender eyes. It was as if a shark had just ripped off an arm or a leg and was now threatening to remove an even bigger chunk from his bottom, and soon there would be nothing left of Georgie, so he was screaming and sobbing for dear life – but where was his Savior?

In the months after he vanished, while seated in the cafeteria with my tin lunch box embossed with a picture of Davy Crockett, I'd often think of Georgie while eating an enormous sandwich. My favorite was a double-decker roast beef, stuffed with juicy tomatoes that came from our Brooklyn backyard, and with everything slathered in plenty of mayonnaise. For dessert I'd bite into a shiny red apple or munch on a chocolate-chip cookie that Bridget, my dear mother, had prepared with love and affection. Absorbed by such alimentary musings, little did I realize the gravity of it all as we practiced our fallout drills along with millions of other children around the world during this precarious October.

Although the nuns had instructed us to cower beneath our desks or to squat beside the wall, they never once explained what good this would do, since a nuclear blast would level everything in sight. But our role was not to question why. Instead, we were trained in the art of blind belief. Perhaps the Holy Spirit knew something that we had yet to learn.

Crouched with our heads between our knees, our palms over our ears, and our eyes shut tight, we passively absorbed Sister Anastasia's latest admonition: *Boys and girls, the most important thing to remember is: Don't go near the windows!* With this sage advice we were assured that everything would turn out fine and dandy ... until the streets were bombarded with radioactivity and engulfed in flame.

Shifting back and forth in my patent leather shoes while the nuns led us in prayer (an exercise that was so tedious that I only pretended to be praying while silently mouthing the words), my mind continued to drift until, once again, I was in the back seat of my father's 1956 Chevy as we wended our way to Uncle Pat's ranch-style house in suburban New Jersey. To get there you had to drive along the Jersey Turnpike, which cut through an interminable stretch of pungent oil refineries. Row upon row of gleaming metallic chimneys scorched the heavens with plumes of iridescent red, yellow, and blue flame. This sickening chemical stink was so putrid that my father, Arthur, would announce in a loud, stentorian tone: *Roll up the windows!* But the fumes would filter into the car anyway, even after the windows were sealed shut; and then suddenly it hit us, and we felt like puking.

Now, all this raced through my mind as a result of trying to envisage a post-apocalyptic world, for this horrific jaunt along the eerily flaming Turnpike was the closest that my juvenile imagination could come to what the nuns had hinted at with such foreboding.

Four years after Kennedy's assassination, it was over this same piping hot, petroleum-fouled horizon that President Johnson and Soviet Premier Alexei Kosygin would each travel – as if they were taking a joyride on their way to a summit in Glassboro, New Jersey. But the Americans had specifically chosen this route because they were secretly trying to impress upon Kosygin that all of America is like this: dotted with heavy industry and crisscrossed with countless refineries. *And Alexei, my boy, Sputnik or no Sputnik, you'll never catch up with our good ole air-conditioned nightmare!*

As a result of the Cuban Missile Crisis, mail-order fallout shelters were back in vogue, and you could even build one in your own backyard. Some were stocked with a year's supply of dried food so that you could hunker down and sit it out; for radiation will eventually dissipate, just you wait and see.

The radiation symbol consisted of an interlocking trinity of yellow triangles starkly imposed on an ivory-black background. The image was engraved on metal signs that suddenly appeared on high-rise buildings all throughout our neighborhood in Gravesend. And it meant that, in case of a nuclear debacle, please enter this building, for the basement is a government approved and federally inspected fallout shelter. You'll be safe here, unless of course your neighbor decides to scratch out your eyeballs or slice your throat while the world is bathed in a phosphorescent conflagration.

The summer before the assassination, concerned that children around the world were consuming milk rife with radioactive isotopes such as strontium-90, President Kennedy had signed the Limited Nuclear Test Ban Treaty. Just before the signing, about fifty members of Women Strike for Peace, a widely respected antinuke group, had assembled in front of the White House to signal their approval. The president's wife,

Jacqueline, delivered coffee and donuts to the women as one of Kennedy's aides informed the group that the president wanted to thank them for their support.

Small wonder that he was assassinated; for now we could return once again to the Cold War, with its booming business of armaments and fallout "shelters."

* * *

Our parish church was built the same year as the Eiffel Tower, in 1889, and it was shaped into a tall narrow rectangle with a towering steeple. According to our gray-haired Irish pastor – a former navy chaplain who, decades later, would be accused of child abuse – it resembled a boat turned upside down, thus symbolizing a vessel that was leading us to some sort of inverted "salvation."

Within this lugubrious structure I wasted so many precious Sunday mornings, dressed to the nines and seated beside my parents in a long wooden pew, while a Latin mass was intoned with sonorous, hermetic phrasing. In chapels off to the side, hundreds of candles flickered in sooty glass jars, while up in the balcony a choir chanted along with the piping notes of an antique fluted organ. But to my young artist's eyes, the cathedral's most impressive feature was its finely crafted stained glass, which cast a panoply of rich, shimmering colors across our flesh as we hovered between the deities of boredom and wonder.

One cold February night, the church caught fire and was burnt to the ground. The priceless stained glass was now reduced to a glittering pile of rubble. Something indescribably beautiful, which I'd always imagined would last forever, was no more.

The word on the street was that a handful of boys had

broken in and accidentally started a fire by tossing around lit matches. But we later learned that the Mafia had paid those boys to set the blaze so that a Mob-controlled construction crew could be handed a lucrative contract to build a new cathedral: one constructed with the Mob's favorite overpriced commodity, concrete.

To finance the new building a fundraising effort was set into motion, and the parish inducted the students to serve as its flunkies. We were told to scour the neighborhood in order to sell raffle tickets, magazine subscriptions, and expensive, deluxe candy. The nuns encouraged us to regard it as a sort of Darwinian competition: those who unloaded the most raffle tickets would be held in highest esteem, while the others would be shamed for their inferior efforts.

Day after day, the boys and girls were forced to reveal how many raffles they'd pawned off on their neighbors or extended Sicilian families, whose patriarchs nipped at this bait and, with a macho flair, reached into their working-class trousers to proudly unroll a wad of cash so that little Tony Formosa or Antoinette Regario could be regaled as a topnotch seller. But my father wouldn't hear of such nonsense, so he refused to buy more than a single ticket.

When the nuns pinned up oaktag charts that revealed the number of raffles we'd sold, I was chagrined to see my name lingering near the bottom. But then Arthur's older brother, Byron, who lived in the basement of our house on West Twelfth Street, came through for me by purchasing two entire books of raffles so that I wouldn't have to go to school empty-handed. I can still picture his broad smile and handsome oval face as he exclaimed: "One book for me, and one for you!" The winner would receive a thousand dollars, and whoever sold the winning ticket would walk away with a record player, which was built into an elegantly designed console cabinet.

Low and behold, when they announced the winner it was Byron. He pocketed the prize money while I won the stereo, which my mother installed in our living room. I would later listen to my first rock 'n' roll records while seated on the parquet floor between the speakers.

Byron used the cash to help finance his marriage to a woman named Rona, an emotionally unbalanced chain-smoker from Dallas. Since Rona was unable to bear children, she and a previous husband had adopted a girl named Laura from an orphanage in New Orleans. But when Rona's husband died from a heart attack, she'd conveniently sent Laura back to the orphanage – an experience that must have wreaked havoc upon the poor girl's soul.

Just as Byron had rescued a small black terrier from being abandoned on the street and had adopted it as our beloved pet, I wondered if he'd married Rona just so that this lost little girl – a strikingly beautiful redhead with luminous green eyes – could come in out of the cold. But instead of being grateful to Byron, like a lowering, sinister cloud Laura soon augured nothing but trouble.

Several months after Byron had married and moved away, one day he returned to West Twelfth Street accompanied by this ill-fated ménage. While the adults were chatting over drinks, Laura sidled up to me, seductively pursed her lips, and whispered, "Come on, let's go for a walk!"

We rounded a corner at the end of the block, where Laura paused before an old-fashioned fire-alarm pole and asked, "What's this?"

"A fire alarm."

"How does it work?"

"You open the cover and yank down the handle."

To my astonishment – and without a moment's hesitation – she reached out and pulled it.

A screeching, ear-splitting alarm went off, and we ran away – as fast as our little legs could carry us.

That evening, when I told Arthur about the alarm, instead of blowing a gasket he just wearily shook his head. Perhaps he already knew that Laura would prove to be an albatross.

* * *

A part of Byron's playful spirit remained behind in the incarnation of Sparky: the mutt that he'd rescued from the barren, inhospitable streets and that soon became my most treasured childhood companion.

One evening when Byron was working the nightshift as a police officer, he and his partner had stumbled upon this frightened little terrier: a puppy with smooth shiny black fur and longing umber eyes that must have pierced Byron's heart. But when he returned home with it tucked under his arm, Bridget was none too pleased:

"We've already got our hands full taking care of these kids!" she exclaimed. "And now you bring home a dog?"

To which Byron softly replied: "Oh, but it's just for a night. Until we can find it a home …" Byron knew that, by the following morning, Bridget would fall in love with this charm-ing creature and that it would remain with us.

The next day he turned to me and said, "Robbie, it's your job to name him!" The delightful pup wiggled his rubbery nose as I scratched my head, stared at his jet-black fur, and blurted out: "Brownie!"

Byron just smiled and replied, "*Wow!* What a *great* name! And can you think of *another* one?"

And with even more élan, I shouted, "*Sparky!*"

What was it in Byron's spiritual makeup that drew him to rescue abandoned pets, orphans, and bereft children?

Years later I came across a clipping from the *New York Journal-American* dated 27 September 1962 (about a month before my sixth birthday), which was slipped into an old family album. It was a human interest story about Byron:

Little Boy in Big City – It's Thanks in any Tongue

When you're seven and a stranger in a big city, you can get into a peck of trouble.

The trouble can be much worse if you don't speak English.

Robert Mailloux understands that now. He understands something else, too. He now knows that those big, gruff men in blue uniforms can be a little stranger's best friends.

Somehow, Robert, who recently came to New York from Canada and speaks only French, strayed away from his home, 3235 Emmons Ave., Brooklyn, yesterday afternoon. A report was promptly sent out to police.

At 9 o'clock last night, Patrolmen Bill McGuire and Byron Couteau saw the youngster ambling along at 71st St. and Narrows Avenue.

To judge from his name, you might think Patrolman Couteau can talk French, but he's American born and parlay-voos not a word.

Just the same, the trio had no difficulty in establishing rapport.

At the Fort Hamilton station, the aura of good fellowship continued. Robert was regaled with sandwiches and ice cream cones. He spoke

French, the cops spoke English, and the lack of a common tongue proved no handicap whatever.

Mrs. Yolanda Mailloux, summoned to the station, picked up her errant son, thanked his benefactors profusely in a tongue they didn't comprehend – yet grasped full well – and Robert was taken home to bed.

Rather strange that the boy and I shared the same first name. And what a journey, wandering from Sheepshead Bay to Bay Ridge – about nine miles by the most direct route – until finally wandering into Byron's arms.

* * *

Decades later, shortly after I moved to Paris, Byron was diagnosed with bronchial cancer. A lifelong smoker of unfiltered cigarettes, his habit had caught up with him, and he started to cough up blood. Upon receiving this dire news, I flew back to the States so that Arthur and I could embark upon a series of deathbed visits at Byron's house in Bensonhurst.

Byron lived for those nights when Arthur and I would do our best to help him prepare for his imminent journey across the Styx. We would position ourselves on a rude wooden bench running parallel to his bed and listen raptly as he regaled us with tales about his earlier life.

But almost from the start, it was as if *we* were doing the dying and Byron was there to keep us entertained – like an impresario hoping to distract us from a looming catastrophe. Ignoring his own discomfort, upon our arrival he'd prop himself up against a threadbare pillow, slip on a pair of horn-rimmed glasses, and glance at a notepad upon which he'd penned a few key phrases that would serve to remind him of an anecdote he wanted to expand upon.

During our first evening there, he placed his index finger upon the phrase "V-2": an abbreviation for a supersonic ballistic missile that the Germans had launched toward the end of World War Two. Sliding his glasses down his nose, he looked at me and said, "The first time a V-2 came zooming overhead, we had no idea what it was. There was this tremendous *BOOM* when it broke the sound barrier. But it was so damn fast that we had no way of blasting it from the sky. After a while, so many sailors were killed that I kept getting promoted to fill their positions."

It was precisely the sort of self-effacing remark that had always endeared Byron to me, for I was convinced there were many other reasons that he'd been chosen to rise in the ranks. At first, he said, he was a gunner's mate, stationed behind cannons that were aimed at those elusive German rockets. But then he was promoted to petty officer first-class, and he wore three red chevrons on his arm.

Despite the heavy casualties, the supply ships kept sailing across the Atlantic, zigzagging back and forth over those treacherous, shark-infested waters. "By the end of the war," he continued, "instead of just delivering food and munitions, we were also transporting German prisoners. And since they didn't want to end up in Davy Jones' Locker either, they'd stand right beside us on deck, helping us to spot the German U-boats."

Arthur was just as surprised as I was to hear about all this, and more than once he muttered: "You never told me about that before!" But Byron wasn't the sort to brag about such tales of heroism.

As we were getting ready to leave one night, I handed Byron several book reviews that I'd recently published. Glancing at the newsprint, he grinned and said: "Remember – language was invented by those who wish to deceive you."

Startled by this remark, I asked, "And who said that, Uncle Byron?"

Playfully raising an eyebrow as he shrugged his shoulders, he replied: "Who knows?" and laughed once again.

I suspect that it was Byron himself who had coined this expression, but he was too humble to ever admit it.

A family doctor had informed Rona that Byron wouldn't live much longer. The cancer had spread into his lungs, and by now it was too advanced to justify any painful treatment. Instead, he was encouraged to stock up on morphine patches and to wait it out at home. Just before we'd arrive each night, he'd pump himself up with morphine; then he'd do his best to ignore the pain as he continued to regale us, delving into the mysteries of his past.

During our second visit, Byron said that when he was in elementary school one of his teachers had decided that he possessed "artistic talent." So their mother, who was nicknamed "Mammie," had arranged for private art lessons. But then the Great Depression arrived, so they had to put an end to such extravagances and to curtail expenses.

Arthur was just a little boy when his mother died from a stroke. It was one of the only things that I knew about her. My father was so traumatized by this event that, even decades later, on the anniversary of her death he would sequester himself alone in his room.

Five days after Arthur's twelfth birthday, Mammie was standing at the top of the stairway, under a colorful skylight in our house on West Twelfth Street, when she began to babble incoherently about President Roosevelt. And then she collapsed. A few hours later, she was dead.

In a diary that probably hosts the last attempt he ever made to pen a personal record of his innermost feelings, a twelve-year-old Arthur wrote:

> The most tragic day I've ever experienced. It all happened so suddenly. My mother felt a little weak a day or two before, but nothing serious. Then, about 5:45 p.m. she began to get slightly delirious, so we called Dr. Holmes. Meanwhile, she got worse. She fell at the head of the stairs. Many times she murmured to Byron not to lose the letter (imaginary) from Mrs. Roosevelt. The doctor did not get here until 10:30 p.m. All the rest is a blur: the ambulance, the police, the priest (whose name I can't even remember) who gave mother her last rites. If only that doctor had got here earlier. But I guess, as Byron said, "God called her." Byron also comforted me greatly by saying "The good go to God first." It must be true, because my mother was the most wonderful person, next to the heavenly leaders, who ever lived. Or died. I hope I will meet her again in heaven, if I ever get there.

How strange, how utterly incongruous it is to see the words *God* and *heaven* coming from Arthur in any sort of positive context. By the time he was an adult he would only speak of such things with abject derision and a scalding, acidic tone of bitterness and contempt.

Ever since I chanced upon the diary when I was a teenager, I was convinced that this tragic event marked the end of Arthur's writing career. Why bother to create if everything ends in suffering and death? If nothing means anything? And how can it, if the world is capable of destroying a little boy's mother?

This was the sort of reasoning that had crushed Arthur's spirit.

I call it a *writing career* because I always sensed such a potential within him. I regarded it as no mere coincidence that Arthur enjoyed little else but endlessly repeating the fundamental stories that composed his earlier life. With writers who fail to honor their creativity, it's often like this: they're stuck in between gears, unable to shift to the next level. Instead, they spin their wheels ... to the chagrin of everyone around them, forced as we are to listen to what amounts to a broken record.

Since Arthur so rarely spoke about his mother, she'd remained an enigmatic figure for me, and I would occasionally search for clues about her past. In photographs from the early 1920s she appeared as a lithe, statuesque brunette with movie-star looks and allure. Byron said that Mammie's father was a brawny Irish carpenter and mason who hailed from Galway and who was known throughout Gravesend for his toughness and no-nonsense manner. And while Mammie's father was laying bricks and building houses, during her late teens and early twenties Mammie worked in vaudeville as a "chorus girl."

In one of the old tin boxes filled with sepia-toned photos that were stored in our basement closet, I came across a professionally composed five-by-seven print of Mammie appearing onstage. She's about twenty years old, which would date the picture from 1916, and dressed in an elaborate costume. She's outfitted with a cone shaped, pointed cap with a furry ball dangling from the top; an open-back scalloped dress that reveals her softly curving shoulders; a long pair of gloves that reach to her elbows and then flare out, like equestrian gauntlets; and a daring set of thigh-high suede boots. A black velvet theater curtain hangs directly behind her. With a beguiling expression, she gazes over her shoulder into the camera lens, her lips puckered into a smile, her bewitching eyes sparkling with merriment.

Mammie knew exactly how to seduce a camera lens. Instead of being intimidated, she played with it like a delightful toy. In one snapshot from the early Twenties she tosses back her head and sticks out her tongue. Rather unusual for the time, when family photos would normally feature a far more somber, serious pose. But Mammie's style was that of the Flapper, the newly liberated feline who played such a key role in the Roaring Twenties.

How did she ever meet my grandfather Merle, whose maternal line had descended from staid, conservative aristocrats? According to family legend, Merle and his friend Harry were "stage-door johnnies." After the vaudeville acts were finished, they'd wait backstage and attempt to pick up the chorus girls. Supposedly, that's how Merle met Mammie and how Harry met his future wife, Mammie's sister Julia, who also worked in vaudeville. And whether it was fact or fiction we'll never know; but I believed it, especially since we had that intriguing photo of her dressed in such an exotic outfit.

In later years the more I studied this image the more it all made sense. I was convinced that Byron's artistry was derived directly from Mammie, along with his playful sensibility – a quality deeply anchored to creativity itself. And the artistic talent that had blossomed within me could be traced back to the influence of Byron, whose enchanting pastel drawings of impressionist landscapes were later rolled up, like incongruous afterthoughts, and tossed on a shelf in my bedroom closet. They would later disappear, falling victim to Arthur's incessant housecleaning routine.

As they say, "An old man is a new broom."

* * *

By her teenage years Byron's step-daughter would become a heroin addict who succumbed to thievery to support her habit. According to Arthur, when all else failed Byron was forced to kick her out. But while Byron and Rona were gone one weekend, Laura broke into the house and walked away with his policeman's pistol.

"How did Byron ever manage to explain *that* at police headquarters?" Arthur wondered, sadly shaking his head.

On our way home from our first deathbed visit, Arthur said that he suspected Laura had something to do with the fact that Byron's house appeared to be stripped of everything but the bare essentials. With his hands gripping the steering wheel and staring with a grim expression into a windswept horizon, he murmured: "It resembles a place that's up for sale." Only a few sticks of furniture remained, and the walls were denuded of ornaments. "Either she's brazenly stolen their possessions," he added, "or else they've placed everything in storage rather than risk her larceny."

Appearing in such stark contrast to all this, my early years with Byron had been shaped like an enchanted idyll. As Arthur drove along Ocean Parkway, my mind drifted back to a Saturday afternoon just a few months after my sixth birthday, when Byron had entered the living room carrying a small package tucked under his arm, wrapped in brown paper.

Greeting me with one of his broad mischievous smiles, he shouted, "Come here; I've got something for you!"

I followed him to the kitchen table, where we sat beside a pair of windows overlooking our backyard. Everything was covered in snow, and it was too cold to go out and play. But now, eagerly tearing off the wrapping paper, I was thrilled to discover a paint-by-number kit.

A few years before, Byron had introduced me to watercolors. My kindergarten teacher later complained to my mother that I'd become such an avid artist that I wouldn't let the other children use the easel. But I'd never before dabbled with oil paint. The set included a sable-haired brush, numbered tins of pigment, a small vial of linseed oil, and a canvas board outlined with the figure of a world-famous "hobo clown" named Emmett Kelly.

Byron spread some newspaper over the table and patiently instructed me on how to proceed. Within moments, my attention was intensely focused on the canvas, while a bouquet of fragrances effused from the various pigments and filled my nostrils with a delightful sensation.

The gangly silhouette of Emmett Kelly was soon transformed into a colorful, fully fleshed out carnival figure. When I finished and held it aloft for Byron's inspection, he took a step back, narrowed his gaze, and pursed his lips into a serious expression. Then he clapped his hands together and complimented me on my handiwork.

"Now, you've had a new experience!"

"*Experience?* But what's that, Uncle Byron?"

Regarding me like a benevolent patriarch, he explained the meaning of this word in such a way that even a little boy could comprehend it.

Thanks to my magical uncle, in that moment I became confident of my creative ability despite the fact that it was little more than a nascent, fledgling potential, which had barely taken root in the wispy dreams of a six-year-old.

How is it that such events can so radically shape us – even for a lifetime? I often wondered how Byron might have continued to influence my life if he'd remained with us a while longer. But as soon as he married Rona and moved away, he appeared less and less frequently on West Twelfth Street. Once he'd adopted his ready-made family, fate had steered him into his own domestic chaos.

But even in his absence, the force that was personified by Byron would continue to flourish within me. Like a lingering childhood ghost, the Byron of the late Fifties and early Sixties seemed to guide me through thick and thin, no matter what challenges I might later encounter. Thus, seeing him on his death bed was a calamitous as well as a euphoric experience, because after losing contact with him for so long we were now linked to each other again, albeit tragically and briefly.

I suspect that, as a "big brother," Byron had also nurtured Arthur during his time of need. I'm certain that after they lost Mammie, and Arthur sank into a bleak, morbid depression, it was Byron who helped to hold him together. A part of Arthur had stopped growing at this point, and he was eternally scarred by this corrosive trauma; but Byron had been older, already sixteen, and perhaps his psyche had been adequately fortified by those extra years of affection that he'd received from his mother.

In any case, never were two brothers so fundamentally dissimilar. While Arthur seemed to be *annoyed* by life, Byron was deeply *amused* by it. I often imagined myself positioned between them, benefitting from the various qualities that they each embodied: Arthur's intellect, Byron's joie de vivre. But my allegiance always remained firmly anchored to Byron's side of the equation.

*　*　*

Shortly after our last deathbed visit, while we were stopped at a red light, Arthur blurted out: "I just don't understand how Byron could have ended up with someone like Rona."

"You mean, because she's at least half mad?"

"He always dated such *bombshells*. Women that you or I would have died for!" According to Arthur, one of Byron's

most comely admirers was a Greek girl named Virginia
Spirodon, who'd lived at the other end of the block, near Kings
Highway:

"Everyone knew that Virginia was nuts about him, yet he
never even asked her out."

When the light changed and Arthur stepped on the gas, his
tone softened, and he added: "One day in the early Seventies, I
was walking along West Twelfth Street when a handsome
woman approached and remarked: 'Your stride is such that you
must be a Couteau.'" Speaking with the diction of another era,
she was referring to the jaunty, devil-may-care bounce of
Arthur and his brother, who sauntered about with a loping gait.
"It was Virginia, who'd returned to visit the block where she
grew up. And the first question she asked was if Byron had ever
married. But I lied and said no, because I wanted to avoid the
whole embarrassing subject of Rona."

"How did she react?"

"She said that she wasn't at all surprised that Byron had
remained a bachelor."

This last remark startled me, for it confirmed something that
I'd long suspected about Byron's enduring love of freedom.
And yet, he'd sacrificed all that to support Rona and Laura.

"By then Virginia was married and had several children. But
I wondered if she'd returned just to seek out her old heartthrob.
I've often thought about how Byron's life might have been so
much better," Arthur concluded, "if only he'd responded to
Virginia's obvious interest."

As further proof of Byron's "bombshells," in the photos
stored in the basement, Byron could be seen posing with a different mermaid looped over his arm in each snapshot: an olive-
skinned siren from Romania, a wide-eyed angel from Belgrade,
a willowy naiad from Mesopotamia. In between imbibing the
nectar of such heavenly hosts he would sail back and forth

across the Atlantic, braving the U-boats that could so easily sink our ships because our depth charges couldn't yet reach them. Week after week, Arthur would sit beside his father at the living room table and study the casualty lists published in the local papers, hoping and praying that Byron would live to see another day.

But somehow, Byron survived ... and with his élan intact. Often graced with that kind of luck, he was one of the golden boys – the blessed few who remain far from harm's way, at least for a while.

As death approached to sweep him away, I realized that it wasn't just Byron, a single man, who was taking his leave. It was an entire generation, with its unique experience and perspective, that was now being obliterated.

One by one, we're plucked like the missing pieces of a vast, collective dream ... until there's nothing left of it.

* * *

On the plane ride back to Paris, I recalled an incident that had occurred when I was no more than four years old:

It's an evening like any other in Gravesend, with the TV blaring and Arthur burying his head as deeply as possible into the centerfold of the *New York Times*, tuning out the rest of the family while studying the catastrophic situation in the world at large. In the opposite corner of the living room Bridget is seated in an upholstered armchair, and her gaze shifts from Arthur, to the TV, and back to Arthur again. Perhaps she was hoping for a miracle: that he might put down his paper and pay her some much-deserved attention.

As I enter the room, I'm gripping the end of a leather leash that we use to walk Sparky; but now it's dangling over my shoulder and dragging along behind me. Pausing at the center of the parquet floor, which Bridget would wax and polish to a sheen, I boldly announce that I've decided to leave home.

It's after sunset, and the streets are veiled in inky darkness. In my childish mind brimming with fantasy, instead of a leash I imagine that I'm carrying a hobo's sack, which dangles from the end of a stick. Thus, I'm all set to embark upon my first great Odyssey, perhaps in emulation of the legendary hobo clowns.

Arthur's head briefly emerges from the side of his paper. He takes one look at me, gestures toward the front door, and with a snapping, staccato beat, replies: "Go right ahead!" Then he disappears again into the alcove of his sheltering newsprint as Bridget's look of disconsolation only deepens.

Now it hits me full force: there will be no more peanut butter and jelly sandwiches, nowhere to sleep, and nowhere in particular to go.

Overcome, defeated, and vanquished ... all within mere seconds!

Gazing at the thick oak door of the vestibule, which leads to the porch and front stoop, I realize that, with no way to sustain myself, running away might have to be postponed. So I turn round and beat a silent painful retreat, once again a victim of Arthur, the dream crusher.

But Arthur only appears to be amused by all this. I can still recall the smug, self-satisfied smirk curling along the edge of his lips.

Little did he realize that what I was impulsively attempting to escape from was Arthur himself. It was no less than an attempted deliverance from the "fatherland."

* * *

In the years ahead, the question of where to seek one's true homeland continued to haunt me. After I said farewell to Byron and flew back to Paris, it occurred to me that perhaps there is no enduring hearth and, instead, only a series of journeys that point first in one direction, then another. But if he's lucky enough, a spiritual hobo may occasionally be endowed with a spectral sack filled with the fecundating largesse of imagination.

But poor Arthur! Instead of rooting itself to the wonder of the moment, his gaze was all too often riveted upon the past, reflecting a forlorn regret that certain events could never be exhumed and relived. Rather than looking ahead with hopeful anticipation, when Arthur contemplated the future he'd focus upon whatever dire calamities were sure to be lying there in wait: bleak handmaidens of gloom and doom. As Walt Whitman's father used to tell his son, "The worst is yet to come!" Not exactly the sort of advice that's most suitable for a young boy's ears.

As soon as I returned to France I phoned Byron, and we spoke one last time. He greeted me with a warm, welcoming tone, but he sounded considerably weaker, so we chatted only briefly. The following week he was shipped to a hospital where he fell into a coma and passed away. Rona would perish of lung cancer just a few years later, but she outlived her daughter, Laura, who became one of the first causalities of the AIDS epidemic; most likely, from using a dirty needle.

While Byron was dying in Brooklyn, I was undergoing my own rebirth in Paris: sorting out the creative tasks that I'd inherited directly from him.

But that's jumping ahead. First, I had to escape from the eight rungs of Satan's ladder, positioned as it was in a grimy hellhole known as Gravesend.

Hell is Catholic School

Like a gnarled and hoary ogre from a Grimm's fairy-tale, on the second rung of Satan's ladder there lay in wait an elderly Irish matriarch named Mrs. McAvoy. But this wrinkled old termagant turned out to have a bark far worse than her bite.

We'd just returned from lunch in the cafeteria when the principal's voice blurted out over a loudspeaker. Following a wave of static, we carefully listened to her words: President Kennedy had been gunned down in Dallas – the city of hate – and he wasn't expected to live.

At once McAvoy spun round, burst into tears, and ran into the hallway. She'd momentarily abandoned her post rather than permit the children to witness her uncontrollable weeping.

I'd never seen an authority figure collapse into grief like that, and I was duly impressed. Little did I realize that, at this very moment all across America, the notion of trusting authority was also being gunned down along with our president.

On that dreadful Friday afternoon we were sent home early. And for the remainder of the weekend, even on the mean, racist pavements of Gravesend, there was nothing but a reign of silence. Never before had West Twelfth Street been so utterly bereft of red rubber balls, squeaking roller skates, and the sound of rice-filled hula-hoops whizzing round and round. Even the meatheads of Bay Ridge and Bensonhurst – who accused the Kennedys of being "nigger-loving" integrationists – remained at home, glued to their TVs and mesmerized by the continual news bulletins devoted to our fallen leader. We were equally shocked when, two days later, a patsy named Lee Oswald was murdered during a "live" television broadcast.

Rimbaud's "Time of the Assassins" was now upon us.

A few hours before his death, Kennedy had emerged from his suite at the Hotel Texas in Fort Worth, where fifteen modern masterworks had been installed at the behest of local art connoisseurs. The first thing he would have seen upon entering, and the last thing he would have passed on his way out, was a bronze sculpture of a long-beaked bird that Picasso had christened *Angry Owl*.

One can easily imagine the president and his elegant wife, Jacqueline, admiring this predator with its fierce, gaping maw just moments before boarding the Lincoln convertible that would deliver him to the talons of his own birds of prey.

* * *

On September 3, 1964, Robert Kennedy resigned as attorney general to run for the position of U.S. senator from New York. That fall, after I'd entered the third grade, he was scheduled to appear on 85th Street, under an elevated train line a block away from St. Anne's. Five years earlier his brother John had also appeared there, during his presidential run. Though I couldn't recall a thing about it, my parents had taken me to see JFK, along with my younger brother, Arthur Junior, who was seated in his baby stroller.

So now, Bridget volunteered to bring us to see "Bobby," and the three of us took off, with much excitement, for the train. We arrived early and positioned ourselves right up front, beside a raised wooden platform. But soon the crowd – which wasn't entirely sympathetic to the Democratic Civil Rights agenda – began to swell. The audience was also growing restless because Bobby was stuck somewhere in traffic and hadn't yet arrived. Finally Paul O'Dwyer, a platinum-haired pol who'd emigrated from Ireland, took to the stage and wove his magic over the surging mass of Brooklynites who stood shoulder-to-shoulder along the avenue.

Bridget and I were just a few feet to O'Dwyer's left – as close as anyone could get to the stage – when a rotten egg sailed over the swarming mass, headed directly toward O'Dwyer. At the last possible moment he calmly shifted a few inches to the side, and it smashed against a wall. O'Dwyer didn't even flinch as he continued to stoke the crowd with his slick gift of gab. Then night fell, and the klieg lights were turned on with a soft *pop*, and everyone surged forward. By now, we were beginning to get crushed.

Bobby Kennedy suddenly appeared under a bright spotlight, grabbed an oversized chrome microphone, and tossed his head back. And that golden lock of hair that made such a perfect curl on his forehead fell into place, and the crowd swooned. Regardless of how many crates of rotten eggs and spoiled tomatoes the mobbed-up vendors of 86th Street had distributed to the bigots of Gravesend to throw at these "liberal" Democrats, soon the crowd was just putty in Bobby's hands. He continued to mesmerize the spectators with his delightful Bostonian lilt – such a strange melody to hear in such a backwater – and, as the lights bathed him in a shimmering halo, the women screamed just as they'd screeched for Elvis and the Beatles on the Ed Sullivan Show.

The crowd again surged forward like a rippling wave, pressing against my scrawny frame. So I grabbed my little brother by the wrist, and we slipped under the platform and out of harm's way – much to Bridget's approval. Seeing the panic in our eyes, and appearing to be flustered herself, she gestured for us to remain there. I was so small that I could almost stand up under the wooden rafters, so I listened to the remainder of the speech crouched just inches below the figure of Bobby Kennedy.

By the seventh grade Bobby would be no more: felled by conspirators who would retake the country from the progressive Kennedy clan, while all across Brooklyn bumper stickers proclaimed: GUNS DON'T KILL PEOPLE, PEOPLE KILL PEOPLE. But who, or what, had killed the Kennedys? In the decades ahead, many of us would invest long hours into examining any reasonable answer to this nagging question. This collective search would eventually result in opening a portal of doubt about anything that was officially sanctioned by the government or by its spoon-fed lackeys in the corporate media.

The shots that felled the president marked the inception of the questioning Sixties; the ones that obliterated his younger brother marked its finale. Neither man was as saintly as my Irish grandmother had imagined, yet they personified a hope or a prayer that perhaps, at the very end, something worthwhile might emerge and a decent outcome might prevail.

And what of Bobby's golden locks? In the end, like an enchanted object in a fairy-tale, it was his hair that preserved the truth. In the words of LA County Chief Medical Examiner, Thomas Noguchi,

> I knew that the scalp hair around the wound area which they had shaved off Kennedy's head before the surgery might contain critical evidence. So I instructed one of my investigators to rush to the operating room to see if the hair shavings were still there. They were found in little clumps which had been retained by the hospital staff. My investigator carefully placed them in a coroner's evidence envelope [...]
>
> The day after the autopsy, a criminologist from the Los Angeles Police Department appeared at my office door. "Dr. Noguchi, we've found

something in those little hair shavings."

"What?"

"Gunpowder residue. Not only metallic elements but what could be soot."

"Soot?" I stood straight up.

As Noguchi goes on to explain, *soot* is coroner's jargon for burned grains of gunpowder – or carbon particles – that, because of their light mass, travel only a few inches. Further tests revealed that the gun had been fired "one inch from the edge of [Kennedy's] right ear, only three inches behind the head." Yet the supposed killer, Sirhan Sirhan, was standing no closer than three feet *in front* of Bobby Kennedy when he fired his gun. The other problem? According to Noguchi, "Tracks of twelve bullets were found at the scene, and Sirhan's gun contained only eight" bullets, since it was an eight-shooter.

Hello, sucker. The fix is in!

While Noguchi had delivered the truth, the *New York Times* concocted yet another fable about a "lone nut." The paper of record never mentioned the fact that it would require a magic gun to produce at least four extra projectiles. A fantasy just as ludicrous as the "magic bullet" that had supposedly injured both JFK and Texas Governor Connelly while doing twists and turns that defied the laws of physics as it pirouetted like a genie from a bottle.

* * *

I look back upon the third rung of Satan's ladder with a certain fondness, for Sister Majella – who occasionally even cracked a smile – was the last halfway decent creature to instruct us for some time to come. Our assignments were fairly easy, and we usually finished our homework in time to go out after dinner and play our sacred games on the street. Perhaps Majella had planned it this way. A sports fanatic herself, one day she was featured in a *Daily News* centerfold, photographed in her nun's habit at a New York Mets baseball game while holding up a sign that read: *Let's Go, Mets!*

That same year, thanks to Bobby Kennedy's push to racially integrate the school system, President Johnson signed the Civil Rights Act of 1964. That September, Bridget made the courageous decision to take my brother by the hand and cross a picket line at P.S. 97: one composed largely of our own neighbors, who stood there cringing in disbelief as Bridget braved the screaming, heckling crowd and escorted him safely to kindergarten.

Besides Arthur Junior, there were only two other students in the building: a wide-eyed Chinese boy and a shy little Black girl. Bridget believed in doing what was right, and there was nothing that would stop her – including a seething crowd of Gravesend racists.

Two months before they killed Bobby, the civil-rights leader Martin Luther King was murdered while standing on his motel balcony in Memphis, prompting riots in 125 cities across the country.

In a famous photo of the incident, while everyone else is pointing to the opposite side of the motel courtyard – where the shots were fired – a fellow named Marrell McCollough is calmly kneeling over King's body, checking his pulse. Unbeknownst to King's inner circle, McCollough was an agent provocateur who had infiltrated the Civil Rights Movement. Originally he worked for the FBI, but during the assassination he was employed as an undercover cop by the Memphis police. Six years later, McCollough was "rewarded" for such nefarious tasks and offered a position at the CIA.

Despite such frightening revelations, which eventually trickled into the underground press, the question of what McCollough was doing there, on King's balcony at the Lorraine Motel, was never satisfactorily answered by the government. But in 1978, the U.S. Congress House Select Committee on Assassinations concluded that there was a strong "likelihood" that the thirty-nine-year-old leader was killed as the result of a conspiracy, although it continued to deny any government involvement.

To honor Dr. King on the first anniversary of his death, my father hoisted an American flag, flown at half-mast, between the front windows of our rowhouse. When our neighbors asked why he was flying the flag and he answered that it was for Dr. King, at first they assumed that he was up to his usual practical jokes – and that he must be kidding.

Three years before, the same clandestine forces had killed Malcolm X, who was threatening the alcohol, tobacco, and drug cartels by insisting that African Americans abstain from addictive substances.

With each new assassination, we lost another degree of faith in the American government.

* * *

The fourth rung of the sinister ladder was by far the most difficult for me to transit. Now, I was burdened with a virago named Lisa Puzo, who for some reason had tacked my image upon her target.

Mrs. Puzo resembled one of those beady-eyed provincial instructors who are so cleverly depicted in the work of Federico Fellini: pretentious stiff-backed martinets who hail from tiny hamlets with absurd-sounding names such as Cannemerda or Porcoputta, but who act as if they're natives of noble cultural centers such as Florence or Rome and are lecturing in prestigious, elite preparatory schools. Although Puzo was a lay teacher, she possessed even less empathy than the iciest of nuns. For Lisa Puzo, the only thing that mattered was an "A+". If you scored less than 100% on a test, the degree of her scorn was in direct proportion to the points that you'd failed to muster.

Whatever it was that had turned her against me I'll never know for sure. At first I imagined that it might have been the fact that, with my turquoise eyes, dirty-blond hair, and French surname I was obviously no Sicilian. In any case, my friend Drew Dunkle, who had some Irish and German ancestry mixed in with his Italian blood, was convinced that Puzo bore a grudge toward anyone who didn't trace his roots directly to the heel of *Italia*.

I also wondered if she was jealous of my mother's other-worldly beauty or was unsettled by Bridget's disarming sweetness. Both my parents were so photogenic that, one day, while shopping for a wedding dress at Abraham and Straus department store, a photographer from *Modern Bride* magazine had spotted them and asked if they'd like to appear in the next issue, for a "Real Life Bride" feature.

In her flowing tulle wedding dress, Bridget resembled a top-shelf fashion model. The article featured beautifully lit black-and-white photos of Arthur, who was tall, dark, handsome, and endowed with crystalline hazel eyes. In one shot he's captured in a glamorous profile: smiling winningly at my mother while seated at a marble bistro table, sipping coffee from a large white mug. Another picture portrays Arthur standing beside a department-store clerk as they examine sophisticated electrical tools and elaborate machinery, which Arthur supposedly intends to purchase for his "future workshop." A caption reads:

After a compact but comfortable apartment had been found, she met Arthur for lunch one Saturday to start their furniture quest in earnest. They talked about contemporary styling: cool, light colors that both are fond of. He will need a study, a book space (they are inveterate readers), and a workshop, because Arthur, like many husbands today, will be a local carpenter and fixer. The workshop will also feature this Cummins tool: a marvel that is seven power tools in one. With this he'll be able to construct bookshelves and cabinets and do all the household adjusting and repairs. When major work is out of the way, he plans to build a special table for their favorite chess game.

Like most American journalism, it was a mixture of fact and fantasy. Bridget wasn't much of a reader; and while Arthur certainly loved books, he only occasionally played chess – and never in his life would he dare to approach a power tool! Instead, he grew fidgety and anxiety-ridden whenever he was forced to wield a simple screwdriver or hammer, being so maladapted to anything pragmatic.

Eventually I realized that, above and beyond all else, what must have piqued Puzo's wrath was the fact that although I'd managed to remain in the top class each year, I was obviously a dreamer and an intuitive type, and not at all a hyperrational intellectual. Thus, I plucked the correct answers to her inane questions out of the ether rather than arriving at them through any carefully ordered logic. Throughout my entire schooling, although at times I was forced to work hard and ingest a tedious jumble of facts and figures, I usually worked only as hard as was necessary, conserving whatever energy I could for the more important things in life: for my own reading and writing, and for meaningful *experience*.

After I scored an eighty-five on a math test, on parent-teacher's day Puzo had the gall to icily inform Bridget that I was in danger of falling to the "bottom of the barrel." My mother never tired of relating this story with an incredulous smirk and in such a manner that it was clear that she regarded Puzo as a gauche loon, a country bumpkin, and a spiteful hick. But in those days, there was never a question of lodging a complaint to the school or of making a personal appearance in the principal's office to defend your child against the sociopaths and ignoramuses who regarded themselves as teachers.

And more than anyone, the children realized that they were out there all alone, come hell or high water.

* * *

One afternoon a middle-aged man in a grey-flannel suit appeared in our living room. With a solemn expression, he unfolded a glossy brochure featuring a photo of an orchestra, laid it on our coffee table, and asked which instrument I wanted to play. But instead of pointing at a musician, I placed my finger on the image of a conductor and said: "Him."

Bridget was seated on the plastic-covered couch beside me, and she burst out laughing as he somberly replied, "No, you can't be the *conductor*. You have to select an *instrument*." So now, I pointed to a guitarist. And then, once a week for the following year, I traveled with Bridget to Maggio Music, a studio on New Utrecht Avenue where a kind, jovial man with a pudgy oval face taught me how to play.

Since we were paying good money for this, we always arrived at least fifteen minutes early. As I sat there awaiting my turn, I listened with delight to three schoolboys who were inside the studio playing the latest Beatles tunes on their Gibson electric guitars. They were just a few years my senior, but they'd already formed a group called the Daze'n'Nights.

By the end of the year I was beginning to get the hang of it. The instrument began to feel different in my hands – as if there were an invisible stream of energy flowing from my fingertips to the guitar neck. But after we left the studio each week, I rarely bothered to practice.

Following my lesson one day, the instructor emerged from the back room and approached Bridget. "Although your son has talent," he said, "he doesn't practice. I can tell that he only plays when he comes here. But he won't learn quickly enough that way." He seemed to be genuinely concerned and was hoping that Bridget might help me to develop some discipline. But as an eight-year-old who was in love with the pure energy of life – and with the various games and adventures that were lying in wait upon the dusty tarmac – the idea of sitting inside on a hot Saturday afternoon and plucking catgut seemed ridiculous to me.

I would have been content to continue to make such slow, steady progress, but in the end Mrs. Puzo's heavy load of homework forced me to drop the lessons. With growing irritation, even Arthur commented upon this excessive amount of work, but only because it affected his own schedule, since he had to help me get through it.

Perhaps Puzo would have been pleased to learn that something as "useless" as music was being eclipsed by her relentless marching orders. As far as she was concerned, there were more important goals in life, and in order to achieve them there was a proper procedure to be followed. Unless you faithfully obeyed such a protocol, your chances of remaining above the fray – and of rising ever higher on the socioeconomic ladder – would exponentially diminish. It went without saying that, in Lisa Puzo's world, childhood was simply something to be outgrown, not something to be indulged in, lingered over, or, heaven forbid, *enjoyed*.

No one knew this better than Lisa's fatherless son, Alfred, whom she'd yoked like an ox to various joyless labors and pushed and prodded along the road to "success." During our final years at St. Anne's, Alfred used the cover of the Civil Rights Movement to form an interracial track team: one composed largely of African Americans with skin so smooth, dark, and shiny that his mouth watered as he sat upon the bleachers and watched them run laps. Mrs. Puzo would never have to fight for the control of her offspring with some ungrateful daughter-in-law, for Alfred concerned himself only with these nice young athletes who flew like champions round and round the parquet court in their flashy red sneakers. Flexing their muscles in the locker room and spraying their underarms with the latest brand of deodorant, they'd say, "Alfred, you're the man!" That is, when they weren't laughing behind his back and calling him a lame little cracker.

The headstrong Mrs. Puzo continued to mold Alfred as he descended to new levels of obsequiousness. Until he finally found himself plowing across the mud-encrusted mulch of the local political machine and running for an obscure county seat. As he zigzagged through Gravesend in a white sedan rigged with a pair of bullhorn speakers that wobbled on top – *Vote for Alfred Puzo!* – we'd occasionally hear his voice blaring outside our classroom as he cruised along 23rd Avenue. And, oh, Mrs. Puzo was so *proud* ... until Alfred lost the election by a considerable number of votes. But of course, Lisa would have been the last person to advise a more modest goal. Modesty was not in her repertoire. Meanwhile, she encouraged Alfred to apply for government grants to expand his interracial initiatives. But then, ineluctable fate stepped in.

One night while Alfred was cruising along Bay Parkway in Lisa's sparkling black Cadillac convertible, the cops pulled him over. They wanted to know what a honky like Alfred was doing seated beside a couple of "niggers" in a neighborhood where, obviously, "they didn't belong." It could only be drugs. When Alfred attempted to explain – in that haughty, patronizing manner that he'd inherited from his obnoxious mother – that he was *Alfred Puzo* and that he was driving these young *gentleman* home from an *interracial track event*, the cops decided to billy club some sense into his thick skull. So they cracked it open and sent him bleeding to Kings County Hospital.

A million-dollar lawsuit was the result. With the prospect of all that fresh loot lining his trousers Alfred grew even cockier, and he began to skim from the till. But when he was caught siphoning grant money, he fell into *merde profonde*, and everything that Lisa had dreamed of went right down the drain.

To make matters worse, Alfred then made the mistake of sleeping with the adolescent son of one of the local mobsters. After being caught in flagrante delicto, Alfred disappeared. His body was eventually found floating in the East River, his throat slashed from ear to ear.

*   *   *

The following autumn we found ourselves seated before the paranoid glare of a rail-thin nun named Sister Iranaeus: a pasty-faced cretin who towered over the fifth rung of Satan.

Even the most empty-headed *gedrools* (cucumber heads) seemed to sense that something was not quite right about Iranaeus. There was also a persistent rumor that she'd once been scorned by a boyfriend who had left her brokenhearted. As a result, Iranaeus had renounced the pursuit of romantic relationships in order to surrender her love – or whatever else one might call it – to the Lord.

Despite her mean-spirited nature, some of us felt a tinge of sorrow for this neurotic woman who beamed at us with such haunted eyes. Iranaeus was as pale, forlorn, and anorexic as the crucified Christ himself, hovering before us like a semimaterialized spirit as she attempted to drill those enervating multiplication tables into our febrile brains. As Knut Hamsun had written back in 1889: "Americans are so absorbed in the scramble for profit" that "their brains are trained exclusively to grapple with monetary values and columns of figures."

As I tried to remember that *nine times six is fifty-four*, suddenly it occurred to me that Iranaeus's womb would never serve to multiply the human species. Then I realized that perhaps this was a good thing, and that religion might have a place after all. Instead of bearing offspring, she'd remain pinned like a dusty butterfly to that lonesome crucifixion of the fifth grade, another childless saint who was martyred not by Romans but by the "spiritual" doctrine of the church itself.

* * *

The television shows of this period were rife with spy stories, no doubt inspired by the Cold War and the terrorism wrought by our own intelligence agencies. In retrospect, it's easy to imagine how such programs served the useful purpose of not only acclimating us to "special agents" but also encouraging us to view them as endearing, loveable personalities. Thus, these fictional spooks served as "cutouts" for the more diabolical figures whose evil knew no bounds.

Perhaps as a result of all this, I created a spy organization called the Snakes, and my archenemy, Jake Pellegrino, formed one to battle me called the Moles. For months on end, secret messages were passed back and forth in the corridors;

espionage files were opened and maintained; dossiers were combed for clues; plots and counterplots were cooked up in shadowy alleyways throughout Gravesend. The turmoil in the school yard, always at a fever pitch, now reached new heights. Eventually it spun so far out of control that the nuns convened a special meeting to decide what to do.

The following day, Iranaeus faced the class with her brow terribly furrowed. Appearing even more funereal than usual, she said: "Class, I know all about the Snakes and the Moles. All this must stop at once! And believe me, I'll soon get to the bottom of it. Now, I want the leaders of each group to act like men and to step forward."

And so, Jake and I stood up and proceeded to the head of the class to face the music – or the lack of it – so deep and sonorous was this ominous silence.

Looking us up and down, Iranaeus demanded to know who else was a Mole. About half the class raised their hands, and Jake beamed with pride at his fellow henchmen. A squat frog-faced fellow whose pimple-ridden face was always suffering from a bad case of acne, Jake looked particularly devious when he grinned.

"Oh, I see," Iranaeus continued, "it's about half and half."

Suddenly I was seized by a strange foreboding as I hoped against hope that she'd leave it at that. But instead, she continued: "Now, everyone who's a *Snake*, raise your hand."

But no one raised a hand. For, in fact, I was the *only* Snake, and I'd *imagined* the entire thing: a baroque organization that existed only in the etheric reaches of my gossamer, intuitive daydreams. And somehow, I'd convinced everyone that the school yard was overrun by a legion of phantom serpents.

Appearing nonplussed, Iranaeus continued to wonder about the location of all those missing reptiles. She turned to me for an explanation, but I simply shrugged my shoulders and remained silent. She even sent a pair of students to the other fifth-grade classes – to 5-2 and 5-3 – convinced that the culprits would be uncovered there. But to no avail.

Once she surmised that I was single-handedly fighting all these Moles, Iranaeus solemnly nodded her head, then proposed a "Christian" solution to the entire fiasco: that we shake hands and become friends. But when I extended my hand to Jake, he refused to touch it.

Without realizing it he sealed his fate. Now Jake was viewed as the less mature one, which served to place me in a positive light despite the "defeat" of having a memberless organization. But as a result of this abrupt confrontation with reality, for the remainder of the term I withdrew even more into my imaginary world. After school each day, I'd spend hours secluded alone in my room: reading, drawing, and daydreaming.

For the conflict wasn't really between Snakes and Moles; it was between reality and whatever hid behind its veil.

* * *

In the fall of 1967 we were introduced to a young nun with pale-blue eyes, ruddy Irish skin, and a sympathetic smile that radiated genuine warmth and concern. It was an expression that informed the more clairvoyant among us that something special was about to occur: something that might even approach the realm of pleasure.

Sister Maryjane had just rolled in with the winds of change that were sweeping across the nation – even into backwaters such as Gravesend. Unlike the other nuns who enshrouded themselves in thick folds of black cloth encircled by shiny rosary beads and festooned with grotesque metal crucifixes, Maryjane's outfit was composed of a cyan-blue fabric. And you could see her entire face, because she wore a simple veil that covered only the back of her hair. Whereas, with the other nuns, not a single strand of hair was visible, so their faces seemed to be popping out of a tiny black portal.

Years later Arthur recalled that when he first met Maryjane it was the only time he'd ever seen one of our teachers with a smile on her face. Indeed, it was startling to realize that Maryjane wasn't quite like the other sisters – and this contrast made everything seem that much more disconcerting.

Although St. Anne's had produced some bright students in math and history, until Maryjane appeared on the scene we'd never once had an art lesson: not even an art-appreciation class. And so, in order to remedy this situation, she designed a new curriculum. As a result, instead of being icily dismissed as something repugnant or maladroit, my intuitive temperament was now viewed as something of value. For, try as they might, the other kids couldn't approach my level of drawing or painting. The more that Maryjane praised my work, the more that I tried to please her by redoubling my efforts. When she finally organized our first art show, several of the drawings that I'd submitted – interpretations of Rembrandt etchings – were mounted on matte board and displayed in modest gilt frames.

Thanks to her sincere display of empathy, Maryjane worked her spell over the parents as well; but unfortunately she didn't last there very long. Rumor had it that she'd finally lost her patience with the other nuns because of the Vietnam War. At suppertime each evening, as the images of protestors flared across a black-and-white TV in the convent the nuns would seethe with rage, and Maryjane began to wonder whether she really belonged in such a den of intolerance. Thus, the "Generation Gap" had finally entered St. Anne's.

After we graduated, Drew Dunkle and Jake Pellegrino visited Maryjane in her new flat in Greenwich Village. No longer a nun, now she was garbed in a peasant blouse and paisley skirt – the quasi-hippie fashion of the day. And she treated the boys to a pot of herbal tea – something that probably didn't even exist yet back in Gravesend.

* * *

In the summer of 1968 Arthur decided that we should take a ride into Manhattan to watch a musician named Pete Seeger pluck his banjo on a rotted wharf at South Street Seaport. As we crossed the Brooklyn Bridge, Arthur lectured us about Seeger's old group, the Weavers, and explained how Woody Guthrie's tune, "This Land is Your Land," which the Weavers often covered, was actually a protest song. Arthur said that Seeger had served as an important figure in the Civil Rights Movement; and, thanks to his masterful reinterpretation of this haunting old spiritual, the song became the celebrated anthem of the marchers. Arthur added that, because of his political advocacy, Seeger had been banned from television and was rarely allowed to play in mainstream concert halls. But now he was helping to raise funds for a budding environmental movement, the Hudson River Clearwater Project. Arthur also spoke fervently about a prescient book published in 1962 titled *Silent Spring*, which featured one of the first warnings about the environmental apocalypse that would soon rear its ugly head.

Once we arrived at South Street, there were only a handful of people seated along a dilapidated old pier. Some of the holes in the planks were covered with strips of tin nailed into place, but many more were left exposed, so we had to take special care as we ambled along.

We positioned ourselves at the edge of the wharf, just a few feet away from Seeger as he strummed his banjo aboard the docked Clearwater. The scruffy members of this select audience – bearded hippies and slender young women in flower dresses

– passed around a cheap bottle of Chianti. As Bridget later recounted, "It was the beginning of an amazing movement."

In the decades to come South Street would undergo extensive renovations after being designated as a historical landmark, attracting crowds of tourists who had never even heard of Pete Seeger.

* * *

When my classmates and I ascended the next rung of the Luciferian ladder, we cast our weary gaze upon a lay teacher in his early thirties named Mr. Tuff. We'd never been taught by a man before, and we didn't know what to expect.

One day Tuff announced that he was organizing a debate on civil rights. Since I was the only one willing to defend the movement, I was asked to represent that side of the argument, while Jack Pellegrino volunteered to be my opponent.

When I told Arthur about my assignment, he threw himself into the good cause of helping me to prepare. A Civil War aficionado, he'd read nearly as many books on the subject as he had on the Second World War. But Arthur's tendency to focus excessively on the past nearly resulted in derailing my debating début.

When the day of the debate arrived, as an opening statement I read from various historical accounts that chronicled the humiliations, floggings, and lynchings in the South, attempting to establish a broader context for the Civil Rights Movement. But with every fact that I summoned to strengthen my case, Jake simply shook his head and replied, "Yes, but all that's changed. Racial injustice no longer exists in America."

After I'd exhausted my logical arguments, as I glanced at this all-white assembly, the words suddenly formed on my lips: "Would any of you ever date a Black person?" And one by one, the boys and girls shook their heads: *No.*

"You see?" I concluded, staring each one in the eye. "*Nothing has changed.*"

At first my remark was met with silence. Then Carmine Miranda, a pug-nosed bully who had yet to learn how to question authority, raised his hand and asked, "But who's *right*, Mr. Tuff?" Now I wondered if even Carmine had been rattled by a scintilla of doubt.

Mr. Tuff glanced at me with an approving smile. Following a dramatic pause, he concluded: "Every Christian should know who's right." With this adroit, strategic rejoinder he acknowledged that I'd fought for a just cause and, in my own way, had succeeded. But thanks to Tuff's subtle, open-ended phrasing, he was also protecting himself should his words be repeated over the spaghetti laden dinner tables that evening in Gravesend.

After returning from work, Arthur approached me with a look of hopeful expectation and asked how it went at school. When I told him about how the kids shook their heads, his eyes began to glower. Shaking his own head in disgust, he grumbled, "I just don't understand it. I really don't."

"Which part?"

"The fact that they could hate anyone with such violence, and virulence, and all that. It's just unbelievable. I mean – *why?* I can't understand it."

Despite his acerbic temperament there was also a native tenderness in Arthur that was never fully obliterated. A sort of humanitarian utopianism was always lingering there, gnawing at his gut … and the impossibility of ever actualizing it served to fuel the core of his lifelong rage.

* * *

With his short sandy hair, black-rimmed glasses, and

starched white shirt, Tuff could easily have passed as a fit gym instructor, a persnickety German bank teller, or a Midwestern drill sergeant. He also evoked the chilling manner of an unhinged psychiatrist: one who enjoyed looking straight through you as he prescribed an interminable course of shock treatment.

One of the biggest troublemakers in our class was a kid named Charles Sorrelli: a blubbery, overweight wiseguy whose rumpled shirttails were always slipping out of his disheveled, wrinkled pants. Sorrelli was whispering a little too loudly one afternoon while Tuff had his back turned at the blackboard. When Tuff spun round and told him to shut his fat face, Sorrelli made the mistake of talking back. Storming across the room, Tuff let go such a powerful punch into Sorrelli's belly that it would have felled a fully grown man.

Right after lunch, Sorrelli returned to the school yard with his mother in tow. But instead of apologizing, Tuff yelled at her, too, his face turning a deep shade of red as he unleashed his fury just inches away from her widening eyes.

Not surprisingly, Tuff didn't last very long at St. Anne's. Even in that rearguard time and place, his disciplinary measures went so far over the line that he was eventually canned, but we never learned anything about the specific details of his dismissal.

If he caught you talking out of turn or passing a note to another student, Tuff's method of maintaining authority was to force you to stand up with your palm held out. With sadistic glee, he'd raise a wooden pointer and hold it stationary for several moments as he absorbed the fright sparkling in your eyes. Then his face would darken with an ugly grimace, and he'd pound you across the hand. If you moved even slightly before the stick made contact, he'd whap you a second time – or however how many times it took before your swollen palm remained still.

There must have been a deep well of sociopathy within Tuff to cause him to attack defenseless children in such a terrifying manner. Perhaps the weight of traveling around the world with a name like *Tuff* – which must have provoked other men to question whether he really was that "tough" – had twisted him in some pernicious and unfathomable manner.

Other than being struck with a pointer, one of the most unbearable things about the seventh grade was being subjected to Tuff's obsessive demand to plow through each and every paragraph of *The Golden Age of Homespun*, a treatise about pre-Industrial America that was published in the early Fifties. Laboring over the driest prose imaginable, we were forced to read about how the pioneers had learned to plant corn, harvest buckets of honey culled from buzzing beehives, and knit their frumpy sweaters from wool gathered from bleating flocks of sheep.

Within minutes the boys would be daydreaming about playing stickball or stoopball – or maybe even caressing the farmer's daughters upon the billowing haystacks. As Charles Sorrelli had so elegantly phrased it one day in the school yard, "What was so damned golden about it anyway? There weren't any transistor radios, Stratocaster guitars, or fin-tailed hot rods, so how did those suckers ever have any fun?"

* * *

The fates had ordained that Renate Lorganina – one of the three "bad" girls of St. Anne's – would be seated right in front of me during the eighth grade. I often whiled away the hours by gazing at the shiny locks of her hair as it cascaded down her back and hung just inches away from my desk. Drew Dunkle sat in front of her, and he told me that Renate would twine her fingertips into his hair when our teacher wasn't looking. For the first time, the boys and girls were no longer positioned in alternating rows but were distributed in alternate seats throughout the room: a chamber that appeared to grow incrementally smaller as the years stretched on.

The three "bad" girls were also regarded as the "hottest" or most desirable ones. While Angela Fischetti was the adolescent incarnation of a russet-haired seductress, and Teresa Travalini was a steaming blonde bombshell, Renate epitomized a pale, auburn haired Fifties starlet with doelike eyes and a wan, woeful smile. But Renate's ghostly pallor was beyond mere paleness. There was a livid tint to her skin, which she claimed was a symptom of the hepatitis that she'd contracted after drinking a dirty glass of water in a Chinese restaurant. Only in later years did we learn that Renate had been shooting up with a dirty needle.

Although she wasn't as pretty as the other two insidious Graces, Renate's withdrawn demeanor lent her a certain mystery and charm. And just like Angela and Teresa, she appeared to be wise beyond her years; but just *what* had wised them up remained a matter of relentless schoolboy speculation. All of which led us to draw one "obvious" conclusion: the bad girls possessed *carnal knowledge*, a "fact" as palpable as the plaster halo that crowned a statue of St. Anne in the church next door.

On the morning that our class was scheduled to pose for a graduation picture, Renate was positioned on the far left of the ensemble; Teresa on the far right; while Angela – bearing a wicked smirk – towered at the center of the top row, her red locks shimmering like a slow-burning fuse. As Nabokov says of Lolita and her classmates: "A fairy princess between her two maids of honor"! When I study certain photos from this era, I'm astonished to see how much I resemble a guileless blond bunny – as naive as naive can be – while the three evil Graces appear as if they're twice my age and many times my maturity.

No wonder that Sister Noel – whose name always reminded me of dolorous Christmas bells echoing across an abandoned Gravesend boulevard – gazed at us with such a mournful regard. For Noel, our little ensemble of lost girls and boys represented only the tip of a looming iceberg. Between the term's commencement in September 1969 and its conclusion in June 1970, something unspeakably malign had engulfed the nation. Even the nuns appeared to realize that the Dark Ages of St. Anne's and the lingering Victorianism of America were suddenly being eclipsed and that Angela and her wily handmaidens would soon be in the forefront of a wicked new generation.

A petite woman with a pointy chin and bookish appearance, Sister Noel wore a veil similar to Maryjane's, which allowed you to see most of her grumpy, sallow face. Perhaps the less enveloped, more open facade reflected a level of empathy that was absent in most of the other nuns; but, unlike Maryjane, her compassion was rooted in fear rather than in an embrace of life's joys or wonders. As evident in her morose expression, Noel was imagining all manner of disaster and distress for us – this most bereft of all lost generations. Nearly every word from her lips resounded with a cheerless, woebegone intonation; yet at the same time she seemed to enjoy delivering such depressing admonitions. And when they didn't sink in properly, she didn't hesitate to use corporal punishment to beat them into us.

Thus, it took a certain measure of courage to rebel while stuck inside this final crucible. And yet, the bad girls – whom I idolized and never ceased to admire from afar – often didn't hesitate to do so. While Noel was positioned with her back turned as she chalked up the blackboard, Angela Fischetti would hike up her skirt, turn round to face the class, and whisper: "You want to see some more, now don't you, boys?" Even then, her adolescent psyche was finely tuned to the immense power she yielded as a precocious tease. And without a doubt, the most impressive lesson I absorbed that year was one that unexpectedly revealed the true nature of what was hidden beneath those beguiling schoolgirl pleats.

Teresa Ravenna had piqued Noel's wrath when she was caught passing a note to Angela. So now, she was bent over her desk with her palms pressed against the tabletop, her butt sticking out at a ninety-degree angle, and her hair hanging straight down from the sides of her bowed head, with her golden locks bathed in crisp afternoon sunlight.

Noel raised a wooden pointer and whipped it through the air with a surprising force, spanking Teresa's firm, cherry-shaped treasures with an impressive *thud*. But then, the rubber tip at the end of the stick caught in one of the pleats. As Noel pulled it back, it lifted Teresa's skirt straight up.

Like a revelation of the Holy Spirit, there they were: her tight white panties, glowing upon a perfectly shaped pubescent sphere, with her bronzed thighs sculpted like the finest Venus, and flecked with honey-colored peach fuzz that caught the fire of the sun as it licked her quivering, undulating flesh.

Despite this humbling chastisement, Teresa didn't lose her cool. Instead, she maintained a sardonic smile throughout the ordeal ... all of which made it that much more enticing.

Sister Noel never tired of informing us that "Life is not a bowl of cherries." But even this late in the game, perched upon the final rung of Lucifer's ladder, at first my mind had a tendency to interpret such remarks in too literal a fashion. Perhaps it was my artistic temperament that caused me to react in this way; for, at once, I visualized a glistening silver bowl, filled with ripe dew-flecked cherries. Nearly fainting in that stuffy classroom – with billows of steam rising from a row of cast-iron radiators that constantly hissed, banged, and rattled – now I imagined sinking my teeth into those juicy, succulent treats:

"But *why* isn't it a bowl of cherries?" I finally blurted out.

In response, Noel threw her hands up, shook her head, and promptly gave up.

With an unwavering resolve, I continued to imagine that life should always be approached as if such a bowl might be lurking there – behind the nearest velvet curtain. For Byron had instilled in me an instinctive belief that we were here to live each and every moment to its fullest.

I had yet to learn that the constant pursuit of joy could also result in a great deal of sorrow.

* * *

Perhaps it was Noel's idea – who was still wringing her hands over the threat of our eternal damnation – or maybe it was just standard operating procedure at St. Anne's, but that spring it was decided that we would spend an afternoon at a Franciscan retreat. The very notion of which, as I sit here typing this, fills my belly with butterflies of mirth and astonishment. I mean – what an absurdity! And to consider that this occurred during the halcyon days of 1970, with an entire globe of hormone-pumping Lolitas shedding their dour Fifties attire and writhing along the sultry sands of the Mediterranean or upon the pastoral fields of Woodstock, perfumed with freshly picked flowers and vials of patchouli, naked under all that solar glory, and impatiently itching for love and adventure.

On the bus ride upstate I retrieved a Richie Rich comic book from my knapsack: a serial about a "poor little rich boy" who could have anything he wanted. Richie usually dressed in a dark blazer, a red bow tie, and expensive leather shoes that his butler, Cadbury, polished to a sheen. Just like me, Richie was blond haired and baby faced, so it was easy to imagine that I was Richie himself, vicariously experiencing the thrilling life of a "poor little rich boy." And this despite the fact that my brother and I nearly had to beg Arthur for our weekly allowance – a mere pittance that was so minuscule we were ashamed to tell our friends about it.

Shortly after the bus pulled out of the parking lot, Charles Sorrelli unlocked his portable record player, and with no one there to stop him – since the nuns were traveling behind us in air-conditioned limousines – he cued a steel needle onto a song by a group called David Peel and the Lower East Side. Every line of their underground hit, "Up Against the Wall," ended with the refrain: *Motherfucker!* (Little did we realize that the tune was originally inspired by Amiri Baraka's poem, "Black People," which had appeared in the *Evergreen Review* only three years earlier.) The boys raucously sang along, relishing this golden opportunity to shout out some truly filthy, soul-enriching vulgarities.

Once we arrived at our destination, David Peel was discreetly silenced, and we disembarked upon a sylvan lawn. There we were met by an unctuous pair of Franciscan brothers who were eagerly rubbing their well-scrubbed palms – hands that had never borne an honest day of labor – while grinning like a pair of demented chimpanzees. They were dressed in burnt-sienna robes engirdled by pine rosary beads, which culminated in a plain wooden cross that dangled at their sides. Appraising us with narrowed, beady eyes, they focused mostly on the cutest boys: the jailbait that would soon enliven their nocturnal fantasies, unrepentant child molesters that they most certainly were.

We were led into a well-furnished auditorium where the slickest of the lot embarked upon a velvet-coated lecture, filled with dollops of false humility and smarmy goodwill, and all of it presented in a butter smooth, melodious manner that stood in stark contrast to the stern caterwauling of our own priests. As he rambled on, Angela Fischetti – who for some incredible reason had deigned to sit beside me – leaned over, whispered in my ear, and asked if I knew what *soul kissing* was. As she tilted her head and smiled, her silky russet hair brushed against my burning cheek. Astonished, I shook my head, no. In response, her moist lips stretched into a knowing grin as she explained that *you slide your tongue* into the other person's *mouth* while your lips are *locked together*.

Whatever the huckster on stage was selling, it paled beside Angela's Mephistophelean revelations.

On the ride home, Renate sat beside me and divulged her plan to "turn me on" to barbiturates. Although I was alarmed by this idea, I also remained too intrigued to immediately refuse her offer.

More than anything I wanted to be *cool*, and now Renate was offering me entrée into the hippest circle of hell. But why? Would transforming a cherub into a demon and stripping it of its wings make her feel even more empowered?

As Sister Noel might say, only God – the cause of it all – could possibly know for sure.

It was thanks to the intervention of a boy named Tony Malatesta that I was saved from certain psychic damnation. One afternoon in the school yard, after he heard about Renate's plan, he took me aside and said that I shouldn't do it.

"Downers aren't cool," he said with a disgruntled expression. "They'll just mess with your head."

But why should I listen to Tony? Because he was by far the coolest kid at St. Anne's. The tallest boy in class, he could easily have passed as a high schooler. And best of all as far as the girls were concerned, he resembled a Hollywood star named Paul Newman – a handsome, charismatic actor who made the

Gravesend women swoon. Lusted after by the girls and vicariously emulated by the boys, Tony was also cherished by the nuns. With his winning smile and gentlemanly manner, he knew exactly how to kiss their habit-swaddled bottoms. Embodying that rare combination of brawn and intelligence, he was a "brownnoser" without necessarily acting like one. Tony could hold his own in a fight, but he never abused the weaker boys, and he only fought when provoked. You'd be hard-pressed to find a kid any cooler than Tony. Although he was well aware of this, he usually assumed a modest demeanor.

And so, after our brief chat, I decided to say no to Renate.

The day before graduation she penned a pithy phrase in my autograph book: "I *wanted* to take you higher." (A remark that caused me endless strife while attempting to explain its meaning to my nosy mother.) When I passed my book around the room, Ann Napoli, one of the "good girls" who loved to tease me about my "liberal" politics, wrote:

> There is a place called Bellevue
> where all the retards go,
> and on the steps
> was Couteau screaming:
> "Let my people go!"

Years later, when I worked at an advocacy agency for homeless schizophrenics and periodically visited the halls of Bellevue Psychiatric Center, I'd often smile upon recalling Ann's uncannily clairvoyant remark.

* * *

Toward the end of the Sixties, the progressive trends that had blossomed across the country eventually took root even upon the intolerant streets of Gravesend. Instead of separating the classes into three hierarchical tiers, now the "dumbest" kids were mixed in with the "brightest." And instead of being taught by a single teacher all day, in the afternoon we were shuttled over to Sister Eleanor, our literature instructor. A lanky, swarthy skinned, melancholy woman who reeked of Old World Victorianism, prim-and-proper prudery, and a relentless fastidiousness, Eleanor was possessed by a withdrawn and brooding soul. And it was because of her that I was nearly left back and forced to repeat the grade.

For Sister Eleanor, literature seemed to begin and end in the staid, dowdy parlors of Queen Victoria's England. Through the medium of such watered down, lackluster, impotent prose she tried to impress upon us the importance of the written word while reading aloud from the gelded abridgements of Dickens, Thackeray, or Charles Reade. With her sullen mien, morose expression, and gaunt, bony frame, she evoked one of those wretched, disconsolate El Greco evangelists of the sixteenth-century. Hovering in her lonesome perch at the front of the room, she seemed to be reaching out of a picture frame: hoping to be plucked by the hand of the Maker himself and whisked away, into that far more sacrosanct world beyond.

In the eyes of this ill-disposed literary saint – who regarded us with palpable disapproval from behind a thick pair of granny glasses – my first serious transgression occurred after we were told to memorize a poem, then present it to the class.

I'd carefully rehearsed the "Celebration of the Lizard," a lyric composed by Jim Morrison, the lead singer of a rock group called the Doors. But unbeknownst to me, Angela had selected the same verse, which began with a haunting line stolen from Frazier's *Golden Bough*: "Not to touch the earth, / Not to see the sun ..." Angela presented it just moments before it was my turn, so now I had to think fast. The only other lyric I knew by heart was "Piggies": a cynical ditty written by the Beatles' lead guitarist, George Harrison. Not knowing what else to do, I decided to go with that, instead.

Although Angela's rendition of the "Lizard" must have sounded bizarre to Eleanor she had wisely censored the more provocative parts, so it was opaque enough to pass muster. But in every line, "Piggies" oozed with contempt for the human race, and Eleanor was visibly disturbed by it. Glaring at me throughout my presentation, when I finished she icily groused: "Rather *cynical*."

Near the end of the term, just as we were about to take our final exam, Eleanor announced that anyone who hadn't yet handed in their term paper on a "Great American" must do so now, or else include it as an essay on the test that we were about to take. Since I hadn't even decided on a subject, I had yet to accomplish a stitch of research. And so, once again, I was forced to think quickly.

The previous weekend, Arthur had driven us to Levittown, Long Island – the location of one of the first prefabricated suburbs – to visit my mother's sister. While I was stuck there against my will, out of sheer boredom I tried to amuse myself by reading through a stack of old magazines. An issue of *Time* featured a story about a pioneer of modern plumbing who was christened with the peculiar-sounding name of Thomas Crapper. As I continued to read, I learned that Mr. Crapper, an Englishman, had invented several devices that led to significant improvements in water closets for flush toilets, such as the floating *ball cock* (what a wonderful phrase to emerge from the age of Victoria!). The author added that, despite certain urban legends to the contrary, the terms "crap" and "crapper" weren't actually derived from the inventor's surname.

I was gazing up at the white styrofoam tiles of the classroom ceiling and waiting for my intuition to kick in when it occurred to me to transplant Crapper to America and to use him as the subject of the essay. I stuck to the facts as best as I could recollect them, all except for this one minor detail: that despite his greatness, Crapper was a bloody Englishman.

The following week, while we were horsing around in the school yard, Tony Malatesta – the golden boy himself – approached with a subtle smile curling along the edge of his lips. He said that Eleanor had decided to fail me for what she'd assumed was a flagrantly crude and completely fictional account of a certain unnamable inventor. But then, Tony had spoken up on my behalf. He informed Eleanor that I wasn't really such a bad kid after all, and that maybe she should give me a second chance.

He added that she'd repeatedly mouthed the word *cynical*. How *awfully cynical* I must have been: not only to compose such filth but also to recite that atrocious poem, which equated the human race with a bunch of wallowing, mud-encrusted swine. But Tony had saved the day, and now he was here to tell me all about it. And no doubt, to glory in his good deed and to bask in his extraordinary coolness.

* * *

As graduation approached, Angela, Teresa, Renate, and a handful of boys and girls from the other eighth-grade classes decided that we should have a prom. As word of this insurrection spread, increasing numbers of students pressured their parents to demand one, until Noel finally organized a meeting in the auditorium to discuss it.

At heart, Noel was a softie, so she eventually gave in. Not only would there be a prom – St. Anne's first – but we could even hire a rock 'n' roll band to perform with electric guitars.

Accompanied by Tony and the unholy trio, I attended about

a dozen auditions throughout Gravesend, Bensonhurst, and Bay Ridge in search of the ultimate rock 'n' roll band. For the next few weeks we met with hooligans who smoked cigarettes down to the filter and blew the smoke in our faces as they blasted tunes from Gibson and Stratocaster guitars, miming groups such as the Stones, the Doors, the Cream, and the Who. Incarnating a weird hybrid that melded the quintessence of a Sixties hipster with a Fifties *cafone* (a "crass, vulgar boor"), these Brooklyn toughs could perform popular ballads celebrating the dawn of a New Age while simultaneously cracking open your skull.

By the early Seventies some would even grow their hair long and sport bell-bottoms, tie-dyed T-shirts, and other typical symbols of the Love Generation. But they never lost their fighting skills or their psychopathic bravado; and they wouldn't hesitate to swing a baseball bat over your head if you made the wrong move and pissed them off. But once they started tripping on LSD they quickly fried their brains, often ingesting four times the usual dose and outdoing each other in a frenetic competition to see who could trip the farthest away from the earth while still retaining a semblance of sanity. Thus intoxicated, they wandered aimlessly through barren midnight lots or raced in hopped-up convertibles while chasing evanescent angels.

Though they were the freakiest of freaks spawned by the spirit of lysergic acid, they left nary a trace in the chronicles of the time. Some melded back into society and became lawyers or accountants. Others never descended from their visionary heights and ended up in insane asylums. Still others abandoned all pretense of normalcy, surrendered to the zeitgeist, and became cultural outcasts living in the marginal communes that sprouted across America, until finally recanting their psychedelic detours and dismissing it all as merely a diaphanous daydream.

We finally decided upon the Daze'n'Nights, who were widely regarded as the best band in Gravesend and whose rendition of "Sunshine of Your Love" always packed a punch. But except for the music itself, the prom evinced all the trappings of a dance party from the early Fifties.

You were expected to buy your date a traditional corsage, usually a white orchid, which she'd pin on a taffeta dress. Once you were fitted into a navy-blue blazer, a white button-down shirt, and a tightly knotted necktie, you'd go to meet her family. Over coffee and Stella Doro cookies, her father would calmly inform you that if anything unseemly should transpire between you and his dear, beloved princess your balls would be hanging from their clothesline in the backyard the following morning. "And don't get any ideas that just because you're taking Suzie to a prom that you can do anything to disgrace my family!"

As you swallowed your cookies, her muscle-bound brothers, bubble-gum chewing sisters, anisette-sipping grandfathers, and stern-faced Sicilian grandmothers would be sitting in a circle in the living room, nodding their heads and grunting in approval. Thus, along with the majority of the boys – who were either too scared to ask a girl out or in no mood to deal with her family – I preferred to go it alone, free and unencumbered.

On the night of the prom, as the Daze'n'Nights blasted music from a bulky set of Kustom amplifiers, with the lights dimmed and the dancers nervously milling about a basement chamber called the "Green Room" (because of its mint-green floor tiles), Renate asked me to accompany her to a stairwell behind the stage.

Once we shut a heavy metal door behind us and entered the darkness, Renate commanded me to smack her face. She'd taken too many Quaaludes, she said, so now she was almost passing out and needed to be revived.

But why didn't she ask Peter Riposo, her date, to handle this thankless task? Renate said it was because Peter was already annoyed with her for getting stoned, so she didn't want to make matters any worse. Instead, she'd invented some excuse to buttonhole me privately.

As she slurred her words, I noticed a shadow flitting across a tiny windowpane that was embedded in the door. Peter was trying to peer in, with his bulbous nose pressed against the glass. I had no idea what she told him, but maybe he wasn't convinced that we weren't trying to fondle each other.

"Smack my face," she whispered.

Her glazed eyes were half closed as I smacked her softly on the cheek.

"No ... *harder.*"

I smacked her again, this time a little more forcefully, but still not as hard as she wanted. I just didn't have it in me to strike a woman.

Exiting the stairwell, I glanced up at the louvered windows near the top of the wall. I could see the bottom half of the legs of the parents who were lingering outside. Every now and then a mother would squat down, cup her hand against a windowpane, and nervously search for her child.

After the prom was over, the students on the prom committee sauntered over to Jahn's Ice Cream Parlor on 86th Street. Commandeering a plush red-leather booth beside a front window, we ordered an exotic array of sundaes, slathered with chocolate syrup and topped with long stemmed glazed cherries.

* * *

The last few times that I attended mass I ran into some of the kids from St. Anne's, but for the most part the children with whom I shared so many mornings and afternoons for eight straight years simply vanished from my life. Most of the boys had enrolled in either Bishop Ford or Xaverian: the "boys only" Catholic schools that were run by Jesuits and Franciscan brothers. And the girls attended institutions such as St. Edmunds, Fontbonne Hall Academy, or Bishop Kearney: the "girls only" Catholic high schools.

I just couldn't imagine being trapped for four more years in such an unnatural setting, surrounded by pimply adolescent boys and without a single girl to admire.

An Experiment

My mother would often meet with our next-door neighbor Josie for coffee and pastries, and in this way she heard about a radical new high school named after the philosopher John Dewey. It had first opened its doors the previous year, but it was already being recognized for an innovative art and music department and for an "experimental" system of allowing students to plan their own curriculum and design their own courses. Classes started an hour earlier than at the other public schools, and they ended at four o'clock, an hour later. But you were given plenty of unsupervised free time throughout the day, during which you could visit resource centers to study, or hang out on a beautifully landscaped campus with your guitar-strumming friends.

Josie explained all this to Bridget with an air of incredulity as well as trepidation and disapproval. How had their daughter Regina managed to hoodwink her, she wondered, into going along with such a scheme? But the more that Bridget heard about Dewey, the more intrigued she became, until she finally exclaimed: "But that sounds just perfect for my son!"

Bridget presented all this to me as if the choice were entirely mine to make, all the while inoculating me with her rosy-tinted vision of the school until I wouldn't have dreamed of making any other choice. Which, in this case, worked out for the best. No longer would I be hemmed in by the narrow-minded parochialism of an all-white Catholic school in Little Sicily. Dewey was attended mostly by secular Jews, and it was racially mixed with Blacks, Latinos, and Asians. In later years, it would be hailed as the greatest experiment ever attempted in an

American high school in the twentieth century.

But of course, from Arthur – with his head buried in the sheltering cove of his *New York Times* – I received not a word of advice. Instead, he was busy scanning the newsprint and grumbling about the injustices in the world chronicled by his favorite reporters. Like many fathers during this period, he remained largely unaware of the needs of his children.

* * *

Disembarking from an elevated line on Bay 50th Street, I entered a sprawling tree-lined campus where a steady stream of teenagers was flowing into a main building. Instead of donning the starched button-down shirts and pleated skirts of St. Anne's, they dressed casually, with most of the boys sporting jeans and T-shirts while the girls wore denim miniskirts, brightly colored leggings, and peasant blouses. And instead of bearing the grave expressions typical of students about to be sequestered into classrooms, there was often a look of merriment beaming from their animated facades.

The art department was better equipped than that of many colleges, and it hosted separate rooms for painting, drawing, sculpture, printmaking, photography, and ceramics. There was even a course for commercial art – the only one that I avoided. The music department was equally advanced. The southern rim of the twelve-acre campus was ringed with practice rooms for musicians, who performed in a full orchestral ensemble twice a year in the auditorium.

During my freshman year a painting instructor gave me the key to his room, where I spent many hours alone, composing watercolors. In my sophomore year, a drawing teacher organized a noncredit course held on Saturday afternoons that featured nude models. How he managed to accomplish this without causing an uproar at the Board of Ed, I'll never know. Perhaps he didn't bother to inform them. After all, it was the beginning of the rebellious Seventies, the decade of "anything goes." I was one of twelve students that were invited to attend the class, and the drawings inspired by these sessions helped me to gain admittance to the art department in a state university. This experience also engendered a lifelong devotion to portraying the female form. I stepped into this tradition unwittingly; little did I realize that, when you draw the nude, you *draw from* the nude, like a bucket drawing water from a well. But the model is also witness to the artist's own unveiling; for he stands there without a shield, his gleamy eyes hungry for beauty – as if he is the truly naked one.

My parents were impressed by the school's youthful instructors, many of whom were in their early twenties. After returning from a parents-teacher's day, with a mixture of astonishment and amusement Arthur exclaimed: "You can't tell the teachers from the students! Half of them have long hair, wear blue jeans, and look nearly the same age as you do!" Bridget was equally delighted. "Yes," she added, "and they're so *enthusiastic* about their work ..."

But what I was most ecstatic about was the *girls*. On sunny days, many of them wore colorful Danskin leotards or nearly transparent blouses, minus any bras. I was amazed to discover that if the sunlight hit the thin cotton fabric at just the right angle, I could see their pert young nipples as they wandered across the campus.

Transcending the tomfoolery of the Holy Spirit, this was a vision that gave a young lad something to believe in.

* * *

It was the spring of my sophomore year, and I was perched

on a hill near the entrance to the school. Two freshmen girls glanced up at me, wandered off the path, and came gamboling up the hill.

Megan O'Malley was a lanky redhead whose long stringy hair was rarely brushed, and it fell to her waist in a sensual disorder. A talented comic who would later pursue a career in stand-up, her emerald eyes would glow whenever she made a louche remark or related a salty joke. But more often than not, Megan seemed to be lost in a hazy daydream, with her mouth hanging half-opened and her eyes glazed and unfocused. Everyone said that she was a bit "spaced out" from all the LSD that she'd imbibed during her adolescent years.

Megan's sidekick, Rachel Carlson, was a petite Jewish brunette who wore her curly hair in a bouncy 'fro. Curvy and well proportioned, she was endowed with bright cerulean eyes that were now twinkling with coquetry. I began to blush when she asked, "So, are you a virgin? We're asking all the boys on campus today ..."

"Yeah, we're conducting a *survey*," Megan added with a straight face.

My cheeks were burning red, but since I'd been trained in Catholic School to never tell a lie, I answered in the affirmative.

"Well," Rachel smiled, "we'll have to *do* something about that!"

So after school that day, the three of us boarded the F train to Montgomery Place in Park Slope, where Rachel led us to a stately brownstone stoop, bedecked with a regal pair of granite lions.

At first we passed through a living room filled with tapestried furniture and antiques; then I followed the girls up a carpeted mahogany stairway. Although Rachel wasn't exactly a member of the haute bourgeoisie, she was a step above our station on West Twelfth Street, as both of her parents were lawyers. But Megan hailed from a more working-class milieu. Her father was a bus driver, and her family lived above a noisy saloon at Park Circle, adjacent to Prospect Park.

Approaching a second-floor landing, I spotted a blonde woman seated at a rolltop desk, in a room softly lit by a Tiffany lamp.

"Hi, Mom! This is my friend Couteau, from school."

With her gold bifocals balanced at the tip of her nose, Mrs. Carlson glanced up. As our eyes met, she nodded and smiled warmly. I noticed that she possessed the same friendly, open gaze as her daughter. Then we continued to Rachel's room, on the fourth floor.

Within minutes, the three of us were sprawled across a queen-sized waterbed. The girls unbuttoned my shirt and grabbed at my jeans, kissing and fondling me, and occasionally caressing each other, as well. After we were undressed they took turns bouncing and squirming on top of me, like a pair of high school cheerleaders enthusiastically rooting for their home team.

Not only was I losing my virginity to two such experienced nymphets, but all this was occurring while Rachel's mother was just two flights below, working on her legal briefs. Despite Rachel's reassurance, I was convinced that at any moment her mother might walk in unannounced. With the heavily carpeted stairway and hall, I figured that we wouldn't hear her approach until the very last moment. Thus, my rollicking entrée to the world of sex was like a roller coaster ride that shifted back and forth between peaks and vales of fear and euphoria.

Once we were dressed again, Rachel leaned across the bed to cue Jimi Hendrix's *Are You Experienced?* on a turntable, while Megan climbed into a rattan chair that was hanging from a chain attached to the ceiling. As I spun her round, she shrieked with delight until finally exclaiming:

"No more! I'm getting dizzy!"

"But that's nothing new," Rachel laughed, "you were already dizzy!"

"So," I asked, turning to Rachel, "how did *you* lose your virginity?"

"Yeah," Megan exclaimed, "give us all the *sordid details*."

"It was last summer," Rachel smiled, "after I turned fourteen. Markus was seventeen. We'd been seeing each other for just a few months, but I considered him to be my boyfriend. So I invited him over one night, when my parents weren't home, and we went up to my room and had *sex*."

Dramatically raising an eyebrow, Megan asked, "And did it hurt?"

"It was a bit painful, but Markus was very sweet. The next morning, my mother asked me, 'Who was here last night?' Of course, I said '*Nobody* was here.' I figured that, if I told her, she'd realize that I'd lost my virginity. How she could she not? But she insisted, 'No, *someone* was here." I'd completely forgotten that it was snowing. When she came home that night, she saw our footprints going up and down the stoop!"

"Oh, no," Megan groaned, "you were busted!"

"*Totally!* But when I told her about Markus, she said, 'Well, that's fine; you don't have to *lie* to me.'"

"Your mom's just *so cool*," Megan murmured, now staring at the ceiling with her mouth agape.

"And how did you feel after your first time?" I wondered.

"The next morning, while I was walking to the subway on the way to school, I thought: 'Now, I'm not a virgin, and I'll *never* be a virgin again.'" Shifting to a more subdued tone, she added: "It felt as if some *momentous thing* had just occurred."

*   *   *

Trish Adler was more introverted than most of the other kids at school, and her gentle hazel eyes effused a contemplative aura. A petite girl with an androgynous look, normally she was possessed by a doleful air. But if Trish smoked pot she'd become overwhelmed by a contagious laughter, which was often accompanied by a self-deprecating wit.

Whenever she read me excerpts from her poems, I'd visualize the lyrics etched in silverpoint across a midnight sky, especially when she portrayed the ephemeral lines of shooting stars. It was a frequent metaphor in her work, and perhaps one that highlighted her own lack of grounding.

My weekly allowance hadn't increased much since the days of St. Anne's, so I took a job at a local butcher shop and saved up enough to invite Trish to dinner and to the movies. We'd usually patronize one of the local theaters that were just barely managing to forestall bankruptcy, their audiences having been winnowed by the growing popularity of television.

Many of these old showcases resembled enormous caverns, suffused with a lingering scent of popcorn and with their floors sticky with spilled soda pop. In the stifling summertime, years before air conditioners appeared in our homes, they also served another purpose: providing temporary escape from the baking Brooklyn pavements. The mere sight of those white-and-blue signs embossed with images of dripping icicles and the words AIR COOLED gave us hope. But upon exiting the theater and hitting a sizzling wall of heat, all hope quickly evaporated.

One of our favorite haunts was an ornate but dilapidated Art Deco dive on Coney Island Avenue called the Kent. The director Woody Allen would later feature its interior in his *Purple Rose of Cairo*, a film in which a character walks out of the projection screen and enters real life. Allen nostalgically referred to the Kent as a "last run theater." It was also notorious for its malfunctioning vending machine. Instead of a waxed paper cup descending first to receive a gurgling stream of soda pop, more often than not the liquid would splash down the chute *sans* receptacle. Only when the dark stream trickled to a halt and drained away would an empty cup finally arrive, neatly plopping into place, filled only with crushed ice.

Far more lavish than the Kent was an opulent establishment on Flatbush Avenue known as the Kings. It was one of five "Wonder Theaters" in the Loew's chain that, along with the Paramount, was once regarded as Brooklyn's most glamorous. The third largest theater in New York, it was dwarfed only by Radio City Music Hall and Madison Square Garden. It was even equipped with a regulation-size basketball court and a gym in the basement, for the staff. But now the court was padlocked, the staff reduced to a bare minimum. And the only films they could only afford to show were over a year old: hence, the nominal fee of a buck and a half. Yet the Kings never lost its glamour. A French Renaissance lobby still featured bronze figurines and walnut paneling. Inside, there were curved ceilings, sweeping arches, lighting fixtures etched with elegant designs, carved walnut columns, and Baroque murals. These garish, brightly colored paintings were framed by glazed terra cotta molding, gilded ornamentation, and pink marble. Seductively shaped plaster maidens loomed over the balustrades of the grand staircases, and a spooky pair of satyrs flanked the stage and leered back at them.

This last detail seemed especially appropriate, since our main purpose in being there was to honor Dionysus. Selecting a secluded spot, we'd anxiously wait for the lights to dim so that we could fondle each other in the enveloping darkness. Although the Kings was equipped with 3,676 seats, on most nights there were barely a dozen paying customers, so we had plenty of privacy.

Covering my lap with a jean jacket, Trish would cautiously run her fingers along the swollen contours of my jeans as if tentatively exploring the landscape of a foreign world. Did she really belong there? Did she really want to be part of it? Her fingertips danced back and forth over this unresolved question mark curving ever upward. But the waves of her desire often seemed to be held in abeyance; perhaps because, until now, she'd only been interested in other girls.

As we slumped across the velvet folding chairs and her hands worked their way into my unzipped jeans, sometimes I'd imagine that we were directing our own steamy drama: one that not even a Marcello Mastroianni or an Anita Ekberg had dared to explore on those gargantuan screens. In between our steamy make-out sessions, we'd vicariously partake in a variety of zany Hollywood adventures; but, for the most part, we simply ignored the flickering specters as we wriggled in our squeaky seats.

Trish and I had first met during my junior year. She was seated by herself on the grass, composing poetry in her journal. As I approached, I spotted a copy of the *Whole Earth Catalog* lying next to her knapsack: a first edition, from 1969.

"Do you mind if I have a look at that?"

As if awakening from a dream, she glanced up and softly intoned, "No, go right ahead." Then she returned to her nihilistic scribbling.

Thumbing through the newsprint pages, I studied designs for cartwheels and wooden footbridges, and ads for fruit presses and Moog synthesizers. Exhibiting typical Sixties hubris, on the inside cover the editors had written: "We *are* gods and might as well get good at it." The catalog also featured a review of *The Year 2000*, a text authored in 1967 by a future-study expert named Herman Kahn, who predicted:

If computer capacities were to continue to increase by a factor of ten every two or three years until the end of the century … then all current concepts about computer limitations will have to be reconsidered.

The front and back covers of the catalog were illustrated with one of the first photos of the whole Earth taken from outer space. From a distance of 400,000 miles, our planet appeared to be no larger than a Roosevelt dime. On the back cover, the word "FURTHUR" (sic) was printed in large white letters on a shiny black background. Though I hadn't noticed it at first, below the image of the Earth, in minuscule font, the word *closer* hovered like a wandering asteroid.

Little did we realize that the catalog was part of a broader attempt to reprogram the counterculture, turning America's youth into a bunch of depoliticized hippies who would merely "subsist" in the margins of society. The publisher, Stewart Brand, had joined (or infiltrated?) author Ken Kesey's group, the Merry Pranksters, and had promoted LSD in the early Sixties: a substance that helped to dissolve the clear thinking and hard-earned discipline of so many aspiring political organizers.

Decades later, in seeming contradiction to his "whole earth" environmentalism, Brand would speak out in favor of using nuclear power plants. He would also support the CIA's top public-relations propagandist in the so-called war on terror, John Rendon, whose PR firm concocted numerous falsehoods for the Pentagon in order to sell the 2003 war with Iraq to the public. Brand would eventually fall under suspicion of being a CIA asset.

And the futurist author Herman Kahn, a RAND Corporation

analyst who believed in "social control," was well-known for proselytizing about how to "survive" a nuclear holocaust. All we needed, he said, were two-hundred million fallout shelters.

Kahn had unwittingly served as one of the models for Stanley Kubrick's "Dr. Strangelove": a sociopathic fascist portrayed by Peter Sellers in a satirical film subtitled *How I Learned to Stop Worrying and Love the Bomb*. Thus, an enthusiastic book review of anything crafted by this atom bomb-obsessed zealot would, on the surface, seem to be out of place in a *Whole Earth Catalog*. But this was a time when even stranger things were covertly lurking beneath the chilly surface of the Cold War.

The following weekend I visited Trish at her home in Mill Basin. As soon as I stepped inside, she introduced me to her mother, a psychoanalyst who worked at Kings County Psychiatric Hospital.

Mrs. Adler was pleasant and soft-spoken, but she possessed an intense, penetrating gaze that was impossible to ignore. Judging from the anxiety that seemed to flash from her eyes, I imagined that, besides trying to figure out if we were a couple, she was also wondering if her daughter would even *want* to have a boyfriend. As we grew closer, Trish confided in me that such concerns were precisely what most worried Mrs. Adler, who had indeed been hoping that we were romantically involved.

"I hate to look into my mother's dark eyes," she said. "I always have the feeling that she's looking straight through me."

I suppose it didn't help that, like so many headshrinkers, Mrs. Adler had a tendency to overanalyze every little word or gesture, no matter how inconsequential they might be. No wonder that Trish seemed to be teetering on the brink of depression.

*   *   *

Perhaps because he bore a close resemblance to the homely figure of President Nixon, who by then had dropped 539,129 tons of explosives on the peasants of Cambodia, I soon came to regard our principal, Sol Levine, with a certain contempt. With his polyester suit and stiff, somber demeanor, he just didn't seem to belong in such an avant-garde institution.

One day after school, he caught me squirming on top of Trish behind some bushes on the south side of the lawn. We were ravenously tongue kissing with our eyes closed when we heard a voice gravely intone: "Do you really think this is *appropriate?*" That dreadful adjective! I looked up, paused for a moment, then replied, "Yes, I think it's *quite* appropriate."

Without another word, I stood up, grabbed Trish by the hand, and triumphantly marched away in satyric glory.

Though I wasn't aware of it back then, Trish had arranged for a series of informal counseling sessions with our biology teacher, Leonard Borg. A young man in his early twenties, Borg wore his long hair parted down the center and sported a pair of granny glasses – all in imitation of the Beatles' rhythm guitarist, John Lennon. According to Trish, Borg had become a teacher in order to avoid the military draft and the Vietnam War.

One rainy afternoon we were seated in a corridor across from his office, near the entrance to the school. We must have looked bored or dispirited. When Borg emerged from his room, his eyes lingered upon us sympathetically, then he motioned me over with a wave of his hand.

Holding up a shiny brass key, he said, "This is the key to my office. I won't be returning until four o'clock. Maybe you and Trish could use some privacy." He paused for a moment, then added: "You can lock the door from the inside."

Instead of doing anything scandalous, once we entered this windowless cubicle we just sat on top of a desk and self-consciously chatted. For, despite our mutual admiration, an invisible wall often seemed to separate us – like an obstacle that couldn't be breached.

*   *   *

Around this time my mother was hired as an office manager in an import-export firm, located on Nassau Street. One morning while my parents were both working in Manhattan, I invited Trish over to my house. Once we snuck inside, I led her directly to my room.

Reclining on a bedspread, I unzipped her jeans, removed all her clothing, and slowly caressed her soft white skin.

All the while she lay there silently, as if frozen with uncertainty over what to do. Her kisses were nervous; her caresses were tentative; and the look in her eyes was pensive and melancholy.

As if by a process of osmosis, I gradually seemed to absorb her angst until I was no longer aroused. The cheerful sunbeams streaming through the window and bathing our youthful flesh in shimmering luminosity now seemed to be mocking us. And more than ever, I sensed that invisible obstacle standing between us.

When we returned to school, we parted with hardly a word. After such an awkward, fruitless encounter we drifted apart – ashamed as well as confused. But then Trish embraced the obstacle and became what she'd been all along: a woman who loved other women.

*   *   *

By the time I began my senior year my hair was flowing down to my shoulders in long feathery locks, parted in the center and layer cut, as was the fashion for hip young laddies in the early Seventies. But since Gravesend still hovered between the Forties and Fifties, my friends and I were always looking for trouble whenever we appeared like that in the rearguard Sicilian ghetto that we ironically called our "home."

One afternoon after a final bell had sounded and classes were dismissed, I remained on campus with my friends Tina D'Angelo and Max Cohen. Tina was a bubbly, convivial girl who devoted several hours each day to her pottery, throwing clay on a wheel in the ceramics studio. Her overalls were usually stained with splotches of dried terra cotta, while Max's eyes were usually red-rimmed and squinty from the fat joints of pot that he'd imbibe with a religious devotion. But on that day, Max was in possession of a far more forbidden substance.

"There's a lot of bad acid going around, laced with ampheta-mine," he said, while lighting a joint and passing it around. "But Rachel Carlson's friend Markus makes his own organic mescaline. It's a hundred percent pure."

It was a few weeks before graduation, and Max was plan-ning on tripping during the commencement ceremony. "Do you want to try some?" he asked. "I can give both of you a few grams to take home. Or we could take some now!" Dangling a baggie filled with a tawny-colored powder, he added, "You'll definitely have a *great* experience."

Tina and I declined, so Max tucked the baggie back inside his jean jacket as we boarded the elevated line heading for Coney Island. It was late in the day, and most of the other stu-dents had already departed, so the train was nearly empty.

Sitting at the end of a car, we were jabbering with a typically unrestrained, teenage intensity when I happened to glance up.

Standing before us was a man wearing a bright silver badge

and a starched blue uniform. In those days, transit cops had a reputation for being out of control and converting their boredom and frustration into acts of violence. As we would soon discover, this one was no exception.

For a moment my eyes focused on the wall behind him. A gaunt black-and-white poster was displayed in a shiny chrome frame, and unlike the other more colorful ads its starkness served to highlight a serious message. It was a list of Governor Rockefeller's new drug laws, and it carefully noted the grave penalties associated with each type of criminal possession.

"Rocky" was waging a war against the nation's rebellious, anticonformist youth, and drug busts were the easiest way to get rid of such renegades. The ad announced that possession of an ounce of mescaline, such as the one now hidden in Max's jacket, was an invitation to live in a federal penitentiary for a rather lengthy stay. Indeed, what better way to nullify an entire generation: first distract them with the "voice of God," then lock them up and toss away the key!

Looming over us, the cop's eagle eyes narrowed upon their prey.

"You should be ashamed of yourself," he barked at Tina, "sitting here with boys who look like girls!"

Max and I immediately assumed that he was trying to provoke us into saying or doing something stupid so he could bash in our skulls and haul our asses off to jail. So we each remained silent and adopted a look of complete indifference. But Tina lost her cool and started shouting: "Don't just sit there! *Do* something!"

Max turned to her and whispered: "Just stay calm. Don't let him get to you. That's exactly what he wants; you're just playing into his hands."

The uniformed sadist continued to rage at us until Tina burst into tears. Max held her hand as I discreetly scribbled the cop's badge number onto the cover of my spiral-bound notebook.

Brandishing his night stick, he seemed to be coming in for the kill. But then the train jolted to a halt at Coney Island, and the doors slid open. Now there were plenty of other commuters coming and going, and he backed off – thus avoiding any witnesses to his violence.

We didn't even say good-bye to each other; we just bolted away in separate directions.

When I returned home, I told Bridget all about it. At that time, she was vice-president of the PTA. "All right," she said, "we're going to call Mrs. Jones, the PTA president. Go up to my room. When I holler, pick up the phone."

Bridget reached for a kitchen telephone as I ran up the stairs. Once I was on the line, she introduced me to the president and hung up.

Mrs. Jones asked me to describe exactly what had occurred, so I related everything down to the last detail, including the cop's badge number.

Perhaps it was my youthful candor, or maybe it was the budding writer in me that knew how to tell a good story; but by the time I finished, my words had triggered a pregnant silence.

"Is there anything else you'd like to tell me? Do you recall any other instances during which the police behaved in a questionable manner?"

I paused for a moment, then added: "They certainly seem to treat the Black kids differently. Sometimes they rough them up for no reason, or push them into the cars when the train's already full."

In the lingering silence that followed, I could sense that my words had moved her, but I wasn't sure why. For, unbeknownst to me, Mrs. Jones was an African American.

The next day the elevated station was filled with an entirely different crew of cops. And they kept their hands off the students and minded their own business. When I told Bridget about it, she smiled and said: "Sometimes, *who* you know is more important than *what* you know."

The following year, when Mrs. Jones stepped down from her position she nominated Bridget. And being so well liked, my mother easily won the election and served as the next PTA president.

The communication of certain kinds of pain often transcends the boundary of mere words. All these years later, I can still hear the sympathetic tone of Mrs. Jones' voice in my mind; but even more resonant are those moments of pregnant silence.

*   *   *

The grim contrast between the carefree kids of high school and the hardened hooligans of Gravesend was growing more apparent to me each day. The long-haired hippies at Dewey, bearing their mellow smiles and stoned-out, dilated pupils, would be tossing Frisbees and strumming acoustic guitars, while the boys of Little Sicily were better known for pastimes such as smashing faces and cracking skulls.

Bearing this in mind, perhaps no portrait of West Twelfth Street would be complete without paying homage to its most terrible and frightening figure, Nunzio Baritoni:

In the years before he lost his mind and ended up as a drug-ravaged zombie, Nunzio's relationship to both domesticated and wild animals was somewhat unusual, to say the least.

One of my earliest memories of him goes back to when we were each about twelve years old. It was the early evening, and Arthur had just returned from work. He said that Nunzio had been standing at the corner, staring at a bird chirping in a tree beside his house. When Arthur asked, *Nunzio, what are you looking at?* he replied, *I'm studying the way that birds speak.* But it wasn't with the soft, empathic gaze of a nature lover that Nunzio regarded his avian comrades. It was with the cold gleaming glare of a lion honing in on its vulnerable prey.

Looking back on it now, it's clear that my father was one of the first to realize that Nunzio had more than a few screws loose in his noggin. And this was in the early years, well before he blew his mind from sampling every imaginable variety of street drug, including such unedifying substances as horse tranquilizers.

A few years later, when he was about fourteen or fifteen, I entered Nunzio's alleyway one afternoon and noticed a mad gleam shining in his chocolate-brown eyes. He was holding a grimy hammer in his hand, and when I asked, *What are you hammering?* he excitedly replied, *Come here, I'll show you …*

He led me to a telephone pole at the back of his yard, where he'd just crucified a frog. It's weblike hands and feet were stretched out – fixed to the wooden pole and punctured by four large rusty nails.

As Vladimir Nabokov says in *Laughter in the Dark*, perhaps "it is best not to inquire into the things he did to cats."

Nunzio's father, Ernesto Baritoni, was a gnarled, wiry man who wore thick horn-rimmed glasses, which had the effect of magnifying his cruel dark eyes. One of the only adults who could, at least for a time, tame Nunzio, he was also the only one that Nunzio would listen to and even obey.

"But Nunzio," Ernesto would moan, "what the hell is wrong with you?" I can still recall Ernesto's dramatic displays of frustration over his son's cognitive shortcomings, yelling and screaming at him as if he were a child. With his patience worn to a frazzle, he would exclaim: "Why can't you be more like these other boys?" – a question that he'd pose right in front of us, as if trying to convince Nunzio's friends that the apple had fallen not near the tree but far away from it.

Nunzio's eyes would glaze over, and he'd regard Ernesto with a slack-jawed expression of befuddlement. With a dumb, beast-in-the-headlights stare, he'd squat on his stoop like a lump on a log, while Ernesto waited for his son's brain to connect the dots.

"*Strunz!*" Ernesto would finally exclaim. "Listen to what they're telling you! Otherwise, you'll end up in deep shit one day ... Do you hear what I'm saying?"

When he was a bit older, sixteen or seventeen, Nunzio purchased a boa constrictor, and he fed it live rats. He just loved to watch it devour those struggling rodents. Beaming with pride, he came walking along the street one day with the serpent draped over his shoulders like an oversized necklace. And with a satanic grin, he lifted it up and gingerly placed it round my neck. But moments later, slithering and squirming, it began to tighten its grip. Soon, it was choking me. So I said, *Nunzio, please. Take it away.*

Somehow I managed not to panic, for I knew that any hysterical response would only elicit Nunzio's prurient interest in witnessing my demise. Instead, I spoke calmly, appealing to him through a combination of reason and camaraderie.

Despite his wicked grin, it was probably only because Nunzio liked me that he waited just another minute or two – watching with glee as the serpent constricted against my Adam's apple – before removing it. But since we were friends, he'd gallantly deprived himself of that ultimate sadistic pleasure.

When Nunzio approached that testosterone-driven age of madness – sixteen, seventeen, eighteen – he could easily have killed anyone in the neighborhood with just his bare hands.

Although he held a record for doing hundreds of push-ups and sit-ups, at first glance he didn't appear to be such an imposing figure. Yet somehow, despite his modest stature, he possessed a superhuman strength – as if he were more of a beast than a man. Hence, his natural affinity for subhuman creatures. Like one of those horrific monstrosities that one reads about in Greek legend, I often imagined him to be a cross between a cobra, a leopard, a ferret, and a hyena.

This bestial nature was further enhanced by the beatings he continually received as a child from his discipline-crazed father. Nunzio bore the brunt of Ernesto's fists until all vestigial traces of humanity were gradually extinguished. And no incident serves to better illustrate this than an event that occurred a few months after he turned seventeen:

Drew Dunkle pedaled up the block one day on a sparkling new "ten-speed." It was a time when such racing bicycles – with their complex system of chains and gears – were all the rage in Gravesend. When Nunzio saw the shiny white contraption, he said, "Lend it to me so that I can go up to the hill and get a pack of smokes." Nunzio had never before ridden a ten-speed, and he was just itching to get his hands on it. But Drew, who obviously wasn't crazy about this idea, hesitated.

"Nunzio, I can't lend you my bike. It's brand-new; I just got it for my birthday. What if something happens to it? My mother would kill me!"

"Don't worry; nothing'll happen."

They haggled back and forth until Drew finally said: "Look, if I lend it to you, you'll have to defend it with your *life*. Do you understand? Because if anything happens, I'll be up shit's creek."

With that histrionic manner that Drew had honed from studying acting at Xaverian High School, he continued to drill this message into Nunzio's brainpan. And like the dimwitted Manchurian candidate that he was, after Drew repeated *You'll have to defend it with your life* Nunzio replied: "If anyone so much as looks at it, I'll *kill* them." And so, against his better judgment, but hoping to avoid Nunzio's wrath, Drew reluctantly handed it over.

Nunzio took off in a flash, shooting down the alley and gliding along the asphalt ribbon, turning east on King's Highway and peddling up the incline to West Sixth, or "the hill" as we called it, to get his cigarettes.

It was one of those glorious spring days in Gravesend; and a golden sheen of light dappled the Norwegian maples that hung so languorously over the street. As Nunzio peddled away, Drew chatted with Danny Brutta's younger brother, Jimmy, and with Jimmy's next-door neighbor Luke, as they played wiffle ball in the backyard. Then Drew went round, to the pantry, to see if Danny Brutta, or "the Buddha" as we called him, was at home.

But moments later Baritoni came racing back, zigzagging along the street and careening up the alley.

Tossing the bike on the floor, he shouted: "This fucking thing almost got me *killed!*" Before anyone could respond, he hopped the fence and leapt up the steps of his back porch. Drew noticed that Nunzio had a slight scratch on his right temple, but otherwise he looked fine.

Since it was obvious that trouble was brewing, Drew grabbed the bike and took off. But Jimmy and Luke just shrugged their shoulders and continued swinging at their plastic ball.

On such a sunny day in Brooklyn, sometimes you felt as if you'd stumbled into paradise. During those balmy, breezy afternoons, as we lingered in our respective yards or sat upon our stoops out front – with the block cradled by the wagging boughs that arced so majestically overhead and tinted West Twelfth with an almost mystical sap-green light as we played our beloved stick ball, stoop ball, or hand ball, or shot hockey pucks while gliding on our squeaky, rusty roller skates – we felt as if nothing could go wrong. You just had to remember to circle back and wait beside the parked cars whenever a lunatic came bolting along the block at ninety-miles an hour ... which is why Gravesend boasted the highest car-insurance rates in the country.

But then, like a rupture in an otherwise idyllic, pastoral space, unforeseen calamities might suddenly rear their heads; and they appeared to be even more incongruous when they occurred on days such as this one: so tranquil, halcyon, and serene, at least on the surface.

When Baritoni tried to enter his house, he realized that he'd lost his keys, so now he had to break in. He dug his fingers into the spaces between the bricks, slowly scaled the wall, then grabbed hold of a louvered window, prying it open with his preternatural strength. Like a boa constrictor, he slithered through this tiny space that he'd managed to wedge open, then dropped out of sight, uncanny contortionist that he was.

Seconds later a carload of gangsters came roaring up the block, screeching to a halt in front of the alley. With baseball bats in hand, they scrambled into the driveway on a search-and-destroy mission.

Jimmy dropped his wiffle ball as the goons closed in and shouted: *Where is he?* And only then did he notice that one of the kids who was standing there shirtless possessed a face that was no longer a face. His mug was bloodied and mangled; and, in between severed gobs of skin and strips of ripped-open flesh, all you could see – bruised and swollen – were the whites of his bloodshot eyes: staring back in horror.

Luke and Jimmy grew so frightened that, at first, they couldn't speak. But Luke finally managed to stutter: "*T-t-t-t-t-there*," pointing a shaky finger at Nunzio's house.

The hoods hopped the fence and circled round, kicking at the doors and banging on the walls. But when they couldn't figure out how to break in they eventually split.

An hour later I came ambling up the driveway, to visit Danny Brutta. When I encountered Jimmy and Luke, they were still shaking.

"Man, they tried every door on the house," Luke exclaimed, "front, back, and side! They went round and round – kicking, screaming, and yelling. That boy who stole the bike had blood and scratches all over his body. It was one of the scariest things I've ever seen."

Jimmy took a deep breath as he stared at the empty driveway. "If they'd gotten their hands on him," he said, "they would have *murdered* him. And not thought twice about it. They just wanted death."

"They demanded to know where Nunzio lived," Jimmy continued, "and we were so scared that we gave him up right away. That poor boy! The swelling, the scrapes, the busted lip that was three times its normal size! His eye was an inch off his face and popping out of his head. He looked like Frankenstein!"

Now my mind flashed back to that tragic figure portrayed by Boris Karloff in 1931: a creature possessing a poignant mixture of loneliness and compassion, but whose brain was so damaged that the merest misperception of reality would short-circuit everything. The wrong synaptic switch would suddenly flip, and then a little girl might be found floating facedown in a lake.

But the real Frankenstein monster wasn't that bloodied boy – it was slack-jawed Nunzio himself.

"So where's the Buddha?" I finally asked.

As if emerging from a trance, Jimmy gazed at me and muttered: "The Buddha is nowhere to be seen."

Experiences such as this one made me realize that, sooner or later, I had to escape Gravesend.

Student Teaching

In the fall of my freshman year at college, Shea Stadium hosted the Eleventh Avant-garde Festival; and it was briefly transformed from a ballpark into a sprawling showcase of conceptual art. My friend Jonathan, a Jewish intellectual whom I'd met in high school, had invited me to accompany him; and, having nothing better to do, I went along.

We were poking around the exhibits when we chanced upon one of Jonathan's professors from Bard College. Tod Meagher was accompanied by his wife, Margery, and by their teenage daughter, Layla: a lithe, sinewy blonde who was studying to be a ballerina. Tod was a conceptual artist, while Margery was a calligraphist who taught at the Dutchess Day School, a combination elementary- and high school that bordered the grounds of Vassar College in Poughkeepsie. A few months before this serendipitous encounter Jonathan had told Margery about me, hoping that she might accept me as an intern when I'd be required to work as a student teacher to complete my undergrad degree in art education.

We'd bumped into the Meaghers right beside one of Yoko Ono's installations: gigantic cardboard boxes, which were scattered in a hodgepodge across the seats of the stadium, as if randomly tossed by the hands of Gargantua. (I later learned that the Meaghers were acquainted with Yoko through their contacts in the art world.) Having no idea what they represented, I wasn't at all impressed.

Briefly glancing at them, Jonathan scratched his head and muttered: "Box seats."

"Yes. Rather literal," added the bespectacled, ever-cerebral

Tod.

Once I was introduced to the Meaghers, Margery and I took an instant liking to each other. But Tod trained his steely orbs upon me for just a moment, nodded, then glanced away, his icy pupils twinkling like remote, hoary stars. Like so many of Jonathan's acquaintances, Tod resembled a lump of cold gray matter connected to a computer by a buzzing bundle of electrical cords.

As I would later discover, Layla had inherited a troubling mixture of her parents' contradictory qualities. At times she exhibited Margery's enthusiasm and passion, but far more often she remained as somberly withdrawn and emotionally remote as her flinty-eyed father.

Four years later, just before I began my final semester at university, the art-ed department approved my placement with Margery at the Dutchess Day School. But the school's close proximity to Vassar made it difficult to find an apartment – or even a closet – to rent, for there were never enough accommodations to host the constant flow of university students.

All this should have been more than apparent to me; but I had no idea that finding housing would remain so challenging. Disembarking from a train, I wandered through the tree-lined streets with a copy of the *Poughkeepsie Journal* tucked under my arm but without even the flimsiest of leads.

I approached a man walking a dog and stopped to ask if he knew of any rentals. He took a step back, looked me over with widening eyes, and exclaimed: "Are you crazy? With all those students from Vassar searching for a place? You'll never find something so close to the university!"

Settling for a moment on a snow-covered bench and scanning the classifieds, I realized that it was just as the man had said. And there was only one week left before the first day of school.

Ambling along a side street, I next approached an elderly woman who was sweeping some snow off her stoop with a broom. When I asked if she knew of any rooms for rent, she pointed a shaky finger at a wooden house halfway along the block. "Ask for a Mrs. Graystone. She might be able to help you."

Just as I approached the building, a stocky woman in her mid-forties emerged from a front door with a bright-red snow shovel.

"Excuse me, ma'am. Would you happen to know of anyone who's looking for a tenant?"

Eyeing me up and down with a suspicious glance, she nodded her head in the affirmative. "One of our boarders is leaving tomorrow, and his room is up for rent. Would you like to see it?" For a moment I was dumbfounded. I could hardly believe my good fortune, so now I was expecting something to go wrong.

I followed her up a creaking wooden staircase. As we approached a landing, she abruptly turned and regarded me with a quizzical look.

"You don't come home drunk at night, do you?"

"Oh, no, ma'am. I'm a teacher at the Dutchess Day School. I'm too busy for that sort of thing. I've got too much work to do. I never touch the stuff."

Now she brightened up. "Well, you're certainly lucky to get a job teaching these days!"

"You bet, ma'am!"

"You can call me Doris."

We padded along a hallway and stopped at an open door. Inside, an elderly man with snow-white hair was positioned on a rocking chair. His back was hunched over as he stared into space.

"That's our tenant, Frank. He's been with us for *thirty-five years*." Proudly gazing at his bent-over form, Doris raised her voice:

"Hey, *Frank!* How's it going?"

As if emerging from a coma, he gradually took notice of us, nodded, then drifted back into his catatonia.

Almost everything in the house appeared to date from the 1920s: shiny oak cabinets covered with white lace; faded green wallpaper garlanded with sepia-toned photos; thick antique rugs that muffled the groaning floor planks. The atmosphere reeked of embalming fluid and evoked scenes from H. G. Wells' *Time Machine*.

It was the same sort of ambience in the room for rent, which was furnished completely in the style of yesteryear. A stout oak bureau with brass handles and an oval mirror on top stood in a far corner. A small bed was enveloped in colorful patchwork quilts and woolen blankets. On the opposite wall, a window overlooked a yard shaded by sycamore trees. Farther down the hall, a white-tiled bathroom featured a tub with clawed feet and a closet filled with neatly folded white towels. Doris said there were two other tenants; but, at the moment, no one else was home.

Once we were back downstairs she slipped behind a curtained doorway in the living room, then emerged with a frail but bright-eyed eighty-year-old. "Before you move in, you've got to meet Ma. She's got the final say on everyone."

"How ya doing?" Ma cackled. Gripping a gnarly wooden cane, she looked me over with a sparkling pair of hazel eyes. As I shook her bony hand, I worried that my beard, although well trimmed, might give me away; or perhaps my hair was a bit too long. But at least I was presentably dressed, donning my brand-new London Fog trench coat.

"You don't come home drunk at night, now do you?"

"Oh, no, Ma," I said, playing the upstanding young fellow to the hilt.

"Well, it's all right to have one once in a while! Ain't nothing wrong with that! Do you stay home on weekends a lot?"

She continued to toss questions at me as if I was a dartboard, and I fielded them as best I could. But after a while, remembering my Dale Carnegie routine, I turned the tables and asked Ma all sorts of questions about herself. She appeared to be so pleased that someone was interested in her life that, soon, we were all smiling cheerfully, bounding off on a lark down memory lane.

When I stood up to leave, Doris accompanied me to the front door and said that I should call in a couple of days, to make sure that the room was ready.

Apparently, I'd made the grade.

* * *

During the first week of February, I awoke one morning to a Poughkeepsie blanketed in enormous drifts of snow and suffering from its worst storm in decades. Even the main roads were cut off. It was as if we'd been transported to the Dust Bowl in the 1930s and were gazing at the mountains of white particles that had decimated the Oklahoma panhandle. And just like the starving minions of that catastrophe, I was marooned in my room with nothing to eat.

Shortly after I finished dressing, Doris stood at the foot of the stairway and shouted out my name. In the most sincere and good-natured manner, she asked if I'd care to join them in a delicious breakfast of ham and eggs, since the entire town was shut down, and food was scarce.

They knew that I didn't have anything to eat or any implements with which to prepare a meal, since hot plates were forbidden. She even assured me that there was no reason to feel shy about it. They were well-stocked with provisions, and I could pay them back later on.

I must have been delirious already, because I replied, "Oh, no, Doris; I wouldn't think of it. Really, I'm fine," or some such tripe. I can barely remember; for, soon enough, I was out of my mind with hunger. Another two or three days would pass before I'd have a crumb to nibble on, but I remained so damned timid that I refused to ask for help.

If only I had finished reading Knut Hamsun's *Hunger* – a novel that I'd briefly scanned just a few months earlier – I might have been forewarned about the "ravenous inner craving" for sustenance that would soon visit me. How unfortunate that I hadn't completed more than a couple of pages of this Norwegian masterpiece, which so accurately described how my guts were being impaled with pinpricks of unsated appetite!

By the third or fourth day of delirium, the snow mountains began to recede. Once the towering drifts were cleared away, I ambled over to a celebrated mom-and-pop diner next to Vassar. According to the gray-haired proprietors, when President Kennedy's future wife, Jacqueline Bouvier, had attended the university, she too had loved to snack upon their carefully prepared double-decker sandwiches – something they were famous for – at this very same zinc countertop.

Nestled among photos of famous alumni that were set in frames above the countertop, the prize of their collection was an elegantly autographed picture of Jacqueline herself, which was prominently displayed at the center of the wall, right above the soda fountain.

I ordered a prodigious double-decker of tuna on rye, but as I gulped it down I tasted nothing. For all I knew, it could have been made of sawdust. By now I'd lost any sense of taste, and the sandwich seemed to fall into a bottomless cavern. I devoured everything down to the last crumb – including generous heaps of coleslaw and pickles – but I merely felt like an automated eating machine, minus any sensory apparatus.

It wasn't until I was in my early thirties, after I'd moved to Paris and was forced to earn my living by dealing with strangers day after day, that I overcame my inherent shyness, which was actually much more than mere timidity. Instead, it was pure dread, based on the realization that human beings can be so exhausting, especially if you lack certain simple tools. That is, a means of talking but not really talking, of listening but not really listening, of smiling but not really smiling, and so on. But minus such vital implements, one is forced to reinvent the wheel at each and every turn of phrase. Thus, any attempt at "socially appropriate" intercourse drained me to the core. In the end, even after learning how to utilize such skills, I was left to wonder whether the effort to blend in was really worth it.

But I also realized that starving for three or four days is one thing, but that one is ill-advised to starve past a certain point – say, for three or four years. As a university student, however, it had seemed like such a monumental task to strike the proper chord, to summon the appropriate phrase, to mask the glimmer of apathy, disquietude, or distraction in my eyes. How to simply say, "Doris, may I please have another dab of ketchup?" And: "Those eggs are just fried to perfection!" All this was beyond me. It seemed as if the most obtuse pataphysics was mere child's play compared to the mechanics of ordinary discourse, so I chose the solitude of starvation as the easy way out.

* * *

As if to emphasize that nothing "square" was happening there, the Dutchess Day School was shaped into a circle and featured a big open space in the center of the ground floor. We'd assemble each morning in a large room at the back, which was well lit from a curving bank of windows that bordered the wooded fields of Vassar. As the sparrows chirped and flittered from branch to branch, the teachers would discuss their upcoming projects, and the students would usually respond with brimming enthusiasm. Everything was conducted in a laid-back, informal, convivial style. Rather than an educational setting, it resembled a bunch of hipsters planning a celebration.

I soon realized that Margery's daughter, who was a senior at the school, didn't seem to appreciate her mother as much as I did. But during this period, Layla was even less enthusiastic about her father. According to Jonathan, Tod had recently been disgraced, because he'd been caught having an affair with one of his students. So now, Layla refused to talk to him.

But despite this, she always remained closer to Tod in temperament. As I say, he resembled a disembodied cerebral cortex stored in a laboratory freezer, while Margery was a woman governed primarily from the heart. Unfortunately, Layla had inherited more than a touch of Tod's inhuman sense of detachment. Her sentiments were often buried beneath a frozen surface; but, once they emerged, they could be molten hot and explosive.

Although Tod possessed an intellectual adroitness, when it came to things such as romantic affairs he was merely a clod. Jonathan said that, until this affair, Tod had never been involved with any of his students. Normally he behaved himself despite the fact that he was bored with Margery. As I would later learn from my own foolishness, how important it is to gracefully accept the specter of boredom and to not run away from it!

As far as I could see, Tod and Margery had almost nothing in common. One understood the other as little as the other understood the other; and it was only this perfect symmetry of mutual incomprehension that united them.

* * *

One afternoon when Margery and I were alone in her house, she confessed that, in the years before she'd met her husband, she'd been wooed by a rich, handsome, refined aristocrat. He was a count, or baron, or prince of some sort: one of those gilded European patricians from a long line of wealthy heirs who'd inherited so much fortune, and who possessed so many acres of coveted real estate as well as liquid and nonliquid assets, that he was set up not only for life but for several lifetimes over. And of course, he was endowed with all the usual accoutrements that such a fellow would normally acquire, including hobbies such as equestrianism, playing polo, hawking, and shooting pheasants. With Margery riding beside him, he engaged in these delightful pursuits while galloping across a seemingly limitless tract of land; for one could ride for days on end yet never reach the boundary of his lush estate.

Smiling wistfully now and even with a glint of pride in her warm watery eyes, she said that, one day, while they were gliding along on horseback, the courtly gentleman turned to her and announced that he wanted nothing more than to marry and to make her his princess, his duchess, his well-appointed maiden, or whatever her actual title would have been.

But then Margery shook her head; and as she gazed at me her voice shifted to a rueful timbre. "But at heart, he was just a *businessman!* He knew *nothing* about being an *artist*, or what art was really *all about*. And so, instead, I married Tod."

Her beautiful blue eyes teared up as she smiled so charmingly, regarding me now with an expression of utter naivete. And I thought: *Nice going, Margery. A brilliant move!* Tod, a self-enclosed mental synapse, who almost completely ignored her and who, for entertainment, would invite one of his haughty, highbrowed pals over for dinner. I should add that these fellows weren't really "pals" such as you or I might say with warmth and affection, *He's my pal!* Instead, the term *associate* or *colleague* would more properly categorize such inhuman monstrosities. In other words, matching sets of test tubes, bubbling and spewing iridescent nonsense once the Bunsen burners of their respective brainpans were heated properly, along with the macaroni and cheese.

One evening Tod had invited as his guest a music critic, or music theorist, or whatever the hell he was, it didn't really matter, because he was simply another one of these droning test-tube boys. As soon as they were seated, they ignored the rest of us – Margery, Layla, and me – as they spouted, bubbled, and fizzed. Even when I made a vain attempt to interject a comment, this monotonous music maniac simply brushed it aside with a curt remark riddled with condescending urbanity. For I was merely a university student; what could I possibly know? Then they continued to engulf each other with noxious fumes of potassium chloride. As Holden Caulfield remarks in *Catcher in the Rye*: "It was the phoniest conversation you ever heard in your life." I mean, it was all so rude and ludicrous that even the cerebral daughter, Layla, said so. The next day at school, she made a pointed remark about how obnoxious this blabbermouth was. Even for Layla, it was too much.

Imagine growing up surrounded by such pretentious poseurs! And having to wade through those spouting gases at your very own dinner table – trying to enjoy a bowl of French onion soup and, instead, having to listen to this claptrap. A crime against childhood! But Tod didn't give a hoot about anything other than such dreary, soulless monologues. That, and his "aerial sculptures," which were driven by his obsession with Japanese kite making. Layla said that one summer he'd dragged the entire family all the way to Kyoto to study under the native kite masters there. As she related this story to me at school one day, all I could think of was: *Tod, why don't you just go fly a kite?*

If there weren't any dinner guests to distract him from his family, then Tod would lecture me about how these *very special kites*, which he'd designed so *painstakingly*, were actually *works of art*. "Kinetic drawings," I believe, is how he categorized such doodles, because they filled the sky with "carefully thought-out shapes and lines," molded as they were by "nature's own nature." Such horseshit, but not even a horse trader could dream up such stuff!

Not surprisingly, since he was a devoted follower of conceptual art, Tod exulted in making offhand remarks about how they should throw away all their books about fine art, because all that was so passé; for painting was so *dead*. He didn't even have to say, "Painting is dead," it was taken for granted. Yet, as far as I could tell, his kites were nothing more than pretty little trinkets that, in the larger scheme of things, meant nothing.

I even wondered if all this kite business wasn't merely the result of Tod's own unconscious tricking him into having some fun. For the poor man didn't seem to know what fun was. Maybe his psyche had pulled a fast one, and he'd been lured into standing outdoors, in the midst of a painterly landscape, where he might begin to behave like a child again. But beyond all that, at the end of the day it was simply enjoyable: nothing abstract or "logical" about it. But if you're going to tell me that all this windblown "kinetic" gibberish represents the conquest of men such as Rembrandt, Renoir, or Picasso ... I don't think so, Tod. Not even Timothy Leary had hallucinated anything as ridiculous as that!

Speaking of visions that would put Leary's fanciful delusions to shame, that semester my most memorable experience occurred early one morning in Margery's quaint and roomy dwelling. Decorated with a carefully acquired collection of Japanese ceramics, the old Victorian house was filled with a rustic fragrance of tree blossoms and spring flowers, as well as a lingering scent of home cooking. It echoed with creaking floor planks and, at dawn, was illuminated by broad shafts of resplendent sunlight. All of which would certainly have inspired those nature loving Japanese bards, Issa and Basho, to no end.

That evening after dinner Margery invited me to sleep over, on a couch in the living room. Early the next morning, while unaware of my presence, Layla pranced across the room without wearing a stitch of clothing. I'd just woken up; and, as I rolled over, my glance fell upon this nimble dance of glowing flesh: her painted toes pitter-pattering across the floorboards; her blonde locks falling in gleaming waves to her slender waist; and, most intoxicating of all, her budding nipples floating under crisp, refulgent beams of sunlight. Lolly pink, and ever so firm, and even a bit stiff from the brisk chill in the air. It occurred, this vision, in a flash: she saw me, gasped, spun round, and darted away – all the while screaming *But I didn't know you were here!*

Those sweet orbs heaved, and then, as she turned, my eyes refocused upon her jiggling, oscillating bottom. As if emulating a *tableau vivant*, Layla was spirited away like a wood nymph surprised by one of Picasso's Minotaurs. As she flew across the kitchen, even their cat, Bardo, lost its royal cool, leapt off the counter, and scampered after her, toward a door at the opposite end that led to Margery's bedroom.

"But you didn't tell me that he stayed *overnight!*" Layla's voice was rising and falling in muffled crescendos: first, cresting into hysteria, then reduced to whispers.

> Red has entered
> the swelling peaches;
> green, the rigid bamboo stalk.

I was grinding some coffee beans when I was next greeted by the tender blue eyes of Margery, who was wrapped in a silky red kimono.

"Good morning!"

"Good morning, Margery."

"Would you like some eggs and asparagus?"

"Ah, that would be very nice."

"You must excuse us for disturbing you. Layla didn't realize that you were staying over." As the French would say, Margery was such a refined, *délicate* woman; for she always approached everything with a well-honed, elegant reserve.

Whatever else we shared in common, I suspect that the lingering shadow of Tod's infidelity had served to foster a certain bond between us. Perhaps it was Margery's way of showing Tod that she, too, could attract such attention, even if nothing intimate occurred between us. Jonathan said that Tod had become embroiled in that scandal because this brazen young woman had pushed herself upon him so aggressively, teasing him to the very limit, till he broke down and fell right into her trap. Then she grew even more demanding, insisting that Tod leave his family. When he finally broke it off and abandoned her, she followed through on her threat of forcing the art department to bring him up on charges. It was something relatively unheard of back in that era of flagrant student-teacher relations. But Tod had picked a real winner, a veritable oyster wench.

So now he was gelded: left to his kites and his sputtering test-tube colleagues. And Layla, his "brain child," would hardly even speak to him.

While I sipped my coffee, it occurred to me that Tod had been entrapped by the very thing that he professed to abhor. For, wasn't this home-wrecker with nothing of merit in her head the ultimate example of "superficial beauty" seducing the "retina"?

If only he'd exerted as much care in selecting a suitable mistress as he had upon his kites, perhaps Tod might have spared his family from such tribulations.

Not long after I graduated, hoping to avoid further embarrassment, he moved the family to Kyoto, where Layla created a ballet school for young girls.

* * *

Throughout the four months that I taught at the Day School, Margery seemed intent upon extinguishing my lingering self-doubts. Under her patronage it seemed as if I could do no wrong, despite the fact that I often felt like an interloper.

For, by this time, I had almost no desire to become a schoolteacher. Instead, I was merely completing what I'd started. I was determined to get that university degree, especially since my interest in schooling was so tenuous that I'd just barely managed to talk myself out of quitting. I bristled at the notion of being told what to read or, even worse, being forced to write about subjects that were inconsequential. But I also realized that a diploma might come in handy one day, especially when applying for some other job.

Instead of being a young, upcoming professional, I regarded

myself as a wayward Dionysus surrounded by worldly Apollos, each of whom seemed to be far more adapted to quotidian reality. While my schoolmates were carefully preparing their résumés on IBM Selectric typewriters, I continued to resist "fitting in." Instead, I dreamed of wandering off, into the woods, and howling with the beasts.

Much to my mother's chagrin, almost from the moment that I obtained my degree, I delayed and then abandoned any earnest pursuit of becoming a teacher. Instead of typing resumes, I began to compose haikus in the style of Issa and Basho, those clever Japanese poets that Margery had introduced me to one balmy spring day in Poughkeepsie.

Flora and Marilyn Monroe

During the spring break of our senior year, Drew began rehearsals for his play, an apocalyptic drama titled "Boom!" which he staged to complete his degree at New York University. And rather unexpectedly, he invited me to act in it.

Introducing me to the cast, he announced that I was a gifted thespian from a college upstate; so no one was the wiser, especially since it was such a minor role. And it was there, at Shimkin Hall on West Fourth Street, that I first laid eyes on Flora: one of the most beautiful women that I've ever been involved with and one of the sweetest, as well. The daughter of a Polish housewife and a brawny Italian carpenter, Flora was modest at heart, perhaps to a fault, and she never attempted to hide her working-class roots.

Flora exuded such ethereal glamour that Lee Strasberg, the mentor of James Dean and Marilyn Monroe, had spotted her and, with that pompous whisper that he had honed so well, said: "Flora, you will be the next Marilyn." Point-blank, just like that – the next Marilyn Monroe! And just like Marilyn, the Strasbergs regarded Flora as a "natural talent."

As Flora had once remarked: Marilyn was gone, but her ghost still lingered, haunting the Actor's Studio. By following the inside gossip that Flora had picked up from Lee's daughter Susan, I slowly pieced together an unsettling portrait of the ill-fated actress. Though it was generally agreed that Marilyn knew how to rely on her instincts, Flora said that her acting abilities weren't really the result of a carefully crafted skill. It wasn't something incrementally acquired, artfully teased out, dutifully exercised, and gradually refined. Instead, Marilyn was possessed by an unconscious force that, at times, had nearly derailed her.

Rumor had it that, as a result of being orphaned during her childhood, Marilyn was a victim who'd been tossed hither and thither, from one dreadful set of "guardians" to the next. All the while being terrorized, twisted, and perverted, so that the final result could not have been anything other than a borderline personality. According to Flora, who also minored in psychology, Marilyn exhibited each of the classic symptoms of this disorder, especially an insatiable need to be mentored in even the most elementary of tasks. Plus, there was that hyperactive relationship to sexuality, not to mention an enduring pattern of manipulating those around her and constantly creating drama. As her husband, the playwright Arthur Miller, had once remarked: "Emotion alone could make her happy, almost without regard for its hostile or benevolent significance, for only in emotion was there truth." Classic borderline! For a sense of palpable *beingness* could arrive only via such exaggerated theatrics. Besides serving as a counterpoint to her fear of abandonment, such highly wrought maelstroms helped to convince Marilyn that she actually *existed*. Such behavior forced others to intensely interact with her and – through this overblown, coercive sort of exchange – further guarantee her palpability. Flora believed that, ultimately, all this endowed Marilyn with a sense of power: something of utmost concern for someone who, in every other sense, feels so vulnerable and powerless. In effect, she became the director of the Marilyn Monroe Borderline Spectacle. And minus all this drama, the only thing that remained was a despairing hole of inner emptiness.

"But as far as borderlines go," Flora concluded, "Marilyn's was a special case." Not only had she slept her way from one casting couch to the next; she did so on the most highly esteemed of couches: not even casting couches really, but the king-sized beds of the most influential Hollywood moguls. Until she manipulated her way into Joltin' Joe DiMaggio's own private baseball field: the most famous athlete in the land, but one who lacked even a basic means of understanding her.

Fortunately, Flora had far less psychological baggage as well as considerably less *mishegoss* surrounding her everyday life, but less only in terms of degree. Perhaps because Flora was also coached by the Strasbergs, who specialized in confusing and disempowering actors so that they'd grow ever more dependent upon Lee's occult powers of "mentorship" – powers that were fueled by sowing a nagging self-doubt into those he was supposed to be helping – during this period Flora grew nearly as bewildered as Marilyn about her life's true purpose.

Flora grew up in the dreary suburbs of Baltimore, where she eventually befriended several other rebels, including a slightly older lad named John Waters. Accompanied by John and his entourage of self-proclaimed weirdoes and freaks, Flora hung out in a local park, smoked cigarettes down to the filter, listened with amusement to their ribald tales, and learned how to be *cool*. John would later become a famous filmmaker while Flora would follow in his footsteps to NYU, to study acting under the questionable tutelage of Anna Strasberg, Lee's "trophy wife," and eventually under Lee himself, a huckster if ever there was one. According to Drew, Lee had stolen nearly everything from a Russian drama theorist named Constantin Stanislavski. Years later, Drew would lend me his "Bible" – a multivolume collection of Stanislavski's writings – to prove it.

But Drew wasn't the only one who felt this way about Lee. The director Elia Kazan had once remarked that "Strasberg's great fault was to make his actors more and more rather than less and less dependent on him." Actor Marlon Brando was even more to the point. He regarded Lee as an "ambitious, selfish man who exploited the people who attended the Actors

Studio, and he tried to project himself as an acting oracle and guru. Some people worshiped him, but I never knew why." Perhaps Arthur Miller said it best when he referred to Lee as "Willy Loman": the traveling salesman in Miller's play, *Death of a Salesman*, who seeks popularity despite having no real substance or talent.

In any case, just like Marilyn, at this stage of her life Flora was falling into the tentacles of a leaden ennui. Strangely enough, despite her natural beauty and innate talent, perhaps even more pathological than Marilyn in at least this one regard, Flora *despised* acting. Or rather, she *acted* as if acting *meant nothing to her*. But Flora's jettisoning of this priceless commodity had left her floating in a vocational limbo ... as if she had an eternity to resolve these crucial matters while her wheel of fortune continued to spin in such uncertain directions.

Though acting came easy for Flora, and although she was born with movie-star looks – with those moist, inviting lips that stretched into a perfect shape across an elegant jaw line; a jaw delicately balanced upon a columnar neck framed by jet-black hair that flowed round those feline cheekbones; not to mention an upturned nose that ascended into an alabaster arch featuring eyebrows that she'd raise, one at a time, to annihilate her admirers with a devastating regard as she stared with cobalt-blue eyes and batted her long lashes – Flora could care less. All this was accompanied by a sharp tongue that could throw barbs that usually hit their mark. But at heart Flora was a softie: not at all hardened or remote.

Her callous exterior masked a native tenderness; for her gentle sincerity was always there. Among her true friends she didn't hide it, despite this Manhattan-bred irony and sharpened, voluble wit. And despite a nimble-footed dark humor that, after all, was a prerequisite if you wanted to be around any of us. If you grew up on the street, you survived only through this existential levity, not through some abstract doctrine. We were a bit like the Australians in that one regard: the modest citizens of Oz who had an expression about knocking down the tallest poppy – the one that tries to stick out from the mass. We harbored no patience for haughty, cerebral types, especially those who were as full of it as the Strasbergs and who had adopted a pose to achieve fame and filthy lucre. But unlike the Aussies, we respected a tall poppy that possessed true artistic merit, even when it was expressed through naive, germinal attempts, such as we were now aspiring to, as young artists. So, in that sense, we were each a tall poppy. Instead of knocking each other down, even though we constantly ribbed each other, we admired such bold efforts to stand out among the herd.

Anna Strasberg had arranged a scholarship for Flora, but she also supported herself by working as a hostess in a mob-controlled topless joint. Unlike most of the women at the club, Flora wore a bikini and never exposed her beautiful breasts to the customers or to the gangster proprietors: muscle-bound goons who would promise Flora the world if she would only agree to accompany them on a single date. But she always refused.

After spring break, when I returned upstate, I never missed a weekend with Flora. Every Friday, I'd take the train down to Grand Central; and even if I called at the last possible moment Flora would cancel her other plans and say, *Yes, of course; come over as soon as you can!* A few hours later I'd be knocking on the metal door of her basement flat on Sullivan Street, with the living room windows that were just above street level. The sun would beam through the venetian blinds, and you'd see only the calves and feet of pedestrians walking by.

Flora's opalescent skin emitted a fragrance as light and buoyant as the finest perfume: subtle yet hypnotizing. What an honor it was to hold her hand and walk along MacDougal

Street as we strolled toward Café Borgia or Caffe Reggio for a cappuccino, then promenaded the crooked lanes of the Village or circled through Washington Square.

* * *

One evening I ran into Flora drinking at a bar on Bleecker Street, and she was a bit tipsy. After she finished her drink we wandered into a playground at the corner of Prince and Thompson, just a few blocks away from her flat.

The streetlamps cast a soft glow on her pale skin as she swung back and forth on a wooden swing, her breasts heaving and wobbling to the rhythm of the clanking, clattering chains; and at once I realized that she'd never appeared more enticing. I stood there silently taking it all in: her bulging white blouse with the buttons almost bursting; her rippling navy-blue skirt; her knee-high white socks highlighting those succulent calves; her shiny hair fluttering in an occasional breeze; her bright eyes reflecting the moonlight as she threw her legs back and forth and the squeaky seat gained momentum. Now, I imagined that even Queen Luna herself was smiling down with approval.

Flora gazed at me with those troubled but ever kind and sensitive eyes, and then she blurted out: *But why do men find me attractive?* Just like that – completely clueless.

Why?

Before replying, I silently recalled how, shortly after we first met, we began to flirt during each of our dress rehearsals. By then, we were in full makeup. It was the week before the opening, and I realized: This is it; the real scene, the real drama is occurring in our dressing room and not on stage. Each evening Flora would sit beside me, carefully applying her makeup while staring into a mirror that ran lengthwise over a narrow countertop as we prepared for scenes of near nudity in the play. And so, there I was in my underwear, trying not to get aroused while Flora was completely naked, seated right beside me.

But now, as she kicked her legs and the swing set rumbled with another groan, again she blurted out: "But why do they find me attractive?" There was such an aggrieved tone to her voice. Perhaps she feared that, if she didn't crack this puzzle right away, disaster might ensue. Or perhaps her bewilderment stemmed from the fact that Flora could never imagine how devious and shallow men could be. As my father had once remarked with an acidic tone of derision, she couldn't grasp that *A man would fuck a mashed potato if given the chance* ... or that he might risk everything just to fondle and embrace Flora's exquisite bosom. Somehow it was beyond her, a woman who laughed at mobsters and their glittering gold cufflinks; their stinky wads of cash; and their vulgar stretch limos, elongated to such absurd lengths in the Eighties – as if they housed prehistoric reptiles. And maybe Flora felt that if *she* could see through all this, then why couldn't *men* see through the superficial allure of her flesh?

"I shouldn't be so nice to everybody." Her voice slurred, then shifted to a bitter tone. "I should just be like everyone else ... *A cunt.*"

"No, Flora," I laughed, "that's ridiculous! You've just got to be more careful about who deserves your attention. And besides, the cunt is not all it's cracked up to be."

"And all these guys," she moaned, swinging her gorgeous legs back and forth as the swing continued to squeak, "why do I get involved with them? I don't even know what attracts them to me. What is it? I could never figure it out."

"You know, maybe it's time that somebody told you." Pausing a moment, I teasingly inquired, "Do you really want to know?"

Regarding me with a glassy-eyed expectation, she nodded.

Then I replied, deadpan: "It's your breasts."

"My *breasts*? That's *it*?"

"Sometimes," I added, "even I myself have a weakness for them."

At this, she burst out laughing.

"Well, no one's ever told me *that* before. Hey, come on! Let's go back to my place ..."

Fumbling with her keys, she unlocked the door, spun round, and collapsed in bed. Within moments, Flora was passed out: her arms stretched across the sheets in the pose of a crucifixion.

Gazing at her fondly, I undressed her, slipped her into a nightgown, and tucked her in. Now, she appeared to be dreaming. Beneath her fluttering eyelids her pupils were darting about.

I briefly fell asleep beside her. When I awoke, I spotted a copy of Josephina Niggli's *New Pointers on Playwriting* wedged into a bookshelf above her bed. But I mused that Flora needed more than just a few pointers; she'd require an entirely new metaphysic to remain firmly ensconced in her profession.

Thumbing through the Niggli book, I learned that a "crisis" or "turning point" ("an unstable state of affairs in which a decisive change is impending") unfolds in three distinct phases:

The first is *conflict*, which leads to one of two possible choices. In this particular drama, although we were in bed, Flora was unconscious. Thus, we'd already entered the second stage:

> *Suspense*: This is usually stated in the form of a question about the character who is making up his mind: What will Hamlet do now? What will Nora do now?

Glancing at her again, I tried to imagine what it would be like to sleep beside her night after night, year after year. Such a confused and tragic divinity, yet one exuding such sincerity and tenderness!

Moments later, I left Flora in peace. Creeping down a creaking stairway, I headed toward West Fourth Street, for a train back to Gravesend.

> *The conclusion*: The character makes his final choice.

That was the last I saw of my divine Flora. A few weeks later she grew fed up with Manhattan and disappeared into the backwaters of Maryland.

But now, in the wee hours of the morn, on a nearly empty subway platform, a drunken reveler was laughing like a besotted hyena. His trilling, warbling notes resonated along the tiled walls and sent shivers up my spine.

Leaning against a rusty pole and closing my eyes, I envisioned the surrounding ziggurats of brick; the obelisks of steel; the craven monuments to the gods of commerce that run north and south beside the grimy harbors of despair.

"How solitary lies the city," proclaims the anonymous author of the Book of Lamentations, "and how her daughters are forsaken!"

Crackpots and Conmen

There's such a thing as remaining in a place a moment too long – an extra day that morphs into a month – until a tangential detour leads your life in one direction instead of another. And when all sorts of trouble begins to brew, you scratch your head and wonder how you ever ended up in such a pickle.

After graduating from university in the spring of '78, I refused to return to Gravesend. Instead, I lived on a shoestring, or less than a shoestring, cadging meals whenever I could, since my parents had cut off my funds and insisted that I return home at once.

Of course, I didn't last there very long as I didn't even bother to search for serious employment. Instead, I read Louis-Ferdinand Céline's *Guignol's Band*: a bizarre account of all the crackpots and oddballs that Céline had surrounded himself with during his sojourn to London in 1915. In fact, this entire crew could have taken a page out of the late 1970s. After a decade of over-the-top, drug-induced nonsense – a "revaluation of all values" that would have done Nietzsche proud or else scared the pants off him – it was as if every available screwball had rolled onto Main Street, just ninety miles north of Manhattan. And no matter how outlandish they were, it rarely fazed a soul.

The powerful influence of Céline's confessional novels had also served to trigger a series of harebrained schemes. For there I was, an inexperienced, green lad having lived nothing yet but already dreaming of portraying my "life story." Equally absurd, I reasoned that Céline's decision to collect his own cast of novelistic cuckoo birds gave me an excuse, or even a mandate, to do the same. For wasn't it all part of a literary tradition?

Thus, one sunny afternoon I planted myself on the cement steps in front of a deli at the end of Main Street – the closest thing I could find to an authentic Brooklyn stoop – and I waited. Spring semester had just ended, so most of the students were gone, and by now the local riffraff had taken over the street. The "townies," as we so derisively referred to them, were appearing in greater numbers in the bars and cafés, where they'd mix with the older students and alumni who lived there all year.

It didn't take long for me to collect my first Célinesque oddball: a goggle-eyed ex-con whom everyone referred to as Friar John. The "stoop," which was a popular hang-out spot, was also his favorite perch, so perhaps it was inevitable that we'd eventually fall into conversation.

Since John cut such an extravagant figure, it was hard not to notice him. A pale-skinned Irishman who was shaped like an onion (à la Alfred Jarry's *Ubu Roi*), he possessed piercing green eyes that he loved to narrow and bear down on you like a glinting pair of gimlets. A wide-brimmed straw hat crowned his flaming red hair and flowing, curly beard. He also donned a faded linen shirt; baggy cotton pants that were unevenly cut with a scissors at the bottom; and open-toed leather sandals. In one hand he gripped an oak cane; in the other, an ebony cigarette holder that he flaunted like a squire. A purple tote bag stuffed with reams of scribbled papers, tattered magazines, and loose cigarettes was looped over his brawny shoulder.

Though he was more widely known as Friar John, I soon discovered that his real name was Billy Doyle; and he was one of those skillful con artists who are rarely caught in a lie. The bigger and more elaborate the fib, the more you wanted to believe it. The other principal actors in John's shady affairs were Marlon Mudnick and Bradley Prescott, who were also in their early forties. John said that Marlon was a truck driver who'd faked a back injury and then collected "relief." Bradley, an egg-headed intellectual, was a former university professor.

During the late Sixties, Bradley had achieved notoriety for conducting his courses while tripping on acid. On the first day of class, he'd announce that everyone was getting an "A" whether they remained there or not. Upon hearing this, about half the class would bolt from the room. Then he'd smile at the ones who'd remained and say: "Now, we can get down to business, and really have some fun ..."

Even in casual conversation, Bradley often spoke in the manner of an intellectually prodigious lecturer. He wasn't trying to show off; it was simply the way his brain worked. But despite this scholarly demeanor, he was also an inveterate con artist. One day while his students were immersed in an animated discussion about his hero – the innovator, architect, and systems theorist, Buckminster Fuller – a sheriff marched into the classroom. The professor was arrested on the spot for passing bum checks. Summarily fired from the university and declared mentally incompetent by a psychiatrist because of his habitual LSD use, Bradley subsisted on disability and lived in a dilapidated shack at the edge of town. But you'd never know that he was busted flat, because he always wore an impeccable suit and tie; and he continued to hold forth like a brilliant if somewhat impractical visionary.

Bradley produced a cable-access television program that featured interviews with leading figures in business and culture. He was one of the first to take advantage of a law that stipulated that cable companies allot a certain number of hours to anyone who wanted to create a nonprofit broadcast on "public access" TV. Beginning with Buckminster Fuller, he eventually hobnobbed with guests such as Vice President Hubert Humphrey; the acid guru Baba Ram Dass; the proponent of behavior modification, B. F. Skinner; the Beat novelist William Burroughs; the CIA whistleblower Philip Agee; the neurologist Oliver Sacks; the antipsychiatry advocate Thomas Szasz; and the controversial president of Libya, Muammar al-Gaddafi. But when we first met he was interviewing corporate figures who were doing things to "change the world" and usher in a "New Age" of technological innovation that, according to the professor, would connect everyone in some complex but immediate fashion.

Shortly after I was introduced to Bradley, I accompanied him on an interview in a swank Madison Avenue office. We were greeted by a corporate executive who proudly displayed a strand of optical fiber in his well-pedicured paw. Bradley took one look at the clear plastic filaments and uttered a prosaic but prescient phrase: "To be connected!" Well before the masses were obsessed by and engulfed within the digital age, he was already jabbering about computers and advanced telecommunications capabilities. But since Bradley was incapable of speaking plain English, the far-ranging implications of this conversation went way over my head. For most of us back then, computers were something that existed only in Batman's cave.

I was basking in the sunlight on my makeshift stoop when John took notice of me scribbling in a journal.

"What are you doing in New Paltz?" he asked. "Are you a student?"

"I just graduated from the Art Department with a teaching degree. But now, I'm trying to write literature."

John's eyes lit up. "Really? I've always wanted to find someone to help me with a memoir. Maybe we could work on it together."

"Have you tried to write it yourself?"

"I'm better at telling stories out loud. Though I never get stage fright, I always get writer's block. Whenever I sit in front of a typewriter," he frowned, now twirling his thick, stubby fingers in the air, "I freeze up. Would you like to hear a story?" Before I could reply, he dramatically cleared his throat, gripped the head of his cane, and assumed an ostentatious, theatrical intonation:

"Bradley, Mudnick, and I looked at each other while we were half-asleep, and we realized that it was Christmas. The sum total of money we had between us was a dollar and twenty-seven cents. Bradley came up with the idea of going into the village to find another unfortunate soul who was lonely, and to invite him to spend Christmas with us.

"'See, we're like the three wise men,' Bradley smiled, 'and we've got to find someone who's in even worse shape than we are and help him out.'

"So we went looking for someone who was less fortunate, but we found no one. No one was lower than we were. The streets were white with snow; the sidewalks were deserted; the stores were closed; and we couldn't even get a cup of coffee. Then I remembered an invitation I'd received a long time ago. There was a commune of holy men called the Bruderhof, who lived just a few miles away in a forest retreat. Several years ago they'd opened their doors and offered me some wood scraps, for heat. So now, I thought about paying them a visit.

"We were drifting aimlessly along a dirt road when I heard a car approaching, so I put out my thumb. Bradley and Mudnick turned and stared at me as if I was delirious. 'What are you doing?' Mudnick asked. Before I could answer, the car stopped, so they followed me in and we bounced along, toward the Bruderhof commune.

"After thanking the man for the ride, we followed a dirt road to the main building. Then I saw a figure dressed in a blue work shirt, walking beneath some trees. It was the gatekeeper,

Brother Tony. He stood there glaring at us until he recognized me, then he broke into a smile.

"'Brother Tony! Any wood scraps you can spare?'

"'Gentleman, the shop's closed for Christmas. But why don't you join us for dinner?'

"'That would be very nice,' grinned Bradley.

"'Sure, why not?' Mudnick replied, barely disguising his hunger with a matter-of-fact nonchalance.

"We followed Tony up the hill in silence. From the outside the building resembled a log cabin resort with thick, greasy smoke pouring from a chimney. But inside, the air was so crisp that you could almost bite into it. It was plenty warm, too, from three big indoor fireplaces. All around us there were women wearing peasant dresses, serving heaping plates of food. Tony must have noticed our astonished eyes and sensed how hungry we were, because he escorted us to one of the longest tables and said: 'Here, help yourself, and God bless!' Everything was homegrown, and it seemed to be alchemically transformed by their love.

"I sat there stuffing my face like a starved winter cowboy. As the food was absorbed by my gut, my eyes began to refocus, and my attention shifted to the friendly smiles, soft-spoken voices, and happy laughter. And most of all, to the colorful dresses that lingered before us, draped with homemade scarves of glowing red, blue, and green. As the Bruderhof sisters strolled past, I thought of how their finely sculpted heads were covered not only in fabric but in mystery.

"'I wonder what she looks like when she's unwrapped,' Mudnick whispered, his eyes darting from side to side as he sliced a turkey with a steady motion.

"'Mudnick, it's not that type of place! Control yourself! Otherwise, they may notice and get angry ...'

"Biting into a celery stalk and swallowing another helping of stuffing, he grunted: 'If I could only eat *her!* It would be like unwrapping a beautiful Christmas present!'

"'If the brothers caught you with a sister, they'd pull you behind the counter and do a number on you.'

"'No way,' Mudnick chuckled, 'they're too peaceful for that.'

"In the midst of our whispering, a brother who was wearing an Amish head cushion invited us to sit beside their visiting dignitaries – high holy men from the other Bruderhofs across the country. So there we were, an exiled professor and two hustlers, positioned at the very center of things. Just hours before, we'd been shivering in Mudnick's freezing house like sardines trembling in a can of ice, with our Saint Bernard looking us over and blinking its oily eyes. But now, we were invited to partake in a sacred celebration.

"We bowed our heads to give thanks, and a group of children suddenly appeared. Laughing and giggling, they began to sing Christmas carols that they'd composed by themselves. The candles flickered and the fires snapped and crackled, and I felt deeply touched. I guess Mudnick was touched, too, because suddenly he sprang up and said, 'Beautiful sisters! And, uh … beautiful brothers!' Reaching into his back pocket, he pulled out a crumpled piece of paper and began to unfold it. Clearing his throat, he continued, 'I'm going to read a poem that I've just written to thank you.'

"But it was really something that he'd composed a few days before, about a slum in Brooklyn. Unfortunately, it was too late to stop him. When he got to the part about walking through Red Hook and blowing snot from his nose, the brothers glared at each other. Obviously not understanding Mudnick's fine, upright intentions, they grew sullen and dismayed. As soon as he finished, they moved in and huddled round him, their smiles now turning into tight, drawn grimaces. They whispered something to Mudnick, and, before I could figure out what was happening, I felt a hand gripping my shoulder.

"When I turned round, two young women, along with a handsome young man, were angelically smiling. The man said, 'Happy Christmas!'

"'Yes, Happy Christmas.'

"'Do you believe in God?'

"'Yes. And once, I was even his servant. I was a monk in a Franciscan order. They used to call me Brother John.'

"'Praise the Lord, Brother John! You're still a servant of the Lord Jesus.'

"'Well, not *officially* anymore ...'

"'But you do believe in Jesus.'

"'I believe that Christ was a good person, who was probably not the Savior or Messiah, so to speak. But he was a holy man, a spiritual being, and a free spirit. And maybe he was crucified because he preached love.'

"'We, too, believe in the Lord Jesus. But we have a slightly different understanding of him. And we'd like to discuss this with you. So we're inviting you to stay for the night.'

"'That would be nice. But first, let me speak with my friends.' I went looking for Bradley and Mudnick, searching in room after room, but there was no sign of them. Then I approached one of the brothers to ask where they were.

"'Your companions have departed. Brother Tony has driven them home.' As he spoke, I could see that he was perturbed about something, so I went to look for a phone, to call the Ice Palace.

"'Mudnick, what's going on?'

"'We left you there,' he laughed, 'because the brothers said that they're going to *keep* you!'

"'Keep me? What do you mean?'

"'Listen, why not lay up there for a while? They probably want to convert you.'

"'But why did you leave so early?' Then I heard Bradley's voice:

"'First, they were upset over Mudnick's poem. Then I got into a conversation with the head brother. I mentioned something about television, saying that I wanted to do a program about him. But he grimaced and said that TV is an evil tool of the devil.'

"'Don't tell me that you laid your whole philosophy on him.'

"'Well, let's just say that we got into a disagreement, then they asked us to leave. But why not stay there? You're in bad shape. You could use some food and a warm bed. They even have a doctor. Maybe you can get a checkup.'

"So I decided to remain with the brothers, especially since Mudnick and Bradley were permitted daily visitation rights. Besides seeing me, they could get a shave and a hot shower. It was a luxury long overdue, and one they couldn't afford to miss. I also had the pleasure of sleeping in my own bed, with clean sheets and strong springs. One without water bugs or cockroaches, without dampness or dirt, and without Bradley and Mudnick sleeping on either side of me.

"I was there for about a week when, early one evening, there were three sharp raps on my door.

"'Good evening, John.'

"'Hello, father.'

"'How are you feeling?'

"'Please, have a seat. I'm feeling good, especially at the end of such a beautiful day.'

"'Thank the Lord.'

"Pausing to roll up the sleeves of his work shirt and to wipe beads of sweat from his brow, he added: 'I'm here to ask if you'd like to come to the shop and work with us one day.'

"'Sure. I could use some exercise to get back into shape.'

"'How about tomorrow? Is that too soon?'

"'No, tomorrow's fine.'

"The next day I was surrounded by shrieking machines. The Bruderhof manufactured Christmas toys out of solid rock maple. Each morning, the factory shook with a chopping sound from the iron-toothed devices that gnawed into lumber: sanding, milling, and transforming the raw stuff of nature into refined, commercial products. The little buggers who slept with these toys wrapped in their arms each night had probably never dreamed of their violent birth: the ear-splitting wailing and buzzing with which these gentle-looking trinkets are produced.

"In the midst of this racket, I was placed in charge of making children's blocks. It was my job to run them through a sanding machine, then stamp them: *Made by the Brothers at Rifton*. To muffle the noise, they offered me a headset that resembled padded headphones. The pressure of it on my skull only compounded the headache that was already brewing, yet no one else seemed to mind this cacophony. Despite the constant din and clamor, they just sat there with Cheshire-cat grins.

"Eventually they said that I'd done enough in the workshop, but would I mind cutting some wood outside? Anything to escape that sweathouse! So they led me down a hill to a woodpile shed, where about a dozen axes were lined up in a row, gleaming in the sun.

"As soon as I grabbed one, they could hardly hold the wood fast enough for me to split it. Compared to my sixteen-pound sledgehammer at Leavenworth Prison, it wasn't anything at all. I kept swinging and chopping, swinging and chopping, occasionally stopping to wipe my brow, and really getting into a rhythm and song about it. The brothers were so amazed at how fast I worked that they shed their cast-iron grins, and a wrinkle of perplexity passed over their faces. But soon enough, they snapped back to their goofy smiles.

"Later that night I was stretched across my bed, staring at the ceiling and wondering what I'd gotten myself into, when the drilling started. It came without warning: a sputtering of engines, then a heavy pounding into concrete and asphalt.

"I jumped up and looked out the window. A hundred yards away, on a road that the brothers used to truck in supplies, a work crew was slicing up tarmac and cutting the pavement into squares. It brought me right back to the racket in the workshop. But then I remembered the headphones. At least, I thought, they'll muffle the noise! So I ran back to the shop, grabbed a pair, popped them on, jumped into bed, and dozed off.

"The next morning, one of the brothers came to wake me for breakfast. As he pulled away a pillow wrapped round my head, his eyes widened, his mug twitched, and a look of confusion shot across his face.

"'John, you're incredible!' He was grinning uncontrollably as I pulled off the headgear and tossed it onto a bureau. 'You're ready to go to work already!'

"When I heard the word *work*, all I could think of, all I could feel, was how every muscle in my body was aching. I slowly realized that he'd assumed I was eager to labor because I'd been lying there with the headgear on, as if rearing to go. Before I could explain otherwise, he had me shuffling across the grounds to the office of Father Momsom, the head brother.

"Momsom regarded me from beneath a thick pair of fish-lens eyeglasses. His stiff expression gradually transformed into a smile as the brother continued to sing my praise. What an eager, strong willed, energetic worker I was! Now Momsom is smiling, the brother is smiling, and I'm smiling, too.

"After whispering to one another they donned their hats, and arm in arm we headed toward the workshop. As we passed the shed with the axes leaning against a pile of wood they must have noticed a hesitation in my gait, because Momsom turned and said, 'No, you've done enough of that. Now we have more important things for you to do.'

"They ushered me into another building beside the workshop. Momsom gestured for me to sit in an upholstered armchair, while he sat at desk directly in front of me. He gazed into my eyes and said: 'My boy, we want to do something for the local community. We've decided to seek out those in need of food and other necessities. We have a fund set aside for this; we have money. But since we rarely mingle with outsiders, we don't really know what's happening out there.'

"I realized that he was offering me a job to work as a liaison between the brotherhood and the surrounding area. Locating those in need and giving them food, clothing, and *money*. As he elaborated on his plans, my mind wandered back to my own father. He was always walking around the house with a glassy look in his eyes and with his mind immersed in the purity of his classical music. Like Momsom, he was an idealistic dreamer. But unlike Momsom, he rarely made his dreams come true.

"My thoughts wandered from the purity of my father back to the hustle of the street: to the conmen who constantly work their territorial beat. When I looked up again, I realized there was nothing fake or phony about Momsom. He was an authentic holy man: a part of nature, like the whistle of wind or the glimmer of morning light, which now covered him with an iridescent sheen. Then I noticed a dead-drop silence. He'd stopped talking; he was awaiting my reply.

"'Father,' I said, "I'm just a street hustler and a conman. There's no place here for someone like me. It did cross my mind that I could take the job and hustle you out of your dough. But I can't even do that, because I respect you too much.'

"With his hands folded beneath his chin, Momsom sat there staring at me. His eyebrows were arched, and one eye was opened wide, as if he were peering through a monocle. Speaking with a firm but gentle tone, he replied: 'Whatever you've been in the past is the *past*. You're welcome to remain here.'

"'I really shouldn't, father.' My voice was shaky, and my throat tightened. 'But thanks for the offer.'

"'My offer is always open, John. Remember that.'

"As a way of saying good-bye, I smiled an uneven, trembling smile. Then I ran back to my room, past the children with their kites and the women with their fruit baskets. After I packed my things, I ran toward the dirt road. Just then, a car approached and offered me a ride back to town. I was out of breath ... and a little out of my mind."

* * *

The following afternoon I hitched a ride to the Ice Palace. Shortly after I arrived, John proudly displayed a sawed-off shotgun: fully loaded and rather impressive looking as he grabbed the barrel and tugged it back – *cha-ching*. Then he pointed it out a window at the apple orchards, which had just been dusted with a thick cloud of pesticide.

"I'd offer to shoot us some apples, but those chemicals would kill us faster than these bullets." He stored the rifle in a closet, cleared a space on a cluttered kitchen table, and said: "You must be hungry. Please, sit down; eat with me." Lunch consisted of instant soup made from dried powder, and English muffins smeared with peanut butter.

"Thanks, John. But first, where's the bathroom?"

He pointed me toward a well-worn staircase that ascended to a landing flanked by three white doors. The central one opened into an old-fashioned water closet. A large index card taped to a medicine cabinet read: *Put cover down on toilet after flushing*. Over the sink, another one said: *Turn on valve in basement when using lots of hot water*.

Returning to the landing and opening the door on the right, I found myself in John's bedroom. The walls were adorned with gaudy prints of Jesus and the Virgin Mary, mounted in cheap metal frames. Plaster statues of Christ, Saint Francis, and several other saints were positioned on a table covered with a white cloth trimmed with lace brocade. The statues were about three-feet high and colorfully painted. I suspected that John had nicked them from a local church.

The third door on the landing opened into a larger room. The ceiling was covered with styrofoam squares that were stained and yellowed from water damage, and the center of the ceiling was sagging – as if ready to collapse.

I approached a window overlooking the orchards and studied a lingering billow of pesticide that was as thick as a fog-bank. In a vain attempt to block the fumes, John had stuffed strips of newspaper along the edge of the window frames.

On the other side of the room a couch was covered by an enormous American flag. When I later asked John about it, he grinned and said, "Yeah, *where* did I get that, *heh, heh!*" John's friend Marlon later told me that John had fingered it while working with Bradley on a TV broadcast inside the White House.

I returned to the kitchen just as the soup was coming to a boil. Despite the newspaper-lined windows, the house was rife with a noxious, toxic stink. Soon, my eyes were itching, and my head was spinning.

We discussed our project for a couple of hours, then decided to go to sleep early, to get a fresh start in the morning. John said that I could crash in the room with the flag, but since the Stars and Stripes were redolent with pesticide at first I had trouble falling asleep.

I was drowsing in the darkness when John crept into the room, wearing only a flimsy dressing gown. When I opened my eyes, he was lingering beside me like a hovering specter and staring with a lustful expression.

A firm, authoritative basso profundo emerged from my chest – a voice that I didn't even know I possessed – and I snapped: "Get back to your room, and go to sleep!" Hesitating for a moment, he turned round and disappeared.

The following morning, while sipping black coffee tainted with a tincture of pesticide, neither of us mentioned what had occurred the night before. In an offhand, casual manner, I suggested that we hitchhike to town, then hunker down to record his tales on a cassette deck that one of my friends had promised to lend me. I didn't want to remain there another night, since I might not be as lucky a second time – between the loaded shotgun and the Friar's devious mind.

Dressed in his boxer shorts, John cleared the table as I studied an array of scars dotting his physique. Several of these souvenirs were remarkably large: one arced across his chest and resembled the scythe of a crescent moon. There were a variety of smaller cuts and bruises, too, including a welt along his bicep, from a fruit dealer's whip. When he was just a little boy, he said, he'd stolen some apples from a peddler's cart, and this was the price that he'd paid.

He also bore an ugly burn on his knee, which he said came from a hot-water pipe at Leavenworth Prison. I also noticed a small bone jutting at an angle on his left foot. While working in a roadside chain gang, he'd asked a cellmate to break his chain with a sledgehammer. But his pal had missed and had accidentally smashed John's foot. This explained the hobble and limp in his walk. At the bottom of his ankle there was another discolored band of skin: a memento, he said, from the leg-iron that had once held him in place, until his time was up.

I soon learned that the Friar had posed as a priest and had married couples at a nearby waterfall, which eventually led to his arrest. He also claimed to have worked as a personal assistant for Governor Nelson Rockefeller, who later became vice president of the United States, serving under President Ford. The Rockefeller story was utter nonsense, but John delivered it with such panache that it was both witty and amusing.

Marlon later informed me that they'd once attended an event where Rockefeller was being whisked through a crowd. As "Rocky" was passing by, John had shouted, "Nelson! Do you remember me?"

The governor turned, paused, and then replied, "Oh, yeah; sure I do, Red," calling him *Red* because, obviously, he'd never before laid eyes on John and had no idea who he was. But the Friar didn't miss a beat: "You see? He remembers!"

Over the weeks ahead I continued to record these elaborate fibs, scams, and immoral machinations, all rendered in the classic manner of a sociopath who attempts to make the listener empathize with his actions as if *he* were really the victim, since the rest of society has turned so unjustly against him. Thus, what else could he do but become a modern-day Robin Hood – or Friar John – and steal from the rich and give to the poor, meaning himself? But I soon discovered that John didn't just steal from the wealthy.

After accumulating oodles of tapes filled with these soft-pedaling, con-artist serenades, I returned to Gravesend to transcribe, edit, and figure out what I'd managed to collect. But as the weeks rolled by and John continued to dream of the gold bars that would fall into his greedy palms as soon as the book shot to the top of a bestseller list, he eventually grew alarmed. What if I absconded with his precious fables and cashed in all by myself? No doubt, he assumed that the rest of the world was as crooked as he was. And so, he'd inevitably reached such a conclusion. And by withdrawing into seclusion, I'd only further fueled his native paranoia. But I was so fed up with the drone of his voice – hour after hour on those cassettes – that the last thing I wanted to hear was any fresh hokum sputtering from the Friar's lips.

Since John was marooned upstate, he decided to set one of the other cons on my tail.

One day, out of the blue, Marlon called to invite me for a coffee at the Dojo café on Saint Mark's Place. Though we had yet to meet, I'd seen a photo of Marlon at the Friar's flat, so I was certain that I'd recognize him. He'd be accompanied by a drama critic, he said, who lived in a basement under Theatre 80, a former Prohibition speakeasy just down the block, which had once hosted talents such as Thelonious Monk and John Coltrane.

When I approached the Dojo, Marlon was relating a story about Bradley to the drama critic, a bespectacled fellow with a slight build and a shiny bald pate. Without being noticed, I slipped into a chair at an adjacent table and eavesdropped:

"Bradley was arrested for forgery while lecturing his class. Later on, he was declared innocent: victim of a set up. But the real reason they wanted to get rid of him was because of the rumors that were spreading across campus – that he used LSD and that he knew Timothy Leary."

Raising an eyebrow, the critic appeared to be impressed. "How did Bradley meet Tim Leary?"

"He requested an interview, which resulted in plenty of wild speculation. During the trial the judge insisted that Bradley meet with an eighty-year-old psychiatrist from Highland, to evaluate his mental competency. Since Bradley will talk to anyone who will listen about his great mission in life, he didn't waste any time in professing his consciousness-raising philosophy ... or his enduring belief in LSD. So she immediately certified him as insane. Since he was now 'legally crazy,' they offered him a lump sum: fifteen thousand dollars from his pension fund, and 250 bucks a month for the rest of his life ... or as long as he stays crazy! Bradley was euphoric. He bought the best tape deck he could find, along with a video camera and plenty of cassettes."

The critic appeared to grow thoughtful, then softly intoned: "How pleased the Establishment must have been to see that we were burning our brains out with LSD rather than organizing political protests and demonstrations. Better to sacrifice a generation to lust, lunacy, and dope-fueled madness than to risk the overthrow of the elite."

When Marlon paused to light a cigarette, I stood up and introduced myself.

"Mr. Mudnick, I presume."

Squinting his eyes, he looked me up and down as he clenched a toothpick in his teeth, slowly nodded, then murmured in a sinister tone: "We've been expecting you." Gulping down the last dregs of his coffee, he suggested that we retire to the critic's basement flat.

The sidewalk in front of the theater was a landmark in itself. Pressed into the cement were the footprints and handprints of film and theater stars such as Gloria Swanson, Joan Crawford, Myrna Loy, Ruby Keeler, and Joan Blondell. The critic paused for a moment to remark upon the biographies connected to some of the lesser-known names, such as Fifi D'Orsay: a Canadian vaudeville actress who worked in the Greenwich Village Follies and who later appeared in films, often playing the role of a "naughty *parisienne*."

As soon as we entered the critic's flat, Marlon spun round and confronted me about the tapes. With his voice shifting to a huskier timbre, I felt as if I were being strong-armed. Now he had me cornered in a basement with nowhere to turn, and he insisted that we drive to Brooklyn so that I could surrender the recordings.

I calmly replied that John was obsessed, as so many amateur writers are, with immediately cashing in on a so-called winning ticket. "As I'm sure you realize, Marlon, the writing process just doesn't work like that." I described the arduous task of transcribing all those tapes and added that I wasn't even halfway through all of John's tedious monologues.

"If he wants me to hand them over, I'd be glad to. But then I'll abandon the whole project, and we'll see if John can make heads or tails of his own babble."

The more I ranted on, the more Marlon saw the logic behind my reasoning. As I later learned, besides being aware of John's paranoia and duplicity, he was also touched by my sincerity. The savviest of the cons, Mudnick – or "Nick" as he preferred to be called – soon realized that I didn't harbor any ill will. As a result, we gradually entered into a warm friendship.

A tall, handsome, swarthy-skinned lady's man who was endowed with sensual lips and a deeply resonant, seductive voice, Nick's bassy timbre seemed to purr whether he was reading from a laundry list, reciting a poem, or ordering a pack of Pall Mall cigarettes. As they say in France: *Une voix des couilles* – a voice from the balls! And he was so photogenic that he'd once landed a minor role in a film starring Sophia Loren. On his bedroom dresser Nick proudly displayed an eight-by-ten glossy that had captured him and Sophia in the same frame. I later dubbed him the "Mana Voice," because it was from Nick that I learned how to modulate my tone and enrapture an audience.

Another thing that drew us together was the fact that, unlike John or Bradley, Nick was versed in a broad swath of culture, including avant-garde literature and obscure Beat poetry, the colorful rituals of Tantric Buddhism, and the medicinal use of plants. This last item thanks to his companion, Kathy, a kind, unassuming woman in her late thirties who originally hailed from Palo Alto. Besides grounding Nick, Kathy provided for him, since she was employed in a lucrative post at the Peace Corps. Although Nick delighted in the exchange of ribald tales, he always remained faithful to her. They impressed me as an offbeat but charming couple despite their difference in age and temperament, Kathy being less intellectual but far more practical.

With Mudnick as my unorthodox literary mentor, I spent the next few months hitching back and forth to Washington, DC, where he lived chez Kathy in a cozy little studio. I'd roll off the highway early in the evening, just as they were preparing an elaborate macrobiotic dinner. After imbibing Nick's richly brewed coffee, we'd leave Kathy to herself, snuggled up on a couch and sipping an herbal tea. Then we'd hop into Nick's 1965 Pontiac convertible: a battered black dinosaur creeping along on its last legs.

Our favorite place to promenade was the elite embassy section on Q Street, a picturesque stretch that featured Georgian-style mansions illuminated by softly lit amber lamps. But if we rendezvoused in Manhattan we'd cruise along the grimy downtown asphalt, always moving at a snail's pace as Nick sat behind the wheel, reciting his poetry as we calmly cruised along. At once we'd pick up where we last left off, embarking on an endless dialogue about Ginsberg's "Howl," Burroughs' *Naked Lunch*, or Corso's "Gasoline." Nick was also fascinated by a resilient sociopath named Ray Bremser, a minor Beat poet who'd been incarcerated for pyromania. He even wondered if the pyromania was a primitive expression of that higher magic, *pyromancy* – divination by means of fire. "For, after all," Nick concluded, "isn't that what poetry is all about?"

I could never decide if his fascination with Bremser had more to do with the poet's raw, unpolished talent or with Bremser's pathological criminality. But on the other side of the literary spectrum, there was Nick's admiration for Charles Reznikoff: a poet-scholar whose masterwork, *Testimony*, was originally crafted as a work of continuous prose, then reshaped into an epic poem. Most of all, Nick admired Reznikoff's love of ordinary people, especially those nameless victims of society that the poet had chronicled with the exactitude of an accountant marking ledgers of hardship and woe. Nick said that Reznikoff was employed by a publisher of legal texts; and, when placed in charge of summarizing court records he realized that a "found poetry" often lurked beneath such sterile accounts of injustice. So Reznikoff proceeded to hone this detached prose style into an art form, eventually giving birth to his finest verse.

Looking back on it now, it's obvious that this strange pair of poets embodied the classic Apollonian—Dionysian split, and I'm sure this is what drew my attention and kindled my interest in their life and work. As a young writer coming of age during the counterculture breakthroughs of the Sixties and Seventies, it was easy to identify with Bremser's gutsy, emotional approach to composing. But perhaps as a result of growing up in a household full of old books, even at that young age I respected the power of literary tradition. The ability to draw from a well-cultivated mind and to slowly craft and patiently polish one's particular link to this creative tradition is something that comes more easily to an older, more mature writer; and no doubt this is what also drew me to Reznikoff. But in due time, I would learn to balance these dueling forces that each have their place in the forge of creation.

Passionately debating such literary minutia, we'd leap from

one theme to the next as Nick's Pontiac crawled to a near halt or until he needed a break from driving. Then we'd amble along a side street, either under the surveillance cameras near the Luxembourg Embassy or on the rat-infested lanes of Manhattan's Chinatown, where we'd stop at Wo Hop's for fried duck at 3 a.m. But then we'd push on until dawn raised its iridescent hackles and we'd cruise back to Gravesend, where we'd sit for another hour in the idling convertible, attempting to wrap up the loose literary ends of the evening. But if I was visiting Nick in Washington, when it was time to leave he'd deposit me on a highway ramp, where I'd stick out my thumb and hitch to Manhattan under a twinkling canopy of stars.

During one such haul back to New York I bummed a ride with a driver who dropped me off in the Bronx, near the base of the George Washington Bridge: back then, a rather dangerous place. All I had left to my name was fifty cents: exactly enough to purchase a subway token. But when I cautiously entered a station on 175th Street – as I say, not the safest neighborhood on earth – there wasn't a clerk in sight. And without a token, I couldn't activate the revolving turnstile door with its interweaving metal bars.

I waited until a train roared onto the platform. An exiting passenger approached and pushed against the bars, and I grabbed them just before the gateway swung back into place. Prying it open, I barely managed to slip through a narrow space – a trick that Nick had taught me a few months earlier – and I safely returned to Brooklyn. But instead of feeling relieved, a frisson of fear crept along my spine. Perhaps, I thought, I was beginning to live too close to the edge.

A few weeks later, Nick called to say that Bradley's cameraman was sick. Or perhaps he'd quit. In any case, he suggested that I give it a try. Although Nick volunteered as Bradley's driver, he could easily have manned the camera as well. But since Bradley was such an egghead, Nick had probably decided that it would be more fun if I accompanied them.

As it turned out, I had a steady hand and a decent eye for the composition of a film frame. Thus, with Mudnick behind the wheel, me behind the lens, and Bradley holding forth in his brainiacal fashion, we'd saunter into executive boardrooms on Park, Madison, or Fifth Avenue, right in the center of that glittering skyscraper dystopia.

When Bradley was still working as a professor, he'd lavishly praised his hero, Buckminster Fuller, and had invited him to lecture at the university. So it wasn't hard to convince "Bucky" to appear on Bradley's first cable-TV program. After featuring this celebrated figure, Bradley soon attracted other notable guests. Thanks to his inspired babble, he could pick up a phone and easily beguile these bigwigs into granting him an interview. With his growing list of celebrity guests, and his ability to speak in multisyllabic phrases that would have gone on page after unpunctuated page if they'd been transcribed, it wasn't difficult to persuade such characters – who were always selling something – to surrender an hour for some free publicity. But what they never expected was that, upon our arrival, Bradley would ask for a handout – or rather, a "donation" – for his just cause. First, he'd introduce Nick and me, then he'd ask to speak privately with his next victim. About twenty minutes later he'd usually emerge from a conference room smiling triumphantly, having impressed the bejesus out of his guest. In most cases, flush with the excitement of a prospective interview, they'd swiftly write a check and the show would go on.

The only time I witnessed this rather dubious affair being called to an abrupt halt was in a glamorous penthouse that belonged to a man named Alan Greenspan. The future head of the Federal Reserve, Greenspan lived in the "millionaires only" section of the U. N. Plaza, on East 44th Street. Shortly after we entered his high-rise flat – or perhaps I should call it his *floating chateau* – things took a turn for the worse.

Bradley was chatting with Greenspan as I stood off to the side, eying an ancient Oriental vase mounted in a plexiglas display case in the vestibule. A spotlight positioned beneath the base illuminated its weblike patina as I lingered there, transfixed by its beauty. Meanwhile, Nick was glancing at Greenspan's attractive assistant, whom we immediately suspected was his mistress: a chic, svelte, considerably younger brunette who smiled enigmatically at Nick and then offered us coffee, served on a glass table in the living room.

Bradley asked for milk and sugar, but Mudnick and I shook our heads and declined. I figured that Nick wasn't in the mood for caffeine yet, having just smoked a fat joint with Bradley; while I abstained out of fear that I'd spill the cup or make some other disastrous *maladroit*. But eventually I realized that Nick was preoccupied with something else entirely. His inscrutable regard was usually so impenetrable that I might never have noticed his shifting mood if I hadn't already spent so many hours traveling beside him.

Unpacking the equipment, I mounted the camera onto a tripod while Bradley and Greenspan slipped into a conference room. Then Nick shot me an intense look, complete with a raised eyebrow and sealed with a frown. Just moments later, the conference room door swung open, and Bradley told us to repack the equipment.

We were nearly given the bum's rush out of there. Though Bradley had maintained a winning smile, I figured that he must have been utterly crestfallen.

Approaching the vestibule, I took one last look at the sumptuous vase. What a waste, I thought, to have such a priceless treasure sequestered here. From the very start, Greenspan –

that handmaiden of the economic oligarchy – had struck me as a type who was incapable of *seeing*. No doubt, the antique was simply a showpiece: a trophy, just like his companion. I couldn't imagine him ever pausing in the midst of his busy day to absorb its colorful, mysterious wonders.

The scenes rendered on the opalescent orb honored the lives of ordinary folk: figures gracefully going about their daily routine, planting seeds and harvesting crops. This was another thing that Greenspan would probably never learn to appreciate: an honest day's labor, working with one's *hands* and actually *producing* something. For a moment, I imagined these noble creatures were mocking him. Then we were seen to the door by the serenely smiling mistress, who exchanged one final enigmatic glance with Nick.

Bradley waited until we boarded an elevator and began our descent to reveal that the mention of his other hero, the economist Louis Kelso, had made Greenspan's head spin. Apparently, Greenspan regarded Kelso as being no better than an insane socialist, a satanic communist, a misanthropic Marxist-Leninist, or however else he'd phrased it.

"*Kelso!*" Bradley shouted in mock hysteria while shaking his head and wringing his hands, "that *maniac!*" He added that Kelso's "employee stock-ownership plan," of rewarding workers with company shares as an incentive to increase production, was the "Close Sesame" term that had cast us as renegades who belonged in a wilderness.

"Instead of admiring a genius such as Kelso," Bradley bitterly exclaimed, "Greenspan is a devotee of that economic fascist, Ayn Rand!"

Nick cut him short: "Kelso had *nothing* to do with it." Nick had a way of intoning Bradley's name that conjured a beatnik school principal reprimanding an errant young poet: with a patronizing snarl, and a bit more vociferously than he'd normally speak. For he knew that, otherwise, it was impossible to grab Bradley's attention, absentminded professor that he was.

"But of course, it was Kelso!"

"No," Nick hissed. "It was the *mistress*."

"The mistress?"

"Yes. Take a guess."

"You mean ... you slept with her?"

"Exactly. An old girlfriend."

"But ... are you *certain*?"

"*Of course*, I'm certain!"

Nearly choking on his own laughter, Nick continued to cackle like a gargoyle as he backed the Pontiac down a curving ramp and out of the building. Then he turned to me and winked: not just to emphasis a point, but to commune in that silent, telepathic manner that we'd developed during our long spins to nowheresville. It was as if he were saying: *Ka-tow, can you believe this jerk?* Nick always pronounced my name in a way that no one else had: a buzzing, thrumming chord that made me feel like a rock star: *Can you believe it, Ka-tow? Cackle! Cackle!*

With his eyes pinned to the traffic on First Avenue, he added: "Bradley, remember when she gave Greenspan that strange look? Then they disappeared into a hallway. Moments later, right after you entered the conference room, out you went. *You* didn't screw up. *I* did. Or rather, I screwed *her*, then she screwed *us* out of an interview with Alan Greenspan!"

"Well," sighed Bradley, "whatever it was, Kelso or the mistress, now, we have to find something to eat."

In order to avoid risking arrest, I asked Nick to drop me off at a nearby subway station. "Finding something to eat" meant that they would select a crowded Midtown diner that was large, well staffed, and thriving; otherwise, it was too risky to put their plan into action:

They'd wait outside until a throng of customers was entering, then they'd slip in beside them, as if they were part of the group, and grab a table at the back. Ordering an elaborate spread, while lingering over dessert Bradley would open his briefcase and spread his papers across the table in an intentional pattern of disarray. When the waitress ambled over to replenish his coffee, he'd charm her by politely asking a few innocuous questions, such as where she hailed from, or what was her favorite dish, or when was it less crowded? Nick would interject with a few witty remarks, perhaps poking fun at Bradley's nerdiness, but mostly he'd just sit there, gazing seductively, until she nearly melted under his molten glare.

Once they were alone again, at a deftly chosen moment Bradley would lower his eyes and nod at Nick. Then he'd bury his head in his papers, ostentatiously fussing with his gold-tipped pen while Nick approached the cash register at the other end of the restaurant. But instead of paying the bill, Nick would order a pack of cigarettes, then continue out the front door. Meanwhile, Bradley would leave a large tip prominently displayed for the now-enchanted waitress. He'd gather his papers at a leisurely pace and dump everything into his briefcase – along with the unpaid check. He'd wait until the cashier was busy with other customers, then he'd calmly stroll outside.

Nick claimed that they'd been apprehended only once, when a waitress had emerged from a diner and politely called after them:

"Sir, did you forget to pay?"

Bradley turned to Mudnick and said, "But I thought *you* took care of the bill." In response, Nick regarded Bradley with an equally bewildered expression and replied, "And I thought *you* did!"

"Well, if neither of us paid, then where's the check?" Scratching his head and apologizing profusely, Bradley added,

"Hey, maybe it got mixed up with my papers!" Kneeling on the pavement, he snapped open his briefcase, fumbled around, then "miraculously" retrieved it.

"Oh, my gosh! How *foolish* of me!"

Nick pointed his knobby thumb at Bradley, rolled his eyes, and chuckled: *"The absentminded professor!"* And everyone laughed, and now the waitress walked away with an even bigger tip than the one that they'd left on the table.

*   *   *

During the first week of May I was invited to crash at Kathy's flat while Bradley slept at a cheap hotel, accompanied by a fourth fellow: an old pal of Nick's named Ray Veshnevski. Ray was a nearly destitute poet, now in his sixties, who'd failed to leave his mark; but he was still plugging away in a half-hearted, distracted manner. Nick said that Ray was so broke that, instead of a belt, he wore a rope tied round his waist. A petite fellow, with his long silvery hair and sinewy frame he resembled a troll. Little did I realize that Ray would later arrive at a key moment to assist me in my own survival in Manhattan.

Taking pity on Ray, Nick invited him to accompany us on a program we were filming that weekend at the White House. Computers – those increasingly miniaturized monsters that were creeping into offices throughout the land – were now being used by President Carter's new administration, so Bradley wanted to interview the president's communications director. He was also intrigued by the solar panels that Carter had installed on the roof of the White House but that the next president – a petroleum-soaked politician named Ronald Reagan – would discreetly dismantle, minus any publicity.

The other reason we were in Washington was to participate in what would later be hailed as the nation's largest antinuclear rally, an event that drew over ninety thousand protestors.

Earlier that year the actress Jane Fonda had starred in a film called *The China Syndrome*, which dramatized a nuclear core meltdown that, theoretically, could burn to the other side of the earth – or to China. In the movie, a physicist claims that such a catastrophe would leave an area the "size of Pennsylvania permanently uninhabitable." Two weeks after its premiere, in a bizarre historical synchronicity, Three Mile Island – a nuclear plant in Pennsylvania – underwent a partial core meltdown. In response, antinuke groups across the country scrambled to organize a demonstration in the nation's capital. Never one to let the grass grow beneath his feet, Nick had arranged for us to read our freshly concocted antinuke poems after the rally, at a downtown café.

By the time we finished breakfast and arrived at the National Mall it was packed, with the crowd burgeoning to the far end of the esplanade. But never fear – and this is what I mean about Nick's cocksure bravado – he simply said: *Ka-tow! Follow me!*

Weaving a serpentine path along the periphery of a shoulder-to-shoulder crowd, he led me to a side entrance at the speaker's pavilion. A young man was stationed there as security, checking VIP passes before allowing anyone to enter.

Nick nonchalantly sidled up to him, and, without a word, flipped open his wallet and flashed it. The guard nodded and waved him inside. But then, as if realizing he'd forgotten something, Nick spun round, pointed his thumb at me, and said: "Him, too." And *Open Sesame*, now, we were circulating among celebrities such as the author Kurt Vonnegut and the comedian-cum-activist Dick Gregory, who had jeopardized a multimillion-dollar career in order to pursue political proselytizing.

I sat on a balustrade right beside Gregory and thanked him

for having spoken at my university the previous year. Perhaps, I thought, he was resting his leg, which had suffered a gunshot wound during the Watts riots of 1965. Gregory had marched beside Martin Luther King in demonstrations since the early '60s, and along the way he'd been beaten, humiliated, and arrested more times than he might care to remember. So now, I exulted in the honor of speaking with this heroic figure. But I also detected a certain wariness and mistrust in his manner. He was trying to size me up, perhaps wondering if I was an agent provocateur. If the Sixties was the Love Generation, the Seventies was the decade of the Paranoid Heebie-Jeebies.

Seated a mere ten feet away, Kurt Vonnegut stood up and approached a speaker's podium to deliver a fifty-seven-word speech to the thousands of demonstrators that fanned out on the esplanade below. As the roaring crowd shouted its approval, the curly-haired author of *Slaughterhouse-Five* accused the nuclear moguls of being "filthy little monkeys," then added: "If we let them, they will kill everything on this lovely blue-green planet with their rebuttals to what we say today with their stinking, stupid lies."

Toward the end of the demonstration we ran into Bella Abzug, a former congresswoman from New York, whose trademark apparel was a wide brimmed floppy felt hat. Bella was widely admired for her political activism and early opposition to the Vietnam War. She'd also attended rallies to impeach President Nixon, thus earning my eternal respect. When we told her about our antinuke poems, she smiled broadly and replied, "Well, I've never been invited to a *poetry reading* before!"

Once we were alone again, I turned to Nick and asked, "What the hell did you flash that guard?"

"Come here," he whispered, his eyes darting about in search of a more secluded spot.

Moving to a far corner of the balustrade, he opened his wallet to reveal a glittering gold detective's badge.

Glancing down at the swarming mass on the mall below, I realized that, thanks to Nick, we'd landed the best seats in the house ... while somehow managing to avoid arrest for impersonating police officers.

*   *   *

When Nick returned to New York a few weeks later, we met late one night in the Lower East Side. Cruising in the Pontiac, upon the break of dawn we parked on Canal Street and wandered over to nearby Chinatown. The storefronts had yet to open, and the streets were nearly deserted.

We were padding along Mott Street when we noticed several somber-faced proprietors peering out from behind dusty windowpanes or cautiously stationed before their shadowy doorways – as if frozen at the threshold. They regarded us with a wary, portentous, unwelcoming glare – as if they were warning us that we'd drifted into a territory where we didn't belong. Nick stopped speaking in mid-sentence, turned to me, and raised an eyebrow. But before either one of us could speak, as we rounded the corner and continued along Broadway, we stumbled directly into a hornet's nest.

A half dozen members of the Flying Dragons gang – dressed in black leather jackets with white dragon wings emblazoned on the back – were milling around. One of them lay there, dead on the pavement, draped across a dirty curb. Another young man was frantically gripping the top of a parking meter, shaking uncontrollably as he tried to steady his wobbly legs, until two other boys staggered over and held him up, from beneath his arms.

Most horrifying and remarkable of all, at the very moment

that we were tiptoeing by, as they attempted to steady their comrade I could hear his wheezing and gasping breath passing through the stab wounds that had penetrated his torso. The air whistled through him like a breeze through a screen door. Then he collapsed in their arms, and I felt him die. I had the distinct, unnerving impression that he'd passed away just as we were passing by, just as our feet were about to take another cautious step.

Though they waved their hands with a panicked animation – desperately trying to hail a ride – nobody would stop until one of the boys threw himself upon the hood of an advancing yellow cab that had slowed for a second, to see what was happening. The cabbie was about to speed away, but the boy leapt, swan dived, and hit the hood with a *bang*, so he was forced to halt.

They shouted bloody murder at this poor devil, who was utterly terrified as they gingerly placed their injured companion in the back seat. They slipped him in as delicately as possible, then ordered the driver to hit the gas, and the cab screeched along Broadway. The back door wasn't even closed as they sped away. Whizzing up the avenue, one of the boys reached out, grabbed the handle, and yanked it shut.

The next day I spotted an obituary in the *New York Times*. A brief column, about two inches long, stated that a member of the Flying Dragons gang was stabbed multiple times – as the French say, *un coup de couteau* – and pronounced dead upon arrival at St. Vincent's Hospital.

From East to West

With the arrival of our teenage years, we wanted nothing more than to escape the narrow-minded confines of Gravesend. Drew Dunkle and Danny Brutta were among my closest friends at that time, and we would often sit together on our respective stoops and dream of our deliverance.

Drew was a tall, loose-limbed fellow who usually wore a deadpan expression and who bore a close resemblance to the comedian Stan Laurel. As a result of studying acting in high school and college, he often liked to treat the world as a stage. Sometimes it was difficult to tell whether Drew was simply reading lines from a script in order to get some attention or if, instead, he was speaking sincerely. Spectacle and performance were the leitmotifs of his life, coupled with a comedic sensibility that verged on the playfully sadistic tradition of Le Grand-Guignol.

The temperament and personality of Danny Brutta stood in stark contrast to Drew; for never was a man more forthright and matter-of-fact in his dealings with others than Danny. While Drew held his actual emotions in check or appropriated them only to fuel his thespian antics, Danny rarely disguised his true feelings and was known for his flashing temper. If he felt he was being short-changed or treated disrespectfully, his ire would flare to match the vivid hues of his carrot-red hair. He was of medium height but was muscular and fit, and he kept himself in excellent shape. He wasn't the sort to pick a fight, but if he got into a jam he could easily defend himself. Drew, on the other hand, had no interest in physical culture and was content to exercise his lungs by puffing away on cigarettes.

Perhaps because they embodied such diametrically opposed characteristics, they developed an enduring friendship that was grounded on this strange balance of opposites. Drew would often glance over at me and laugh while witnessing one of Danny's fits of ire; conversely, Danny would raise his eyebrow and make a dry remark about what a madman Drew was, all the while being thoroughly fascinated by his performance. Meanwhile, I would position myself between them as a sort of touchstone and referee, egging each of them on.

One balmy June morning while I was seated on my stoop, Danny came sauntering along the block with his ducklike waddle and broad smile. Seating himself beside me at the top step, he asked, "So, what do you say to a cross-country trip? Me, you, and Drew. Would your father lend us his camping equipment?"

"As long as we don't allow Drew to drive," I replied, "you can count me in." Although Drew was a decent driver he'd never used a stick shift before, so we were apprehensive about letting him sit behind the wheel of Danny's Pinto.

Pooling what little cash we had, that summer the three of us embarked upon a trip that would take us all the way to California and back. No doubt, it was in imitation of Kerouac and his *On the Road* crew that, come July, we drove in such a frenzied manner across the continent. But the national obsession to hit the tarmac and escape from something had begun well before Jack Kerouac. It hadn't escaped my attention that J. D. Salinger's *The Catcher in the Rye* not only leads to but also strangely anticipates Jack's celebrated chronicle:

> I decided I'd go away.... I'd start hitchhiking my way out West. What I'd do, I figured, I'd go down to the Holland Tunnel and bum a ride, and then I'd bum another one, and another one, and

another one, and in a few days I'd be somewhere out West where it was very pretty and sunny and where nobody'd know me and I'd get a job. I figured I could get a job at a filling station somewhere, putting gas and oil in people's cars.

On the Road? Not at all. It's from the final pages of *The Catcher in the Rye*, just before the protagonist cracks up. And just like Holden Caulfield, Jack Kerouac cracked up, too, although his alcohol-induced decline was far more prolonged and incremental.

The author J. D. Salinger had also weathered some profound personal challenges. First he suffered a nervous breakdown in his mid-twenties, which he drew upon when writing *Catcher*. But later on he went bonkers on the other side of the psychic spectrum, neurotically obsessing over organic food, enemas, and yoga meditation. While Salinger never matured past the age of fourteen, unlike Kerouac he wanted to live to be at least a hundred and twenty.

In any case, in our growing obsession to reach the Coast, we outpaced even the frenetic flight of Kerouac and his pal Cassady … perhaps because, unlike either of them, we felt there was so little to hold our attention between Greenwich Village and the San Francisco Bay. Thus, we drove for stretches of twenty, forty, or even sixty-hours.

In an essay that I later chanced upon in an obscure literary journal, an *On the Road* scholar says that although Kerouac flew in and out of various locales like a whirling dervish on a magic carpet ride, one wonders if he really came to know anything essential about quotidian life in America. I mention this because we, too, didn't linger very long in any one place. It was more like taking a speeding taxi across the country. We were obsessed with reaching the West Coast but, once we arrived there, we grew equally obsessed about completing the journey back east.

Between east and west at least we visited Buffalo Bill's house in North Platte, Nebraska: a modest tourist attraction run by the first pair of semiretired hippies that I'd ever encountered. We'd just crossed the great Mississippi – Huck Finn's mythical river – and at once we felt something grand open up: the country was remarkably different after you transited this legendary divide. Sometimes, merely crossing a state line would give birth to an entirely new sensibility. Even Danny, that eternal pragmatist, sensed this ineffable psychic shift. But perhaps it isn't all that surprising, since so many western states are carved along natural boundary lines such as meandering rivers, abrupt mountain ranges, or a variety of other geological impediments that separate one section of that vast, untamed wilderness from the next.

Of course, we couldn't drive continuously; we were forced to stop at certain points along the way, so we did witness some extraordinary things, such as the mineralogical wonders of Yellowstone, especially those bright iridescent pools painted in such otherworldly hues – now dried up and perhaps gone forever. While exploring the park we promenaded over a series of wooden planks where the earth's crust is exposed, and the rising steam engulfed us until we could hardly see each other. We were surrounded by the ghoulish, lifeless claws of petrified trees – calcified and skeletal – which resembled a den of prehistoric beasts. Geologically speaking, there's such a rich variety of things out there that are unique to America and that you'd never encounter in Europe, such as the Mars-red canyons of the Southwest that are featured so prominently in cowboy movies, or the ancient Pueblo cliff dwellings of New Mexico. Not to mention that picturesque drive along the coast as one travels south from Washington State. We entered northern California just as the foggy mists of Oregon were clearing away, and suddenly we were gazing over that placid, dreamy Pacific: so markedly different from the roaring Atlantic of the East.

We finally pitched our tent at Humboldt State Park in the redwood forest. Despite being Brooklyn boys, that's where we felt most at home: seated beneath those majestic boughs known as the *Sequoia sempervirens*, or coast redwoods. But what impressed me almost as much as the towering trunks was the forest floor itself. It was carpeted so deeply, from centuries of fallen redwood needles, that the padding produced the most profound silence that I'd ever experienced. You were just enveloped in it.

The following day we ascended a leafy mountaintop at Big Sur. As I wandered along the cliffs and gazed at the sparkling undulating waves of the Pacific, I mused that it was no wonder that the author Henry Miller had chosen to live here. In terms of natural beauty, it was a crowning point: a pinnacle in America. Henry must have been overwhelmed by this vista, I thought, especially after living for so long in dusty, smog-encrusted Paris. Big Sur was the antidote to all that.

I'd often marvel over Miller's ability to stretch the English language like taffy, especially in certain pellucid passages of trancelike proclamation that mark the *Tropics* with an incandescence that one normally associates with visionary or spiritual literature. Those early masterpieces were spawned from the vivid, fecund atmosphere of France, but then the expatriate returned home – very much against his will, when Americans abroad were compelled to flee from the obscene penumbra of Hitler's looming silhouette.

Seven years before Kerouac's trip out West, and seventeen years before the publication of *On the Road*, Henry embarked upon his own cross-country tour, in 1940. In comparison, it was a far more leisurely expedition than Jack's maniacal blast into space. Miller's trek lasted 354 days, and, unlike Kerouac, he lingered at various points along the way: interacting with ordinary folk, soaking in the flora and fauna, and all the while raging over the culturally barren, desolate pavements that stretch from one dreary state to the next.

But by far, the most glaring contrast between the two authors centers around Henry's profound dislike of America. After discovering himself in Lutèce (the ancient Roman name for Paris) and visiting the paradise of prewar Greece, as the world braced for conflict he was forced to return "home" again; and what was there? Just an open road cutting through all this wilderness. Yes, there were plenty of picturesque geological formations, but what of human culture? Where could one encounter the monumental cathedrals, the ancient museums, the haunts of Dante and Shakespeare? While wandering around Las Vegas one evening, he recorded his dismal impressions in a journal:

> The sense of utter desolation. Loneliness. Madness. Two days in Vegas and I'd be a raving lunatic. The walk in fields at night. The stars clouting me. The sinking feeling of being again in my own country, amidst empty souls. And the name so beautiful. Vega! A great star! And this awful desolation – this appalling nothingness. Nothing anywhere in the world to compare with it. The loneliest spot in Tibet or Mongolia couldn't produce in me such a feeling of devastation. I am no longer a man, no longer a human being. I am a lost soul – a haunted man.

An *appalling nothingness* – the horror of the vacuum! Miller's despair is so all-consuming that almost nothing he experiences during this arduous trek serves to inspire his daemon. The only exemplary thing about his chronicle, which was later published as *The Air-Conditioned Nightmare*, is its title. Otherwise, it remains the author's only major work that I can't sink my teeth into – for it lacks the beauty and mystery of his other rollicking prose. But fortunately, he maintained a journal during this trip, which was later published as *The Nightmare Notebook*. Besides his ruminations on Vegas, there's a line in there that sums up the author's harebrained scheme to portray the mid-century American soul – or lack of it. When he ran into Gypsy Rose Lee at the 1940 World's Fair in New York and told her about his project – to drive across this vast wasteland and record whatever he experienced along the way – she dryly remarked: "I could think of a lot better things to do than tour America." Rather reminiscent of what Humbert Humbert says about his own road trip with Lolita: "We had been everywhere. We had really seen nothing."

Perhaps Henry would have been better off staying right there and writing a biography about Gypsy Rose. For, without realizing it, he'd finally encountered a woman as wily as himself. (She was said to have committed two murders, and her mother had once shoved an uncooperative female journalist off a fire escape, plunging to her death.) But instead, he set sail for the ironically named New Hope, Pennsylvania.

Yet, eventually, this wild-goose chase led Miller to precisely where he was supposed to be, and to where we were now standing: gazing upon this foaming, churning, *heavenly* ocean – to use an odd turn of phrase – which often brought the author such bliss.

* * *

After our cross-country odyssey we ended up right where

we started: sipping a cool beer in Danny's backyard at midnight. And without missing a beat, we were plotting to escape from Gravesend once again. But now, at least we had a better idea of where we might be headed.

Drew was most impressed not by what we'd seen, but by what we *hadn't* seen. "Before we left," he said, "I imagined that America was filled from coast to coast with big thriving cities, just like New York. But there's almost nothing out there! You have to drive hundreds of miles just to get from one dinky little town to the next ..."

Drew and I were city boys at heart, but Danny more resembled a country bumpkin. Upon our arrival in the Southwest he'd grown enchanted by the picturesque landscape, the laconic manner of its inhabitants, and the dazzling array of twinkling constellations that lend such places an otherworldly wonder.

"My aunt and uncle are moving to Taos next year," he said. "So that's where I'll be headed as soon as I can save up enough dough. I can live with them until I find my own place, and rent's a lot cheaper out there than it is in New York. Besides, I'd never want to live in Manhattan. It's loud, dirty, and filled with too many crazy people."

"But that's exactly what makes it so exciting!" Drew laughed. "And with that pale Irish skin of yours, how will you survive the sizzling sun of New Mexico? After just a few weeks on the road, you already look like a baked lobster!"

Ignoring Drew, Danny turned to me and asked, "What about you? You haven't said anything yet."

I was gazing at the constellation of Orion. The reddish-tinted star, Betelgeuse, which marks the tip of the hunter's left shoulder, was shimmering just over Danny's head, on the eastern horizon. But the blazing orbs of Orion were exceptional, as so many other constellations that had burned so brightly out West were invisible now, due to Brooklyn's floodlit streets. Orion's radiant light reminded me of Dylan Thomas' poem about death, with its marvelous line: *They shall have stars at elbow and foot.*

"It's certainly beautiful out there," I replied. "But like Drew, I need to live in a big city, and one with some culture. Now that we've seen America, I'm more convinced than ever that, one day, I'll have to make my way to Europe."

"But there's plenty of culture in Manhattan," Drew interjected. "Think of all the great museums, theaters, and music halls ..."

"Yes, but what Danny says is also true. It's exciting, but if you remain there too long it burns you out and tosses you into the gutter. Perhaps I could live in Manhattan for a few years, but eventually I'll need something more humane, and with a touch of the Old World. A slower pace, and one that offers some solace to the soul."

"But you've only *read* about Paris," Danny said. "What if it isn't like anything that you imagine it to be?" An eternal pragmatist, his first impulse was always to search for the proof behind any conjecture. "How do you know that it isn't just a pipe dream?"

"Well, one thing I know for sure is that there isn't anything for me in America. The next step is Manhattan, to escape Brooklyn. But then, if I'm lucky, one day I'll set sail for a foreign shore."

At that moment, I promised myself that by the time I reached the age of thirty I'd be walking along the streets of Paris, the city of my paternal ancestors.

A few days after we returned I received an urgent call from Mudnick:

"Did you hear about John?" he asked. "He's been arrested for theft!"

"No, what happened?"

"He tried to slip a few bucks out of a cash register, after a grocery clerk stepped away from the counter. And now he's in big trouble."

"Oh, no …"

"But listen, there's something you've got to take care of. When he mentioned your tape-recording project to his lawyer, the guy almost had a fit."

"What's that got to do with anything?"

"The lawyer said that you have to destroy those tapes, because you've inadvertently created a trail of evidence linking John to all sorts of crimes. Now that he's facing jail time, if those recordings ever got into the wrong hands, his goose would be cooked. He said that, in a court of law, they could be regarded as a confession."

Upon hearing this, I could only imagine how John's paranoia must have spiked.

"Don't worry, Nick. I'll take care of it right away."

As soon as I hung up I called Danny. "Meet me in front of your house in ten minutes. I need you to help me with something …"

I arrived with a burlap bag, stuffed with cassettes. Once I apprised him of the situation, he broke out laughing.

"But how did you ever get yourself into such a jam?" he grinned.

"Never mind; what should we do?"

"The sewer."

"You mean, dump them?"

"Of course. Once you drop them into that stinking hole, they'll melt into nothingness." As always, Danny got right to the point.

"The stinkiest sewer's got to be the one on Kings Highway."

"Then let's go."

We nonchalantly strolled to the corner, where I knelt beside an open sewer main and slipped the bag into the hole. A few seconds later, we heard a *splash* echoing from the foul-smelling pit.

"All those hours of work," I sighed, "right down the drain. But at least the rats will have something extra to munch on."

"And now, no one will be able to rat on old Friar John. But if I were you," he added, assuming a serious demeanor, "I'd cut myself loose from that entire bunch. Otherwise, you're asking for trouble."

"You're probably right about that."

"Come on, let's go have a beer."

Although this put an end to my project, thanks to my work with Bradley a seed had been sown. Not only had I absorbed his interviewing technique; I'd also learned how easy it is to approach important figures that one might otherwise have regarded as unapproachable. Eventually I would publish my own collection of conversations with leading literary authors, some of whom had directly inspired my writing.

But first, there was the untrodden road to Paris.

The Butter-yellow Rays of Edward Hopper

I was seated beside a gurgling fountain at Washington Square one afternoon when a petite young woman with large green eyes approached, holding out an unlit cigarette.

"Would you happen to have a light?" She spoke softly, with an elegant British intonation, and was formally dressed, in a dark skirt and heels.

"What a delightful accent you have," I said, offering her a lit match. "You must be from England."

"No, South Africa. My name's Jenny. Would you like me to roll you one?"

I nodded as she sat beside me and opened a satchel of tobacco. "What about you? Where are you from?"

"Gravesend. But not the one near the River Thames."

"Brooklyn? But that's so far away!"

"Yes, but I come here often." Looking her up and down, I added: "You're dressed as if you've just returned from work."

"Believe it or not, I work as a debt collector in a stuffy Midtown office. It's a job I simply detest," she sighed, speaking quietly now and shaking her head in resignation. "But for the time being, it pays the bills."

We exchanged phone numbers, and the following week I invited her for dinner at a Japanese restaurant on Bleecker Street. As we relaxed at a table facing Sixth Avenue, Jenny seemed to be fascinated by every figure that walked by, looking them over and commenting on how they dressed, gestured, and promenaded along the avenue. When she lifted her teacup, I noticed that she wore a brass ring round her thumb, decorated with tiny figures that were reminiscent of ancient African art.

"I just love it here. It's so uninhibited and so much more energetic than South Africa." Jenny added that she was from Cape Town, where the ruling Afrikaners had established a state of apartheid: something she was deeply opposed to. The daughter of an investment banker whose roots went deep into the colonial past, whenever Jenny spoke at length about her upbringing she would absentmindedly twirl her brass ring.

We were waiting for the check when she invited me back to her studio. "Why don't you come over for a beer? I live just a few blocks away, on Downing Street."

"You mean, near Father Demo Square?"

"Yes, beside the Church of Our Lady of Pompeii."

Upon entering her flat I glanced at the contents of a small bookcase in the living room. Sandwiched between Dante and Montaigne were several volumes of Céline, Jean Giono, and Hubert Selby. An eclectic assortment, it included many of my favorite authors.

Seated on a rug on her parquet floor and drinking bottle after bottle of beer, we talked long into the night. But finally Jenny frowned and announced that I had to leave, because she had to wake up early for work.

"But maybe you can come back next weekend?"

The following Saturday I returned with a bottle of Bordeaux. As I sat beside her and stared into her gentle eyes, her face seemed to metamorphose. Was the wine going to my head, I wondered, or were her shifting moods altering her facade?

Staring back at me, her face tensed. "My God, your eyes seem to look right through stuff – like an X-ray!" She tilted her head and asked, "What is it? Do you think I'm crazy?"

"No," I laughed, "but it's like witnessing a changeling." When I explained what I meant, she sighed.

"What a relief! I thought you were going to say, 'I can't work you out.'"

"What a funny expression. That must be British English. But no, I don't think you're crazy; I think you're quite normal."

"Normal!" Now, she was frowning.

"Of course, I don't mean that in the perverse, ordinary sense of the word ..."

"Well, I think you're good going," she grinned. "Yes, you're absolutely *lovely*."

"Lovely? Good going? No one's ever called me *that* before! But has anyone said that they can't work you out?"

"Oh, sure. Plenty of times. Almost *all* the time. Especially in South Africa."

"Those poor devils! Imagine getting so nervous in the face of a little mystery. Besides, what's normal and what's crazy?"

"No one seems to know anymore."

"Maybe you're just too *intense* for them."

"Yes," she laughed nervously, "perhaps, it's true!"

Despite what she'd said about X-ray vision, Jenny's gaze was far more penetrating than mine. That night as I slept beside her, I dreamed that as I was staring into her eyes I saw a flicker of images rolling past, like a cosmological newsreel. First, I observed the earth spinning round, as if seen from outer space. There were also trees bending in heavy winds, with their leaves torn to shreds. One image would transform into the next with such celerity that they appeared to occur almost simultaneously. And all the while, like a double exposure, the image of Jenny's eyes hovered beneath this deluge of luminous forms. When I finally awoke, she was sitting there staring at me with an enigmatic smile.

Jenny had impressed me as being an inherently kind woman who wanted nothing more than to enjoy the simple things in life. That is, to smoke her hand-rolled tobacco; to leisurely sip her cinnamon-flavored espresso; and, after surviving the daily torture of the debt collection agency, to return home, pull off her skirt, and make passionate love.

It was difficult to imagine Jenny in such a ludicrous profession. She said that such positions were usually manned by cutthroat, unscrupulous, testosterone-driven bastards who'd sell their own mother if it meant settling a claim and collecting a percentage. It was a setting that she absolutely *abhorred*. From what I'd gleaned from her description of this grind, it was plain to see that it was only because she was so sweet and good-natured, and because she possessed such an impeccable, sterling character, that the clients would often repay their debts, or at least part of them, doing whatever they could to please Jenny. And it was due to this remarkable success rate that her employers begged her not to leave. Whenever she'd grow determined to resign, they'd plead with her to change her mind. They appeared to be experts at taking advantage of Jenny, as if they sensed that she didn't have the heart to say no. But while the bosses grew ecstatic over her performance, and while the clients felt less beleaguered, the dark circles, the ever-widening rings round Jenny's adorable eyes only deepened.

And so, after such a spiritually nullifying, gut-wrenching day, she wanted nothing more than to uncork a bottle of wine and snuggle up beside me on her futon, which faced a courtyard shaded by an abundant foliage of ailanthus trees. Tucked into this cozy little corner, under shafts of glowing sunlight, our flesh would be dappled by the colorful shadows of the autumn leaves. By late afternoon the sun would illuminate the red brick wall beside her bed with a luscious, butter-yellow hue. It was the same color that Edward Hopper had once captured so deftly in *Early Sunday Morning*: that widely celebrated landscape featuring a crooked barbershop pole slanting over a warped Manhattan pavement. The bricks and mortar in Jenny's flat would glow with those same golden rays: an opalescent mixture of Naples yellow, titanium white, and a hint of cadmium orange.

While sitting under this nearly palpable light, Jenny would say that she wanted nothing more than to kiss and caress, and sip her Bordeaux, and listen to my tales of growing up in Gravesend. And then for me to reach under her dowdy black skirt – her *work skirt*, as she so derisively referred to it – and slowly fondle her. And then to yank off her blouse and unhook that capacious brassiere so that her breasts could jiggle and bounce so proudly under the setting sun. She just loved to linger there naked in the warm glow, she said, with her legs crisscrossed like a Buddha as she rolled her tobacco.

*　*　*

Jenny would occasionally amuse me with one of her own delightful anecdotes about growing up in Cape Town with her older sister, Dorothy, with whom she didn't share much in common. Dorothy's abundant red hair was cinched into a long ponytail, and her most prominent feature was a steely pair of icy-blue eyes. In many ways, Jenny said, Dorothy was a product of that postwar "what you see is *all* you get" sensibility of superficial materialism and existential nihilism: a cynical way of thinking that eschewed anything nonrational. While Jenny's sensibilities were far more cultural and artistic, Dorothy and her world-weary cronies always made fun of anything that didn't fit neatly into their atomistic, hyper-intellectual perspective. In the words of Ken Kesey, they worshipped "only the rattle of insects in the dry places of Eliot, signifying nothing." That is, until quantum physics had uncorked one too many inexplicable conundrums. And then that professorial figure, the author Joseph Campbell, had appeared out of the blue on television one day, and Joe boiled it down to a pithy phrase – almost like an advertising slogan, which, after all, is the most that the average American can digest – and he said, *Follow your bliss*.

An offhand, seemingly castaway comment, presented merely as an afterthought, to which Campbell added that one must carefully consider which wall to place your ladder upon: the goal of your life being the wall, and the ladder the means of ascent. *Pay attention*, he said, because if you don't follow your heart – that is, your bliss: the thing that gives you radiance, purpose, and meaning, and the thing that gives you joy – you'll spend your entire life moving in the wrong direction. Which was sort of the predicament that Jenny was now facing.

Perhaps because he'd spoken from the heart, Campbell's message had spread far and wide. Even those who couldn't comprehend it intellectually had somehow absorbed it emotionally. But at that moment, entwined together as we imbibed our goblets of wine, we didn't speak much about such things because, most of all, Jenny wanted nothing more than to *live*. And everything else, including merely speaking about life, remained secondary.

But there were still those dark circles under her tender green eyes, which lent her such a pensive, mournful appearance. For at heart, Jenny was a stifled coyote. It was as if she'd met every obligation – all the banal responsibilities that life demands – but there still remained this unslaked thirst for adventure on a road that would lead to one's joy.

As if unwittingly spinning a parable about her own entrapment, one evening she reminisced about another free-spirited coyote that she'd befriended in Cape Town.

Bessie was a young Black maid who was employed at Jenny's parent's house and who was, in essence, a servant. At that time, white Afrikaners such as Jenny's family still lorded it over the native Black Africans. But unlike everyone else in her immediate environment, Jenny detested the entire setup. She said that, once a month, the ruling families would meet at their respective homes to display their latest weaponry and ammunition. It was *insane*, she said, shaking her head in disgust while her voice shifted to a tone of palpable ennui. And the only one she really identified with, the only person she admired and even loved was this adolescent maid: a good-natured teenager who possessed an infectious laugh. Jenny added that although Bessie was as slender as a reed, she was also big bosomed, just like Jenny, and the boys were constantly chasing after her.

Shortly after Bessie had turned sixteen, one night she experienced her first sexual encounter, and Bessie told Jenny all about it: how her boyfriend had scaled the side of the building and snuck in, through her window. And how she'd lifted up her shirt and offered her breasts – "Like a pair of melons on a silver platter!" Bessie exclaimed – and how they didn't stop making love until the arrival of dawn. While she related this to Jenny, Bessie giggled and groaned and repeatedly hugged herself as she exclaimed, "Oh, Jenny, I *love* that thing; I just *love* that thing!"

And Jenny looked at me and burst out laughing, and suddenly the dreadful malaise that had engulfed her was eclipsed. Not completely vanquished, but checked and held at bay as her eyes sparkled and brightened. I can still picture her glancing away for a moment as she began to laugh, then turning round again and gazing at me fondly. All that love, just waiting. All I'd have to say was: *Yes, I love you, too, Jenny! I love you right back! Let's run away, then I can save you from this awful grind. Or maybe you can save me!*

But I really didn't know what love was, back then. And the last thing I wanted was to hurt or deceive someone as kindhearted as Jenny, whose affectionate gaze always cut right through my soul. It was so harrowing and haunting that, in mere seconds, I'd be dissolved in it. While staring back, I'd fall into those kaleidoscopic pupils once again.

Perhaps ours was a tale of a love found and a love lost, but also of an unrequited love screaming for recognition. We were living the myth of Guinevere and the Green Knight, but I'd stumbled upon my Guinevere far too prematurely.

And so, whenever I emerged from this entranced state, it became painfully obvious that all would not end well between us. For, without knowing my heart, how could I follow my bliss? Instead, first I would have to – in Campbell's own words – *follow my blisters.*

One day a brisk winter wind whistled through the November boughs and ushered in my twenty-second birthday. Being several years my senior, at that moment, under the waning sunlight, Jenny was nearing thirty. And now, she wanted to settle down: to find her "Prince Charming," as she put it, and to raise children. Jenny finally confessed that, more than anything, this is what she wanted most of all.

But as soon as she realized that I wasn't going to sweep her off her feet and hunker down and make babies, she resigned herself to relocating to San Francisco. A rather drab, boring, but reliable man whom she'd first met in Johannesburg – a pharmacist – had asked her to join him and raise a family.

The evening that she explained all this there were even bigger circles round her eyes, and she seemed to exude a more palpable sense of melancholy than usual, especially when I remained silent and didn't utter a word of protest. For I knew that I wasn't ready for such sobering responsibilities. And so, not long afterward, Jenny faded into the San Francisco fog.

* * *

In the decades ahead, while traveling back and forth between Paris and New York, occasionally I'd wander past Jenny's old digs on Downing Street. I'd approach the tall cement wall that encircled the courtyard behind her flat, and I'd gaze at the finger-like foliage of the ailanthus trees, with their leaves still casting those colorful shadows on the adjacent windowpanes. And I'd shake my head and wonder how we could ever have imagined that, at the mere age of thirty, Jenny was "growing old" – rather than ascending the spire of life's most rapturous summit! Only the stupidity of youth might conjure something so absurd!

Then I'd continue toward the Church of Our Lady of Pompeii, where I'd stop for a moment and call out:

Our Lady of Downing Street! I've come on a special pilgrimage, hoping to penetrate the enigma of the past! Unveil your mystery!

But the oracle always maintained a mocking silence.

Feasting with Panthers

Like a Hollywood drama from the Golden Era that depicts a hero leaving a "good girl" to instead fall into the clutches of an irredeemable femme fatale, one cold December evening while meandering through Soho I fell prey to a triple-jinxed voodoo. For I stumbled directly into the arms of a modern-day Hecate: that intoxicating wraith who, especially to sailors and shepherds, may appear as a beatific maiden but whose triune sorcery, steeped with honeybee venom, belladonna, and aconite only a seasoned Odysseus can survive.

Danny Brutta and I were lingering under the dimmed spotlights at the Spring Street Tavern, leaning upon a slick black bar deck while a woman in her early forties was lurking at the far end: a face in the crowd, glancing at us. After ordering drinks, when I looked up, her eyes locked into mine. Within moments I was hooked – as if gagging on a bobbing bait of bloody red mullet, stuck upon a tantalizing tackle.

Perhaps it was my own dangerous fascination with madness – a desire to flirt with delirium right up to the very brink – that brought her into my world. In any case, I momentarily tore myself away, scooped a bill from my pocket, and paid the tab. But when I glanced up again, there she was, standing right beside me in her black leather pants, with her hand gripping the silver handle of an ebony walking stick.

Her devious gaze seemed to burn with the viridian sap of a Venus flytrap – or rather, a Venus mantrap – yet I was foolish enough to offer her a drink.

Looking me up and down, she replied: "I'm wondering how I can invite you back to my place and still appear to be a lady."

At first, I protested that I was with a friend and gestured toward Danny.

"Just square it with him," she frowned, "then meet me outside."

This reference to a Masonic "square" should immediately have warned me away. Staring into her narrowing pupils, it occurred to me that Dinah resembled one of those opaque gemstones that – no matter from which angle you view it – reveals only your own reflection staring back at you. But despite such overt omens, I sheepishly followed her first command. That night, Danny drove back to Gravesend alone. Little did I realize that, by avoiding her temptations, he'd been dealt a far better deal. What a mistake to abandon, even for a moment, the heartfelt companionship of a true friend! As those timeless fables always warn us, taking even a single step off a beaten trail can result in unmitigated disaster. For one's path may swiftly become obscured amidst an entangling mass of brier, an engulfing maw of quicksand, or an intoxicating outcropping of Dinah's tawny pubic hair.

Dinah lived behind one of the cast-iron facades on Soho's Grand Street, at the southeast corner of West Broadway. Speaking of Freemasonry, as we approached her abode, I noticed that it was just a few doors away from the original location of a nineteenth-century printing press that had once published my great-grandfather's Masonic journals. But now, a hardware supplier rented the ground floor: a wholesaler of industrial *screws*. (Perhaps, a fitting metaphor for what was about to transpire.) Dinah said that her younger brother, Luther, resided on the second floor, just below her; while a top-floor loft remained empty. I later learned that her father owned the entire building. Its innocuous battleship-gray exterior served well to conceal its most flamboyant occupant.

As Danny approached the Holland Tunnel and continued to wonder what I was doing with a woman at least twice my age, Dinah and I boarded a dingy freight elevator. I could hear dogs howling in the distance. Handing me her walking stick, she yanked a greasy metal chain and we rose with a lunge into a dimly lit shaft. Holding the cane aloft, I noticed that the silver handle was shaped into a serpent's head.

The lift halted on the third floor, where we stepped into a 2,500-square-foot loft: a big open space with a row of wooden columns, painted silver, rising from a shellacked parquet floor.

Dinah, who now informed me that she preferred to be known as "Java," wasted no time in leading me toward a queen-sized bed that stood midway between the northern and southern end of this mostly empty rectangle. There I would hunker down for the next three months as she initiated me into that hermetic knowledge that young men crave despite the life-threatening obstacles that continually crop up along the way.

A treble-headed sorceress she most certainly was, for it was no easy task to escape the diabolical jinxes and demonic mischief spawned by that damned triplicity. Java-Hecate-Lagina was also proud to display an abundant collection of un-sheathed knives, castrating swords, and poisonous toxins culled from hemlock, mandrake, and opium poppy. Being one part bronze, one part steel, and one part onyx, she was three-parts deadly.

Since Java was a liminal divinity, each of her vaginae opened into a different trapdoor, camouflaged portal, exit or entrance wound, or secret escape hatch. And à la Picasso, each faced a different point on the compass. As a young man who was terribly lacking in practical sensibilities such as a sense of direction, I found this to be particularly challenging.

If you were lucky, along the way you might stumble upon a flaming torch or a rusty skeleton key; but you could just as easily collapse into a squirming nest of vipers. In one cleft there barked a rabid dog; in another there slithered a slimy serpent; while in the third a cow cowered mournfully in a corner, shifting restlessly upon oxidized bronze hooves. While attempting to gain a foothold upon this slippery riverine embankment, I realized that if I blinked at the wrong moment all would be lost.

To avoid her wrath, each night I prepared scraps of meat soaked in honey, which I discreetly dropped from my pockets at the corner of Broome Street and West Broadway, careful to never turn round or cast my gaze anywhere but straight ahead – smooth sailing. On high holy days I was required to travel to the Upper West Side to a swank specialty shop that served Park Avenue heiresses, where I would purchase the throat of a ewe. Afterward, I'd dig a shallow pit in a secluded spot in Central Park and dump it – still dripping with blood – but not before squirting a few drops of honey from a plastic container that was shaped into the figure of a waddling black bear.

A native of Lagina, Java had developed a fondness for being served by castrati and eunuchs: a final step that I refused to take, which led to endless arguments. Hecate grew even more furious upon learning that I admired the work of Henry Miller, especially his *Tropics*, which she condemned as being nothing other than filthy, depraved, antifeminist diatribes. I'd also made the mistake of mentioning that I particularly enjoyed Miller's use of the term *venereal*, or the way that he spoke of a woman's *libidinousness* or *lubriciousness*, as if quoting from turn-of-the-century Victorian pulp, which was notorious for protagonists that denounced licentiousness in such a manner that the reader – overwhelmed by such lecherous detail – can't help but to become aroused.

"If I ever met him," she growled, sputtering and seething, "I'd kick him in the balls! The characters in his books are such *sick* people! They weren't *real* people; they didn't *exist*."

"Of course they did. I could even show you their photographs."

"No, no ... he made them up out of his own *sick* head. And there's never any mention in there of the feminine principle, of female intuition, of women's wisdom."

"Sure there is. You just have to read between the lines."

"He's *sick!* And besides, I don't regard *starving* to be such a wonderful thing."

"Nobody does. But some people *do* starve, you know."

"No, he's got this great notion of starving! Norman Mailer's *Deer Park* is a much better story."

"*Deer Park?* Ha! Not even close. And not even Norman Mailer would agree with you."

"I know, you already told me."

"Listen, Dinah. Since you're as stubborn as a mule, we shouldn't even talk about it. You have your way of seeing things, and, with *Tropic of Cancer*, either you see it or you don't. And obviously, you don't."

"He's a pig! He's sexist! And it's *not* a book for *girls*."

"Actually, there are plenty of women who admire Henry's work."

"Well, then, they're *sick girls!*"

Attempting to regain her composure, for a moment Dinah paused, then concluded: "I'm a girl, and you're a boy, and that's it."

"Meaning *what*, exactly?"

"Everything comes down to being either a boy or a girl. It's the first thing, the primary thing."

"*That's* what always comes first, that you're a *girl?*"

"That's right."

"And what comes second?"

"That I'm a human being."

But I still maintained some serious doubts about that.

"Some people are so *sick*," she continued with a snicker, "that they're not *even* human beings. Like that *sick* Henry Miller. And *stop* saying that I don't see it."

"What it boils down to is that you just don't *like* it."

"You don't realize how *wrong* you are. I know it; you're wrong."

"Of course you know I'm wrong! Dinah's the only one who's always right!"

"That's right!"

"And that proves just how deluded you are, my dear."

If only Dinah could have severed Miller's nuts and fed them to a cat! Though she didn't own any pets, I imagined that there was an entire menagerie living in her entrails. But at least, in this way, I learned that any attempt at serious dialogue was doomed to failure. Dinah's high-handedness also extended beyond literary matters. Filthy lucre and abject power were the only things that really mattered: the very hobgoblins that I'd remained least interested in. She even claimed that, soon enough, she'd be wheeling and dealing in a lucrative scheme with a bank called Shanghai International ... just you wait and see!

Shanghaied, indeed.

If she felt that way about Miller, I wondered, what would Dinah have thought of "Walter," the anonymous author of a scandalous English chronicle titled *My Secret Life*. I was especially impressed by the opening lines of this gloriously obscene confession, which feature a witty portrait of Walter's own proud, stalwart member. What a marvelous idea, I thought: to commence with a first chapter devoted to one's "manhood"!

If Walter had ever wandered into Dinah's loft, "Off with his cock head!" would have been her first command. Yet Walter's opening is perhaps less provocative than Laurence Sterne's in *Tristram Shandy*, which begins with a father's ejaculation into a mother's womb and a description of the homunculus thus formed: that of the protagonist. Quite an innovative opening for an English novel of 1759! And what if Dinah's jaded eyes had fallen upon this passage from Pushkin's *Secret Journal*:

"Each time I get a hard-on, it means that my cock is turned to Heaven and to God. And whenever it is hard, I know that God is with me." Pushkin concludes with an unconventional eulogy to the female sex: "This pink, moist flesh … this hypnotizing sight of a vagina, is the face of God." Hadn't William Blake himself proclaimed: "The head Sublime, the heart Pathos, the genitals Beauty"?

In any case, as a result of all this, instead of an edifying exchange Dinah and I maintained an almost uninterrupted flow of silence. For the next three months, we carried on like a pair of muted songbirds.

Following our initial argument, instead of pursuing any logical discourse I bedded down upon her enveloping, downy mattress "Where, each year, Hecate's temple drew celebrated, festal assemblies." But contrary to tradition, and perhaps as a result of being such an innovator, instead of a night-walking "crone" Java emulated the behavior of an early-morning hellcat.

I'd usually stir from the love nest around noon, when the enchantress was nowhere to be seen. After checking to see if my testicles were still intact, I'd carefully study a collection of gilt-edged tomes, many of them rare first editions, that were displayed on a wall-length bookcase perpendicular to a set of enormous windows overlooking Grand Street. From there I could also gaze at another cast-iron facade across the way. The adjacent building was painted black, and it hosted a loft in which I never saw another living creature; though I wondered if the restless demons that always accompany Hecate had claimed it as their own, for I often felt as if I were being spied upon.

A dining room table featuring an inlaid mirror on top was the only other prominent piece of furniture between the windows and Java's bed, other than a clothing rack that held the goddess's veils, paradoxes, enigmas, and illusions – as well as her various *schmates*. At the far end of the loft a kitchen counter was attached to a brick wall, where Hecate cooked her bloody victuals and dished up platters of red mullet to celebrate my first month of entrapment.

Although Hecate rules over storms, equipped as she is to either cause or prevent them (thus explaining her connection to sailors and shepherds), Java was herself a living, breathing hurricane, and the tempests in her teapot were never held in abeyance. Instead, they were ever brewing, and only the savviest of mariners could avoid them.

In ancient Thrace, Hecate governed those "in-between" realms such as gates, passageways, and wild forests. Known to render aid to childbearing women, she also served a special role in the mentoring of green, young men. And just like Hecate, Dinah was adept at spinning illusions of bliss as well as visions of terror. (Hadn't Emily Dickinson written that "Bliss was most to blame"?) But as I later discovered, after being abused by an ex-con and surviving some sort of physical assault, her secret mission – instead of enabling men – was to destroy them.

At first, I remained unaware of such occult subterfuge. I naively assumed that this well-heeled princess was simply a former hipster now transformed into a pretentious socialite. But then, as I studied her heavily lidded eyes, I noticed that they often seemed to sparkle as if amused by some secret knowledge that only she possessed but would never reveal. Unlike the magic carpet ride that I traveled upon when I encountered Jenny's sweet, loving gaze – those dreamy orbs that constantly unveiled her tender soul the longer you lingered over them –

Java's eyes were frosty, impenetrable, and glazed with a superficial shine, just like her mirrored tabletop. Instead of embracing a warm, empathic, loving woman, I often found myself confronted by visions of radiant ghosts or mechanically winking voodoo dolls. Not to mention a bubbling vortex of treacherous seas, a clapping thunder of stormy skies, or an ominous silence reminiscent of vaulted mausoleums looming in an ivy-festooned necropolis. Hence, Java's skill in discharging clods of earth, soapy sprays of sea foam, or sparks of static electricity in lieu of crackling bolts of lightning.

* * *

No matter how much I probed, I could never uncover any significant details about Dinah's personal life. Perhaps there had never been one and, instead, she'd come into being whole, like a reptile hatched from a prehistoric egg. Wherever she disappeared to each day also remained a mystery. Even something as simple as that was enshrouded in intrigue. Dinah claimed that she was attending a secretarial school where she was learning dictation; but since she was incapable of listening to anything other than the echoes of her own commands, at once I discounted this.

In the early afternoon I'd wander through the picturesque streets of Soho, visiting art galleries or lingering at cafés along Prince Street. Seated beside a bistro table facing West Broadway, I'd observe the fashion models who wandered around in white togas – as if we really were in ancient Greece and Hecate ruled above and below us. But eventually I'd return to the burial ground, perhaps to scan one of the gilt-edged tomes that were lushly illustrated with engravings depicting scenes from the animal and vegetable kingdom. Besides the *Romance of Plant Life,* Java's eclectic collection featured titles such as *Sunshine and Starlight, History and Practice of Magic, The Book of Truth or the Voice of Osiris, Isis Unveiled,* and – as if highlighting the overarching theme of our amorous conjunction – *The Romance of Insect Life.*

By now I was certain that I'd stumbled into a lugubrious corner of Rider Haggard's *She* – tunneling ever deeper into dank, bat-manure encrusted caves, with only a kerosene lantern in hand. But with the distinct difference that, instead of *She who must be obeyed,* I was simply ignoring or brazenly vetoing most of Java's highfaluting, enervating commands. Instead of succumbing to She, I bided my time and tried to imagine what fresh hokum, what newly concocted *mishegoss* this rabbit-nosed Hecate might unveil before I finally flew the blood-splattered coop.

As Oscar Wilde had once remarked: "Like feasting with panthers, the danger was half the excitement."

Indeed, a most dangerous liaison.

* * *

Upon returning from her clandestine appointments, Dinah would roll a hefty joint of marijuana from her stash. Spiraling along the liminal caverns of her seductive haunches, and in keeping with my total immersion course, participating in this ritual marked one of the few times past the age of sixteen that I'd ever indulged in such toxins. After imbibing, I'd attempt to amuse Dinah by engaging in one of the various Tantric positions that I'd faithfully examined in the *Kama Sutra* and which I'd absorbed with a greater avidity than anything else that I'd studied at university. But whether we embarked upon the Three Steps of Vishnu, the Cranes with Joined Necks, or the Pawing Horse position, nothing seemed to affect her in the slightest. While I was huffing and puffing away, she could easily have been filing her nails, reading a glossy women's magazine such as *Cosmopolitan*, or speaking on the phone with one of her glamorous yet vacuous girlfriends. *Go, Blade, go*, she'd mutter – all the while surveying me with clinical detachment, like a genetic researcher observing a monkey in a cage. "Blade" was a *jeu de mots* that Dinah had coined based upon the fact that, in French, my surname means *knife*. Even if she phoned me at my parents' house in Brooklyn, where I'd briefly return to retrieve some belongings, if they answered the phone she'd ask for *Blade*. I had to warn them: "That's for me; don't hang up. And, please, don't even ask ..."

Following a romp on her bed, Dinah would amble over to the kitchen to concoct an elaborate repast. While she immersed herself in this gastronomic ritual, I'd select another forbidden text or reread certain passages from William Burroughs' *Naked Lunch*, a macabre chronicle that was remarkably consonant with Java's own depraved and twisted psyche. But whenever she grew bored with cooking, we'd wander over to nearby Chinatown.

One afternoon as we were walking along Mott Street, I saw that we were approaching the same location where I'd once witnessed a murder with Mudnick. Moments later, Java and I were seated at a table overlooking the exact spot where the Furies had exterminated that unlucky member of the Flying Dragons gang. Visions of that troubling day filtered through my mind as we sipped our sweet-and-sour soup and cracked open our fortune cookies: *When hoarfrost is underfoot, solid ice isn't far off.* And, *They should come together, free of ulterior motive; otherwise harm results.* And even more to the point: *The maiden is tainted; therefore, one should not marry such a maiden.*

All the while, as we downed our fried rice, we hardly spoke a word. Instead, everything was transmitted in an oracular, vegetative lingo: a shuddering of finely haired roots that would swell whenever Java was fully engorged. Her leaves would unfurl, then she'd burp demurely, as if she'd just swallowed a pair of testicles and was experiencing momentary indigestion. Or her nipples might imperceptibly dilate, indicating a drop in barometer or a forecast of rain.

Then we'd follow the bloody trail back to the boneyard, but only after wandering like tourists through that meandrous warren's den of Chinatown, whose passageways unfold like the coils of a firecracker that you inspect on a Gravesend pavement the day after the Fourth of July. Silently padding back to her loft, I recalled how, as children in Gravesend, we'd ardently search for the unexploded duds lying amidst the cellophane tatters that covered the street like colorful confetti. After assembling a few pristine explosives, you'd gut them of gunpowder and ignite the silvery lump. A panoply of iridescent hues would flare up, like a cavalier's torch in the Ming Dynasty, until it sputtered into ash, as spent as a childhood reverie crumbling to dust. And then you'd go searching for more.

* * *

The entire time that we lived together Dinah hosted only a single visitor: a slender Italian model named Serena Rota. A graceful woman with eyes that resonated with shades of the Black Death, Serena was dressed in the latest Eurotrash fashion. Her glittering silver bracelets lazily clinked and most appropriately clacked as she rigidly sat there, on a black-enamel folding chair, while Dinah and I reclined on the bed, facing her.

Patiently absorbing their babble, I realized that never in my life have I listened to such pointless drivel. Such an absurd conversation: on and on about nothing, and reminiscent of what Walt Whitman had once referred to as "brilliant flashes of shallowness." Rather than merely skimming across the surface of things, it skittered *above* the surface, hovering like a zany moon-beam. But it's impossible to reproduce here, for it contained nothing substantial enough to anchor it to memory. Yet it was phrased – or rather *intoned* – with such sophisticated pauses, such sonorous emphases, such italicized nuance! I recall only that it was mostly about the *furniture* that Serena had acquired for her *new chateau*. Then there followed a sprinkling of lighter-than-ether banter about the "chic" clothing she wore, and, *Oh, how it suits you to a T!* And how the Marquis de Sissiberry and the Countess du Fancipants were ever so charmingly pettifogging around …

After we were introduced, Serena never again deigned to gaze directly at me or to ask even the simplest of questions. Like all superficial surface skimmers she seemed to be lacking in curiosity. For, as we all know – and as some greatly fear – curiosity may lead beneath the surface of things and, *Oh, dear me, we don't want to go there!*

Perhaps Serena was put off by the irritating manner I had of actually looking, of really staring into someone's eyes – and right out the other end. Perhaps this explains why the Countess Serena de Wigglebottom was so fidgety that day. It was as if my unauthorized, uninhibited leer had burned a scorching tunnel that reached from her eye sockets, down into her dainty esophagus, and out the escape hatch of her perfumed buttocks. And so, her well-cushioned bottom was now aflame, smoking like a chimney in February; and, *Oh, wiggle-wiggle,* she just couldn't find the right spot to rest it upon! And before she could discover that sweet spot, suddenly, she bolted up and beat a retreat.

The only other sighting of sentient life from within the loft had occurred on New Year's Eve. Dinah was preparing to attend some swank affair, and she wanted to bring me along. But

I refused, since I had better things to do … such as read *The Time of the Assassins*: Henry Miller's reflection on the quixotic adventures of the boy poet, Arthur Rimbaud. (The phrase, "Behold, the time of the assassins," comes from Rimbaud's poem, "Morning of Drunkenness.")

Just before she departed in her black-sequined gown, and with her hair perfectly coiffed and her makeup professionally applied, Java rolled a fat joint of pot. But I declined to join her and, instead, lingered over my text.

Finally the buzzer rang and she kissed me good-bye. But moments later I heard the chains in the shaft clanking, and I spotted her hovering there in the elevator, along with her consorts. Once again, I could hear dogs barking: Cerberus, Anubis, and Keelut. Or perhaps it was the bees buzzing, searching for juicy scraps of honey soaked, sacrificial meat.

Instead of opening the elevator door, Java and her laminated guests dillydallied in the lift, gazing at me through a chicken-wired windowpane as if I were a creature in a zoo and they had nothing better to do on New Year's Eve than to gawk as I read about how Arthur Rimbaud had nearly walked himself to death across the African continent in pursuit of filthy lucre.

As I would later discover, the story of Rimbaud in Africa was a bit more complicated than that. As far as I know, it wasn't until the biographer Charles Nicholl published *Somebody Else* that we learned that Arthur had done quite well for himself in Abyssinia, in Aden, and in Harar. But like all good Frenchmen, he carefully hid the truth – along with the loot – from his family. As I will continue to reveal, dear reader, money is the real taboo in France! *Heaven forbid* you speak openly, candidly, or directly about such a forbidden topic! And so, while Arthur was stashing away his booty – hundreds of thousands of francs that were discreetly transferred to a Crédit Lyonnais bank account – his mother, Vitalie, and his sister, Isabelle, were kept in the dark regarding his worldly success. *Oh, dear mother*, he'd write in that typically flowery, indirect French manner, *how sad life is! How shall I ever make it here? But persist, and toil, I must*, and so on and so forth.

Little did his family realize that Arthur could easily have achieved recognition as a remarkable explorer – except for the fact that he refused to sign his name to the expedition reports that he composed for the French trading company that employed him in Africa. One such narrative, a travelogue of his voyage from Ethiopia's Mount Entotto to the walled city of Harar, was presented to the French Geographical Society in 1887 and later published in a prestigious journal. But at this juncture in his life, instead of immortalization, what Rimbaud really craved was anonymity: to vanish without a trace, and to turn "Arthur" into a ghost. The ultimate dream of a true expatriate: to incrementally and irrevocably disappear in a foreign land. Perhaps Rimbaud said it best in a letter written to a friend when he was only sixteen years old:

"I is somebody else."

Legions of biographers, especially the literary ones, would later scratch their heads and wonder why in God's name he would sacrifice such a promising career to instead settle in that forsaken backwater – an elephant-dung heap in the middle of nowhere. After rising so swiftly to a pinnacle of poetic genius, Rimbaud would eventually be recognized as one of the great masters of the lyrical form: not only in France, but throughout the world. Yet he stopped writing poetry by the time he was twenty.

As far as I was concerned, however, it all made perfect sense. For what could be more in keeping with an honored Gallic tradition than to jettison your adolescent dreams in order to stash away heaps of bright, shiny bullion? That's all they ever dreamed about in France: untaxed, unregistered profit! *Sécurité,* as they call it, which is simply a coded term for *argent, dough ray me, moola!*

The other unsurprising aspect of all this is that artists of all stripes will temporarily abandon their craft in order to *experience* something – a life-altering drama that they can later continue to mine, plucking from such *prima materia* the rubies, sapphires, and diamonds that comprise the invaluable elements of their craft. One thinks of how, forty-two years before Arthur's death, Dostoyevsky stood before a firing squad: an event that would provoke his deepest transformation and allow him to engender works such as *Crime and Punishment*. The same was true of America's greatest poet, who had dropped everything to nurse the sick, wounded, and dying during the bloody Civil War, placing his creative pursuits in an almost complete abeyance. The list goes on. Yet, when critics pause to study Rimbaud's life, they appear to be stupefied: *How could he? How dare he give up literature for life?* An absurd question, but there it is.

Of course, if he hadn't perished at such a tender age – only thirty-seven years old! – the question might never have been raised. Or at the very least, it would have been phrased in a less strident fashion. For, no doubt, Rimbaud would eventually have returned to his writer's desk, to his rude wooden table in Charleville or in some other outlandish locale, to compose an epic: transforming guns, coffee, gold nuggets – and whatever else he was smuggling – into an even more priceless commodity: *poetry*.

But when Miller composed *Time of the Assassins*, so many of the facts concerning the poet's life had yet to be uncovered. Since he wasn't privy to Rimbaud's actual biography, Miller instead focused on the story of his money belt, laden with gold bullion, which the poet refused to relinquish even when forced to walk for miles across the savanna, now deprived of his horses, which were supposedly stolen by duplicitous Arab traders. Weighed down by this unmanageable load, Arthur's knees gave out and he had to be shipped back to France, to seek medical attention and to have his right leg removed.

After undergoing an amputation, Rimbaud died in Marseille; that much is true. But he didn't walk himself to death; nor was he less canny than those Abyssinian horse traders. And the bulk of the bullion wasn't in his belt. Instead, it was accruing interest in a Crédit Lyonnais bank account. According to Nicholl, it may still be there, sequestered in some dusty vault; for Arthur was so secretive that not even his mother knew of his savings. And the illness moving up his gangrened leg wasn't from walking; more likely it was an inherited condition, probably bone cancer. His sister also had a tumor sprout from her knee, which spread throughout her body and killed her in 1917.

Never one to mince words, the poet had nicknamed his mother the "Mouth of Darkness." From her, Arthur had acquired his stubborn nature, his vituperative tongue, and his enduring tightfistedness. From his father, Frédéric, he inherited only his dreams.

The ultimate mystery of life is often projected upon that which can only barely be seen or grasped – such as the distant constellations that twinkle overhead and form the celestial zodiac. And so, not surprisingly, Rimbaud had created an idealized father out of a fugitive figure who, in reality, was an army captain who had deserted his family when his son was less than six years old. (Was the vagabond son trailing after his father's ghost? For Captain Rimbaud had also spent many years in Africa, as part of the infantry in the shameful conquest of Algeria, for which he received the Legion of Honor.)

Such was Arthur's innate talent, carefully honed skill, and abundant, overflowing imagination that, well before he'd ever seen an ocean – landlocked as he was in a tiny, gossip-ridden, embittered netherworld known as Charleville – before he'd ever witnessed the crash and foam of a salty wave, he composed *Le bateau ivre*, or the "Drunken Boat." It's a poem about a ship that's abandoned, just as Arthur was himself forsaken by Captain Rimbaud.

This twenty-eight-line vision portrays an empty vessel that wanders and wavers as aimlessly as a Parisian flâneur – a flâneur of the sea, one might call it – heaving, cresting, cutting across the brimming swells and reeking with a stale, sour scent of wine and vomit, which the crew have left behind. Just as Rimbaud himself would later attempt in Africa, the ship strips away all remnants of its past and washes itself clean until it's resurrected upon the rosy-fingered breakers at dawn.

And then, with a miraculous sleight of hand, the poet ingeniously transforms this craft into a paper sailboat, which Arthur – now on his hands and knees – pushes across a muddy puddle in the street.

Is the boy poet playing beside a cracked Parisian pavement? Or is it a sinkhole in Charleville that cradles this glittering microcosmic sea?

> If there's a European water
>   I crave,
> it's that cold black puddle
> where, in fragrant twilight,
> a squatting child
> full of sadness
> launches a boat
> as fragile
>   as a butterfly
>   in May.

Perhaps most mysterious of all, "The Drunken Boat" – now considered to be a modern classic – was composed when Arthur was only fifteen years old.

* * *

As I finished the final pages of *The Time of the Assassins*, I was struck by how the author focuses upon two principal themes: Rimbaud's ability to listen to a divine, inner voice and capture it upon the page; and the obstacles that a writer often confronts while attempting to earn his daily bread. Miller continually hones in on this duality, this counterpointing of the sacred and profane – or perhaps one should call it the *divine* and the *absurd*.

The stark contrast between a money belt and a seer's sacred vision also reminded me of Dinah herself: a creature who'd survived decades of her own nonconformist, Dionysian shenanigans to now consider the possibility of moving to Ohio to marry an accountant. It was the sort of fate that I could barely imagine for her, yet there it was. But perhaps I was being naive, for she never pretended to be a Romantic.

According to Dinah, everything was simply a "confluence of atoms." I can still hear her countering my soliloquy to the wonders of life by flatly stating: "No, Blade; you don't understand. It's all molecular."

And unfortunately, for Dinah, perhaps it was just that.

Monkey Business

A couple of years after Hecate returned to the Underworld I was back at the Spring Street bar, sipping a glass of Médoc when news of John Lennon's assassination filtered across the room. Customers were arriving and departing with various tidbits about what had occurred at Lennon's Dakota Hotel as Bruce, the bartender, kept me posted while simultaneously refreshing my glass, gratis.

A petite and nattily-dressed man in his late twenties, Bruce possessed the manner of a nineteenth-century gentleman. An aspiring novelist who suffered from writer's block, he loved to analyze the work of our favorite authors while attempting to unravel the secrets of inspiration and creativity. But that evening he introduced me to a blonde woman named Steph, who just happened to be seated beside me.

In her early thirties, with her sunken cheeks, pageboy haircut, and almond-shaped eyes she immediately reminded me of a Modigliani. Steph also possessed a self-confident bearing that lent her a certain charm.

At once the three of us fell into animated conversation as we reminisced about the hit singles of Lennon and McCartney, whose popular songs had punctuated the milestones of our adolescence. Pouring us another round, Bruce said that although he'd initially favored the Beatle's charismatic lead guitarist, George Harrison, he later switched his allegiance to Lennon, whom we both agreed was the most talented one.

"Everyone has a favorite Beatle," Steph laughed, adding that she'd always had a crush on Paul McCartney and his "big brown eyes."

"My first concert was George Harrison's benefit for the flood victims of Bangladesh," I said, adding that the show had featured the Beatles' drummer, Ringo Starr, as well as Bob Dylan and the Cream's former lead guitarist, Eric Clapton.

"So, you managed to see half the Beatles!" Scott exclaimed.

Steph raised an eyebrow: "But that was back in 1971! You must have been very young."

"It was three months before my fifteenth birthday. I was so skinny that I managed to sneak in a portable reel-to-reel audio deck, hidden under my dungaree jacket, so that we could record the show."

"A reel-to-reel?" Steph laughed good-naturedly. "You must have been a string bean!"

"Yes, but it was so bulky that I still had to suck in my stomach. That was before portable cassette decks even existed."

Bruce stepped away to pour someone a glass. When he returned, he said that crowds were now amassing along the sidewalk at the Dakota. I openly wondered if we should join them in this historic moment, which seemed to mark the end of an era. But Steph smiled and said that she had a better idea:

"Let's go back to my place, for a drink."

The prospect of spending a night with Steph certainly seemed to outshine any candlelit vigil glowing around the hotel.

We waved goodbye to Bruce, then lingered beside the shuttered art galleries of West Broadway, where we hailed a cab. I silently mused that John Lennon would have approved.

Steph's studio overlooked the corner of Seventh Avenue and West Twelfth Street and was just a block away from my favorite *café con leche* joint, which served a delicious Spanish omelet. The first time I ordered a coffee there, a fiery-eyed Puerto Rican woman who worked the counter asked: "Do you take sugar in that darlin', or are you sweet enough as it is?"

The décor in Steph's apartment was chic, elegant, and sophisticated. Posters mounted in expensive chrome frames adorned teal-blue walls, along with a few of her hard-edged acrylic paintings, mostly self-portraits. Everything was stylish and in good taste, but the atmosphere was a bit impersonal, like the waiting room of a hip Madison Avenue advertising agency.

I relaxed on a black leather couch as she opened a bottle of wine. Steph said that she hailed from Boise, Idaho, and had first arrived in Manhattan about a decade ago, disembarking from a Greyhound bus. She was a freelancer now, but she'd initially been employed as a copywriter and graphic designer for a leading ad agency.

It was a world that Steph was deeply immersed in, but one that remained completely foreign to me. The way that she spoke about magazine ads and TV commercials, you'd imagine that such things rivaled the splendors of the Renaissance. But despite the irreconcilable differences of our aesthetic taste, I couldn't help but to admire her devotion to her work. Steph was driven and in control of her life, at least on a professional level, which was something that I had yet to achieve.

She was also proud to have created an ad for women's leggings that was plastered across buses, trains, and billboards all around the country. In the ad, several pairs of stockinged legs are reclining horizontally, intertwined so as to resemble a colorful mountain range, with the women's knees forming the "peaks." As she discussed the genesis of her idea she pointed to an oaktag poster board, mounted on a wall above her worktable. The original mockup resembled a collage; for, in the days before so-called personal computers, designers did indeed "cut and paste" actual pieces of paper with rubber cement.

As often happens in such agencies, she said, her boss, the ever-ambitious Jane Trahey, took all the credit for the design, which was commissioned by the Danskin brand. And so, nobody knew that it was actually Steph's baby. Steph said that Jane was a legend in the advertising world who'd become an icon for the feminist movement, being one of the first women to achieve such celebrated corporate success. Winner of the Advertising Woman of the Year award in 1969, Jane ran major campaigns for clients such as Bill Blass, Elizabeth Arden, and Olivetti. She also published a book illustrated by Edward Gorey: *Son of the Martini Cookbook*. Steph said that the playful idea behind this work is that, as the reader follows Jane's recipes and becomes increasingly drunk, the font size of the text grows larger, to match the reader's state of growing inebriation.

"Jane was my mentor. I learned everything there was to learn about corporate etiquette, advertising, and design from her. So, in the end," Steph sighed with a lingering tone of exasperation, "I had to look upon it as a sort of trade off." But it was plain to see that it was still driving her batty to lose such a sterling credit.

*　*　*

It was clear from the start that we were merely having an affair – as I was neither a highly paid executive nor a corporate lawyer – so in the days ahead Steph openly wondered why her professional life was so well ordered and fulfilling, yet she could never find an ideal partner or "soul mate." Since she seemed to approach relationships with the same sort of emotional detachment that she extended to any other business proposal, I wasn't at all surprised that she'd grown a bit isolated. With her busy schedule, and with such a demanding set of professional priorities that guaranteed to eclipse anything more personal, Steph always came up empty-handed.

Whenever I dropped by on weekends, we'd begin the

evening seated on her cozy couch, preparing to watch a video of the latest *divertissement* spewed from Hollywood. Although artistic titans such as Fellini and Truffaut were still releasing their final masterworks, the era of great auteurs was coming to a close. The "industry" – so fitting a term for a "glamour" factory – was increasingly cranking out ridiculous fairy-tales labeled as "adventure films," which were guaranteed to satiate the masses.

Instead of popcorn and soda, we'd sip Bordeaux from crystal glasses and nibble on Graham crackers smeared with Camembert, with everything neatly laid out on a silver serving tray. After the film, Steph would lead me into her capacious bedroom. Following some relaxed chitter-chatter, we'd gradually twine into various positions such as the Monkey's Attack or Splitting the Cicada, often ending with Steph's favorite: the Mounting Tortoise.

Despite the limitations that were inherent in our odd coupling, these strangely detached yet erotic interludes always offered me a sense of respite. Even today, they stand out in my mind as a sort of exotic archipelago: a string of islands providing temporary relief from whatever chaos was reigning outside, whether it be the assassination of a Beatle or the uncertainty caused by losing one's path along the dispiriting labyrinth of *Mannahatta*.

Though Steph always maintained a detached persona, she was also possessed by a spirit of generosity and did everything in her power to make our moments together pleasurable. Down to the finest detail, she always took care to arrange things properly. It was as if we were two elements in a three-dimensional poster board, anchored to a carefully constructed *maquette*. During this prolonged period of flânerie and folly, no matter what challenges I was facing, I knew that I could always phone on the spur of the moment and return to the shelter of Steph's "waiting room" … while we each attempted to anticipate the course that the fates had lying in store for us. It was an easygoing, informal, and drama-free affair that lasted on and off for a number of years, interrupted only by those more "serious" relationships that either of us engaged in. Even decades later, when she finally left New York and married a real estate developer in Maine, we still remained good friends.

In between such monkey business I continued to bounce around from one idiotic job to the next. This was the real "lost boy" period of my life, the kind of thing they refer to as the *lost years* in an artist's biography.

In one last halfhearted attempt to avoid the teaching profession and to live *la vie de bohème*, I even applied for a job at a movie theater. One of the more celebrated teachers in the NYU drama department – Jack Garfein, who founded Actors Studio West, in Hollywood – told Drew that Cinema Five was accepting résumés. And since Drew wasn't interested, he passed it along to me.

Little did I know that the owner of this well-respected "art house" was an eccentric but visionary businessman named Donald Rugoff, whose principal backer was Mrs. David Rockefeller. Rugoff had established a chain of about a dozen theaters that were regarded as the most prestigious art-film venues in Manhattan. There, he introduced American audiences to directors such as Costa-Gavras, Werner Herzog, and Nicolas Roeg. Not surprisingly, his clientele included the cognoscenti of cinema buffs.

My initial interview took place in a cramped Madison Avenue office with Rugoff's assistant, Marv Dillard. A gregarious easygoing chap, for some reason Marv took a liking to me. Perhaps it was because, the day before, I'd carefully brushed up on my Dale Carnegie routine. Following Dale's advice as laid out in his classic tome, *How To Make Friends and Influence People*, throughout the interview I maintained steady eye contact, feigned intense interest, smiled a lot, and encouraged Marv to talk about himself by posing a few innocuous questions.

By the time we were finished, he was beaming: "Not only do I like you very much, but I think you'd be *perfect* for a certain key position. It's just *made* for you! Of course, *every* job in the theater is important. But when pedestrians approach the marquee, there are two things that make an immediate impression." Leaning across a creaking desk and pausing for dramatic effect, he asked: "Do you know what they are?" Pursing his meaty lips, Marv raised a bushy eyebrow and peered at me with an expression that alternated between childlike glee and benign, patrician sobriety.

"I'm sorry, Mr. Dillard, I have no idea."

Clasping his hands beneath his chin, Marv patiently continued: "One thing is the *environment*. But the other is *who* they see working there. The woman selling tickets in a booth and … the *doorman*." With his face stretching into a fanatical grin, he concluded, "And *that's* what I have in mind for you!"

Pretending that I'd just been handed the crown jewels, I feigned delight and returned his winning smile.

"Now, I'd like you to meet Mr. Rugoff, the president of the company. He'll conduct a final interview and have the last word. A nice man at heart … but a rather *serious* one." Handing me a scrap of paper, he added: "This is the address. You can walk there; it's just a few blocks away." Marv said that he'd meet me at Rugoff's office to sing my praise and to personally introduce me to the grand poobah himself.

A petite blonde receptionist said that Rugoff was expected shortly. Meanwhile, several other applicants trickled in and sat in the folding chairs behind me. Moments later a barrel-chested man waddled into the office. Resembling a bespectacled bear, he possessed even larger and more rubbery lips than Dillard.

Stooping over the diminutive receptionist, he inspected a dozen pink memos that were lined up along the edge of her desk. Carefully surveying the room's inhabitants, he glared at each of us with a fierce grimace. Speaking with a heavy German accent, he asked:

"Who was here first?"

Pointing at me, the receptionist replied, "He was."

"*Vollow* me!"

I goose-stepped behind Rugoff into a brightly lit room that hosted a panoramic view of sparkling skyscrapers. Gesturing for me to sit in front of his oversized desk, he glanced at some paperwork but then abruptly stood up and ambled outside.

Gazing round, I noticed a deluxe edition of Michelangelo's artwork lying on a chic glass-and-chrome tabletop nearby. Predictably, the cover featured a close-up of "The Creation." I was tempted to thumb through it, to relieve my boredom, but I managed to restrain myself. As I stared at the hand of God reaching across the heavens and animating the limp form of Adam, I wondered if it was there simply for display or because Rugoff possessed an authentic appreciation for the arts.

But poor Adam! Soon, he'd be kicked out of the garden – cosmic exile! – and forced to earn his daily bread. The alienation of the soul! Now, such ruminations only served to darken my mood. As the minutes ticked by, an undertow of apathy gradually enveloped me, and my mind drifted like an unmoored canoe. By the time Rugoff returned, I was unable to offer any resistance to this lassitude.

But Rugoff appeared to be more energized than ever. Glancing up and peering at me through his large oval glasses, he leveled his gaze as if sighting prey in a crosshair.

"Mr. Couteau," he began, pronouncing my name with a

perfect French intonation, "tell me *all about yourself!*"

With a wavering tone, I mumbled something about my schooling. Rambling on monotonously, I almost made myself yawn. Perhaps, I thought, he might find a place for me in a sequel to *Night of the Living Dead*. I also wondered where Marv had disappeared to, since I'd counted on his boyish enthusiasm to serve as a buffer to my own mounting indifference.

I continued to mumble as Rugoff glanced at my résumé and studied my checkered work history.

"And what exactly are you doing with yourself right now?"

Before I could answer, Dillard popped his head into the office, slipped into a chair beside me, and handed Rugoff my application.

Marv's persona had undergone a radical transformation. Now, he seemed to be shrinking in his chair, overwhelmed by the presence of this overbearing boss.

"I'm unemployed, Mr. Rugoff."

"When was the last time you were working?'

"About two weeks ago. As a market researcher, for a telephone-interviewing firm."

"For how long?"

"Oh, about a week and a half. Then I quit."

"What was your last job before *that?*"

"I was a cameraman, for an independent TV program."

"But on your résumé," he grunted, "it says that was in July. What were you doing from July through September?"

"I drove across the country," I replied, barely suppressing a yawn, "to visit California."

Staring at me with a look of unvarnished contempt, he leaned across his desk and demanded: "Tell me, Mr. Couteau. What exactly do you want to *do* with yourself?"

"You mean, in connection with Cinema Five?"

"No! With your *life!*"

Absorbing this magnificent explosion, my mood shifted and my malaise evaporated. With an unexpected rush of clarity and purpose, I calmly replied, "Actually, Mr. Rugoff, I'm a *poet*."

As soon as the words were out of my mouth, Rugoff's eyes lit up. He fell back in his chair, and his tone shifted to a sweet, honey-coated resonance:

"*Well!* I have *never!* Had the *pleasure!* Of interviewing a *poet* before! How do you do?" So saying, he stood up, stuck out his big hand, and offered me a hearty handshake.

Turning to his obsequious assistant, he continued: "Mr. Dillard, we have the perfect position for this young man. No, I don't think a *doorman* is the right thing at all. Instead, we'll give him a job as an *usher*. Then he can stand in the darkness, study the moving images, and get some ideas for his poetry!"

Emerging from behind his desk, Rugoff placed his arm around my shoulder and offered me another firm handshake. "Good *luck* now, Mr. Couteau," he added with a wink. Then he nodded to Dillard, who jumped like a marionette and whisked me away, into another one of his cramped, windowless offices down the hall.

Once we were alone again, I found it difficult to suppress my laughter. Summoning my best Stan Laurel imitation, I feigned disbelief and asked, "Did he really mean all that, Mr. Dillard?"

"Mr. Rugoff never says anything he doesn't mean, even if it's 'You're *fired!*'" Amused by his own cornball humor, Marv's face was animated with a goofy grin, so I dryly laughed along with him.

"Now you're to report to the Plaza," he continued, assuming a more serious demeanor. "It's just around the corner, on East 58 Street. Ask for a Mrs. Thomas. She's in charge there. I'll give her a call right away."

Upon exiting his office I lingered in the hallway, hoping to eavesdrop. Once Dillard had Thomas on the line, he launched into the tale of my "poetic" encounter, all the while chuckling with amusement.

It was hard not to like a guy such as Marv, who seemed to relish his ringside seat at Cinema Five. What stellar performances he must have witnessed!

I was about twenty feet short of the Plaza when I felt something give out from under me. Glancing down, I noticed that the sole of my boot had become undone. Flapping like a long leathery tongue – *shades of Charlie Chaplin!* – it was making such a racket that pedestrians on Madison Avenue were pausing to stop and stare. I wondered what the world's most famous "Tramp" would do in a situation like this.

Spotting a stationery store, I purchased a tube of glue, squeezed a glob of it under the sole, and jumped up and down, hoping it would stick. As it began to adhere, the booming *slap* was modified to a less audible *squeak*. Hobbling along, I appeared to be incapacitated – probably the last thing a theater manager wanted to see in a prospective usher. But thanks to the Plaza's plush carpet, the sound was muffled as I padded into a lobby and approached an usher.

"I'm here to see Mrs. Thomas."

"You must be our new man. She's too busy to meet you right now, but I'll help you to get fitted."

We descended into a grimy basement corridor lined with rusty lockers. Wanting to escape as quickly as possible, when he held out a livery I said that it looked fine.

"I'd better go; I have another appointment. But please give Mrs. Thomas my regards."

"Sure, buddy. But you'd better call her first thing in the morning before reporting to work. She still wants to speak with you."

* * *

"Despite what Mr. Rugoff says about writing *poetry*, I don't want you rambling around with your head in the clouds!" Mrs. Thomas' voice had reached such a shrill pitch that scenes from Hitchcock's *Psycho* were flashing through my mind. Perhaps I'd mistakenly dialed the Bates Motel.

"You've got to *pay attention* to what's going on around you!"

"Don't worry, Mrs. Thomas. I've got my feet planted firmly on the ground."

As soon as I hung up, I realized that I never wanted to subject my eardrums to such discord again, so I didn't even bother to show up. With my employment in the cinema having come to an abrupt end, I dozed off while contemplating my next big "career move."

Shortly after my encounter with Rugoff, due to a shareholder's battle in the stock market, control over Cinema Five had slipped through his fingers. When I read an account of the debacle in the *Village Voice*, I discovered who Rugoff really was and what a priceless contribution he'd made to the cinematic art.

According to several articles in the press, in the 1950s his theaters were the first to offer double features and to forbid patrons to enter toward the end of a film. Instead of soda and popcorn, in some of his establishments he served only coffee. Taking a personal interest in the design of each showcase, he oversaw everything from the color of the walls to the pattern of the bathroom tiles.

Unlike many other theater owners, Rugoff never cut a movie without a director's approval. In the various venues that he nurtured as if they were his children – including the Art,

Beekman, Gramercy, Murray Hill, Paramount, Paris, Plaza, and Sutton – films were shown on an exclusive basis. This attracted Manhattan's most impassioned and sophisticated movie-goers, who keenly anticipated such unique events. His theaters were regarded as the most "prestigious" in the world not because of glitz and glamour but because of Rugoff's impeccable taste in art. I finally realized that his Michelangelo tome wasn't a mere prop. Instead, it reflected what this great man had always carried in his heart.

I also learned that Rugoff's Gramercy Theatre had specialized in foreign and independent films. There he introduced audiences to directors such as Costa-Gavras, Werner Herzog, and Nicolas Roeg. He also featured work by American filmmakers that had fallen into obscurity. In the early 1970s he screened ten films by Mary Pickford that hadn't been seen since the 1930s.

In 1977 director Stanley Kubrick made plans to premiere *A Clockwork Orange* at Cinema One. Following a brief visit to the theater, Kubrick decided that the white cement wall upon which the film was projected produced too much glare, so he stipulated that Rugoff have the area surrounding the movie rectangle painted a dull, matte black. Well aware of Rugoff's quirky, quixotic temperament, Kubrick insisted that Warner Brothers secretly send an executive to the theater to make certain that the repainting proceeded according to spec. Either as a result of a misunderstanding or because of Rugoff's everlasting mischievousness, when Kubrick's man showed up unannounced he discovered that the wall was being painted an eerie tint of *orange*.

But perhaps it was just as well that I'd quit. Rugoff was said to be so hard on employees that they either resigned in frustration or were unexpectedly fired. According to one article, if Rugoff happened to enter a theater just moments after a light blew the manager would immediately get the ax. And he hired two assistants to do the job of one, because, more often than not, one would be canned before the week was over and, with two, he'd at least preserve a modicum of continuity. Rugoff himself confessed: "I have one fault. I train good people, then I want to do their jobs." Having come from a privileged background, he was probably accustomed to bossing the servants around ever since he was a child.

But according to another journalist, as gruff and cantankerous as he could be, what Rugoff secretly admired was someone with the courage to be just as difficult and brash right back at him. What may also have worked in my favor was the deep respect that Rugoff harbored for artists and craftsmen, whom he never pestered or badgered as he did the "hired help." Perhaps the best illustration of this was when he employed Noelle Gillmor to create a more accurate version of subtitles for Costa-Gavras' film, Z. Paying Gillmor $100,000 and leaving her to work undisturbed for six months, the result was the finest – and most expensive – example of subtitling in the history of cinema. When it came to preserving the artistic purity of the word, for Rugoff money was no object. Which might explain why, by the end of his life, he had very little of it left.

After absorbing all this I called Drew, who filled me in on the one missing piece of the puzzle: "Jack Garfein told me that when Rugoff was a student at Harvard, he majored in English because his first dream was to become an author. Garfein said that the one class of men that Rugoff truly respects is that of the creators – the artists and writers. They're the only ones that he doesn't try to walk all over. So when you told him you were a poet, he must have admired your courage. Or your audacity. I'll bet no one else had the balls to talk back to him like that!"

Despite his elite upbringing, Rugoff knew that artists transcend the boundaries and limits of class, and for that I couldn't help but to admire him.

* * *

Late one night after exiting a bar in Tribeca and ambling along the woebegone waterfront, I heard a scream:

"Please! Just don't cut me!"

I peered ahead into the darkness. A hundred yards away, a yellow cab was parked at the center of the road. Tiptoeing a bit closer, I noticed a faint billow of exhaust fumes. The headlights were off, but suddenly the brake lights flared with a fitful pulse.

Gradually I made out a pair of silhouettes. A man in the back seat was holding an enormous cutlass against the driver's Adam's apple. When he tilted the blade, it caught the moonlight. The cab hadn't yet been fitted with one of the new plastic partitions that separate the front from the back, so the passenger had simply leaned forward and held this monstrous knife against the poor man's throat. The driver was scared out of his wits, and his voice was trilling: *"Take the money! But please! Don't cut me!"*

I retreated to a pay phone and dialed 911. Moments later three cop cars bolted in from the north, south, and east, pinning the cab against the waterfront.

Emerging from the shadows, I briefly spoke with the cabbie and asked if he was all right. A stocky, balding, middle-aged man, from head to foot he was trembling uncontrollably. He just barely managed to remain standing on his wobbly legs. His throat was nicked with a fine, hairline cut, but the knife had severed only the outermost layer of skin – just a tad deeper than a paper cut.

Clearly, it wasn't the wound that had unnerved him but rather the certainty that he was about to be sliced in two. God only knows what that screwball – who was now handcuffed and tossed into a squad car – had threatened him with or what was spewing from his lips, but this driver was in luck. Now, he could continue to bust his hump and earn his daily bread.

Once I saw that he was all right, I slipped back into the shadows. Bless those courageous cabbies, I thought, for without them *Mannahatta* wouldn't be the same. And hadn't Walt Whitman himself loved to ride beside the stagecoach drivers of yesteryear?

But as I headed back to Brooklyn, I realized that such flâneur-inspired peregrinations wouldn't pay the rent or set me along my path – wherever the hell I was traveling. So now, I decided to bite the bullet and apply for a job as a substitute teacher. Though I wanted to be locked inside those dreary classrooms even less than the children did, at least I wouldn't have to deal with a knife pressed firmly against my throat.

How I dreaded those mornings when the phone would ring at eight a.m. and I'd be ripped from the bliss of a rapturous dream. In one moment I'd be scaling the walls of the Himalayas, visiting Buddhist lamas in Tibet; in the next, my mother would be screaming at the foot of the stairs: *Robbie! Wake up! P.S. 95's on the phone!*

Groggy, disoriented, wiping the sandman's crumbs from my eyes, I'd next be subjected to the monotonous drone of a secretary with an overblown Canarsie accent who was informing me that Mrs. Aiello was sick with the flu, and could I teach her third-grade class for the next three weeks?

Downing half a pot of coffee, I'd stumble into a cacophonous school yard, searching for my class amidst the roaring thunder of that lion's den where the children were encouraged to run themselves ragged – screeching and hollering during that first forty-five minutes of utter delirium.

Those were the days when certain classrooms were packed

with over thirty-five kids, stuffed like sardines into a greasy can. And now that their regular teacher was out of commission, perhaps suffering from laryngitis after so many weeks of yelling and screaming, they were in no mood to be absorbing such tedious information. For, as everyone knows – and no one knows better than a horde of savages from Gravesend – a substitute teacher is not to be taken seriously.

* * *

One morning as I was surveying my latest bunch of insurrectionists in the yard, I devised a plan. When it was our turn to enter the building, I led the class into a ground-floor stairwell, but I waited there until the students in front of us had completely cleared the staircase. From the yard it appeared as if a momentary jam had occurred, and no one was the wiser. But once the stairs were empty again, I ran at top speed up four steep flights.

The kiddies exploded with merriment, perhaps thinking that their teacher had gone mad, and they raced after me – their centipede legs whirling along as they hollered with delight. But by the time they straggled up to the fourth floor they were exhausted, with their pasty tongues hanging from their dried little mouths. Stumbling along, they were nearly out of breath as they waggled, wavered, and wobbled along the hallway.

Next, I buttonholed one the brownnosers and plied her with questions about how far they'd progressed in their various text-books. For I knew that if I asked any of the incorrigibles what page they were up to in math, English, or geography, they'd point to a lesson that had already been completed weeks ago, ingenious little demons that they were.

During this brief intermezzo while they were catching their breath, if I could collect the pertinent information then I'd maintain control for the rest of the day. But if you failed to grip the reins during this crucial moment, you were doomed. A few minutes later, as if awakening from a revivifying slumber, they'd crackle, hiss, and steam like locomotives; and then I'd say, "All right, boys and girls. Here is the deal:

"If you follow my instructions and complete your various and sundry assignments – and if I do *not* have to yell, scream, and carry on like a banshee from hell – then you will be granted *an entire afternoon off.* Yes, and we'll do something fun and frolicsome and easy, such as drawing pictures or playing guessing games. But if you don't follow my instructions – then, *oh, boy* – you will be saddled with *mathematics all afternoon!* And such a drudging, tiresome application of subtraction, multiplication, and division! And maybe even *I shall be a good little dybbuk* written one thousand times ... or some other pointless exercise designed not only to make you crazy but to make you feel as if you've been abducted by a time machine and are now serving on a Roman galley, rowing endlessly across a bright blue Mediterranean with your aching wrists feeling as if they'll drop off at any moment. Yes, 'I shall be a faithful, quiet, well-behaved little golem for the rest of my days' – *one thousand times!*"

Within seconds the class would be split between those who just couldn't help being obnoxious little pricks, despite such lures and incentives, and those who were terrified by the prospect of descending into a disciplinary hell, surrounded by a crazy dance of meaningless integers, and deprived of a rainbow of Crayola crayon ecstasy and the joy of doing nothing taxing for the remainder of the day. And so, the kiddies who dreamed of reaping a reward would attempt to gang up on the malefactors who just couldn't help but rock the boat. Divide and conquer! Thanks to this devious strategy, we'd usually manage to quash a rebellion, maintain our course, and cruise into the final hours of a carefree afternoon.

Back then I was still absorbing the Beat classics published by City Lights and Grove Press, so if I was in a particularly good mood I'd share a few excerpts from this subversive literature ... perhaps reading a passage from Allen Ginsberg's "Sunflower Sutra," that tender homage to a dried-out stalk that rises from a junk heap on Fisherman's Wharf as Kerouac – ever identifying with the tragic horror of the torn and tattered World Soul – proclaims: "Look! A sunflower!"

Thus, I'd attempt to nurture these cultural orphans who were themselves so beat and beaten, not to mention beatific, and encourage them to consider for a moment the dusty gray bloom and its lonesome plight. On another day, to a group of fourth graders, I recited a few lines from Tristan Tzara's Dadaist ravings: "Art is an amoeba! Art is a spook! Art is a tomato!" They couldn't understand a word of it, but it sent lightning bolts up their wriggling spines as they howled with laughter – for their spirit caught the gist of it.

I soon discovered that the administrators of P.S. 95 would contact me only when the other substitute teachers lacked the temerity to enter one of these especially difficult classrooms. They'd never hire me for the more easygoing kids, for the well-behaved pushovers. Instead, I'd only be summoned when no one else dared to tread beyond Dante's fifty-ninth circle of prepubescent hell. And upon learning this, I was convinced that it was my big bushy beard that had marked me as a pariah: one unsuited for a more civilized classroom.

I'd stumbled onto this information accidentally, while speaking to a secretary in the office. One day, she'd let it slip: *Oh, you're the one who never says no when we call!* Thus, she'd unwittingly revealed this villainous plot: to place me in charge of those distressing varmints in need of constant supervision.

They'd even separated the worst laggards and troublemakers of each grade, herding them into these clusters of thirty-five or forty kids. And with my dreadful Whitmanesque whiskers – which I wore in a secret homage to the poet – they regarded me as an antisocial boogieman who might at least serve to scare the bejesus out of such louts, scamps, guttersnipes, and misfits. All this occurred in the years before the beard had returned as an acceptable accoutrement for socially adapted men, so they continued to treat me as an uncouth interloper. But at least the stockbrokers of the Eighties who would soon don such bristle kept it well trimmed. Mine was a bit too unkempt and free-wheeling for such stiffs.

One morning the beard had even made a young girl weep the moment she'd laid eyes upon me in the yard. She was a new student; and when her Russian mother brought her hand in hand to the line, this adorable little goldilocks shyly gazed up at me and shrieked – with a flood of tears cascading along her rosy cheeks.

Her mother tried to reassure her that I wasn't a Billy Goat Gruff, but it was only by the most delicate of maneuvers that we managed to comfort her. I even insisted that the mother briefly join us in the room, to help calm her daughter, while my outlaws hung up their coats and I culled the latest lesson-plan information, hoping to remain at least one step ahead of this dunderheaded bunch of scalawags.

I finally decided to I shave off the beard as an experiment, just to see what would happen. Sure enough, suddenly the administrators hardly seemed to recognize me. Instead of treating me as an outcast, at once the calls increased. Soon I was graced with polite invitations to teach the most well-behaved bevies of mollycoddled darlings. Not to mention the cutest bunnies, the first graders, who were usually too timid to talk back, as well as the more brainiacal second- and third grade classes: sweet little automatons who wouldn't dream of misbehaving. Not only was I inundated with calls; I was even offered a full-time position by the principals of two different schools: offers that I promptly rejected. For the notion of settling into such a "normal" routine horrified me.

Instead, I grew back my stubble and then, of course, the calls dropped away. Once again, I was happily condemned to the dungeon of those endearing demons who proudly proclaimed their latest acts of mutiny and insurrection as I tugged at the reins and forced order down their throats. But oddly enough, they seemed to like me. And the bizarre mixture of extreme discipline followed by extreme disorder fascinated them more than a ride on the bumper cars at Coney Island.

Though I maintained an iron fist, they knew that, beard or no beard, somehow I was different. As soon as I'd arrive – zigzagging through the yard and searching for my class – the kids would shout, *Look! It's Mr. C!* Jumping up and down, they'd holler and scream: *Mr. C, Mr. C, which class do you have?* hoping it would be theirs. But then they'd moan "Oh, *no!*" when I sailed past and, instead, stopped before some other slowly forming double line.

And now, those kids would yell: *It's Mr. C! We have Mr. C!* They'd grow crazier by the second, but I never bothered to contain them, even when some other teacher would stalk over and try to stifle their outbursts. Instead, I'd smile – ever so slightly – as if signaling my subtle approval.

* * *

The salary for such a thankless task was a mere thirty-five dollars a day. And I waited for my first paycheck for so many weeks – and then months – that, one morning, utterly infuriated, I phoned the Board of Ed to complain. Such a plodding, anachronistic, woolly mammoth of an institution! Such a fossil-encrusted labyrinth! Even the byzantine corridors of Southern Italian bureaucracy would put you to shame!

But no matter how much I ranted and raved, at first I wasn't getting anywhere with the various drowsy, indifferent, be-numbed functionaries ... until I claimed that I was a freelance writer who occasionally authored diatribes for the *Village Voice* (a complete falsehood); and if I didn't get that goddamned check within the next ten days I'd publish a full-length polemic denouncing their archaic, obsolete administration. What an abysmal lack of regard for such exploited laborers, such assembly-line pieceworkers known as substitute teachers! Imagine, I said, paying us such a pittance for the torture we endure! I went on and on, but now, suddenly, they appeared to be listening, and I was quickly transferred from one Beelzebub to the next. But instead of being shunted sideways, now I was ascending a ladder of authority. And with each respective func-tionary my story grew even more elaborate, as if were erecting my own byzantine monument.

And then, miracle of miracles, the following week I had my first paycheck in hand. Eventually they raised our salary to fifty bucks *per diem*, though it still wasn't enough to properly compensate the hired hands who actually wanted to labor for such a crusty, mind-molding institution. For what else is a teacher, especially an elementary school teacher, but a mind crusher, a maker of zombies, and an assassin of the soul?

As I shuttled in and out of such forlorn, desperate hollows in the remote hinterlands of Gravesend, I tried to imagine what would happen if those pedagogical victims known as students could somehow read my mind as I lingered at the windowsill and gazed down at the handball and basketball courts, past the wavering treetops – and all the way to the horizon. How I yearned for those exotic lands of adventure that must lie out there somewhere! Hovering beside those dusty windowpanes, I'd wonder what it was like to live in Lisbon, Rome, or Paris. I mean, to really *live*, and to wander for hours through dimly lit streets, minus any rhyme or reason, accompanied only by the song of the open road.

* * *

To escape the tedium of Gravesend, I'd often take the train into Manhattan after work. Usually I'd roam around the Village, but one night I found myself padding under the flashing billboards of Times Square. It was well after midnight, when Broadway assumes its most dazzling aspect: windswept, drained of burgeoning crowds, festooned with a necklace of traffic lights flashing mint green or blood red all the way to the horizon, and with the skyscrapers ever looming … and mocking anything as insignificant as a human being.

After wandering for a few hours, I entered a subway just as an express train roared to a halt at the platform. Selecting a seat in the middle of the car, I retrieved my copy of Jung's *Structure and Dynamics of the Psyche* and buried my head in the thick tome. I was concentrating on a passage about narcoleptic utterances, periodic amnesia, and pathological dreaming when I suddenly noticed, seated directly across from me, an attractive woman with shiny black hair and large ebony eyes. She was scanning a ream of paperwork and occasionally thumbing through a copy of *Cosmopolitan*. Impeccably dressed, I wondered if she was a corporate executive heading home after a long day at work.

At the next stop, a teenage girl wearing garish red lipstick and bearing an insolent smirk boarded the train and pranced into the aisle between us. Her head was completely shaved. On the crown of her scalp was perched an albino rat with a leather collar, attached to a chain that was linked to the girl's necklace.

The woman looked up from her magazine and, noticing the girl, appeared to be startled. As our eyes met I raised an eyebrow and made a comic expression, and she broke out laughing. Then she shuffled her papers and returned to her magazine.

I continued to sneak peeks at her as the train rumbled along. Occasionally she'd dart a glance my way, but only when the train was approaching a station, as if she was wondering if I might disembark.

We continued in this manner until 59th Street in Brooklyn, when she gathered everything into her bag. I assumed she was about to leave, perhaps to catch a local train, so I stood up and waited by the door, pretending it was my stop as well.

She exited behind me, along with most of the other passengers, to board an awaiting train. Once again, we assumed the same positions: seated directly across from one another as we continued to glance back and forth.

Suddenly I sprang up and sat beside her. She smiled demurely as I said hello; and as we began to speak I realized that her grasp of the language was rudimentary. A native of Spain, she said that she was studying English and working for the airlines, adding that she lived on Shore Road. As the train approached Bay Ridge Avenue, she frowned and announced that it was her station.

"Perhaps," I said, "we can exchange phone numbers on the platform."

"Yes, good idea!"

When we disembarked she continued walking along, chatting about her job as we approached a staircase. Once we were outside, she halted at a taxi stand and removed a notepad from her bag.

"Now, I take a cab home. This is my residence number," she said, writing on the pad, "and this is my work number." As she wrote her name – *Monica* – I could see that her delicate hand-writing was beautifully formed, as if penned in another century.

We lingered under a flickering streetlamp as her eyes beamed with a warm intensity. I leaned forward to kiss her goodbye, but at the last moment she turned, ever so slightly, so that my kiss brushed against her soft cheek instead of her full, pulpy lips.

That weekend I borrowed Arthur's car and drove into Bay Ridge. We'd originally planned on a dinner date, but, when I phoned, Monica said that her doctor had advised her to remain indoors, as she'd contracted some sort of mysterious skin disorder. "But don't worry," she added, "it's not contagious!"

I arrived with a flower in hand – a single rosebud – and rang the bell. A young Black woman answered the door, dressed in a nurse's uniform.

"You must be here to see Monica," she smiled, leading me inside. "Have a seat. She'll join you in a moment."

I tossed the rose onto a table, sat in an armchair, and waited. Moments later Monica appeared, looking a bit pale. She turned her cheek toward me, and I gently kissed it.

"This is my friend Marie," she said, gesturing toward the nurse. "She works at a hospital and lives upstairs." With a look of amusement, Marie's gaze shifted back and forth between us. Then she smiled at Monica and nodded, as if she approved of our rendezvous, and wished us good-night.

"Aren't you going to take your flower?" I ask, pointing at the table.

"Oh, how nice!"

She retrieves a vase and plops it inside, then sits across from me on a small velvet couch. "I'm sorry I have no whiskey for you. Last night, two of my friends come over and drink it all up. Next time you come, I have *plenty of whiskey*. Yes?"

"Sure, Monica."

"*Leeson*. You married?"

"No, are you?"

"I have boyfriend for two years, we engaged to marry. But then, two months before we marry, he die."

"Oh, I'm sorry."

"Make me very sad. You want some tea? I get you some."

She returns with a teapot and pours me a steaming cup as I slip into the couch and sit beside her.

"Tell me about your family," she says. "They're in Brooklyn?" I nod and explain that I still live at home.

"Oh, you lucky! I have five sisters and three brothers, all in Spain." It's another thing that makes her sad, she says, for she misses them and often gets lonely.

"I *soofer*. Terribly. Make me very, very sad. When I twenty-three, I come to America and learn to take care of myself. How old are you? I twenty-five."

"I'm twenty-two." As she absorbs my words, she appears to be crestfallen. "Does it bother you," I ask, "that I'm younger than you are?"

She nods, then presses her hand against her bosom and adds: "But I very young in heart, yes?"

Her response startled me. How many Americans would have responded like that, I wondered. Suddenly I remembered the girl with the shaved head and the albino beast slouching toward 59th Street: the augur of a new generation, about to emerge from its nightmare cradle. But Monica epitomized the Old World woman that I'd encountered only in classical works of literature: an amanuensis who takes special care to reassure her companion of her devotion.

"It is very ... Wait." She retrieves a Spanish-American dictionary, thumbs through it, and points to the word *rare*. "How you pronounce it? It is *rare*," she continues, "for man to bring flower to woman these days. I am very impressed. I will keep it forever. I will press it into my diary to remember you. *Forever*."

Pointing to the word "flirt," she adds: "I like the way you do this on the train. Most men, they use too many words. I no like. But you, you use your *eyes*." Pointing to her own pupils, for a moment she assumes a serious expression, as if miming me on the train, until we both burst out laughing.

Glancing over her shoulder, I notice a stack of records piled in a corner of the room. "Monica, should we listen to some music?"

"Yes!" Tossing a couple of pillows on the floor, she gestures for me to sit there beside her as she sorts through the collection.

Selecting a few albums, she carefully places them on a turntable. Traditional Spanish ballads, they're profoundly sentimental, melancholy, and romantic.

> Love me, love me again,
> As if this tender night
> Will be our very last

Singing along with the crooners, she occasionally pauses to translate the lyrics. Whenever the songs shift into a refrain, I ask if I can kiss her. After each kiss, we unlock our lips as if nothing unusual has happened. Then she selects another record.

*   *   *

"*Leeson*," she says, holding my hand, "when I see you again?"

"When would you like to see me?"

"Tomorrow!" she grins.

"I'll give you a call this week."

Standing beside the front door, we kiss one last time: a long, passionate, tender embrace.

"Oh, that was a *good* kiss! Bye-bye!"

"Goodbye, Monica."

As the Great Bard once said, youth is wasted on the young. For, instead of calling her back, I allowed Monica to vanish into the ether.

After my experience with Jenny, I was fearful of giving Monica any false expectations about marriage. But despite that, when she said that she would press the rose into her diary and keep it forever, I felt assured that at least a part of me would remain in place, under the empathic gaze of those warm ebony eyes.

Sitting beside her on the floor, listening to those charming love songs, and kissing during each refrain was one of the sweetest, finest things that I'd ever experienced. It was all so simple, pure, and human. I even imagined that the rose, dried and mounted, would somehow preserve such ephemeral joy.

But as any Old World woman would tell you, such relics mean nothing. For the only thing of lasting merit is what persists and grows from one living, breathing moment to the next. And instead, thanks to youthful folly, I'd nipped all that in the bud.

But when I look back on it now, I'm sure that meeting Monica was one more sign that Europe was indeed calling.

> Kiss me, kiss me again,
> For I'm afraid to lose you
> Once again

Freddie and the Mobsters

One afternoon while I was mulling over my vocational limbo, my friend Drew called. There was a pressing matter he wanted to discuss, so I invited him over.

Slipping on a heavy coat, I waited outside. Gravesend was blanketed in snow, and the pavements were icy and treacherous. We lived so close to the sea that the temperature often dropped precipitously during the winter. If you could survive an adolescence of hanging out on such blustery streets as an icy gale shot through your bones, then you felt as if you could survive anything. As Proust says of the wind at Combray, this shrieking merciless blast was the "presiding spirit of the place," especially during such a brutal, inhospitable season.

But there was something else to consider, I mused, turning up the coat collar. In all its varying degrees – of slight gust to full-blown gale – the wind reminded us that there were other forces at work within this deadening, concrete landscape.

Here the presence of nature was often subtle and lacking in drama. The sharp smell of autumn leaves, crunching underfoot, scraping along an endless pavement. Or the baying of a neighbor's dog, straining on a rusty chain. Subtlest of all was a soft breeze caressing a cheek as one carried on a dialogue with the twinkling stars.

Being otherwise deprived of such a natural phenomenon, when it arrived we passionately embraced it. How impatiently we awaited that blazing summer sun, which seemed to find its own pleasure in caressing human flesh. Once the hoarfrost had melted away, perhaps we'd linger in my tiny Brooklyn backyard, seated beside luxuriant rows of irises, hollyhocks, and tulips – their colors seeming to burst in the air – with creeping tendrils of delicate morning glory dangling from the back fence. But along with the heat came an incarnation of nature that was utterly repulsive:

As you lift the lid of a garbage can positioned beside the front stoop, suddenly there's a hungry rat staring up at you. You slam the lid shut just in time to avoid its leaping claws and rancid teeth. During one summer they appeared to be every-where: crawling out of sewer mains, wobbling along the gutter on uncertain feet after consuming a heap of rat poison, or climbing up the sheer facades of brick buildings, their claws digging into the mortar joints. One of our neighbors walked into his kitchen while a rat was nibbling on a chunk of cheese on a butcher block; he grabbed a butcher blade and with one fell swoop sliced the rodent in half.

I amused myself with such idle thoughts until I saw Drew rounding a corner at Highlawn Avenue. Donning one of his father's gray fedoras, now he resembled an extra in a vaudeville troupe.

He greeted me with an exaggerated grin, then broke out laughing – as if acknowledging the absurdity of our pointless existence in Brooklyn. Although we were twenty-four years old, we were still trying to figure out what to do with our lives, and sometimes all we could do was laugh about it.

Chatting in the midst of this wintry tempest, at first we didn't notice the approach of a tall skinny shivering Black man. Not only did he lack a coat; his feet were bare. Shocked to see an African American still alive on the racist *trottoirs* of Gravesend, I wondered what would get to him first: frostbite or a baseball bat smashing open his delicate skull. Before I could ask if he was all right, he muttered: "The garden. Call the garden."

"The garden?" His teeth were chattering as I attempted to

decipher his muffled speech.

"Garden of Eden," he replied, shifting from one bare foot to the other as he paused on the slippery ice.

"Why don't you come inside," I asked, "and warm up?"

We helped him up the stoop and into the kitchen.

"Maybe you'd like some hot tea?" He nodded his head, so I placed a kettle on the stove.

"Now," I continued, "what's this about a garden?"

His face was so numb that he had difficulty speaking more than a few syllables, but finally he repeated: "Call the Garden of Eden."

I noticed that his eyes appeared to be coated with a cloudy blue film. Bearing a stoic expression, he seemed to be looking through me – as if I wasn't there.

"Whom shall I say that I'm calling for?"

"Claude."

I picked up the kitchen telephone. "Operator, I want the Garden of Eden."

"Is this a business or a residence?"

"I'm not sure, but I know it's in Gravesend."

"There's a Garden of Eden on Ocean Parkway. Would you like to be connected?"

Moments later a receptionist answered: "Garden of Eden. How can I help you?"

"I believe that one of your occupants has escaped."

"Oh, you must mean Claude!"

"Yes. He's here with us on West Twelfth Street."

"But that's over a mile away! Give me your address; I'll send a car right away."

"Make sure to bring some shoes; Claude's been walking barefoot."

"Barefoot? Oh, dear Lord!"

"I doubt that the Lord has anything to do with it."

"Oh, my!" she rambled on, conveniently ignoring my last remark. "Sometimes he goes out and forgets where he lives. It's not the first time. But he's never left without his *shoes* before ..."

When I handed Claude a cup of tea, his manner changed abruptly. "Put it on the table," he snapped, "let it cool off!" Studying his faraway gaze, I suddenly realized that he was nearly blind. Perhaps, he was afraid that he might inadvertently burn himself.

While waiting for the tea to cool, I cleaned his bony feet with a hand towel, then covered them with a thick pair of socks. When the doorbell rang, Drew returned with a middle-aged man who said that his father was a friend of Claude's.

"Years ago," he said, "my father was a superintendent in a high-rise in Flatlands. One day, some fool left a garbage bag in the basement filled with turpentine and paint thinner. Not knowing what it was, my dad threw it into the incinerator, and it exploded in his face. The solvents melted his skin, and he lost his vision. Now he lives at the Garden of Eden. I just happened to be there when you called."

Removing a pair of patent-leather shoes from a paper bag, he knelt beside Claude, slipped the shoes on his feet, and carefully tied the laces.

"There you go. Well, you're lucky that you found such nice folks to help you along your way."

A man of few words, Claude nodded and replied: "Thank you."

After they left, I turned to Drew and exclaimed: "The Garden of Eden! What do you make of *that?*"

"I know; it's mind-boggling."

"Remember our eighth-grade teacher, Sister Noel? She always liked to say that life is not a bowl of cherries. Maybe she was right. Instead of a happy-go-lucky garden where a lion lies down with a lamb, suddenly there's a can of turpentine exploding in some poor sap's face."

Before I could continue, Drew pointed at a manual typewriter that was positioned on the dining room table.

"Were you in the middle of writing something?"

"Yes. But around here, you'd think that was a capital crime. When my mother returns from work each day, the first thing out of her mouth is: 'What's that typewriter doing there? Why don't you leave it downstairs, in the basement?' Of course, they never ask me *what* I'm writing about.'"

"Listen, my parents are just as bad. My father scowls and frowns, but I never know what's bothering him. And my mother yammers on for hours about nothing – like an empty rattling pot. She can't comprehend that I don't want to work for a bank, just like her. You know," he grinned, "I still remember the first time I had supper as a teenager at your house. Your father ignored my existence, then sat there reading the *Times* as if he were on a train. But your mom actually looked me in the eyes when she talked to me. Whereas *my* mom would just look at the dishes and food whenever she spoke to me."

"How did they ever get this way, I wonder?"

"That's a long story. But listen, I've been meaning to ask you … One of my friends from acting school lives in the East Village, and his next-door neighbor is getting ready to move out. It's a two-bedroom deal. A fifth-floor walk-up, but the price is right. I think we should grab it. Would you like to live in the Lower East Side?"

"Why not? Maybe it's time to leave the Garden."

* * *

For the next three weeks we were busy cutting sheetrock,

coating parquet floors with polyurethane, and sealing cracks along the baseboards in the vain hope of cutting off the cockroaches. So many came crawling out each night that they would have walked across our faces if we hadn't positioned the bed legs in sardine cans filled with kerosene.

The ground floor of the building featured a jewelry store, but Drew said that it was actually a money-laundering joint, staffed by mobsters with thick gold chains hanging from their beefy necks. A few weeks after we moved in, it was busted and shut down by the Feds.

The building next door, toward First Avenue, hosted an Italian American club, and the cigar-chomping man who ran it, a short stocky fellow named Freddie, was our landlord. Although we didn't realize it at first, the real landlord was a Mafia don who was imprisoned in a federal penitentiary, and Freddie was merely fronting for him.

Freddie owned an overweight mastiff named Peggy, a beast that was so obese that it took five minutes for it to climb the three cement steps that led into the club – with its flabby stomach dragging across each step. The club members fed it filet mignon, lasagna, and spaghetti with mushrooms and tomato sauce. Peggy swallowed everything without the slightest hesitation. Her favorite toy was a regulation-sized football, which she munched as easily as another dog might chew on a small rubber ball.

Freddie seemed to take an instant liking to us, and especially to me for some reason. At first we thought it was because, coming from Gravesend, Drew and I knew how to talk respectfully and in a certain down-to-earth manner to men such as Freddie, even though it was obvious that we weren't quite like Freddie, being a bit more schooled and polished. But we never behaved pretentiously or felt awkward in his presence, which he seemed to appreciate, especially since there were so many yuppies searching for flats in the neighborhood, which was rapidly changing. But we eventually discovered that Freddie's gregariousness was motivated by something that neither one of us would have ever guessed.

* * *

A few months after we moved in, Freddie hired me as his "right-hand man," and together we'd renovate the empty apartments in the building.

A typical day would begin in his flat on the ground floor, where we'd eat a lumberjack breakfast of three or four eggs, along with heaping slices of ham, sausage, or bacon. The chef was a congenial gentleman named Jimmy – the only nonmobbed-up man around – who weighed about three hundred pounds. Hence his nickname, "Bonzet," a Sicilian word meaning "little fruit." A fair haired, blue eyed, slightly nervous fellow, Bonzet enjoyed the simple things, such as relaxing in the sun in his folding chair, devouring an enormous spread, or chatting about whatever nonsense happened to be the order of the day. He also possessed a delightful sense of humor and, more than anything, he loved to laugh. Only something stressful, such as Freddie's snide comments, endless ribbing, or gruff commands could flip his switches and trigger his more anxious, jittery side.

Well fortified by Bonzet's cooking, Freddie and I would clamber up the slate steps inside the building, where he'd lead me into some ancient, dilapidated tenement. These were the same flats where the nineteenth-century immigrants had once lived, gaining their first foothold in America. And there we were, Drew and I, college-educated guys from solid, middle-class families, *And what the hell is wrong with you kids? It's as if your grandparents' American dream is running in reverse! And how on earth can you afford such an astronomical rent? People are paying seven hundred bucks a month for these dumpy, roach-infested rat-holes!* Freddie would exclaim, all the while insulting us, berating us, and puzzling over why we'd let him take such advantage of us.

For the first few hours of each day, Freddie and I would be busting hump and rearing to go, perhaps crawling on our hands and knees as he taught me how to lay linoleum tiles:

"You heat the edges with this here blowtorch" – pointing the flame of a propane burner directly at my face and nearly singeing my eyebrows – "and they'll melt right into place. Then you trim them to fit those oddball angles, and they'll cut just like butter." Freddie loved his burner, which he also used to melt away decades of lead paint from wooden moldings that ran along the entrance to each room. Having been spawned by the devil, he was immune to such toxins, so there were never any gas masks to protect us.

By midafternoon, when we were making some decent progress on the job, he'd mutter: "Damn it, I forgot my Scotch. Do me a favor, go get it. It's in the club."

So I'd saunter down to the club, knock on the front door, and tell Nicky or Ralphie or Harry that Freddie wants his Johnny Walker Black. They'd invite me inside – the only non-mobster other than Bonzet who was allowed in there – and hand me a bottle, but always with a sly, witty remark, such as: *That lush! Ain't he had enough already? Make sure he don't drink it all in one gulp!* And I'd nod and smile, never once talking back to these killers, maimers, and torturers. Although I had no idea what they were up to, I sensed that these were not the sort of men to be messed with.

I'd return with the booze, and Freddie would begin to suck on his bottle. Soon, the tiles would have gotten laid sideways if

I hadn't volunteered, in the most diplomatic fashion, to finish the job:

"Hey, Freddie, why don't you save your knees and take a break? You're working your butt off; let me take over. Come on, relax, enjoy your drink. You did enough for one day. Let me practice a bit and get it down."

Ever the drama queen, Freddie would take a deep breath and murmur: "Yeah, maybe you're right. OK, but do me a favor. Reach over there, on the floor behind that toolbox, and hand me one of them cigars."

I'd pass along one of his cheap De Nobilis, and he'd offer me a slug of Johnny, and I'd say, "No, I better not. I can't handle it like you can. If I do that, the tiles will end up gettin' glued to the walls!" And Freddie would laugh, especially since the joke was on me. Then he'd take a few more slugs and begin to slur, and that's when the workday would end: about three in the afternoon, when he'd abruptly announce: "OK, that's it. I've had too much to drink. We better call it a day." So we'd leave the tools and half-cut tiles right there, on the floor, and return to his flat and wash up.

Once we were in the club again, he'd hand me cash for a day's work and insist that I join him in a drink. There was no way around that, so I'd sip the Scotch as slowly as possible; because if I downed it, Freddie would pour me another, and then another, until I'd be unable to think straight for the rest of the day. So instead, I'd sip and try to blend into the woodwork as Nicky "The Cook" turned on the espresso machine, and somebody knocked at the front door, and Frankie "The Foot" slid the curtain open just a hair and said, "It's them fuckin' junkies ..."

Two skinny, scruffy, beady-eyed guys would stand at the threshold and unbutton their long trench coats, which were stuffed with an assortment of filet mignon, nicked from a local supermarket. Freddie would offer them six bucks a package, then settle accounts and say, *Scram*. Then he'd throw me a steak, and Nicky would hand me an espresso, and I'd thank them profusely, but not too profusely – just the right balance. For, as Walt Whitman says: *Be profuse, be profuse, be profuse. But be not* too *damned profuse.*

Once we were back at Freddie's apartment, he'd stick his head out the window facing the courtyard and yell: "Oh, *Bonzeeeeet?*" as if Jimmy were his downtrodden maid or over-wrought housewife.

Moments later Bonzet would appear, snapping at Freddie in short, clipped beats: "What the *fuck* do you want? Why are you always *yelling* like that? What the hell is *wrong* with you?"

Only Bonzet could get away with that, because he really was a sort of wife to Freddie. And because they possessed the informality of old pals who had grown up on this very street. And because Freddie, sadist that he was, enjoyed cranking him up and bringing out his hysterical side.

Once Bonzet had simmered down a bit, he'd turn and offer me a warm, benevolent, respectful nod, and maybe murmur *How ya doing?* Then he'd unstack the aluminum pots and pans and begin his elaborate preparations.

While we were devouring our chicken parmigiana, filet mignon, or baked ziti, there would be knock after knock at the door, with Freddie barking *Who is it?* and someone answering *It's Paulie,* or *Tommy,* or *Ralphie.* Then Paulie "The Pipe" or Tiny "The Tank" or Ralphie "The Rope" would saunter in and hand Freddie a scrap of paper marked with a three-digit number, along with some cash.

Freddie would make small talk with these goons while Bonzet and I lingered over his delectable spread. And I'd say "Bonzet, this is magnificent; I can't believe how good this tastes."

In response, Bonzet would assume his most serious demeanor, because now we were talking about that most holy of holies. With a concentrated expression, he'd hesitate for a moment as if gathering his thoughts and searching for words – words often being so unnecessary to a man such as Bonzet. Who needed them when, instead, you had sun, wind, food, drink, and life itself right there, in the palm of your hand? But eventually he'd say, "Look, it ain't hard. This is what you do. You boil some water ..." He'd spend the next twenty minutes describing in minute detail how he'd prepared the filets, or how to chop garlic, or what to look for when you shop for red and green hot peppers.

Freddie would finally lose his patience and shout: "Bonzet! What the hell are you wasting your time for? He ain't never gonna cook nothing for himself! He's an upper-class man! He even has a college degree! And *now* look at him. He's working for *me*. What does *that* tell you? What's more important, book knowledge or life knowledge? *Nothing* beats real experience ..." But the "experience" Freddie was jabbering on about had nothing to do with what most folks would regard as an uplifting existential adventure. Instead, it referred to his various incarcerations in Sing Sing, or the Tombs, or wherever he'd slept behind county walls. But Freddie never spoke openly about being in the Mob. He even tried to lead us off the trail, making a seemingly innocuous remark about how, once, he'd met a guy who had *seemed to be in the Mafia*. A red herring if there ever was one, as I later realized. But he made no bones about how he'd done time for various crimes. In fact, he was proud of it, as he knew it would bolster his image as a tough guy.

Freddie even taught me some of the odd little things that he'd learned in prison. One afternoon while we were looking for a nut to fit a bolt, he lifted a tray from his toolbox that was filled with an assortment of nails, screws, nuts, and bolts, and said: *Hey, grab that there newspaper!* Spreading it open, he dumped the contents of the tray onto the centerfold. Poking his knobby fingers through the mess, he finally found what he was looking for. Then he gripped the paper by the edges, formed a funnel, and neatly poured everything back in.

"I'll bet you never learned how to use a newspaper like that in school, did you? You know where I learned that? Same place where I got all my best education. In the can."

* * *

One evening while we were feasting on calamari with sautéed garlic, a stevedore named Eddie "The Breeze" appeared at the door – bug-eyed and pale as a specter – accompanied by a strapping Longshoreman named Ronnie. Eddie was distraught because the guys on the job had pooled their resources and played a winning number, but Eddie had scrawled it so carelessly that it resembled a 451 instead of a 431. So now, the numbers men refused to pay. To make matters worse, some of the Longshoremen were convinced that Eddie had pocketed the prize money and was bullshitting about not getting paid because of an ambiguous scrawl.

As we munched our corn on the cob and I complimented Bonzet on his cooking, Eddie said that the other Longshoremen had nearly lynched him when he claimed that he hadn't collected anything. That's why he was here now, with Ronnie, so that Freddie could explain what had happened and that they could receive a final verdict about what the "numbers guys" at the top had decided to do.

Freddie treasured any opportunity to lord it over other men – especially when they were three times his size – so he was in no rush. In between succulent bites of calamari he'd pause, burp, and savor each morsel of his story, recounting how he'd gallantly marched into Mikey "The Meat Hook's" office and said: "Mikey, these Longshoremen are stand-up fellas. We've been doing business with them for years, and they ain't never pulled nothing like this before."

"Never mind about that bullshit. What happened? When he handed it over, did you look at it or not? And if you did, why didn't you ask: *What is this? I can't read chicken scrawl! Are you sayin' 431 or 451?*"

"I didn't ask nothing because Eddie said: 'Say a prayer for the 431! If I hit it, I'm taking Suzie' – that's his wife – 'out on a cruise.'"

Mikey drilled his eyes into Freddie and asked, "You sure about that?"

"Absolutely. He repeated it twice: *'I'm praying for the 431!'*"

Mikey scratched his chin, spit on the floor, lit a cigar, then asked Freddie if he wanted one. But Freddie declined, saying "No, thanks; I'm good."

"Because Mikey loved them fuckin' cigars," Freddie laughed. "They were fifty-dollar Cubans. You ever smoke a good Havana, Eddie?"

By now, Eddie was nearly crawling through his skin. He was so choked up that he could hardly talk. He just shook his head, no, while his partner stood beside him, mute. Eddie must have told Ronnie not to say a word, because he knew that Freddie didn't care to converse with strangers. So Ronnie just quietly bit his lip.

Letting go a long, reverberant burp, Freddie wiped his chin and made like he was about to reveal the final decision. But then he turned to me and asked if I wanted to watch *Buck Rogers in the 25th Century* or *I Love Lucy*.

I said, "Let's go with Buck," so Freddie hit the remote control just as Buck was coming on. And we both agreed that although this Buck was slick, he wasn't as smooth as the original Buck from the 1930s. How I loved to watch the old *Buck Rodgers* and *Flash Gordon* serials! In those ancient, black-and-white shows, the sets were constructed of paper-mache and cardboard, and sometimes they'd shake while Flash or his angelic heartthrob, Dale Arden, ambled across the stage. But the best part was the spaceship, which sputtered like a sparkler and moved so slowly, and in such a wavering, crooked line, that it appeared as if it were about to fall from the sky.

Yet there was something terrifying about those old fables, because so many of the characters were killed ... even some of the main protagonists, whom you'd never expect to get offed. Nonetheless, they were zapped by aliens and vaporized into nothingness. Thus, there was something so lifelike – or death-like – about those vintage serials. It was just like the Mob: one wrong move, and it didn't matter if you were Joe Blow or Mikey the Meat Hook – *poof* – you were gone.

Swallowing one last chunk of calamari, Freddie burped, said *Excuse my manners*, then drilled his eyes into Eddie and grumbled: "Listen. Mikey said, 'Next time you write a three, make sure it looks like a fuckin' three.' But for now, you're good."

Meaning, the Mob had decided to fork it over.

When I consider it now, it's amazing how unabashed Freddie was about that whole gambling racket. At one point they'd even positioned a small blackboard in front of the club, where they'd chalk in the numbers, one by one, as soon as they were announced. But the cops finally told them to be more discreet, so the kindergarten chalkboard was 86'd.

* * *

It wasn't just the numbers racket that made us suspicious of Freddie, who claimed that he was handling it as a favor for one of the local hoods. What really did it was a story he related one night while Drew, who occasionally worked with us, was seated beside me at Freddie's kitchen table. We were wolfing down cheesecake that Freddie had portioned into what he called *humungous* slices, passing it back and forth until we could eat no more.

I can no longer recall how we drifted into this horrendous tale, but Freddie had been drinking too much and let it slip that, a few years ago, his sister had phoned to complain about her neighbors: "A 'free-loving' couple who were nudists." She'd politely asked them to erect a fence so that she wouldn't have to see them cavorting around naked in the yard, but they did nothing; they refused.

So Freddie said, "Alright, sit tight, I'm coming over." He flew out to LA, and one evening when the neighbors were away he set their house on fire.

Once he returned to New York, he phoned his sister and asked: "How's the barbecue coming along?"

"Everything's done to perfection," she laughed. And that was the end of those troublesome nudists.

Upon hearing this Drew and I shot each other a look, and we nearly gagged on our cheesecake. At that moment, I realized that we needed to distance ourselves from Freddie.

A few days later, Freddie offered to take me to a bordello: a proposition that I successfully managed to avoid. When he first introduced this subject, he'd made some peculiar remarks about male anatomy: something that seemed to be a bit out of character, but eventually it fit snugly into the Freddie jigsaw puzzle.

Freddie later confided that, when we'd first moved in, he'd assumed that Drew and I were a gay couple. It wasn't until one of my girlfriends showed up that he realized that we were just "regular guys." But he related this to me with a lingering tone of uncertainty, as if hoping that he might be wrong.

One night after work when he was really hitting the bottle, Freddie insisted that I accompany him to his other flat in a building a few doors away, where he'd grown up with his immigrant parents.

From what I'd gleaned from our previous conversations, Freddie regarded his mother as an unblemished saint. His eyes would tear at the mere mention of her name. And now, prominently displayed in a cheap, gilt-edged frame on his dresser, there she was:

Garbed in woebegone widow's attire, and staring into the camera lens with a malevolent glare, she resembled a black widow spider that had just swallowed her son's meager soul ... and was about to burp it up. Without a doubt, she was the most hideous-looking woman that I've ever seen. And as I later learned from one of the old-timers on the block, the spider had died a most fitting death.

One day a garbage truck had come careening round a corner. A heavy metal chain that was normally attached to the back of the vehicle had slipped off one of its hooks; and, as it flew out and unfurled across the street, it wrapped around the waist of Freddie's mother. Lifting her up, it snapped her back into the gaping maw where the trash was being crushed to a pulp. Which is precisely what it did to her.

All this filtered through my mind in brief, fleeting moments as I stood there and Freddie confirmed that, yes, it was indeed a photo of his mother. Then he stepped into the kitchen to pour himself a bumper glass of Scotch. When he returned, for once he seemed to be at a loss for words.

Hemming and hawing, he finally said: "You know, it's late. Why don't you stay over? Here, you can sleep in these" – handing me a pair of silk jammies.

All at once it hit me, naive little bunny that I was: Freddie wants me to be his *chicken*. And *that's* what he learned in the can!

Of course, I scrammed. Then I really distanced myself, working with him as little as possible and only for as long as he remained sober. Whenever Freddie hit the bottle, I'd make some excuse to split.

*   *   *

I was circling round the northeast corner of Washington Square one day when I encountered the raggedy figure of Ray Veshnevski, Nick's poet friend. From head to toe he was covered with a fine white powder.

"Sheetrocking, Ray?"

"How did you guess?" he grinned. "I'm working as a laborer on a construction site in the Upper West Side." He paused to smack at his jeans, and a puff of dust rose with each strike of his hand. "What about you? Are you looking for work? Maybe you should give this guy a call. There's a building boom going on, and he can use all the help he can get. The pay is pretty good – fifty bucks a day, in cash."

"Do you need experience?"

"Nope. It's simple. Ripping up old floors, carting away rubble, helping the carpenters with their tools and materials. Plus, you couldn't work for a nicer guy. Reggie isn't a native New Yorker; he's a country boy from Minnesota."

I absorbed all this during one of those split-second Manhattan encounters: me going one way, Ray the other, but pausing to telegraphically dictate the details before rushing past and disappearing. And that was the last I ever saw of Ray.

My first assignment was a demolition job at Boerum Hill, and since Reggie said he could use all the men we could muster I brought Drew along. Together, we had a ball: swinging our sledgehammers, knocking down walls, and joyfully smashing everything to bits. We even finished the job in half the time that Reggie had allotted: twice as fast as the other laborers, who couldn't understand why we were working so frenetically. But we were lucky we did so, because when he required fewer workers Reggie hired only the two of us. That extra effort had placed us at the top of his hiring schedule from then on, so we managed to stay afloat.

Nonetheless, there were some unexpected challenges. The following weekend I was placed in charge of setting up a table saw on the roof of a high-rise. Moments after I turned it on, an electrical cord became intertwined with a fan belt. The jam catapulted the far end of the table up into the air. Then it came crashing down, with its spinning blade coming directly at me. The serrated metal teeth roared toward my torso as I leapt back, narrowly escaping. I was nearly sliced in two from throat to scrotum.

Upon witnessing this, one of the carpenters dryly intoned: "You should have lost something."

Reggie then asked me to polish the windowpanes that formed a slanting glass ceiling over the kitchen, which was positioned at a corner of the roof. So there I was, teetering and tottering on a two-foot-wide parapet that hovered fifteen stories above Fifth Avenue. In the midst of this task – gazing down at pedestrians who resembled ants – I suddenly took a step back and inched my way toward safer ground. Overcome by a wave of panic, I realized that I'd reached my limit, and I told Reggie to find someone else to take over.

Reggie's most lucrative contract was for a penthouse renovation in the Village. The owner, an ochre-eyed redhead named Susan Sarandon, was best known for her small part in *The Rocky Horror Picture Show*. The film was one of the first to develop an "audience participation ritual," and it soon became a cult classic. In 1976, after it opened for midnight screenings at the Waverly Theater on April Fool's Day, rice, toilet paper, and hot dogs were hurled at the screen during key moments; and lines of dialogue were shouted out in unison by the film's devotees. Following a run of ninety-five weeks at the Waverly, it moved a few blocks north, to the Eighth Street Playhouse. There, for the next fifteen years, it continued to be shown every Friday and Saturday at midnight, a run that made it world famous.

Though Sarandon had acted in several films after that, by the summer of 1983 she feared that her career was dropping into limbo. Now she was trying to decide whether to accept a role in a TV series or to hold out for a more prestigious part in a film. Meanwhile, as she fretted over her starry future, we – the common laborers, carpenters, and painters – wandered about her spacious digs and built her a new pleasure palace.

At that time in Hollywood, women past a certain age were hard-pressed to land major roles, but all this was about to change. After appearing in a television mini-series, Susan eventually resurrected her career and starred in *Thelma and Louise*, a popular film that she completed at the age of forty-five.

But what did she do in the meantime? She continually flirted with every construction worker on our "set," even dropping objects "accidentally" on the floor so that she could bend over – slowly and deliberately, in her ribbed summer T-shirt minus a bra – and allow us a peek at her breasts as they spilled forth (those legendary Hollywood icons!). Such an insatiable thirst for attention!

But apparently Susan had never performed before a crew of hardboiled Manhattan carpenters, whose showmanship easily eclipsed her own. As soon as a silver spoon or a gold-tipped pen slipped from her fingers and she stooped to conquer, the workers would turn their backs and ignore her as she retrieved the prop from the floor.

It was a premier performance that I witnessed innumerable times and never grew tired of ... especially since I lacked the resolve of the carpenters, and I always allowed my eyes to wander. After Susan ambled away, the men would circle round as I grabbed a pencil and drew a picture from memory that illustrated the *belles formes* of her seductive *coquetterie*.

A month after we started working for Reggie, Drew was hired as a clerk for the FBI. I made sure to mention this to Bonzet, knowing that he'd relay this unsettling tidbit to Freddie. But I never said what, exactly, Drew was doing there, claiming that I wasn't sure. So now, just as I'd hoped, they wondered if Drew was in training to become a federal agent.

Since I'd agreed to help Freddie finish a job on the third floor, the following day I waited for him there, in an empty living room.

A few minutes later he banged open the door with a thrust of his toolbox and silently stared at me, a half-chewed cigar jammed into the corner of his mouth. A consummate exhibitionist, he knew precisely how to milk every little gesture for its full cinematic effect. But this time, all he could mutter was: "You boys work in strange ways. That's all I'm gonna say. Strange ways." He was waiting for an explanation, but when I feigned ignorance of what he was referring to he left it at that.

We silently laid the floor tiles, then called it a day. But instead of paying me in the club, Freddie handed me a wad of cash in the hallway. Perhaps, by now, his suspicions had gotten the better of him.

Thus, we finally managed to escape from the manacles of the Mob.

*   *   *

I was walking along the block one afternoon when I saw Freddie seated in his black sedan, idling at the curb. When he spotted me, he waved me over. He said that he'd just sold the building and was about to move back into his mother's old flat.

"Call this number," he added, handing me a scrap of paper. "It's the Manhattan housing authority. Tell 'em you're being overcharged."

Drew and I had always assumed that Freddie was ripping us off, but we never dared to mention it. But now he was giving us carte blanche to take the new landlord to court.

Perhaps, it was his going-away gift.

Freddie managed the club for a few more years, but then he received orders to relocate to California. A lucky move, because the Feds soon came down hard on the Italian Mob in New York.

But one thing Freddie couldn't escape from was AIDS.

I didn't hear about it till decades later, but that's how he died. Especially at that time, when the illness was newly discovered and the treatments were harsh and ineffective, a bullet to the brain might have been more merciful.

When I learned of his demise, I tipped my hat to Freddie: son of proud immigrants, and the craziest motherfucker on the block.

The Walt Whitman Asylum

During my junior year in high school I befriended a bookish intellectual named Bernie, a literary bibliophile who also possessed an abiding interest in Eastern philosophy. Over the years, we remained in touch; and one day he called to invite me to a lecture by Jiddu Krishnamurti, author of numerous tracts on spirituality such as the *First and Last Freedom* and *The Only Revolution*.

Born in 1895 – the same year that Gauguin had settled in Polynesia and that Oscar Wilde was arrested for "gross indecency" – Jiddu had recently celebrated his eighty-eighth birthday. Little did we realize that we would be witnessing one of his last public appearances, just a few years before his death.

Upon entering Manhattan's capacious Felt Forum, we slipped into a pair of seats about a hundred feet from the stage. Bernie said that, unlike many other gurus, Jiddu had disavowed an allegiance to any particular religion, philosophy, or nationality. Instead, he devoted himself to writing, traveling, and cultivating audiences both large and small.

"At the age of twelve," Bernie continued, "he was raised by Annie Besant and Charles Leadbeater, who were prominent figures in the Theosophist movement. They were convinced that Jiddu was fated to become their next leader: an avatar of the Lord Maitreya. But twenty years later, he turned the tables and set out on his own." Bernie added that he considered Krishnamurti to be a sort of "spiritual anarchist."

While absorbing all this I couldn't help but wonder if Jiddu had maintained any lingering resentment over having sacrificed those precious years of adolescence, which were ripped away by these "mentors" who'd insisted upon initiating him during such an impressionable age.

The Forum was now filled to its capacity of five thousand, and the audience was patiently awaiting their guru with a respectful, reverential silence. At the precise stroke of the hour, Krishnamurti slowly approached the stage. Instead of a flamboyant spectacle of pop music celebrities prancing under flashing strobe-lights – which was the typical fare at the Forum – now there was only the stooped but regal silhouette of a diminutive elder dressed in a three-piece suit. As he ambled toward center stage, a thunderous applause echoed across the cavernous space. When he paused to survey the scene, I was struck by Krishnamurti's bushy black eyebrows and crown of snow-white hair, which was brushed back from a large forehead. His hooked nose and pursed lips, shaped into an expression of disdain, lent him the appearance of an eagle swiveling its head before diving down and ripping the heart from its prey. Despite the deeply engraved lines that etched his wizened facade and marked him with the imprint of a weary knowledge, there remained something youthful about Jiddu's open regard and penetrating gaze.

An Indian physician named Deepak Chopra was also seated in the audience that morning. Three decades later, in a memoir titled *Brotherhood*, he made special note of the confrontational quality of Krishnamurti's talk. As Deepak recalls, Jiddu's opening gambit was: "Who are you clapping for? Perhaps for yourself?" And he adds that, throughout this lecture, his belligerent tone "was challenging to the point of being abrasive." But in fact, this was an understatement. Over the next two hours, every word that Jiddu uttered seemed to be laced with a molten anger that only barely managed not to fully erupt.

For a moment I imagined that he was holding out a palmful of diamonds; but before carefully selecting one and handing it over he wanted to remind the recipient that these gems had been plucked as the result of an enormous labor: a product not only of blood and sweat but even death. "Look closely," he seemed to be saying. "Although I can appraise this for you, once I hand it over you'll never realize it's true value, because you yourself weren't down in that mine, risking life and limb, knee-deep in muck and slime, and forced to carry on while your comrades were falling like flies all around you. Here, take it. But don't forget, you're a worthless little fool who doesn't even deserve the cloth that it's wrapped in. But that's my job: to hand over treasures to utter morons."

And yet, his scathing diatribes were delivered in a sonorous, melodic timbre: one resembling a reed instrument oscillating playfully in a balmy Indian breeze.

After exploring such ponderous topics as "man's relation-ship to God" and "the loneliness of the spiritual desert," Krishnamurti paused to glance at an old-fashioned pocket watch that dangled from a gold chain pinned to his suit. Then he opened the floor to questions.

The first "seeker" was foolish enough to shout out: *Krishnamurti, what is the meaning of life?*

Without a pause, Jiddu unloaded his full artillery. Twisting his face into an even darker, grumpier mask, he now evinced the hauteur of an irate barrister. With an impeccable British accent, he castigated this lost lemming while harshly bellowing: "What an *idiotic* question! Why should I have to sit here and listen to such ridiculous blabber?" With a vehement huff, he added: "Don't you realize that I have better things to do than respond to such *nonsense*?"

Bernie and I turned to each other and burst out laughing. But the rest of the audience sat there in mute silence, apparently stunned by Jiddu's flinty style. For the term "condescending" doesn't even begin to describe what we'd just witnessed.

Besides appreciating his "school of hard knocks" approach, I could also sense his pain; for he effused the discontent of an intelligent man surrounded by nincompoops. But I suspect that we were also witnessing the festering rancor of a man who, when he was only twelve, hadn't yet been strong enough to escape the Theosophical yoke that had been forged to bind him. Once he escaped, he never again let his guard down.

It finally occurred to me that Jiddu was living proof that the ego must not only be "transcended"; it must also be *defended* daily from the inane onslaught of meaninglessness, which is often embodied in lost souls who gravitate round a bright light and seek – often inadvertently – to extinguish it. Maybe that's what Krishnamurti was referring to when, just before he died, he remarked that no one had ever grasped his true message. He also claimed that the "fireball" of spiritual energy that had gathered round him and had fueled his quest would be dissipated upon his passing – thus preventing the possibility of an imposter usurping the throne. The most that anyone could hope for, he added, was to merely "live the teaching": to obtain limited proximity to this force and to an inkling of the truth it had engendered.

Despite harboring such an elevated assessment of himself, nothing he said that afternoon left any lingering impression of profundity upon me. By the time he finished, I realized that I'd gained far more spiritual wisdom from contemplating a work of art than from anything a guru had ever uttered in my presence. Perhaps what they were after transcended the limitations of language. Or maybe they intentionally cloaked their message or watered it down to make it more accessible to the inchoate masses. But at least Krishnamurti had kindled a fire in his belly and had succeeded in upending everyone's expectations.

After the lecture we headed for a café in the Lower East

Side. Bernie said that, for the last year, he'd been working at the Queens Day Center, a treatment program for the chronically mentally ill.

"A few blocks south from where I work, there's a privately owned psychiatric nursing home, supervised by Catholic Charities. It's called the Walt Whitman Asylum. In the nineteenth century, it was known as the Walt Whitman Hotel. There are all these strange references to Whitman in the neighborhood. The Queens Public Library, located nearby, even contains a small collection of rare Whitman miscellany."

As I later discovered, the hotel was named after Walt because, in the summer of 1839, he'd worked in the neighborhood as a typesetter.

"What an amusing idea," I laughed, "a Walt Whitman Asylum!"

"There's also a job opening there, for a case manager." Pausing to sip his cappuccino, Bernie regarded me with a pensive smile. "I was thinking of applying for that position myself, but maybe you should instead. Just give me the word, and I can call the director and arrange for an appointment."

I didn't have to think twice about it, as I knew that I wouldn't last much longer as a common laborer. Thanks to the spectral presence of Walt, there appeared to be something providential about Bernie's offer, so I felt as if I had no choice but to accept it.

"Set something up for me this week." But moments after I spoke, I felt an undertow of uncertainty creeping in. "What about my lack of experience? It's going to be a bit nerve-racking to walk in there without any previous training."

"All they require is a college degree. Besides, you're already more well-read on the subject of depth psychology than any of the other case managers there. Just maintain a relaxed, confident air, and you'll ace it. What's the worst that can happen?

And it's a lot safer than what you're doing now. Occasionally you might have to deal with a mean-spirited psychiatrist, and of course there are plenty of busybody social workers. But at least you won't have to dodge leaping table saws – or risk slipping off the edge of a high-rise! In your shoes, I'd have been dead already. I mean, with my luck? But you ..." Bernie smiled a peculiar grin that was tinged with melancholy. "Ever since we first met at school, I've always felt that you were blessed with uncommon luck. No matter how far out on a limb you teeter and totter, eventually you return to your senses and float gracefully back down again."

"But what about those heavenly visions of Susan Sarandon, walking around in a ribbed T-shirt with nothing on underneath? How can I just walk away from all that? You wouldn't believe how desperate she is for attention!"

"What a tease!" he laughed. "Well, as the Buddha once said, in selecting one path, we must sacrifice another."

*   *   *

Following a lengthy subway ride into Jamaica, I approached a seven-story building that featured a gray brick facade. Dressed in my only decent suit and tie, and carrying an empty briefcase as a prop, I paused to study several leafless, skeletal trees that stood gaunt and Edgar Allen Poe-like beside this lugubrious structure. With their fingerlike branches, the November boughs were gripping a fluttering pair of pink bloomers; a billowing green dress; and a faded orange hat, pinned with a fake carnation.

Standing beneath this flittering refuse I felt strangely at home; although why, I couldn't say. It was as if the occupants had abandoned all pretense of a persona, jettisoning their clothing to instead stroll about unencumbered in the great outdoors beside the naturist specter of Walt Whitman.

A bank of glass doors opened into a lobby where several dozen patients were sauntering back and forth, their trembling hands gripping styrofoam cups filled with watered-down coffee. A battered desk stood off to the side. There, a woman with a platinum bouffant smiled as I introduced myself. With a reedy nasal drone, she replied: "The director is expecting you." Pulling a long yellow pencil out of her hair, she pointed it toward an elevator.

I boarded a mildewed platform, and several schizophrenic clients ambled in behind me. I noticed that they were dressed in a mismatched assortment of clothing. All around me, tattered shirts frayed at the edges and mottled with food stains fell out of trousers that were either too large or too small.

Instead of being met by one or two principals, I was seated at a long conference table and grilled by nearly the entire staff. Without Bernie's assurance, I probably would have suffered from stage fright.

Positioned at the far end was the boss, a man a few years my senior named John Dougherty: an Irish American who frequently smiled and possessed sympathetic blue eyes. Among the case managers seated closer to my end were three figures that caught my attention. One was Sister Evelyn, a stocky middle-aged nun dressed in a Prussian-blue habit. To her left was a lanky Franciscan brother: a mild mannered, soft-spoken man named Bill Taylor. Brother Taylor often seemed to be distracted by a young woman seated directly across from him, a young Greek beauty named Malama, whose long shimmering hair neatly framed her blooming charms.

What's left unspoken during such an interview often remains more important than whatever is directly stated. Although I'd read most of Carl Jung's collected works – a task that represented my only serious credential in the field – it was perhaps for the best that I avoided any discussion of their more esoteric contents. Otherwise, I might have been forced to explain the author's fascination with things such as the grove of transformation and the heart-shaped blossom; the false and true nightingale; the twelve pairs of golden shoes; epilepsy among mediums; the squaring of the circle; the soul as a homunculus; teleological hallucinations; the love fire of Venus; vinegar as *prima materia*; and the three-legged toad that lives on the moon. But I later learned that what had really clinched it for me was particular response that I've given to one of Dougherty's first questions:

"Why do you want to work in this field?"

Pausing a moment, I replied: "I'd like to lend a sense of hope to all those who have lost it" – paraphrasing one of Jung's more salient remarks about the role of a spiritual mentor.

Once we were finished, Dougherty grabbed me by the elbow and accompanied me to the lobby. As we approached the exit, he turned and asked: "So, when can you start? How about tomorrow?"

"I can be here bright and early Monday morning," I replied, hoping to buy myself a few extra days of freedom.

"Fine – see you then!"

* * *

It gradually dawned on me that case managers bear a certain resemblance to bodhisattvas; for their main task is to straighten out some "bad karma" – or rotten luck – as if in preparation for an eventual rebirth. But despite the teachings of Mahayana Buddhism, the odds remained rather slim that any of our clients would become enlightened within his or her own lifetime. To wit, I'd inherited a caseload that included Carmine "The

Catastrophe," a gambler who'd once frequented gaming halls from Las Vegas to Havana; but then, following a bad tumble of the dice, besides losing the shirt off his back he also lost his mind. And now, the primary focus of Carmine's day was to hope for lasagna for dinner instead of that dreadful roast beef and gravy – for how could anyone be expected to consume such slop? But Jeremy van der Clove, another one of my charges, continually argued with Carmine over this point, claiming that the *quantity* of food was far more important than its *quality*. Since Jeremy could consume as much of it as he liked, he concluded that he had "no fundamental complaints."

While Jeremy was cerebral and verbose, my most laconic client was Louie "The Lip," a middle-aged man who'd suffered a lobotomy for his "antisocial behavior." Louie couldn't care less about what he ate for dinner; he was content to seat himself in the rec room, imbibe a lukewarm coffee, and stare off into space. Occasionally he'd scream out a disjointed phrase in a seeming fit of rage; but then, just as suddenly, he'd calmly sip his drink and forget that he'd ever uttered a word.

Louie's only companion was an obese, loudmouthed sadist named Stuart Abromowitz, who always looked forward to his "free coffee," as he called it, but who bemoaned the fact that his leisure time was constantly interrupted by one Angelica "Pin," who could often be seen dispensing clothing donations from a shopping cart. Stuart had christened her with this moniker because Angelica was a "Born Again," and all she seemed to care about were things such as *how many angels can dance on the head of a pin?*

I was lingering nearby one day when Stuart pointed at me and said: "Angelica, it's not the angels who are important but the man who grabs that pin and sews our souls back together again. Like this gentleman here, God bless him, except that God doesn't exist!" Turning to me he continued, "Didn't Nietzsche discover that? Didn't he prove that God is no more substantial than the devil himself?"

Reacting as if a cloud of sulfur was rising from Stuart's steaming cup, Angelica grabbed her cart and bolted from the room.

Perhaps my most tragic case was that of Lonnie "The Loon": a young man with bushy carrot-red hair who'd consumed so much LSD that he was never the same again. After one too many hits of Purple Haze, his eyes continued to glow like a lava lamp. Attempting to escape from the asylum one night, he walked barefoot through Manhattan's heavily trafficked Holland Tunnel: a task even more challenging than walking on water, especially since Lonnie possessed none of the Lord's various magic tricks.

Lonnie would lecture to anyone who might listen about the questionable behavior of Jesus Christ, whom he alternately regarded as a spiritual mentor or sex abuser, with his assessment of the Savior constantly vacillating between these two disparate possibilities. Whenever Lonnie grew convinced that Christ was the source of his trouble, he'd complain about the Lord's "inappropriate sense of boundaries."

I was trying to talk sense into him one day when he bolted up and ran over to the Queens Day Center. Bumping into Bernie there, he screeched, "The devil is in the Whitman Asylum, and he's coming after me!"

Not having the slightest idea of what was afoot, Bernie escorted him back to the asylum. But when Lonnie spotted me in a corridor, he turned to Bernie, pointed at me, and silently mouthed: "Satan."

* * *

Once Malama and I became intimate, she didn't dare to tell

her Old World parents that she was spending the night at my place, so she was forced to invent all sorts of complicated stories, often relying on her friend Roseanne to serve as a beard. Considering all the time she supposedly spent with Roseanne, I wondered why her mother, the fretful and ever-vigilant Athena Panagopulos, never suspected that Malama was a closet lesbian.

During our first night together, Malama introduced me to ouzo: that powerful liqueur imported from the island of Lesbos. Seated on my couch and sipping this anise-flavored aperitif, we leafed through several photo albums that she'd smuggled from her parents' house in Elmhurst. In each snapshot, whether she was a pubescent girl or a ripe young woman, she'd invariably be posed with her hip jutted out, her eyes burning a hole through the camera lens, and her luscious lips puckered – as if awaiting a precocious kiss.

In my favorite snapshot, a nineteen-year-old Malama is wearing a pair of bright-red athletic shorts, her thighs deeply bronzed under a pellucid Mediterranean sun. She stands a few yards away from the crumbling remains of a towering white column, the sole surviving detail of an ancient temple. Staring with her head tilted coquettishly and her lips shaped into a bawdy smirk, she seems to be asking: *Isn't that a phallic symbol looming overhead?* And indeed, when I pointed this out, she said it was precisely what she'd been thinking of when the picture was snapped.

"My cousin Demetrius had no idea why I'd insisted upon stopping there," she laughed, "but that's exactly why I chose that spot!" Taking another sip of ouzo, she added: "But if she knew, she wouldn't have been surprised. I'd already told her about the first time that I ever had an orgasm."

"How old were you?"

"I was still in high school. When I was an adolescent I'd held hands with boys, but this was the first time that I'd experienced anything sexual. I was with a handsome Italian guy who lived around the corner. One day I saw him riding his bike, and I felt an electric bolt shoot through me. He was really shy; it took him about six months to get the guts to speak with me. But then we started to fool around, by the rocks."

"The rocks?"

"There was an abandoned lot near the railroad tracks, where there were two huge boulders. I'd lie down on the rocks, and he'd grind into me. I'd feel the hardness of the rock underneath, and, in front, the hardness of his *cock*. What a great sensation! But on that day, we were just standing there. It was the first time I let him put his finger in my panties, and I was soaking wet. I mean, I was *dripping*, but I had *no idea why!* I'd never experienced anything like this before. I remember feeling so embarrassed – '*What's going on? What is it?*' – because I didn't realize what was happening. But since it felt so amazing, I didn't stop him. All of a sudden, just as I was coming, my knees gave out. Since he was holding onto me, we both fell to the ground!

"Later on he confessed that I was his first lover. Oh, my God, I was so *hungry* for him! I felt as if I wanted my skin to be *stuck* to his. Such passion! But you know what's really sad? Years later, we met one last time. He was driving by while I was walking along the street. So he parked and I entered his car. We started to fool around … But, oh, it was *gone!* There was just no *passion*. I was *so* disappointed! It just wasn't the same as it was on the rocks …"

Glancing up at me, she added: "Do you realize that those mischievous eyes of yours change color all the time, depending on your mood?" Her voice shifted into a purring, sensual tone. "And did you know that, after we made love, they turned into a silvery gray? Like a panther's! Maybe that's what you were in a past life …"

Malama's lascivious laughter was so infectious that even Brother Taylor and Sister Evelyn were making goo-goo eyes at her. Although Evelyn had managed to restrain herself, Taylor just couldn't resist Malama's seductive allure.

One day after work she made the mistake of accompanying Taylor to a local bar, for a beer. By now, he was visibly suffering from the torture of his unrequited passion. Thanks to a few stiff drinks, Taylor suddenly gained a speck of courage and asked Malama out on a "date." He even confessed to having a crush on her.

All this came as a complete surprise to Malama, who rarely seemed to comprehend the effect that she produced upon others. At first she didn't know what to say; but, after thanking him graciously for his "compliment," she replied that it was *inappropriate* to date, since they were each working together.

Although we'd managed to conceal our relationship, later on, after several clients had spotted us necking on a subway or holding hands on a side street, rumors began to spread. But since we occupied the same professional rank and never made a show of our affection while at work, there was nothing anyone could do about it. And besides, although Dougherty suspected that we were romantically involved, if the subject of Malama came up he'd always smile his big, toothy grin and look at me with a sparkle of approval in his eye. Soon, everyone except for Taylor considered it to be charming.

The "good brother," I should call him, because Taylor wasn't a bad chap, just a bit muddleheaded because of the way he'd been raised. The poor man had been spiritually crushed by a puritanical upbringing. And what parents in their right minds would encourage their son to become a *priest*?

A few days before he discovered that we were an item,

Taylor requested my assistance in unraveling the meaning of a rather disturbing dream.

"Maybe you can help me analyze it," he sighed, all the while blushing from collarbone to forehead. "Malama said that you have a talent for that sort of thing. Do you think you might find some time?" There seemed to be a sense of urgency behind all this, so at once I agreed.

Seeking some privacy, we retired to one of the building's unoccupied suites on the top floor. In the nineteenth century they'd served as elegant sitting rooms, but now they featured dilapidated furniture and cracked windowpanes that loomed over an empty asphalt courtyard.

After making me promise never to reveal the contents of his dream, Taylor confessed something that truly astonished me. It was the first, last, and only time that I've ever heard of a dream that seemed to be composed entirely of sexual components. For despite the baseless hokum that Freud had so skillfully propagated, dreams that focus primarily on sexuality remain the exception, not the rule. Even the ancient dramatists were well aware that, instead of "repressed sexuality," they more often contain a strangely encoded wisdom that transcends our ordinary level of awareness. But now, Taylor had been graced with this highly erotic vision that featured images verging on the pornographic. Perhaps even Freud would have been perplexed by how "manifest" and "overt" it was – leaving nothing to the unseemly psychoanalytic imagination. Therefore, in the most diplomatic manner that I could muster, I carefully chose my words.

"Brother, as much as you might not like to hear this, being a man of the cloth and all that, there is such a thing as *instinct*. You might think of it as the wisdom of the flesh – God's way of speaking to us directly through the body. And when it's blocked, it doesn't just evaporate. Instead, it's trapped like a tiger in a cage, and it grows more and more menacing. A very unhealthy condition!"

"But what exactly do you mean by *instinct?*" By now, Taylor's cheeks were flushed with a luminous glow of embarrassment.

"Why, it's the same force that, burning bright, draws men and women together! For, without it, why should men bother with women or women bother with men, being such vastly different creatures, after all? But the heat of passion unites us, and we're left to make the most of it. And then children pop out, not because a stork tosses them into a chimney, but because life must go on. For no matter how ridiculous it may be, this silly little drama must be repeated *ad infinitum.*"

Taylor let go one of his throaty, rumbling moans as his hands nervously cradled his oversized forehead. He continued to stammer, mumble, and blush as I silently recalled how, over breakfast one morning, shortly after I'd graduated from St. Anne's, I'd asked my mother if it was true that premarital sex was forbidden by the Church. All at once and completely out of the blue, the absurdity of this unnatural restriction hit me full blast. Perhaps it was one of those fleeting adolescent moments wherein one momentarily becomes a conscious individual. And then, one begins to question each of the ludicrous notions that, previously, one has inherited so unquestioningly. Suddenly I found it hard to believe that such a *human* act could be regarded as *sinful*. Quite the contrary – for wasn't the ecstasy of physical passion, especially when twined with romantic love, one of the Lord's greatest creations?

But my poor, dear mother! Bridget's watery eyes gazed at me with a combination of sadness and disbelief. She was truly shocked that, despite so many endless hours of catechism instruction – or, I should say, *indoctrination* – I'd failed to retain such a fundamental Catholic notion. In one of her rare displays of pique and anger, she dropped her cereal spoon and said, *But how could you possibly go through eight years of Catholic school and not know that? Were you daydreaming the entire time? And think of all the money we spent! Sending you to a private institution and scraping together all those dollar bills – one by one – that your father had to work so hard to earn! Were your ears plugged up with wax?*

And it was true; I *was* daydreaming. But this was also my saving grace. It was as if I'd slipped a condom over my brain to guard against the rubbish they were constantly cramming into our noggins. How fortunate that whenever my interest in a subject waned, I was gone in a flash – immediately dreaming on higher, more fecund ground!

Taylor continued to moan and groan, but at least I'd managed to couch my "analysis" in a diplomatic language. And so, once we finished, he dispiritedly nodded his head and murmured *Thanks!* in that sonorous fashion of his as he exited the room.

Alone again, I recalled a marvelous tale spun by a lyrical Greek novelist named Nikos Kazantzakis. It's a story about a man of the cloth who, like Taylor, is forced to question his religious conviction as a result of encountering a sensual young woman. It's featured in his memoir, *Report to Greco*, which Nikos never finished editing, because he died shortly before its completion. Throughout this chronicle, traveling from one Greek isle to the next, he effortlessly converses with seers, saints, and sages. He also relates a series of profound intellectual voyages as he delves into mind-altering books and works of art. In particular, Nikos is moved by the ramblings of Friedrich Nietzsche, a thinker who influenced so many seekers of Nikos' generation. Whereas I myself prefer to read Nietzsche simply to absorb his mad passion: his exultant, overblown enthusiasm and vituperative contempt. But I never attempt to

grapple with what he's actually driving at in a broader, philosophical sense, since so much of this remains of interest only if
you're a student of philosophy and are obsessively counting
how many Hegels one can balance on the head of a Kantian pin.
But if you scan through a work such as *Ecce Homo*, even if you
read only the chapter headings, Nietzsche is always good for a
few vivifying laughs: *Why I am the greatest philosopher; Why I am
the wisest sage; Why all men are mere shitpiles as compared to
Nietzsche Zarathustra Dionysus*, and so on.

In any case, in the midst of this cerebral adventure, Nikos
relates how, one day, while visiting a remote Greek island, he
encounters a man whose life was turned upside down by the
unexpected presence of a young enchantress. Just as her older
sister is about to give birth to her first child, they call for a
priest. Word goes out as if by telegraphic tom-tom, and then
this naive man of the cloth – who appears to be as square and
clueless as Brother Taylor – arrives at their threshold.

The younger sister – a ravishing, raven haired, comely Greek
goddess – answers the door wearing a peasant blouse. As she
pulls open the heavy wooden portal, the loop of her blouse slips
and falls to her forearm and her pert breast pops out – now
shining in the glorious sunlight. It even wiggles slightly, just
inches from this befuddled man's face. Her budding nipple
appears to stare at him like a Cyclops until she cradles it in her
palm and tucks it back into her garment. Then she silently grabs
him by the wrist and brings him inside, where he delivers his
first baby.

In the days, weeks, and months ahead, this bedeviling breast
continues to haunt him. Shivering in fright, he'd leap from his
bed after a series of so-called nightmares – I mean, obviously, to
me, these would not have been nightmares – of a gargantuan
mammary trailing after him. With each reoccurring *cauchemar* it
grows larger, until finally it's a leviathan breast: attached to

nothing and completely self-sufficient as it tracks behind him like a monstrous snail, minus its shell. At least, that's how I myself imagine it, although Kazantzakis doesn't actually refer to it as a snail. Instead, he describes how this wretched fellow had nowhere to hide, and the poor man even feared that eventually he'd become smothered or enveloped by it, as if by a fleshy amoeba.

Of course, when something "monstrous" comes after you, the first thing to ask yourself is whether this "horrible thing" is actually a neglected aspect of your own being: a vital ingredient that one requires to become whole. Perhaps it's chasing you because it seeks companionship; and the more you avoid it, the more difficult it will be to do what this fellow finally did, and which caused his nightmares to cease. Namely, he sucked on the nipple and then he awoke, refreshed.

Just before Taylor made ready to leave, I casually spoke about this autonomous breast and what had befallen the forlorn priest. But I neglected to comment on it in the same manner that I've utilized here, because sometimes it's best to just lay an egg and let it hatch of its own accord and in its own proper time and place. So I delivered the breast with the same care and concern as the priest had delivered the infant, then I let Taylor mull it over on his own. But I have no idea whether it hatched or if, instead, it grew into a golem or a heavenly *gandharva*, because, shortly afterward, Taylor discovered that I'd been dallying with Malama.

And so, in another one of his bathetic, liquored up confessions, he blubbered to Malama about how he was convinced that I'd told her all about our conversation, and that he was humiliated to realize that his confessor had been cuckolding him all along. Though I'd never uttered a word about it to anyone, he refused to believe it. I even began to wonder if Taylor would be challenging me to a duel, for he seemed to be that far removed from our contemporary era – as if we were just a step away from the sordid machinations of the Inquisition and that the Church continued to reign supreme.

Later that evening, with greater avidity than usual, I lingered over Malama's sumptuous bottom – as if to offer a propitiatory sign of thanks to Dionysus. When she looked over her shoulder and asked, "Just what are you thinking?" I was struck by her melodious lilt, which had helped to plunge Taylor into demon alcohol and, no doubt, Sister Evelyn into guilt-ridden onanism. But I simply replied: "An enormous breast." And I wondered why the nuns of St. Anne's had neglected to inform us that the Lord may just as easily incarnate into the shape of a jiggling bosom as that of an emaciated man dying on a cross. Perhaps this was the ultimate spiritual message lurking behind Kazantzakis' enlightening parable. But I suspect that I've taken certain liberties with his rendering; for it's been years since I first studied this tale, and I can't swear that my account follows the original to a T.

But wait ... I'm scanning it now ... it seems that I've got it all wrong. The priest, or rather the monk – one Father Ignatius – dreams of this breast only once, not repeatedly. And instead of being chased by it, it simply hovers there, as if floating in space. Also, he first encounters the young mother while she's nursing an infant in a doorway; there's nothing about a baby being delivered on an island, or a younger sister answering the door. Instead, after Ignatius glances at her exposed bosom, he upbraids her for nursing a child in public; so she covers her nipple and scurries away. Later on, she returns to his room to offer him a delicious spread of food. Day after day, she thrusts these carefully prepared morsels before him, but the monk refuses to eat a crumb. Then this seductive young woman, who always appears with a scent of laurel oil in her hair, summons the courage to break her silence:

"Why haven't you eaten these last few days, Father Ignatius?"

At first he mutters "Get thee behind me, Satan." Then he explodes: "Go away!" and banishes her from his presence. When she turns to leave, however, he becomes heartbroken, and he loses all control:

"Dashing forward, I seized her by the hair ... I threw her down on the bed.... I grabbed hold of her bodice, tugged at it, and with one motion undid all the buttons of her blouse." Then follows the most intriguing and – for some – disturbing passage:

> For the very first time, I felt God come near me ... with open arms.... how completely my heart opened and let God enter! ... For the first time in my inhuman, cheerless life I understood to what degree ... he loves man, and how very much he must have pitied him in order to have created woman and favored her with such grace that she leads us to paradise along the surest and shortest of roads.

Ignatius spends the night with her, but at daybreak she silently departs. Now he's overcome by tears of "inexpressible sweetness," for "it was Woman, God bless her! who brought the Lord into my room."

How lovely that the author capitalizes both *Woman* and *Lord*. With this subtle gesture, Kazantzakis underscores their equivalence. It's as if he's saying: All the nasty, horrible things that life has in store, but then – as if balancing the scales – the Creator fashions this ultimate counterpoint.

And how does Woman accomplish all this? Simply by offering her tender, soothing touch. Through her charm and grace, the eternal verities promised by all the major world religions become null and void. Instead, in her ephemeral embrace, we are made one with life's miracle.

But – contemptible youth! – I was still a virgin to such revelations.

* * *

When I first met Jeremy van der Clove he was dressed in a tweed suit, a yellow necktie, and wing-tipped leather shoes. A tall, thin, distinguished-looking gentleman, with his high cheekbones, slate-gray eyes, and regal posture he cut an impressive figure. From a distance he resembled a literature professor in an Ivy League college. But up close, you could see that his shoes were scuffed and worn; his suit was tattered and stained; and, most disconcerting of all, his gaze seemed to be oddly vacant.

On my first day at work, Jeremy was lingering in the hall outside the main office, asking for me.

"Mr. Couteau, I presume?" His tone was formal, even highfaluting. When I answered in the affirmative, he continued, "Ah, permit me to introduce myself. I am Jeremy van der Clove, Esquire."

"Pleased to meet you, Jeremy."

"But the pleasure is all *mine*, Mr. Couteau …"

For a moment I imagined that, instead of lingering in a musty corridor, we were at Oxford University seated in a pair of plush leather armchairs, surrounded by mahogany bookcases and preparing to smoke a fine Havana while discussing T. S. Eliot's "The Waste Land." But I also wondered if something more intriguing than Eliot's arid wilderness lay in store.

"Perhaps," he continued, "you might know who it was who once said, 'All men are mad.'" Tilting his head, he calmly stared into my eyes as he completed his opening gambit.

"I'm afraid that I don't, Jeremy."

"Ah. I believe it was Descartes."

"You may be right."

"Yes," he continued, "Mr. *René* Descartes."

Masterful chessman that he was, in one deft gesture Jeremy had staked several positions at once. First, he displayed his impeccable credentials as a philosopher. Second, he questioned not only my own sanity but my role as a counselor whose job it was to categorize another man's mental health. And lastly, he unwittingly hinted at my eventual expatriation to Descartes' homeland: a country rife with its own brand of culturally imposed lunacy.

Not surprisingly, Jeremy quickly became one of my favorite charges.

* * *

Jonah Israel was another client whose tales had deeply captivated me. Besides having fallen into a psychic deluge, Jonah believed that he carried the "fate of the entire Jewish race" on his shoulders.

It gradually occurred to me that Jonah and Jeremy resembled a pair of brothers who had little in common other than the unavoidable bond of belonging to the same "family" of the deranged. But while Jeremy was obsessed with maintaining the lofty bearing of a lecture hall master and always took care to match his necktie with his shirt, Jonah never bothered to coordinate the disparate items of clothing that he'd selected from Angelica's donation cart. A red-checkered tie would adorn a green pinstriped shirt, and the ensemble might then be completed with a pair of ankle-high construction boots that were separated from his trouser cuffs by five or six inches, since the pants were several sizes too small.

On any given day, one might find Jeremy meandering through the asylum and pontificating to no one in particular about the relationship between Egyptian cosmology and quantum physics, repeatedly emphasizing that the essence of the god *Aton* is reflected in the structure of the *atom*. Meanwhile, Jonah – slack-jawed and wide-eyed as if freshly traumatized – would remain seated on a rickety chair for hours on end, entranced by a cacophony of inner voices. Like the main chord sung to lead the orchestral improvisation hovering beneath, the oedipal intrigues that were enacted in the figments of Jonah's fluid imagination remained his primary leitmotif. This was augmented by decades of Freudian brainwashing, which had been foisted upon him while he was incarcerated in the state mental health system.

Although Jonah was fascinated by the demons unleashed by his schizophrenia – contemplating his symptoms with an attitude that approached religious awe – Jeremy refused to believe that he was suffering from any such illness. Instead, he was convinced that the label *schizophrenia* was merely a ruse through which he was unjustly imprisoned, adding that the Queen of England – the "ruler of the Anglo-American Empire" – owed him at least $895,321.37 in compensation for all those years spent in enforced labor. How else to account for the vapid "therapy groups" that the social workers had insisted he attend without paying him a red cent for his precious time? Rather than adopting the label "mental patient," Jeremy referred to himself as a *philosopher in exile*; and the return-address stickers that he ordered from a local printing shop bore titles such as *Knight of Cleves*, *King of New Year's Island*, and *Emperor of the World Almanac*. Jonah, on the other hand, was not only convinced of his own madness; he reveled in it. He never tired of informing me that Freud had been enraptured by every detail of Jonah's "billion-year" self-analysis:

"Freud listened to the analysis for a million years. He wouldn't eat, he wouldn't sleep. Instead, he'd sit with my father by the television, and he'd listen to the analysis. He didn't want to miss one *bit* of it! My first doctor, Leon Leiben, also listened to the analysis. He wouldn't eat; he wouldn't sleep; he wouldn't anything. Many doctors listened to the analysis with Freud. They wouldn't eat; they wouldn't sleep ..."

He'd nervously glance at me while relating these tales, and in his watery blue eyes I could detect a haunting glimmer of despair as well as a flickering scintilla of pride. On sunny days I'd encourage him to sit beside me in the courtyard at a rusty picnic table, where I'd commune not only with Jonah but also with his auditory hallucinations. I'd ask him to pose certain questions to these "voices," then I'd await their reply. Though it was impossible to fully comprehend such occult symbolism, the fact that I listened so intently seemed to imbue Jonah with a sense of importance – something he was otherwise sorely lacking. As a result, eventually his appearance began to change, in that he shaved more frequently and dressed more carefully. He also grew energized, as if awakening from a narcoleptic slumber, and he'd seek me out as I wandered like a flâneur through the lugubrious corridors.

Jeremy also flourished as a result of receiving so much attention, and he acted as if, at long last, he was gaining belated recognition for his philosophical ingenuity. Soon he made certain cryptic promises about eventually showing me the *manuscript*: a treasure that he'd plucked from this "most heinous and unfortunate of affairs." Titled "Love, Lithium, and the Loot of Lima," this handwritten tract was replete with mind-bending neologisms and featured several poignant aphorisms:

> We might look on ourselves not so much as the
> sons and daughters of God when we believe in

God, nor as domestic servants of God, but rather
as the responsible (or irresponsible) agents of God.
The Creators.

I felt drawn to both Jeremy and Jonah through a strong
current of empathy. Perhaps it was the result of my youthful
naivete, but knowing that I could change their lives, even in
some small way, served to endow my own life with greater
meaning and purpose. As a young man who aspired to leave a
mark on this rotten vale of tears, this seemed to be as good a
reason as any to extend a helping hand. But I was also drawn to
the challenge of surveying the unique patterns of madness that
had shaped them: to unraveling the mysterious series of events
that had shattered their souls and entangled them in such a
reticulate web, with its stubborn strands of delusion, derangement, and hallucination.

*　*　*

When Miriam Ravinovitch wasn't following Malama
through the corridors, she'd spend many long hours applying
her makeup and carefully dressing while expecting an "important guest": her beloved sister, Nancy, who was supposedly on
her way over for a visit. Miriam would stare expectantly out a
window or linger at the entrance to the lobby, awaiting a car
that never arrived. For it was all just a dipsy-doodle delusion: a
pernicious hope as evil as the plagues driven from Pandora's
malignly glinting box.

But this wispy, nebulous daydream was also the one thing
that kept Miriam afloat. I advised Malama to never puncture
her illusions; for, once Miriam's hope had been vanquished, it
might be replaced by something far more debilitating. Without
it, she had nothing; and, upon realizing this, she might be

scattered to the four winds – or land headfirst upon the moon.

Malama was also trailed by a beady-eyed client named Santini Ferrara: a former racecar driver who, unbeknownst to Malama, was obsessed with the sight of her lithe young form. He finally cornered her in a suite one day and exclaimed: "I can't stand it anymore! I want to perform *cunnilingus* on you!"

"But what's *that?*" Malama asked, having never heard the term before. To which Santini replied:

"You sound so young and fertile!"

In order to escape, Malama employed a trick that she'd learned from our crafty resident nurse. Turning her back on Santini, she altered her tone and shouted: "Santini! This is your new voice! I command you to go to your room!" Taken aback by this mysterious outburst, Santini was convinced that he was now under the spell of a new dybbuk, so he paused just long enough to allow Malama to slip away.

* * *

On my way to lunch one day, I spotted Dougherty lingering in the lobby beside one of my clients: a shy, introverted African American named Sam Frazier. Dressed in a somber gray suit jacket and donning horn-rimmed glasses, Sam could easily have been mistaken for a scholar of jazz. But now, in a florid state of psychosis, he was raving about the image of a pyramid engraved with an eye that adorns the back of a dollar bill. And his own eyes were blazing like a pair of incandescent coals as he wildly gesticulated with an opened wallet in his hand.

I took a step forward to approach him, but Dougherty shot his arm out, held it across my chest, and warned: "Be careful; he might get violent." In response, Sam bolted out the front door. Without pausing to consider what I was doing, I ran after him.

Almost getting sideswiped as I crisscrossed through roaring

traffic, I followed Sam up a side street, where he finally ran out of steam. Positioning himself behind a parked car, he eyed me warily. Huffing and puffing, he was trying to catch his breath as I attempted to reason with him. I was especially concerned about what might happen if he had a run in with the local police.

"Don't worry," he said, "I'll return to the Whitman. But first, I have to finish talking to the magic eye." Then he bolted away, disappearing round the corner.

What made our encounter even trickier was that I knew very little about Sam's background. Besides being one of my more reticent clients, his dossier was as opaque as a polished slab of Egyptian granite, and the hieroglyphs etched upon his records represented nothing more than the usual psychiatric mumbo-jumbo. All the typical psycho-babble, but lacking those more meaningful anecdotes that might help one to piece together the tragedy that had once befallen him.

Until this very moment, Sam had remained so stable that I was assigned to meet with him only once per month. Since he was a classic introvert, I'd respected his privacy and didn't attempt to pry. But now it was as if a doppelganger had erupted upon the scene. I even began to wonder if Sam's puzzling reports had stemmed from his uncanny ability to remain invisible – even when confronted with the most stubbornly probing of headshrinkers.

Although I returned to the lobby empty-handed, Dougherty was delighted by my effort.

"Nice try! Let's see what happens next. Meanwhile, we'll keep our fingers crossed ..."

A few hours later Sam's stomach led him back to the dining hall, where we had a long talk. I did my best to warn him about the effect that such drama might have upon the proprietors of the home. They'd recently hired a particularly vicious director named Abigail Zucca: an aspiring dictator who supervised the patients from behind a glass-enclosed office in the lobby. Zucca possessed the same sort of disheartening glare had animated the otherwise stony expression of Nurse Ratched in Ken Kesey's *One Flew Over the Cuckoo's Nest*. With a snap of her freshly manicured finger, anyone who appeared to be rocking the boat or making life difficult for Zucca's staff could be quickly transferred to one of the notorious wards at Creedmoor Psychiatric Center.

"From now on, Sam, you'll have to keep a low profile and blend into the wallpaper. Otherwise, they're liable to haul you into one of Dante's innermost circles of hell. And then there's little I can do for you, because it's 'Abandon hope all ye who enter here.'"

Sam understood what this meant better than I did, having survived innumerable wastelands where the patients did little else but wander listlessly back and forth along a brightly lit corridor, like hamsters trapped in a plexiglas tube. And if you acted particularly "inappropriate" – a social worker's favorite mantra – you could be punished with shock treatment, which was back in vogue in many psychiatric settings.

Almost as an afterthought, I handed Sam a copy of Ralph Ellison's novel, *Invisible Man*, which I'd recently plucked from a donation box, having planned on rereading it myself. From that point on, Ellison, or rather his protagonist, the Invisible Man, seemed to provide Sam with a basic code of survival. Whenever he'd pass me in the corridor, he'd mutter an enigmatic phrase such as: "Good stuff. *Invisible*, man." Then he'd nod or wink in a conspiratorial fashion that eerily conjured the omniscient Masonic eye.

Sam also made certain hermetic remarks that indicated that he was getting deeper into the text, but they were always camouflaged between innocuous comments about what he'd had for breakfast or the latest weather report. It was as if he were providing me with benign "appropriate" fodder for my case notes while simultaneously keeping me abreast of the more meaningful developments that were unfolding within him.

Since *Invisible Man* chronicles a Black man's life-threatening encounters with racism and how he feels like a walking target that might, at any moment, be turned into a casualty if he utters the wrong word or gestures in an "inappropriate" manner, it was remarkable to observe how Sam's modus operandi was to hush up and withdraw to an even greater extent than was his native inclination. Soon he did so even with me, as if to discreetly inform me that he'd mastered this fine art. I imagined that, in this way, he was helping me to prepare a final series of banal, unprovocative notes:

"Sam said that everything was fine. In the evening, he ate turkey with cranberry sauce and said that he enjoyed his meal." Indeed, in the months ahead, he appeared to grow even more spectral than Ellison's protagonist. He'd carry the novel tucked under his arm, cradled like a Bible from which he might draw a steady stream of inspiration. But to ward off prying eyes – Masonic or otherwise – now it was covered in plain brown wrapping paper. Perhaps "Bible" isn't the right word, however, since Sam also used it as an operating manual to keep the psychiatric hounds at bay. In the protagonist's own words:

> the world is just as concrete, ornery, vile, and sublimely wonderful as before, only now I better understand my relation to it and it to me. I've come a long way from those days when, full of illusion, I lived a public life [...] Hence again I have stayed in my hole, because up above there's an increasing passion to make men conform to a pattern.

* * *

A few weeks later Dougherty applied for a directorship in the newly formed Bronx Psychiatric Shelter. Although he'd asked me to transfer there along with him, the setting was so dismal that I never seriously considered it.

He was eventually replaced by a petite social worker named Holly Moorman. An anxiety-ridden woman with fiery red hair that she wore in pigtails, Holly appeared to be as nervous as a squirrel, and we soon realized that she was out of her depth. Though she feigned friendliness, I sensed that behind her feverous grin there lurked trouble: the sort that usually follows someone who's constantly covering her ass by hauling yours over the coals instead.

Almost from the moment that she arrived, Holly developed a crush on Malama. She even encouraged her to remain an extra half hour during her weekly supervision, all the while salivating over the poor girl with a predatory leer. But whereas Malama was a born diplomat who could easily mask her contempt, whenever I glanced at Holly my eyes glistened like a pair of daggers.

Things finally came to a head one morning when Vickie, our staff nurse, informed me that one of my clients was displaying the symptoms of an impending heart attack. Besides shooting sensations in his arm, he was experiencing sharp chest pains and a shortness of breath. Vickie said that unless I brought Billy to a hospital, there was a good chance that he'd drop dead.

It remained a ticklish situation, however, because she'd already taken Billy to see one of the quacks who was assigned to the Whitman that day: an incompetent lush who would rapidly examine dozens of patients, rushing them in and out so that he could suck up even more of their Medicaid payments. Since the home was owned by those heartless, tight-fisted bastards, hiring a competent physician who would actually improve the care of such lost souls was something that was never considered. Instead, they were ripped off of every cent they possessed.

The charlatan told Vickie not to worry; it was merely the flu. But when I took one look at Billy, I suspected that she was right. Against the doctor's orders, I hailed a cab and rushed Billy to a nearby hospital. Two hours later, a heart attack rippled through his chest like a thunderclap, but they saved him.

Since I was the one who'd violated the doctor's decree, now, thanks to Holly, I was accused of being a renegade. She even contacted her supervisor, one Alice Goldberg, the regional director of Catholic Charities, to file a complaint.

Once I got wind of this, I made some carefully calculated remarks during our staff meeting about what an interesting story this would make for the local newspapers. Since the administrators of Catholic Charities were always fearful of bad publicity, I knew this would make them think twice before attempting to discipline me.

Billy was still recovering at the hospital when his X-rays revealed an extensive collection of teaspoons, coins, and other assorted bric-a-brac that was permanently lodged in his big happy gut. A chronic "swallower," he'd decided there was no safer piggy bank than his own belly, a place that not even the greedy proprietors could crack open, brazen bastards that they were.

* * *

I lasted only nine months at the Whitman Asylum. Oddly enough, when I informed Holly that I was quitting, instead of urging me to leave she almost begged me to remain there. Even during my final afternoon, when I bid farewell to the case managers but pointedly ignored her, she discreetly approached and said: "I think you're making a mistake. I wish you'd reconsider." Perhaps Holly feared a mass exodus because of her lack of leadership, or maybe she was worried about me becoming a loose cannon.

Just before I exited the building Sam stepped forward, stuck out his hand, and said: "I've been waiting for you. I wanted to say good-bye."

"Thank you, Sam." As our eyes met, we regarded each other with a palpable fondness. "And remember, Sam. As the Invisible Man himself says right at the beginning, 'Hibernation is a covert preparation for a more overt action.'"

Smiling affectionately, he squeezed my hand, then slipped back into the shadowy stairwell.

Stepping outside, I glanced at the fluttering scraps of clothing that were still dangling in the branches overhead. It was a mild June afternoon, and the verdant leaves rustled with a gust of wind. The baggy pink bloomers inflated like a balloon, while the hat with the carnation twirled round and round.

Looking over my shoulder at the glass doors, I spotted my reflection staring back at me.

It was as if I'd emerged from a mirror. Now I was outside, looking in.

As I turned to amble away, the colorful images of the asylum drifted through my mind like an evaporating dream.

Beethoveniana Edda Maria

In the mid-1980s the Lower East Side was "the place to be." Mobsters such as Freddie were renting flats to young aspiring designers and entrepreneurs; and art galleries were sprouting up like weeds, featuring talents such as Jean Basquiat, whose work would soon command record prices at Sotheby's. But if you ventured farther east into Alphabet City – toward Avenue B or C – heroin was still being sold on street corners; from zinc countertops in bodegas; and from the basements of abandoned buildings. Many of these crumbling structures resembled the rubble of postwar Germany and consisted of three barely standing walls. Where a fourth wall had vaporized, the interiors were exposed to view, some coated with fading wallpaper from the Thirties or Forties.

"Young up-and-coming professionals" – or *yuppies*, as a recently coined term had it – soon found themselves at odds with Puerto Rican dope dealers, Caucasian skinheads, and wannabe artists and writers who looked down upon the newcomers because they weren't *poètes maudits* and – so went the reasoning – only "damned poets" had a right to remain there, since it was usually the artists who pioneered such wastelands and, in the process, inadvertently made them desirable enough for the other crackers to live there, too.

The neighborhood hosted a variety diners staffed by Polish and Ukrainian émigrés who'd made it their home since the 1930s and who didn't know what to make of these starkly clad waifs with insolent, zombie-like stares; overdone Kohl eyeliner; pierced noses; stockings sliced with razor blades; and black leather boots. The latter attire was all too reminiscent of Hitler's

Nazis – a none-too-distant memory for many of these expats. But they would serve them anyway, despite the meager tips left by such pale, junk-riddled addicts.

In Leshko's diner at the corner of East Seventh and Avenue A, a doughy-faced Ukrainian with a distant regard stood like a sentinel beside a cash register. I never saw him smile, though he effused melancholy rather than anger. He was always garbed in a short-sleeved starched white shirt, and when you paid your bill you couldn't help but notice a number tattooed on his forearm: a souvenir from a Nazi concentration camp.

Veselka's diner, located on the corner of East Ninth and Second Avenue, was another popular Ukrainian eatery where I'd often stop for pierogies and cabbage soup – although I always passed on the jellied pigs' feet – and where the poet Allen Ginsberg had been wolfing down such fare for decades. Allen lived in a tenement on East Twelfth and Avenue A. Built in 1905, this unassuming structure had sheltered some of the women who perished in the Triangle Shirtwaist Factory Fire of 1911. In the days ahead, while visiting my schizophrenic clients who were scattered throughout Alphabet City in their roach-infested hovels, I'd occasionally pass Allen walking along a side street, each of us communing, in such different ways, with our great gray father, Walt Whitman.

Browsing through the help-wanted ads one day, I noticed a listing for a case manager position at a community-residence program just a few blocks east of my flat. A nonprofit agency providing advocacy and counseling for the homeless mentally ill, it operated out of a storefront on the corner of East Fourth and Avenue A. The organization was called Continual Access, and it boasted a reputation for innovation. Following several weeks of unemployment and not finding anything else, I decided to give them a call.

When I arrived for my interview, I was introduced to a short pudgy man with a florid complexion whose chestnut eyes seemed to be far too large for his tiny head.

Stanley's glance darted across my résumé, then he paused to ask about my construction job. When I casually mentioned that I'd worked on Susan Sarandon's penthouse, he seemed to be far more intrigued by my experience as a common laborer than by my work as a case manager at the Whitman.

I soon noticed that whenever I attempted to answer one of his questions he'd grow fidgety, bouncing his knee up and down as if he were still ten years old and his mother had just announced that he couldn't go out to play until he finished washing the dishes. But now, he calmly absorbed my words with rapt attention as I elaborated upon my various interactions with the famous Hollywood movie star and my role in assisting the carpenters who constructed her West Village pleasure palace. Since he was so curious about all this, I decided to make it sound as grand as possible.

With a nervous tick rippling across his facade, he finally asked about my work as a case manager. "I see that you taught *Hamlet* to a group of schizophrenics at the Whitman." He seemed to be equally perplexed and intrigued. "What was *that* like?" Fortunately, I'd prepared an answer in advance.

"We each had to design two groups for the patients. I taught painting to one group and literature to the other. One day, after I explained that certain lines from the bard's dramas – such as 'To be or not to be' – had found their way into our everyday speech, I asked if they recognized any other familiar lines from Shakespeare. My client Jonah raised his hand and, reading from the text, replied: 'Wretched queen, *adieu!*' Of course, it was the furthest thing from a common expression, but I complimented him on his 'discovery' anyway, since I'd never want to find fault with any of them. And really, what did it matter, except that they enjoy themselves and feel worthy of something?" I added that, with schizophrenia, the ego structure is so terribly fractured that even the slightest critique can trigger a psychotic episode.

"Perhaps as compensation to such psychological deflation," I continued, "the schizophrenic psyche produces delusions of grandeur, buttressing the damaged personality with a belief that, for example, one possesses messianic powers. So instead of being a tortured 'mental patient,' now one can assume a more illustrious role: as a Christ, a Mohammed, or a modern-day Queen Elizabeth. Anything with which to prop up a deeply ruptured sense of self. It's as if the personality has been swallowed whole, but then replaced by a more grandiose incarnation, one radiating power and prestige. It's crucial to understand this," I concluded, "but such a perspective often remains anathema to contemporary psychiatry."

Stanley nodded his head while his eyes glazed over. Although my words seemed to have impressed him, he appeared to have little or no idea of what I was talking about.

The following week I was interviewed by his new program director, Priscilla. We were seated at a round table at the back of the office, in a large open space with a staircase that led to a basement, which Stanley had remodeled. I soon learned that he'd been intrigued by my construction job because, although he ran a mental health housing agency, his real love was wielding power tools and renovating buildings.

Priscilla was a vivacious Polish blonde a few years my senior who carried herself like a polished diplomat. She appeared to be sincere about wanting to help those in need, but otherwise she was difficult to read. Her eyebrows darted up and down as she spoke, as if highlighting certain words. With her hair pulled back into bun and her penetrating, inquisitive gaze, she could easily have played the role of a Victorian schoolmarm. But her intelligence and drive also lent her a certain charm.

As she methodically grilled me, I fielded her questions while Stanley nervously grinned, fidgeted with his pencil, and bounced his knee. All the while his eyes shifted from me, to the résumé, then back to Priscilla, whom he treated deferentially even though she was his subordinate.

A few days later he called and asked if I could begin the following Monday.

* * *

As I interacted with various so-called mental health professionals, I gradually realized that the further up the professional ladder one travels the more the garrulous psychobabble increases – along with the pay and power. The higher one ascended, the crazier they seemed to be, with the shrinks being the most insane as well as the most likely to inflict serious harm. The Austrian novelist Thomas Bernhard isn't clowning around when, in *Wittgenstein's Nephew*, he laments the fact that such characters "employ the most inhuman, murderous, and deadly methods" and that "of all medical practitioners, psychiatrists are the most incompetent, having a closer affinity to the sex killer than to their science."

Just as I'd learned to do at the Whitman, whenever I was forced to deal with such *sickiatrists* I secretly played games with their heads. If a client complained about being overmedicated, I'd call his psychiatrist and, assuming the most fawning, obsequious tone, say: "I'm so sorry to bother you, doctor. I wouldn't have called if it wasn't such a pressing, urgent matter. But our client seems to be exhibiting some rather peculiar symptoms today." It was an outright lie, but it was the only way to get their attention. With a copy of *Physician's Desk Reference* in hand,

I'd place my finger upon a list of contraindications for the pre-scribed medication and recite every major symptom of impend-ing heart attack, seizure, or stroke: "Jaundiced pallor, shaking hands, heart palpitations, dry mouth, green tongue ..."

"Send him right over!"

Although the patient would be lacking such symptoms when he arrived at the doctor's office, the shrink would usually be too busy to second-guess what had no doubt transpired just hours before, and he'd usually lower the dosage.

Negotiating with such professional lunatics was relatively simple, for they approached everything as if they were mechan-ics who harbored no interest in the "study of the soul" – as the word *psychology* implies. But it remained a bit more difficult to deal with psychotherapists, and especially with Freudian "ana-lysts" who, at that time, were still thriving in the field despite being indoctrinated with such obsolete, antiquated notions.

I was even forced to listen to one psychoanalyst rave about how our client William – a manic-depressive who was also a master violinist – was merely sublimating his masturbation in-stinct because, surely, the movement of a bow across a string imitates the motion of wanking. I was immediately struck by how this little anecdote encapsulates all the tomfoolery of Freud and his so-called object relations, with its attempt to reduce the greatest mystery of life – art itself – to an utter banality. But of course, to the analyst himself, I simply replied: "What a *fascinat-ing* theory!" – meanwhile making a note to find William another therapist as soon as possible.

When I was promoted to assistant program director, I made it a long-term goal to yank each of our clients out of the jaws of such bumblers and to search for more down-to-earth therapists, especially ones that didn't subscribe to any particular school of thought. But this remained a daunting task because down-to-earth therapists so rarely exist, unless one considers gardeners to be well-grounded healers. But since gardeners don't accept Medicaid, we were forced to regard this as a Platonic ideal.

I also attempted to rescue our clients from the clenches of those fruitless, time-consuming "day treatment" programs: concentration camps of the soul, where they were encouraged to reveal their most intimate secrets while attending "group encounter sessions" – something akin to Maoist thought reform – and to study the "art" of basket-weaving or finger-painting. Instead of pursuing such infantile, kindergarten-like activities, I urged them to seek volunteer work in ordinary settings such as libraries. And then, afterward, we would try to arrange for some serious job training.

To his credit, since Stanley was a pragmatist, he immediately saw the point in all this, and he never stood in the way of such developments. Many of our clients were younger than those at the Whitman and hadn't suffered as many hospitalizations, so their prognosis was somewhat better, especially if they could be helped in a timely fashion. And it was primarily for this reason that I wanted to work there.

The following year, when I managed to get a few of our clients off medication and to "graduate" them from the program into normal jobs and somewhat normal lives, Stanley was ecstatic. But I knew that we were up against overwhelming odds, because all too often the social workers, therapists, and psychiatrists in the other treatment programs didn't really want the patients to become independent. Instead, they preferred to keep them right there, in place. For if a client left a day treatment facility, the shrinks and social workers could no longer milk them of their Social Security benefits. It was all about the money … as if, one day, there might be a shortage of mental patients! Thus, the cards were stacked against them, since there were just a handful of advocates who dared to knock down those cards and scatter them to the wind.

* * *

Back then the Lower East Side hosted an influx of upper-class South American immigrants. Since I rarely cooked at home and instead took advantage of the diverse international cuisine that was available within a five-block radius, I'd frequently encounter these well-educated, cultured travelers at the local bars and restaurants.

It was around this time that I met Vanessa, a slender Uruguayan waitress who worked in a café on East Thirteenth Street. As she hovered beside my table, I was mesmerized by her gentle manner and tender, light-green eyes. Since the place was nearly empty, Vanessa had some extra time on her hands and we made small talk. The daughter of a diplomat, she said that her real vocation was acting, and that she was currently starring in a play that would soon make its debut at one of the local theaters.

I attended her performance the following weekend, then invited her to a candlelit dinner at an Italian restaurant around the corner. We were relaxing over dessert when I asked, "So, what's the main difference between North and South American women?"

Smiling coquettishly, she replied: "If there is a difference, it's that although we can appear to be just as aggressive as women from the States, we behave this way simply as a means of *testing our man*, not out of a desire to usurp his role. Therefore, if you're interested in seducing me, you must first imagine a bullfight in which I am the bull. I may rush you, attack you, or even act as if I want to kill you. But in fact, I'm simply testing you. And waiting for you to …" Pausing to sip her wine, she tilted her head and carefully considered her words.

"Waiting?"

Her lips curled into a seductive smile. "Waiting for you to *master* me."

"But if the man fails to master you, you simply toss him out of the ring, then await the next challenger."

"Precisely!"

At this we clicked our glasses, and, over flickering candlelight, toasted to her metaphorical corrida.

Vanessa was imprinted with many of the more conventional notions that upper-class Uruguayans so often bring to bear, such as dressing conservatively, speaking with a certain formality, and adhering to an exacting etiquette. Thus, in many ways she remained rather traditional, especially regarding what she expected from a partner. For all these reasons, I suspected that our time together would be short-lived; for I was left with the choice of either censoring myself or aggravating her should I choose to truly speak my mind. But I postponed this inevitably for as long as possible.

When we made love, Vanessa's throaty moans would combine with an ethereal cooing, which streamed from her lips like a soulful *bel canto* emitting a pervasive *vibrato*. It was all I could do to hold on, hold back, and wait until she was teetering on the brink. Then she trembled like jelly and gripped me so tightly that I was afraid my back would snap. But in this way, she unveiled a side of herself that I regarded as the true Vanessa, uninhibited by any formal persona.

A few weeks later she invited me to an event hosted at the Uruguayan Consulate General in Midtown Manhattan. Several opera singers were scheduled to perform arias, she said, accompanied by a virtuoso *pianista*.

Little did I realize that our rupture would arrive as a result of meeting this talented musician, a far less conventional woman from Argentina who'd been christened with the delightful name of Edda Maria. I'd later learn that although Edda hailed from Buenos Aires, she was the daughter of Italians and, as a child, had studied under the highly esteemed master, Vicente Scaramuzza. At the age of eighteen Edda won a scholarship to study classical music in Paris, where she would remain for the next twenty years. Then she decided to cross the Atlantic again, to study conducting at the Julliard School of Music in Manhattan.

Until this particular evening I was utterly lacking in any appreciation of operatic music. But now, I found myself seated in the midst of a small group of aficionados as one singer after another utilized her entire body as a powerful instrument, filling the room with an intense, reverberating resonance that riveted through my flesh.

Edda sat with her back to me at a nearby grand piano. Thick streams of raven-black hair cascaded to her waist, and her scarlet dress shaped her bottom into an enormous red pear. Following her performance, she was quickly surrounded by a half dozen male admirers, who ardently buzzed round. When she turned her head, I was impressed by her almond-shaped eyes, her fluted nose, her wide nostrils, and her full sensual lips, which puckered into playful expressions of irony.

Moments later, Vanessa, along with Edda's admirers, disappeared in order to retrieve some drinks. So I made a beeline for Edda and introduced myself:

"Where do you hail from, Edda? Your features could just as easily be South American or Italian. Yet your English is graced with a slight French accent."

Looking me up and down, she replied, "Do you really want to know? I'm warning you, it's a very rich, complicated itinerary!" Raising an eyebrow, her expression communicated a playful naughtiness. "My surname, my appearance, my musical character all come from Sicilia. But I have several other roots:

originally in Piemonte, Liguria, Euskadi, and Aquitaine, and finishing up in that Argentinean land where I happen to be born. Now, is your curiosity satisfied? A long way, isn't it? The combination of Sicilia and Piemonte is more present in me than the others, but it's equally meaningful, this Argentinean-French acquired affinity. But *don't* try to figure me out just by knowing all that – you *never* will!"

There was something provocative as well as audacious in her tone, as if she were saying: "Young man, as you can see, you have plenty of competition here, so let's not waste our time. You must prove yourself worthy; so, what have you got? Something sophisticated enough to draw my interest – or not?"

Yet there was nothing pretentious about Edda. She wasn't *pretending* to be brilliant and refined; she really *was* all that, and more. Besides, her challenge was wrapped in a fine silk of playful seduction. It was all a game to her: one enacted on her own terms, but at least she was inviting me to participate.

"And you?" she asked with the hint of a smile curling at the corners of her lips. "What exactly do you do with your life?"

"Actually, Edda, I'm a poet."

Suddenly she no longer appeared distracted as her eyes honed in on me with an expression of budding interest. "Oh, really? And *what* do you write poems about?"

Time was running out; it was my last chance to impress her. In just a moment Vanessa and her companions would return, and once again Edda would be swept away by her admirers.

"I write about women who wear dresses that shape their bottoms into a voluptuous red pear."

Her lips stretched into a gleeful grin. "Ah, so you are a *specialist* then! *Well!* You should have seen my ass ten years ago. Mother always said *that* was the side I should show."

"You talk like a Charles Bukowski poem!"

"Bukowski? Never heard of him ..."

Out of the corner of my eye I saw that Vanessa was approaching, so I discreetly handed Edda my card. "I'd like to invite you for a coffee. Please, give me your number."

With the mention of the word *coffee*, her dark-sienna eyes dilated – as if I had chanted a magical incantation.

"What a coincidence," she murmured, again raising her eyebrow. "I see by your card that we live in the same neighborhood. I rent an apartment on East Ninth Street."

I memorized her number and promised to call the following day. The moment I stepped away, once again she was surrounded by a gaggle of fans. The Latin boys, arriving with drinks in hand, were now buzzing round the hive.

"Ah," chirped Vanessa, "I see you've become acquainted with our famous *pianista*. What were you two chatting about?"

"I was complimenting Edda on her exquisite form."

"Impeccable. You know, she was a child prodigy."

"And her delivery! So impassioned. I must say, it left me feeling rather libidinous."

"*Libidinous?* But I'm not familiar with this term. What, exactly, does it mean?"

"Let's see ... how do you say it in Spanish? Ah, yes – *romántico.*"

"Opera makes you feel romantic? I just *knew* you were a gentleman. Come, let's go back to my place. We'll have a nice candlelit dinner. I, too, am feeling wonderfully libidinous!"

My poor Vanessa! The following week, she confronted me with a dire revelation: She'd just attended some swank dinner affair, a Uruguayan-American exchange of some sort, and had related something to the assembled guests that had stopped the conversation dead in its tracks. Now, bearing a stern expression, she blurted out:

"Libidinous does *not* mean romantic!"

"What are you talking about? Of course it does."

"No. I was so proud to tell everyone that I had such a *nice* American boyfriend who made me feel *libidinous*. But then, my friends took me aside and explained ..."

"Well then, their English language skills leave much to be desired. The nuances must escape them."

"No. You are a *very bad man* ..."

And yet, I could still detect a certain sparkle in her eye.

Having grown up in a house equipped with a half dozen pianos and a father who was himself an accomplished pianist, Edda had been raised by the same sort of classically trained, sophisticated family as Vanessa, but she remained far more open to contemporary forms of expression as well as to the eccentricities of artists. However, as a devout follower of Beethoven, she knew almost nothing about popular music. And so, as if conducting an experiment, I decided to play some selections from my old record collection, just to witness her response.

Convulsing into laughter, she almost fell off my couch as we listened to a screeching Janis Joplin moan an off-key version of Erma Franklin's rhythm-and-blues classic, "Piece of My Heart." But moments later, while absorbing some Jimi Hendrix, she grew reflective. Then she turned to me and remarked: "*Sophistication.*" Coming from Edda, this was quite a compliment.

I never dared to mention that the only highbrow music that I'd ever absorbed as a child had blared from a television speaker instead of a record player. I'd been exposed to everything from the blues of Ma Rainey to Beethoven's Ninth Symphony via the *Bugs Bunny* cartoons that we'd listened to as children, which often utilized such classics as musical scores.

When we first met Edda was forty-two years old, while I

was only twenty-eight. But I never doubted that the instruction that I might gain from this refined older woman was exactly what was called for, especially since she possessed such a rich cultural background.

Edda's more serious side might emerge at any moment, whether she was mentoring me about the genius of Beethoven or about how to shop for espresso. At that time America's relationship to the coffee bean was undergoing a transformation; and the bitter slop that was served in Manhattan diners was now being regarded as a poor substitute for the cappuccino brewed by the old Italian cafés in the Lower East Side. There were even a few shops where a variety of coffee beans could be scooped from creaking wooden barrels.

When we entered one such establishment, Edda's eyes narrowed and her expression grew intense. With the same elegant fingers that had teased the mysteries of classical composition, she carefully selected a bean and inspected it as if searching for a flaw in a diamond. Then she tossed it into her mouth, gnashed it into a pulp, and whirled her tongue round, as if deliberating the merits of a fine wine.

"After you crush it," she said, "you can taste how it will brew."

Back at her flat, she boiled water in a small sauce pan. "Beethoven was also devoted to this divine elixir," she smiled. "His breakfast consisted of nothing else. For each cup, he counted exactly sixty beans, a dose that he considered optimum."

Fastidiously scattering the grinds over the bubbling water, Edda extinguished the flame and let the concoction simmer. Once it grew placid, she sprinkled a large spoon of ice water across the steaming surface.

"This is the difficult part. But if you do it just right, the icy droplets will bring down the grinds."

And indeed, when she poured it into our mugs, the java was nearly free of sediment.

* * *

One day I noticed some newspaper articles scattered across her desk. They bore headlines such as *Beethoveniana Edda Maria* and *Una pianista argentina y su triunfo en Europa.* (An Argentinean pianist and her triumph in Europe.) They were clipped from German, Argentinian, French, and English papers.

"Edda, I didn't realize you were world famous."

Regarding me with an annoyed expression, she replied: "But what do you know about me? You know *nothing*." Then, with a softer tone: "Not really *world* famous. Only famous through Occidental Europe, and Latin America."

She was in the midst of preparing for a trip to Buenos Aires, she said, to visit her arthritic mother. When I called the following evening to invite her to my place, she hesitated for a moment but then declined.

"I'm still packing. Besides," she added with a rare display of affection, "it's good that you don't kiss me too much. Otherwise, I might miss you." But she followed this remark with a delightful demand:

"Monsieur Couteau, I expect at least one poem from you for each day that I'm gone."

A few days after she arrived in Argentina I decided to surprise Edda with a phone call. When she heard my voice, she shouted my name in excitement. Once again, I'd caught her off guard.

"What are you doing right now?"

"What else, but writing poems about you? How was your trip?"

"I was sad on Sunday, waiting for hours alone at the airport."

"Edda, the whole city was sad. New York had dropped an octave when you boarded your plane for Buenos Aires."

Just as I'd promised, I'd composed at least one poem for each day that she was away. In the evening, I'd travel to the all-night post office on West 33rd Street, to mail her the results. The next time I phoned, Edda laughed and said: "I was having breakfast one morning, when my mother stepped into the kitchen and noticed all the poems and envelopes scattered across the table. Incredulous, she asked: 'But at your age, men still do this sort of thing for you?'"

Upon hearing this I wondered if Edda's urbane manner of speech – of turning phrases so artfully, of concocting such witty replies – had been directly inherited from this sage matriarch.

> Edda is good to me:
> even in her demands
> I can find
> a comfortable niche
> for my soul.
> She wants thirty poems
> when she returns,
> just so she'll know
> I gave her thought
> at least once a day
> all through the month
> while she was gone.

In the weeks ahead I continued to edit the poems, hoping to transform Edda's witty repartee into something worthy of publication. I finally managed to place two of them in an obscure poetry magazine, Z *Miscellaneous*, and I eventually managed to publish the others in a variety of literary journals.

As I searched for my authentic voice, I soon came to realize that the Edda poems contained a crucial cipher, as did poetry itself. For I was convinced that if I struggled first with this most condensed and difficult-to-master medium, then the secret to unlocking each of the other literary forms might follow. But more importantly, Edda's heartfelt words had unleashed something essential in me: a tenderness, yet one without mawkish sentimentality.

This essential ingredient allowed me to overcome the limits of my previous efforts, which tended to be overly cerebral. At their best, the poems combined the insight of a mature, mentoring lover with the joy and laughter of youth. It was a balance that I'd capture momentarily but then lose again; for, without Edda seated beside me and providing such elemental inspiration, I was at a loss over how to incarnate it all by myself.

Thus I learned that the writer and the fruit of his labor is never the product of a vacuum. Edda – or the voice that spoke through her – served as an intercessor that would deliver me to my own voice; for Edda also taught me how to *listen*.

* * *

Once she returned from her trip, we celebrated with a good bottle of Médoc. Wine glasses in hand, we were lingering on my fire escape under a blood-red sunset when, as if entranced, she suddenly began to speak about the beauty of Venice, Florence, and Rome. Edda knew Venice rather well, having lived there for a year, in a *pensione*. An American widow had occupied a suite directly below her, she said, and one day this lady fell into a state of panic, because her plumbing had sprung a leak.

"She was wading through her room with water up to her knees and screaming bloody murder," Edda laughed. "Hours later, when the proprietor arrived, he addressed this panic-stricken woman with a toothy grin and a mellifluous, soothing tone. She flailed her arms about like an octopus," Edda said, "but he simply regarded her as one might an errant, foolish child. 'Signora,' he smiled, 'look outside. The sun is shining. The canal is glittering. In a few years you won't even recall this day, or anything as insignificant as a plumbing leak! It's nothing to get excited about. Here, sit down, relax' – pushing a chair toward her trembling figure – 'and have a glass of wine while I take care of this.'

"'But it's a catastrophe! And my beautiful rugs! They're ruined!'

"The landlord just continued to chuckle while twisting the ends of his mustache. With a thoughtful tone, he added: 'No, Signora. Illness, injury, death – perhaps those are catastrophes. But even then, one can't be certain. For who knows how one thing may lead to another? Even something as dreadful as death may, in a manner that we can never fully comprehend, be as much of a blessing as a curse. But wet carpets? Signora, I can assure you, this is *not* a catastrophe.'"

Edda added that this fellow had certainly earned the right to speak in such a manner. Having lived through Mussolini's Fascist uprising and having lost a wife and a brother to that Nazi grotesquerie, he knew precisely what he was talking about.

"So, you see, *mon cher Couteau*, there's something called a *mentalité*: a way of thinking and being that's different in Europe. And I'm certain that it will be much more to your liking than anything you'll encounter here. For, in some way – and I knew this from the moment we first spoke – you are *not* really an American."

* * *

That fall, Edda was forced to return to Argentina to assist her ailing mother. Seven years later, upon entering a bookshop in Paris one night, my attention was drawn to a woman standing with her back to me about ten feet away. Though I couldn't see her face, I immediately recognized Edda's exquisitely sculpted *bella figura.*

"Edda Maria!"

She turned round, our eyes met, and she regarded me with a confused expression.

"Yes? Do I know you?"

"Have you already forgotten that young man who composed a poem for you each day that you were away?"

"Mon cher Couteau! But how can it be?" Taking a step back, she looked me up and down as her eyebrows remained furrowed. "But did you have plastic surgery? You look *younger*, not older."

"It's from living in Paris," I laughed. "The old rebirth routine."

Twilight was descending across Lutèce as we strolled along the *quai*, absorbing the glittering beauty of the river and confessing our mutual love … for the City of Light.

Priscilla and the Locked Doors

"Something awful has happened at the Whitman." It was Malama, calling from a pay phone a few blocks from the asylum. "Last night, Jonah fell asleep with a lit cigarette. He wasn't hurt, but his roommate, Raymond, wasn't as lucky. After the room caught fire, Raymond died from smoke inhalation. Abigail Zucca was furious, and she discharged Jonah from the home." As if meting out punishment, this veritable Nurse Ratched had sent Jonah to one of the most horrific locked wards at Creedmoor Psychiatric Center. Jonah's case manager at the Whitman had kept Malama informed about all the latest developments, knowing that she'd pass along the information to me.

We were both concerned about Jonah's safety. Besides being unable to defend himself in such a dangerous setting, there was hardly anything for a client to do there except to pace back and forth in a locked corridor. What better way to drive someone to suicide?

After I hung up, Priscilla called me into her office.

"Is everything OK?"

"I just received some bad news about Jonah Israel, my former client at the Whitman. He fell asleep with a lit cigarette, his room caught fire, and his roommate died in the blaze. Now they've shipped him off to Creedmoor, where I doubt that he'll survive."

Priscilla shook her head and frowned. "If you'd like, I can take you to meet the director there. I know all the bigwigs at Creedmoor. Maybe we can figure out a way of helping your client."

The following afternoon we drove out to Queens. A nurse at the hospital led us into a hallway that ended in a cul-de-sac where we faced a stainless steel door. A small glass pane was embedded in the center, as thick as bulletproof glass and reinforced by steel mesh. After we were buzzed inside, an attendant checked to make sure that the door had automatically locked behind us. Then we were escorted past a dozen patients shuffling back and forth in a narrow passageway. Truly a lost, despairing lot, they reminded me of the caged beasts that had once paced the cramped cubicles of the old Central Park Zoo.

We were brought into a plush office at the end of the hall and instructed to wait there, for the director. Unlike the rest of the ward, it was nicely furnished, like an isolated oasis, with curtained windows overlooking a concrete yard.

Before we could even catch our breath, a wiry young man with a mop-top of coarse black hair appeared at the threshold and stared at me. Our eyes locked, and he angrily shouted, "What are you looking at? When I get my hands on you, I'll break your face!" Mistaking me for a new patient – one who would soon be tested by his crew – he added that he'd fracture my limbs if I uttered a word to the director. Just as suddenly, he spun round and vanished.

A few minutes later a tall, thin, steely-eyed woman entered the room. She went right into a spiel about what a safe place it was and how we shouldn't be concerned for Jonah's welfare. In response, Priscilla broke out laughing, then addressed her in a patronizing tone:

"Now, please, Sadie, you know who I am. And not only do I know this isn't a safe ward, but my colleague here was just threatened by one of your patients."

A consummate bureaucrat, Sadie reached right into her bag of tricks. Without a moment's pause, she asked, "Oh, really? And who was that?" When I described the client, she chuckled with a light-hearted trill and replied, "Oh, that's just Johnny Pellerito. And I can assure you, his bark is far worse than his bite. He's absolutely harmless."

"Even if that's true," I replied, "how is someone such as Jonah supposed to know that? *I* certainly felt threatened." Before Sadie could respond, Priscilla, now assuming a somber tone, took the ball and ran with it.

I watched with amusement as they played point and counterpoint. But beyond any particular logic that was tossed back and forth, one thing that remained in our favor was that Priscilla was a big shot in the mental health system. If she wanted to, she could make things difficult for Sadie. And if she really wanted to cause some trouble, she could gather her henchmen at the National Alliance for Mental Health to back her up. Though she rarely visited Creedmoor, when she made an appearance she was listened to intently; for she picked her battles wisely.

We both knew that the last thing a social worker wanted – other than the headache of adverse publicity – was additional work. The simplest way to avoid all this would be to transfer Jonah to a safer setting and to wash their hands of him.

Priscilla leaned back in her chair and acted as if she had all the time in the world to wait for a desired outcome. Parrying and thrusting like a master swordsman, she finally ended her discourse with a simple declaration:

"A twenty-four-hour supervised setting such as this one seems rather excessive and will only exacerbate Jonah's mental illness. His careless manner of smoking is regrettable, but otherwise he remains a highly functioning patient. What about a placement in a more relaxed setting?" In this way, she was providing Sadie with an exit strategy. But Priscilla also made it clear that, if we didn't get what we wanted, there would be a price to pay.

It was with a sigh of relief that I exited the ward and returned to the outside world. "I don't know about you, Priscilla, but I sure didn't like the sound of that door locking behind us."

"I've been in and out of so many locked wards that you'd think I'd be used to it by now. But it always gives me the creeps. Most of all, I feel sorry for those poor people locked away, with no one to even visit them."

As we entered her car she glanced at me with a peculiar expression, as if she was nervous about something. "After all that," she continued, "you must be hungry. There's a fantastic restaurant just around the corner from my place. Would you like to join me?"

An hour later we were seated at a leather booth in a softly lit room. Though she was rarely at a loss for words, Priscilla seemed to be speaking primarily with her eyes now, which burned with an ardent glow.

Though I'd never dared to breach the boundary established by our professional roles, I was certain that something was about to change. Just as we were finishing our dessert, she looked up from her plate and asked: "Would you like to come up to my place for a drink?" As soon as the words were out of her mouth, she blushed. In response, I merely nodded – as if it were a fait accompli.

As we entered her flat and she closed the door behind us, I was amazed to discover an impressive array of locks and bolts, including a steel bar that was secured to the floor on one end and to a door plate on the other.

"Talk about a locked ward – it's like Fort Knox in here!"

Pausing a moment to regard me with a puzzled expression, she replied: "But don't you understand? There are all sorts of *bad men* out there!"

Sliding the last lock into place, she awkwardly turned to face me, then grabbed my hand and pulled me directly toward her bedroom. Without even turning on the light, we ripped off our clothes and ravaged each other.

Later that evening, just before I fell asleep, I turned to her and asked: "So, what led you to invite me here?"

"It excited me to see you advocate for someone like that."

And I thought I'd heard everything! But the more I pondered her reply, the more I realized how well it reflected what she carried in her heart. For Priscilla had always imagined herself to be a Great Mother in a world sadly bereft of nurturing. Certain remarks that she would later drop led me to believe that she, too, had been victimized early in life. Perhaps, only by reaching out to other victims could this unredeemed part of herself be revived, resuscitated, and replenished.

"Actually," she continued, "I fell for you when we first met."

"During my interview? I never would have guessed. You seemed rather cold and distant."

"That was just a facade. I didn't dare to do anything until now."

"But what changed your mind?"

"I've decided to leave the agency. Now, it doesn't matter if anyone finds out, because soon I'll be gone."

I was taken aback by this latest revelation. "But where are you going? Did you land a better job?"

"I've decided to take care of some personal matters."

Sensing her reticence, I remained silent.

In the morning the harsh glimmerings of dawn streaked through a set of Venetian blinds. The glowing bands of light fell upon a stark black-and-white poster above her bed. It depicted a dark silhouette of high-rise apartments dotted with rows of tiny white windows. Written across a foreboding black sky were the words:

HOUSE THE HOMELESS

This was the only "aesthetic" decor in an otherwise unadorned apartment.

After working hard all day and treading in and out of those dour, grimy flats that provided our clients with a basic shelter and tenuous escape from the hospital, I couldn't imagine returning home to an image such as this one. Where were the Fauve-colored Matisse prints that so many women of Priscilla's generation would normally have hanging on such otherwise cheerless walls? Or the playfully composed Klee's? Or the joyful rainbow spectrums of Robert and Sonia Delaunay?

As I soon learned, for Priscilla, art was merely a "distraction" that only the most callous could enjoy without having a guilty conscience. After all, as long as the world was beleaguered with poverty and homelessness, we were obliged to focus on far more urgent matters.

* * *

Our visit to Creedmoor caused quite a commotion back at the Whitman. Holly was now convinced that Malama had tipped me off about Jonah; but since Malama denied it there little that she could do about it.

Still hoping to keep Jonah imprisoned at the hospital, Holly had managed to track down Jonah's one surviving relative, a cousin named Eddie Levin. Eddie was a stock broker who, in his own words, didn't know his ass from his elbow when it came to things such as mental illness. Therefore, at first he didn't know whom to believe, so he simply picked up a phone and called me.

Fortunately, we hit it off right from the start. Perhaps he could sense my sincerity as I elaborated upon Jonah's travails and described how I'd worked so hard to assist him. I also tried to help Eddie understand what a rotten break Jonah had suffered with that damned conflagration, since he'd been doing so well until then.

"You seem to be far more informed about Jonah's life than I am," Eddie said, adding that the last time he'd seen Jonah was during childhood.

"Jonah was dealt a terrible deck of cards," I replied. "His life hasn't been that easy."

"But why did you go so far out on a limb to help a mere stranger?"

I was taken aback by such a question, but I tried to answer it as best I could. "If someone is drowning and you happen to be standing nearby, isn't it your duty as a human being to offer a helping hand?"

Following a thoughtful silence, Eddie said that Holly had tried to convince him that I was suffering from a "countertransference": a pathological obsession over a client. But since Eddie didn't know a transference from a hole in the wall, this remark didn't seem to faze him. I gradually came to realize that he was bowled over by the fact that, instead of someone from Jonah's own family coming to his aid, here I was: an outsider, who had nothing to gain by helping him.

By the end of our talk he said that he'd stand by whatever recommendations I might make for Jonah. "And I won't stand in the way of his transfer out of Creedmoor, if you think that's the best alternative."

So now, with Eddie on our side, there was nothing to stop Sadie from moving Jonah to a more humane setting. With a family member brought into play, and with so much attention bearing on the case, Sadie instructed her assistant to find Jonah a nice, cushy residence that would make everyone at Creedmoor look splendid – as if they were actually doing their job and keeping an eye out for their clients' welfare.

A month later I received a call from a therapist named Larry Lorenzo. At first Larry seemed to be taken aback when I replied, "Yes, this is Mr. Couteau, how can I help you?" Chuckling with a sense of relief, he explained that, until this very moment, he wasn't sure if I really existed: that is, as an actual, sentient creature instead of a schizophrenic hallucination. For, by now, Jonah had incorporated me into his lexicon of semimythical figures who sat beside Freud, listening raptly to Jonah's billion-year self-analysis.

When I grilled Larry about the setting where Jonah had landed, he said that it was top-notch and remarkably difficult to gain admittance into, since the waiting list stretched on for years.

"Someone must have pulled some very heavy strings to obtain his placement so quickly. You must have a hell of a rabbi," he laughed, using the local vernacular for a "powerful contact."

"Yes, indeed," I replied, "Jesus Christ himself."

*   *   *

On our way home from the cinema one night, as Priscilla and I boarded a subway platform I held her hand and gazed into her eyes.

"What is it," I asked. "Didn't you like the movie? What's bothering you?"

"I want to know whether you're *serious* about me."

"After all this time, if you still don't know how much I care about you …"

"I know that, but that's not what I mean." Pausing to catch her breath, she blurted out: "I want to get *married* … and have a baby!"

What is it about women and babies, I wondered. But when I didn't reply, tears began to stream along her cheeks, which appeared even paler under the flickering fluorescent lights.

"I haven't told you why I've decided to leave the agency. It's because it's time for me to raise a family … even if I'm forced to adopt a child. I was hoping that we could do it together. But if you don't want to, then we shouldn't remain a couple."

I was never one to suffer ultimatums, and this was no exception.

"Well, then," I sighed, "it's over."

With a deafening roar, a train rumbled into the tunnel, rattled toward the platform, and screeched to a halt. When the doors opened, Priscilla stepped into a car and glared at me with a wounded expression. She wasn't expecting such a reaction; but now, there was no turning back.

I refused to budge from my spot as an automated bell rang out – *ding dong* – and the doors slid to a close. She continued to stare with a mournful regard as I watched her figure recede into an engulfing darkness.

How easy it is to be swept into a torrent of "love" that seemingly rises of its own accord, until one wonders how a mere human container can hope to serve as its host! But then, how difficult it is to sustain all that. Who was it who said that love is too precious a thing to entrust to lovers?

The next day, Priscilla met with Stanley to break the news that she was leaving. Utterly bewildered, he responded by offering her all sorts of incentives to remain there. But as thickheaded as Stanley could be, even he knew that once

Priscilla had made up her mind it was pointless to protest.

Try as I might, nothing I said would serve to convince her not to leave yet. But in retrospect, she probably didn't have a choice, as she just couldn't stand to be reminded that our love had perished.

The following afternoon Stanley approached my desk with a boyish grin.

"How would you like to take over as program director?"

I knew that I had no choice but to accept. The chances of Priscilla being replaced by a competent – or even sane – social worker were far too slim to consider. And the raise in salary would help to finance my first trip to France, just a few months before my thirtieth birthday.

Raped and Kidnapped

It's a brisk morning in May during my first day in Paris. I'm wandering through the ancient streets, searching for the apartment of a retired sculptor named Bernardo, the father of a friend from university, who's agreed to put me up for the next two weeks.

After I unpack, he treats me to a lunch of rice and beans, served in a handmade ceramic bowl. Three of his bronze figurines are displayed on a table, and I compliment him on their exquisite form.

A Colombian expatriate with bushy eyebrows and a dusky complexion, Bernardo's heavily lidded coal-black eyes often appear to be darkly brooding. Seated cross-legged on a couch, he looks up from his rice bowl and stares at me. "In a little while," he announces with a sententious tone, "after you've rested from your trip, we'll take a tour of the most beautiful city in the world."

In the early evening we promenade on rue du Temple, which runs from Bernardo's flat near Place de la République all the way south, toward Notre-Dame. Short, squat, pigeon-toed, he waddles along unhurriedly. His love of France is unconditional, and he waxes on, evangelical, about all things *parisien*.

As we amble upon the magnificent lanes – more striking than anything I'd imagined – I'm forced to listen to his "computer theory": a hyperrational monologue about how everything in life is "programmed." Yet with each passing step, the suprarational wonder of Paris seems to mock every phrase that rolls from his lips.

Although Bernardo means well, he possesses the bearing of

le grand seigneur out to school the world. His lecture is so completely over the top that it eventually becomes amusing – like the voice-over of a satiric film – and at times I have to force myself not to break out laughing. But I'm also grateful for his hospitality, as France turned out to be far more expensive than I'd planned for.

At Hôtel de Ville I see couples seated beside fountains, holding hands and kissing. Just as we enter the square, amber-colored lamps flicker on, casting everything in a golden glow.

Bernardo murmurs: "Here, the sidewalks are made of rubber." In the days ahead he'll repeat this phrase on various occasions. It's his way of saying that in Paris one can walk for hours, buoyed by a panoply of beauty, without ever growing fatigued.

After a brief visit to the majestic cathedral of Notre-Dame – which I'd once failed to properly identify during an art history exam! – we circle back to Centre Pompidou, then continue north along rue St-Denis. Bernardo remarks upon the prostitutes dressed in candy-colored lingerie who linger in sun-lit doorways along the street. A voluptuous Madame wearing black-lace panties is seated on a stool pretending to read an Emile Zola novel, which she displays prominently while never actually turning a page.

Bernardo casually adds: "I hear they don't charge very much. I'm told it's only three hundred francs." He speaks in an offhand manner, as if discreetly encouraging me to sample one of these fallen angels.

Back at his flat, which is a converted *atelier* featuring a frosted skylight, we dine on another bowl of rice. I hungrily devour the meal while studying an original Picasso – a painted ceramic plate – that hangs from a hook on a living room wall. Bernardo says that it's unsigned because it developed a hairline crack while baking in the kiln, so it was dumped into a refuse pile at the pottery. And somehow (I didn't ask for details), it ended up here in his flat. The face of a bearded man gleams on the glazed terra cotta. As I imbibe my espresso, I imagine that it stares back at my own bearded facade.

The following morning Bernardo scratches his bald pate, then announces: "I hope you don't mind. Soon, we'll have some charming guests."

Moments later three petite Latin American girls appear at the front door. They're from Bogota, freshmen at university, and their fathers are friends of Bernardo's. Two of them, whom he's invited to sleep in the living room, are daughters of ambassadors. The third one is the daughter of a police chief, and she's booked a room at a hotel around the corner. They're delightfully pleasant and friendly, filled with overflowing enthusiasm about visiting Paris on their way to Greece.

The youngest-looking one, Luciana, is boney and gangly. Her body hasn't fully developed, and her clothing drapes from her figure as if from a manikin awaiting a fitting. With her short curly hair and narrow hips she almost resembles a boy, but her androgynous facade imbues her with a certain pixie-like charm.

The tallest girl, Gabriela, is endowed with a precocious expression that lends her the appearance of a slightly more mature woman. A ballerina, her auburn hair is tied in a bun, and it falls in bangs over her long expressive eyebrows. She's also graced with dark emerald eyes and a pretty oval face. I can easily imagine what she'll look like as a fully developed woman in her thirties or forties, for even now she radiates a self-assured, confident regard: one stamped with an upper-class breeding.

Although Gabriela is the most attractive one by any conventional standard, it's the third girl who really draws my attention. Mariana possesses a sweet, open expression; whenever she smiles, I imagine a desert flower blooming with uninhibited splendor. Unlike the others, her bronzed features are clearly Mayan: a broad forehead; high cheek bones; full, succulent lips; and jet-black hair, tied in a short ponytail with a purple ribbon. She looks precisely her age, not a year more or less, but her well-rounded hips and hefty thighs evoke the image of an earth goddess stationed at an ancient temple. More than anything it's her kind, gentle manner that lures me. She hardly speaks, but when she does it's with a soft, suggestive, feminine timbre.

After they unpack Bernardo suggests a stroll along Île Saint-Louis, to sample some ice cream from Berthillon's: "a world-renowned shop."

It's a balmy, sunny day, but once again he shifts into his dreary, somber tone, trying to impress the girls with his "philosophy." As we enter a narrow lane, I linger behind and study their doelike gait.

At Île Saint-Louis we're forced to wait on a ridiculously long line for the famous ice cream, which in fact is nothing special. Then we approach the *quai* at the western end of the island, where the girls sit at the riverside and lick their dripping cones. This panoramic view of the Seine is breathtaking, and I photograph it from every angle.

Crossing Pont de Sully we continue east along the opposite shore, passing Pont de la Tournelle and approaching a sculpture garden at the far end of the Left Bank. Gabriela leaps upon a cement pillar and strikes a sensual ballet pose: a living, breathing sculpture that puts the neighboring Zadkines to shame. With arms extended and one leg flung out like a jack-knife, she pirouettes on her tiptoes. I grab my camera, pretend that we're engaged in a professional photo shoot, wave my hand, and encourage her to spin round as the girls laugh and bask in the sun.

Once we return to Place de la République, Bernardo takes

me aside and says that I should invite them for a drink. He points to a nearby *brasserie*, adding that he's going home alone, to take a nap.

Moments later we're seated at a table with the sun gleaming along the brass railings. I order a round of beer to celebrate this fine moment, and the girls drink it greedily. Then we order another round. They seem to come alive now, jabbering in Spanish in an intense, conspiratorial fashion.

Luciana and Gabriela glance at me sidelong, laugh, and gabble with a machine-gun staccato. Suddenly they stand up, nod their heads, and solemnly shake my hand, offering a polite, sincere farewell. Now I'm left with Mariana, who turns to me with a tender gaze and shyly smiles. We finish our beer, then she invites me back to her room.

Cutting across a capacious hotel lobby, we approach a stairway as a grumpy-faced clerk at the front desk spots me and shouts something in French. I have no idea what he's saying, but as I approach and study his vicious regard I imagine it must be about money. Reaching into my pocket, I slip him a fifty-franc note. This immediately silences him; he palms it, nods approvingly, turns away.

Upstairs in her tiny *chambre*, Mariana dims the lights and excuses herself. While she's in the bathroom, I undress and slip under a blanket, covering myself from the chin down. When she returns and sees me lying there, her dreamy eyes widen and she climbs in beside me, fully clothed. Once she discovers that I'm naked, her kisses grow even more impassioned.

We gently caress each other as I help her undress, then I shut off the light and we make love in the darkness.

Finally she murmurs: "You must go now."

"But why?"

"Don't you understand? Until a moment ago, I was a virgin. Now, I must take care of myself."

Shocked to hear this, I kiss her one last time, then leave, wondering if I'll ever see her again.

Of all the dazzling, monumental beauty of Paris, I knew that hers was the treasure.

*   *   *

Mariana's daintily inscribed missives were always a balm for my soul. Whenever they appeared in my rusty Manhattan mailbox, I'd carefully study each beautifully sculpted word that flowed from her delicate hand. She'd often send postcards with messages that chronicled her travels and that were brimming with the joy of youth.

The first one was postmarked in September and mailed from Caracas, where she was attending university. A photo on the card depicted Colombia's Basilica of Our Lady of Las Lajas, a Gothic-style church built on a spot where a girl who was a deaf-mute claimed to see and hear the Virgin Mary.

"How are you? And New York? I'm really good here in my country and with my people (finally) .... How was the rest of your time in Paris? I hope pleasant. Me, I was two months in Greece, then I met my parents in Paris, and I was traveling with them for about a month. Greece was wonderful. I met a lot of people, places, and everything. Now, here in Caracas. It looks nice. The weather is fine, and the people not so bad. Now tell me about you. How is your work and everything for you? By the way – can you understand me? I hope so. If not, try, and anyway write to me. Soon. I'll never forget you. And Paris either. Love, Mariana."

Can you understand me? The words pop out at me now; for there was so much I didn't understand about what might be beating in a young girl's heart.

The following April I received another joyous card, this one from the Virgin Islands: "Hola! You see? I think of you even here. I'm very good. This is great; I'll be home next weekend. How is your work, and how is everything for you? What about your trip to South America? Did you forget it? I hope to see you soon. Mariana."

In June, a card arrived from Cartagena bearing a photograph of Castillo San Felipe de Barajas: an impressive fortress castle from the sixteenth century. It contained one of those short messages reminiscent of a note penned from a lover who just wanted to say, *Hello; I'm still here; I'm thinking of you; and isn't life wonderful.*

"Hi Dear! How are you? I got your letter last week; I'm here now. I come because of the university. I took the examination, and I think it was okay. (I really hope so.) Next Sunday I'm going home to Caracas. I'm so good and happy here; this city is lovely. Write me soon. I love you. Mariana."

She would always sign each card with a flourish, with the *M* written big and bold and reminding me of the Arc de Triomphe. She'd often conclude a message by saying that she hoped to visit New York one day. Or perhaps I could visit her?

Meanwhile, month after month, almost as if playing a game with myself, I tracked the exchange rate of the bolivar – toying with the idea of a trip, but never actually daring to meet Mariana's father, the police chief. How I deluded myself into believing that I had all the time in the world for such distractions! But time did indeed pass; and, the following year, I found myself living with a terribly unsuitable companion named Dochma, an Austrian expatriate whom I'd reluctantly invited to move in.

As bad luck would have it, shortly after this new arrangement, a letter arrived embossed with the familiar postmark of Bogota – a sight that would normally have lifted my spirits. But now, I felt crushed. In July, Mariana would be arriving in Manhattan with her father, who had some business to attend to. Perhaps, I thought, he was on the way to Fort Benning's notorious School of the Americas, where so many Latin American police units received training in methods of torture, repression, and assassination. But in any case, what to do?

I decided to do nothing: to wait and see how it would pan out.

One sunny afternoon, just as I was sitting down with Dochma for our lunchtime meal, the phone rang and my answering machine clicked on. Fortunately, the volume was turned off. But something about the sound of the ring startled me.

Dochma left for an appointment, and I rewound the tape and played it. And there, as resonant as a harpsichord, were the golden notes of Mariana's melodic voice. She'd just arrived with her father, and where was I? She was hoping that we could all get together for lunch …

The thought of meeting a Colombian police chief sent a chill down my spine – especially one whose daughter had been devirginized by yours truly. And what if she asked to accompany me back home? It seemed like a hopeless situation, so in the end I simply pretended to be away. But it was a decision that I came to deeply regret.

A week later I received a card postmarked from Miami, but a photo on the front depicted the frenetic hubbub of Times Square. "I was here ….. I promised you one day to come and see you, but it was impossible to find you. I don't know where you was, but anyway I remember you a lot. Now is your turn to come visit me at home. I really hope to see you soon. Please call or write. I'll be waiting for you … I love you. Mariana. (I'm the girl you met in Paris one summer day.)"

We remained in touch, but once again the months turned into years. I was living in a tiny garret in Montparnasse, near the Academie de la Grande Chaumière: a legendary art school, where occasionally I'd arrive with a sketch pad and draw from the model. It was October of 1993, and the crisp autumn leaves were filling the nearby Square Ozanam with a fluttering profusion of reds and yellows.

One evening, just as I entered my flat the phone rang – and behold, it was Mariana. It had been seven years since our first encounter. And now, in broken English, she said that she'd been kidnapped, held captive, and raped.

Those horrific words – *raped* and *kidnapped* – stunned me; and for a moment I thought I must be imagining things. Since Mariana spoke such basic English, at first I figured that, surely, I must be mistaken. There was also the matter-of-fact tone of her speech, which I later realized was a symptom of her trauma. *Ray-ped* is how she pronounced it. It took me a moment to decipher, and a longer moment to digest. But then, it all fell into place.

For, these were the final days of a sociopathic drug lord named Pablo Escobar, who had terrorized the nation of Colombia with his countless abductions and murders. As the daughter of a high-ranking officer, Mariana had made for a perfect target.

Two months after our call, Pablo was shot dead in a showdown with the National Police. But while he was still out on the lam and sneaking through the countryside, entire villages were executed by death squads so that his whereabouts might remain a secret. It was only by tracking his cell phone transmissions that the authorities had finally nabbed him.

My poor Colombian angel had been dragged into this pit, yet somehow she'd survived. Following a thoughtful pause, she added: "Thank God you were my first man. I thank God for that."

I was nearly speechless, but I offered whatever words of solace I could muster. I can still hear – and feel – the gentleness in her voice. I only wish that I could have embraced her and held her tightly, even though she remained so far away, on the other side of a vast ocean.

There are experiences that make you question everything. And which force you to realize that life isn't only unfair, vicious, and malefic but also incredibly stupid: a design riddled with such infuriating fault lines that you can only throw your hands up in dismay. And perhaps only someone with a spot of benevolence in his heart can serve as a counterpoint to nature's brutal foolishness and to its capricious, malicious whims.

It wasn't long after this that Mariana decided to enter a nunnery, in a convent located in one of the cathedrals from which she'd previously sent me a picture postcard.

Once again, it was as if the unbelievable had come true.

Art Cloche

About a month before I embarked for Paris, my friend Jonathan suggested that I contact one of his old acquaintances: a Jewish painter from Turkey who'd settled in France decades ago, while she was still a teenager:

"Odile is a wild, crazy artist – *complètement fou! Mais très charmante*. Perhaps, she can show you around."

A few days after Mariana and her friends had departed, I called Odile, and she invited me over for dinner. As soon as I entered her studio apartment, which was just north of Sacré-Coeur, I could see that she lived on the very edge of reality. A petite surrealist who worked with iridescent inks and vivid watercolors, she sliced her paintings with razor blades and hung the shredded canvases from the rafters in her room.

Odile insisted that I join her that afternoon for a day trip to Auvers-sur-Oise. A small town about thirty-two kilometers north of Paris, it hosts a lugubrious cathedral that Van Gogh had immortalized in a painting, which is now hanging in the Musée d'Orsay. But far more impressive than the church, the town featured a municipal cemetery with a pair of gravestones that were inscribed with the names of Vincent and Theo Van Gogh.

As I studied these modest markers that were dappled in sunlight, I recalled my first exposure to the miracles of the flinty-eyed artist. It was at the Brooklyn Museum of all places, a few months after I'd turned fourteen. That fall, my father had spotted an article in the *Times* that announced this historic exhibit: the last opportunity to see nearly all of Van Gogh's works before they would wind their way back to Amsterdam, to form the basis of a new museum.

Bridget must have convinced Arthur to bring us there; for, unlike his brother Byron, Arthur harbored little interest in fine art. And he was completely incapable of appreciating the work of a modernist such as Van Gogh – an artist whom he freely admitted was well beyond his ken.

But once we arrived at the museum, Arthur suddenly realized that he couldn't afford the exorbitant entry fee for an entire family.

"Bridget, why don't you take Robbie inside to see the show, while Junior and I explore the part of the museum that's free ..."

Besides being treated to the marvels of the master, I was doubly thrilled to do so minus the overbearing presence of my father. Bridget always appeared to be calmer, less harried, and more centered in the genuine core of her being when I was left alone with her. But my poor younger brother! He looked none too pleased about being exiled to the ground floor with only Arthur by his side.

Bridget and I wandered in awe from room to room as we encountered an electrifying collection of portraits and land-scapes. Much to my surprise, when I looked more closely, I discovered that the paint seemed to be *carved* into the surface, so thick was its application. Little did I realize that, forty years earlier, a critic named Frank Mather had written of the artist's work: "The whole thing looked *harrowed* in the pigment."

In a corner of one salon we paused before a rendering of a lovely peach tree in blossom. The delicate petals appeared to be fluttering in a soft Provençal breeze. Bridget read the caption aloud: "'As seen from his asylum window.' Look, Robbie! He painted this while he was in the hospital!" Now we were truly astonished. Though he'd been struggling between bouts of seizure, the artist had still managed to produce this miraculous creation.

As Bridget spoke, her cornflower-blue eyes appeared to be more brilliant than anything on display. At that moment I felt her empathy reaching out: not only to Van Gogh but to all those who suffered so unjustly. It was as if she were telepathically communing that there could be no higher calling than to create, and no greater tragedy than to do so while under the dismal pall of such inner turmoil.

After stopping at a local tavern for a delicious dinner of smoked rabbit, we departed from Auvers-sur-Oise and boarded the train back to Paris. As I gazed out a window I could see a small group of painters, huddled beside their easels, working in the same field where Van Gogh had once labored. In a letter to his brother, Vincent describes the landscape as "Vast fields of wheat under turbulent skies." What a fitting metaphor with which to portray the artist's own vast production, I thought, which was also reaped under a turbulent burden of pain.

I silently absorbed the scene while Odile laughed and said that she often imagined that she was making love to Van Gogh under the cypress trees, which now appeared to be flashing by the window.

"You're only a hundred years too late! None of those prissy demoiselles of Auvers-sur-Oise would even deign to pose for the lonely painter," I groused. "They regarded him as a bizarre *étranger*, with his fiery-red hair and deeply haunted gaze." They'd even christened him *le fou roux*, "the redheaded madman." The *Arlésiennes* had treated him no better. As he writes in one of his embittered letters shortly after slicing off an ear: "I've been powerless to paint them as other than poisonous, the women of Arles." But this was the least of his problems. His last words, spoken to his loving brother, were: "The sadness will last forever." And yet, the miracles culled from his aborted life still shine so brightly.

* * *

Though she was as assertive Priscilla, Odile remained far more in touch with her feminine aspect. While I was photographing her in Auvers, she gathered a handful of wild flowers and posed with her head tilted, her gaze softened, and her expression resembling that of a starry-eyed sylvan fairy. She was never afraid to display her tender, vulnerable side; but she was also a willful and determined woman, and one of the only female members of a male dominated artist's group. Composed of a mélange of anarchists and rebels, they squatted in abandoned factories or shuttered railway stations, transforming such forgotten sites into illegal *ateliers*. Not only did she hold her own there; Odile soon became one of their most respected leaders.

Odile occasionally sold a few paintings, but to stay afloat she milked the French welfare system. She also received regular child-support payments from her former lover, to help raise their five-year-old daughter, Edna. I wondered what Priscilla would have thought of Odile – and whether she would be envious of her.

And while Odile loved the company of men, she said that getting married had never been a priority. "The only thing that's important is *love* – to find a soul mate. Until then, there's the life. *C'est la vie!* Very important, to live the life." While so many Americans would dejectedly shake their heads and mutter, *Well, that's life*, Odile never ceased to celebrate it.

That night we fell into a frenzy upon her bed. She laughed, screamed, paused to smoke hand-rolled cigarettes, and twisted and turned into every conceivable position. As I glanced around, I realized that we were hemmed in by a clutter of stacked canvases, wooden picture frames, rolls of drawing paper, and – hanging from the ceiling – a sliced canvas that hovered over the bed like a colorful phantom.

Indeed, her quarters were cramped. A kitchenette faced a modest living room, where her daughter, Edna, slept on a convertible couch. Another tiny room was rented to a German philosophy student, a *Sorbonnette* named Claudia. Not having enough space for an easel, Odile tacked her works-in-progress upon the paint-spattered walls.

What a remarkable contrast to Priscilla's grim, black-and-white poster! Now I was surrounded by a dance of pigment: drops of paint streaking, splattering, and glowing under the glare of a single light bulb.

Pausing to roll another cigarette, she regarded me with a devilish grin.

"*C'est la vie!*" she exclaimed.

Wreathed in a halo of tobacco smoke, we resembled a pair of fallen Baudelairean angels.

"*Oui, Odile, la vie …*"

But life with Odile also posed certain problems that would never have cropped up in Priscilla's world.

The following morning, after I'd finished showering, Odile announced that she needed to visit her *atelier* to prepare for a visit from an art dealer. I'd just slipped into my jeans and was reaching for my socks when a loud, persistent knock sounded at the front door.

In walked a short, stout, noticeably drunk young Russian. His eyes were gleaming, and a waft of vodka and cigarette smoke blew in with him.

For a moment he just stood there and glared. At first he studied the wet locks of my hair, which were still dripping from the shower. Then he cast a prolonged stare at my bare feet. His suspicions now confirmed, his eyes assumed a more fiery aspect.

Having seen so many French films in which infidelity triggers a heated argument but then ends with all three principals seated round a table consuming croissants while reasonably dealing with such peccadilloes, I assumed that all would end well. So I delivered what I regarded as an appropriate opening. I simply said: *Bonjour*.

In response, Grigory raised an eyebrow, regarded me with a feverous grin, nodded emphatically, and shouted *"Oui! Bonjour!"* Then he screamed at Odile and smacked her across the jaw.

Apparently, Grigory and I had not been watching the same films.

I yelled at him to leave her alone. But as soon as I stood up, I realized that it would be pointless to fight barefoot. So I sat down again, slipped on my socks, and grabbed my boots.

Meanwhile they shoved each other back and forth, roaring like a pair of lions about to rip the flesh from each other's hides. Then he smacked her again, on the other side of her mouth.

He was standing with his back to the front door, which was still opened, while Odile stood beside the entrance to her bedroom. Fortunately, a little birdie chirped that I should position myself on Grigory's other side, at the entrance to the kitchen.

By now, he was nearly out of his mind with rage. He mouthed a certain phrase repeatedly; but due to his thick Russian accent, his garbled French was difficult to decipher. But gradually I realized that the word he was shouting was one that I was actually quite familiar with – *couteau!* He was saying something to the effect of: "I'm going to get a knife" – *un couteau!* – "and slice you up! Where's that butcher blade?"

He turned toward the kitchen and attempted to push past me. At first I pretended to offer no resistance, but then I snaked my elbow round his neck and pressed it down, into a headlock.

Grabbing him round the waist with my other hand, by sheer force of adrenalin I lifted him up and tossed him into the hall. He landed flat on his bottom, with his feet arcing back and his head slamming on the tiled floor.

He appeared to be stunned, but then he bolted up and charged. So I kicked the edge of the door and – thanks to the paranoid design of French architecture – it locked as it slammed shut. And not a moment too soon. *Blam!* He crashed into the door, then we heard him collapse again onto the floor.

After a moment of silence he began to kick and punch at the portal, screaming and yelling until finally beating a retreat.

Odile was grateful that I'd protected her and her daughter, Edna, who was now sobbing as her mother tried to calm her. But another problem soon materialized. Odile was adamant about visiting her *atelier*; but since Grigory occupied an adjacent room, he might be lying there in wait for her.

I tried to talk her out of it, but she insisted that it was her *right* to be there. After all, it was *her* studio! And she needed to prepare for the dealer, who was due to arrive later that evening.

I redoubled my efforts to dissuade her, but all in vain. As we walked along the street, I kept my eyes peeled for the madman. Here I was, on a *holiday* in France, but instead of bistros, sightseeing, and promenades, I was forced to deal with Van Gogh's reincarnation as a witless Russian drunk.

Despite all this the intoxicating beauty of Paris slowly enveloped me. A diffuse light cast the street in vibrant tones of Payne's gray, which made the occasional patches of crimson or viridian from the café awnings that much more vivid. Where else on earth, I wondered, does a city assume the vibrancy of a dream?

Thus entranced, I followed Odile into an illegal squatter's den. A former Citroen factory, it was now inhabited not only by artists but also by the homeless, or *clochard*. In honor of such forgotten figures, her radical group had dubbed themselves "Art Cloche."

Odile suggested that I remain out of sight, so I waited in a vaulted lobby while she continued inside, to the makeshift studios.

Moments after she left, a high-pitched scream resounded throughout the building. I ran inside. At the far end, a staircase ascended into a catwalk. There, on a balcony, Grigory and Odile were lunging at each other – as if rehearsing a scene from a Jean Genet play.

A handful of young men were scattered along the ground floor, passively absorbing these theatrics as they stood beside their easels. One appeared to be frozen in place, absentmindedly holding a brush as he gazed up, while a drop of red paint slowly descended from the tip. Others continued to work unfazed – either oblivious to such distraction or behaving as if they'd witnessed this drama so many times that it no longer held their interest.

I pleaded with them to assist me, gesturing that Grigory had imbibed too much booze. Emerging from their torpor, a few of them ran with me to the base of the staircase. But plainly, their hearts weren't in it; for they halted right there and, without taking another step, regressed to the role of being passive witnesses.

Leaving them behind, I bolted up the steps. Just as I approached the landing, a courageous young fellow with a bushy red beard emerged from a studio and wrapped his arms round the madman, gripping him tightly at the far end of the balcony. But then Grigory broke loose, grabbed a long wooden beam that was lying on the floor, and charged like a medieval knight jousting with a lance.

He was headed directly for Odile, who was just a few paces ahead of me. At the very last moment the bearded redhead tackled him again, from behind. Once they fell to the floor, he pulled Grigory away.

By now I'd had more than enough of this nonsense, so I shouted at Odile to retreat. I coaxed her toward the stairs while Grigory was pushed and shoved into a back room.

One of Odile's girlfriends helped me to convince her to return to the main floor, where the two women continued to bicker in French. While Odile maintained that she must remain there, her friend insisted that Grigory was a dangerous, deranged creature, and that it was wiser to leave. Once I comprehended the gist of their conversation, I tried to talk sense into Odile. After all, I reasoned, he was drunk and in love. Our presence would only infuriate him. Why not just let him sleep it off?

Eventually she agreed to a compromise. We would step outside for a coffee and – as Parisians love to do – "talk it over."

A stubborn woman to the very end, she took her time to get out of there. I felt as if we were on tenterhooks. How much longer might we stave off the next sally from the lunatic, who was still yelling and screaming from his lair?

The women continued to argue; and while no one was paying any attention, Grigory escaped from his room, approached the edge of the balcony, and propelled a six-foot beam through the air. It narrowly missed us as it crashed just a yard away, bouncing along the floor. But then the redhead rushed out again and restrained him.

Strolling toward the exit at a leisurely pace as if nothing extraordinary was occurring, the women finally exited the building, accompanied by each of their daughters. Entering a local bistro and engaging in some animated chatter, they eventually decided to retrieve Odile's work from the *atelier*. She would meet with the dealer *outside* the building, while I would remain at the bistro.

Once they departed, I moved to the bar deck. Sipping a cool

beer, an urge was kindled to share my story with the Moroccan bartender – or at least as much of it as I could render with my broken French.

That I struggled so to communicate something of seeming import impressed him. Listening intently but comprehending little, he finally shouted at a group of North Africans who were assembled in a back room, entranced by the vapid drone of a blaring TV.

The bartender motioned to a man dressed in a smartly cut tweed suit, who was fluent in English. This olive-skinned gentleman was appointed – with many approving nods – to serve as translator.

As the tale of my encounter with the impassioned artists unfolded, a warm laughter broke out at the bar. With the mellifluous babble of their respective tongues, several of the men began to add their own asides and commentaries. Now the TV was shut off and the place assumed a lively, carnival atmosphere as they circled round.

The translator was a well-mannered, genial fellow, who remarked that he didn't care much for Paris or for the French. Many North Africans felt this way, he said, because "there's nothing to learn here." As he continued to speak, I realized that his remark referred to the fact that there were so few economic opportunities for immigrants. He concluded that French society, which had ostracized all but its native sons, could offer him very little.

He added that he was a tailor, and although business was adequate it wasn't booming. Few had the money to spend. When I admired his herringbone suit and complimented him on his handiwork he smiled proudly, adding that it was worth eleven hundred dollars. But when I asked if he was married, his expression suddenly changed. His wife had abandoned him, he said, and, in retrospect, he felt as if he had no one to blame but himself.

"I'm the guilty one. She allowed me my freedom, but I abused it." Now he was alone, and he didn't care for such solitude.

"*Oui*," the bartender chimed in as he brought us a round of drinks on the house, "*un homme a besoin d'une femme*" (a man needs a woman).

By the time Odile returned I'd begun to lose patience. Three hours had elapsed since our excursion to the *atelier*. I felt that I didn't have time to waste, especially with the entire City of Light gleaming within reach. And I suspected that her business with Grigory was far from finished.

As we made ready to leave, I shook hands with each of the men. Their eyes sparkled with curiosity as they regarded Odile, and I discreetly nodded as a few of them whispered: "Is that her?" – amused to encounter the protagonist of the tale now standing before them.

Once we returned to her flat, I silently mulled over the situation. I grew concerned that Grigory might arrive while we were asleep and that Odile's roommate, Claudia, would let him in. So I insisted that Odile leave Claudia a note to explain the situation.

I knew that I'd merely been lucky during my first encounter with Grigory. If he hadn't been so soused, I doubt that I would have been a match for him. Instead, I might have ended up in a puddle of blood.

That night I slept poorly. The pillows were limp and soiled, and the threadbare blankets were insufficient for a damp Parisian night. And where was the Russian psychopath? I began to wonder if this entire affair was really worth the trouble.

Early the next morning Odile lightly fingered my back to say good-bye, but I pretended to be asleep. After she left, I wondered what to do.

I was pulling on my boots when a flaxen-haired woman wearing a beige nightgown poked her head into the room and greeted me. Encountering Claudia just before I departed proved to be a blessing. First I pointed to the note that we'd left for her, which she hadn't even noticed, then I filled her in on the details.

"My God," she murmured with a heavy German accent, "I can't believe it!" She repeated this several times, then spoke to me in confidence about how difficult it had been to live there. Odile frequently had visitors over, she said, and they often partied all night.

"She smokes too much and drinks too much. And when she can't afford a drink, she grows desperate. What's just as bad is that she obsessively craves the company of men. She sleeps with one after the other," Claudia said, shaking her head despondently. "I even had to convince her to practice safe sex!" She concluded that Odile was searching for an emotional security that she would never obtain. "Living in Paris only makes things worse for her," she frowned. "All too often, Frenchmen will attempt to preserve their independence at any cost. They have trouble committing themselves to a more serious relationship."

Claudia struck me as the sort of European intellectual who loves the feel of another's dirt in her hand. Studying it under the lens of her analytical microscope, she nearly waxed poetic. But most of all, she was concerned over the fate of Odile's daughter, Edna. "Odile's far too childish to be raising a daughter on her own."

As I was absorbing this, I suddenly grew hungry. "Can I invite you to get a bite to eat?" I asked. "Perhaps you know of a decent place?"

"There's a *brasserie* around the corner. Just give me a moment to change."

Over scrambled eggs, croissants, and coffee, Claudia concluded that Odile was "just impossible." Now, she would
search for a place to live all by herself. She added that Odile
needed to find employment to augment her income; but since
she was obsessed with her artwork, she continued to postpone
any serious search.

"What she really needs," Claudia exclaimed, "is a *psyche*
analysis!"

"You mean, psychoanalysis? Well, maybe what she needs is
a friend who can to straighten her out. Anyway, you two strike
me as a pair of radically different types. It's amazing that you
even live together."

"Yes! For one thing, I'm the monogamous type. I prefer to
concentrate on one man at a time. But now," she sighed, as her
eyes assumed a tragic cast, "I'm in love with someone who
won't even commit to me."

"Is he a Frenchman of the sort that you've just described?"

"No," she shook her head, "he's an intellectual Greek
Marxist."

Upon hearing this I burst out laughing. "I can just picture
the two of you arguing over the dialectic of love while consuming your morning Nescafé!"

"Oh, I don't even know what I'm doing here anymore!" she
groaned. "What a *depressing* city,". "It's like a beautiful woman
who, once you get to know her, reveals how *mélancolique* she
feels inside. When you live here day in and day out, you never
even go to see anything – you never have the time! Look at this
foul, inclement weather. It's like this *all year!* Oh, God, how
enervating ..."

"I was thinking of visiting Arles. Have you ever been
there?"

"Yes! You should leave Paris and travel to Provence! On

your way to Arles, make sure to visit Avignon and the Palace of the Popes. The medieval ruins are amazing! Also, Aix en Provence, where Cézanne painted ..."

Claudia grabbed a pen and, on the reverse side of our bill, drew a tiny map and plotted a course that wended its way through certain key spots in southern France. She even escorted me to the metro, all the while explaining which line to take to the appropriate *gare*. Then – *voilà!* – I bid her *adieu* and headed toward Gare de Lyon, where I wandered from one clerk to the next, speaking in broken French, studying their replies like an imbecile, yet somehow deciphering it all.

How invigorating – to venture forth into the unknown!

* * *

I arrived in Arles at dusk and approached an establishment called Hôtel Terminus Van Gogh. There was something ghastly about its name: the "end of the line" for poor Vincent!

A middle-aged *Madame* at the front desk smiled when she heard my accent. Without asking for my name or passport, she handed me a brass skeleton key for room number one.

I unpacked my bags and walked toward the city center. It was faintly lit by antique lamps that were bolted to the facades, casting a golden glow along the narrow cobblestone streets. Rows of squat, medieval dwellings featured mint-colored shutters and thick oak doors riveted with iron studs and pock-marked metal bands. Though the ironwork appeared to be decorative, it had once served as a protection against intruding axes, swords, and rams. Now I was surrounded by the same enchanted cosmos that Van Gogh had rendered in stunning detail in so many of his works.

I ambled on for hours, occasionally stopping to purchase cheese and fruit. The citizens of Arles aren't particularly warm,

I thought, but, unlike the typical Parisian, at least they're polite and patient. They stand by your side and allow you to struggle with your broken French while hoping to assist you.

The next morning I woke up early and continued my tour. One of the more memorable sites I encountered was one that remained unmarked by any plaque: a crumbling, abandoned building that had once been graced by a special guest. It was all that remained of a hospital where Van Gogh was briefly interned, before being treated at Saint-Rémy. I found it only with great difficulty, as even the *fonctionnaires* at a local tourist bureau were mystified by my inquiries.

Once inside, I explored its hollowed out, shell-like structure. The concrete floors were fractured into massive planes, which I gingerly tiptoed across as if navigating a Cubist landscape. The rooms were stripped bare and the ceilings were punctured with gigantic holes, exposing cerulean skies and billowing clouds that called to mind the landscapes painted by the starry-eyed Dutchman. Despite its ruined state, I recognized certain vistas that had once been featured in his portraits of the asylum, such as a winding path in a courtyard or an arched, vaulted corridor that loomed eerily inside. Even while interned there, the master had painstakingly transformed such imagery with his visionary, courageous labor.

Decades later, while scanning through the memoirs of the painter Vlaminck, I chanced upon these words: "Coming away from an exhibition of Van Gogh in the rue Laffite, I was so moved that I wanted to cry with joy and despair. On that day I loved Van Gogh more than I loved my own father."

I could well understand such a sentiment. And it should be noted that Vlaminck *truly loved* his father.

* * *

From the moment that I disembarked in Paris I felt as if I were enveloped in a dream – but what sort of dream? One boding grace or malevolence? In any case, certain cities strike a chord within us; others either fail to do so or trigger a sense of disharmony. And just like any love affair, the cause of it all remains a mystery. One might describe it or portray it but never define it … and only a fool would attempt to do so. My only regret was that it had taken me so long to arrive.

When I returned to the States these sublime visions rapidly faded away. They were replaced with an abiding sense of discontent, which soon transformed itself into a lingering depression.

What was I even doing here, I wondered, and how could I return – and remain – in Europe? This seemed to be the only question worth considering.

Back at the office, Stanley was positioned exactly where I'd left him: hypnotized by his computer monitor while bouncing his knee, staring at blank grant proposals, and taking several weeks or even months to compose a simple declarative sentence. Yet, he gradually accrued the necessary funds for expanding the agency. He also spent long hours on the phone, cozying up to the board members, wooing potential donors, and doing everything he could to avoid looking into a mirror and asking: "But who am I?" Indeed, rarely had I ever encountered a man so completely extroverted in temperament. Stanley reminded me of an envelope folded inside out and bereft of any interiority. Only later would I come to realize that he was merely one among many: a new breed, whose lives were being reshaped by the glowing pixels of a computer screen.

A stack of applications had piled up on my desk from psychiatric hospitals, seeking housing for clients who were supposedly ready to be discharged. I silently recalled how

Priscilla had trained me to deal with the fabrications woven by overly zealous functionaries who were hell-bent on releasing as many homeless schizophrenics from the hospital as possible, regardless of whether they were able to deal with the pressures of the outside world. Thus, the patients' dossiers were always heavily redacted and intentionally left incomplete; for the bureaucrats assumed that the average program director wouldn't bother to conduct any in-depth investigation. But Priscilla and I made certain to contact all the institutions that were mentioned in these reports and to request their complete records in order to construct as solid a chronology as possible. And then – lo and behold – one might discover that, although a social worker had claimed that her client Billy Larson is exceptionally well suited for our less supervised setting, in fact, just six months ago, Billy nearly succeeded in crashing through a plate glass window on the tenth floor of a psychiatric hospital. But fortunately, after cracking open his skull, he fell back to the floor into a pool of blood, and the medics were rushed in and saved him from bleeding to death. And now, "Although Billy continues to talk about suicide, we've concluded that he's no longer *serious* about it." Oh, *really?*

Once I was promoted to program director, I made it a policy to conduct at least two separate interviews before a patient was admitted to our agency. And to insist that, once a social worker arrives with said patient in hand, the worker must be escorted to a back room, so that he or she cannot butt in with some ridiculous excuse in order to coach the client during a crucial moment of disclosure. It was also necessary to isolate these meddlers because I didn't want them to learn anything about our diabolical methods of penetrating to the truth, to the core of the matter, which concerned questions such as: *If we accept this patient, will she jump off the roof, or kill her roommate, or set the entire building ablaze?*

In the long run such tedious investigations saved us a considerable amount of time and energy. Besides helping such unfortunate souls, by carefully selecting our clients we could accomplish this in a manner that didn't entirely exhaust the staff and quickly burn them out. Therefore, such cunning preparedness was worth every ounce of energy that we invested into it.

As if to highlight once and for all the dangers of dealing with such rigged and redacted dossiers, a few months after I returned from Paris a tragedy occurred in a community residence program run by one of my colleagues.

One afternoon, just as the summer heat was beginning to bake the tarmac, softening the asphalt and transforming Manhattan into one big stinking hellhole, I found Stanley hunkered down at my desk, sipping a coffee while absentmindedly absorbing the wide-angled view of Avenue A. On this particular day, Gerald – a shirtless, six-foot-four barrel-chested homeless man – was in the midst of constructing his weekly "sculpture." That is, he'd fill the wire-mesh garbage cans that stood on the four corners with a towering mass of detritus, which he'd collected in a shopping cart. Upon completing this daunting task, he'd dial a pay phone right outside my office. Flailing his arms, Gerald would shout so loudly that his voice was audible even through the thick plate glass.

After several months of witnessing this weekly ritual, one day I noticed that he never actually dropped a coin into the slot. Instead, it was an imaginary dialogue that he carried on with his mother. Judging from Gerald's antics, she'd done quite a number on her poor son, who'd spent decades being shuttled from the locked wards of Bellevue to the graffiti-mottled pavements of Alphabet City.

Letting loose a final high-pitched screech, he'd slam down

the receiver, then pretend to place a call to a stock broker: "That's right, I said *Caterpillar*, up six and seven-eighths! Dividend on split, and sell on margin! *Coca-Cola*, up three and three-quarters! *General Motors*, up five and an eighth ..."

Just as Henry Morton Stanley was said to have traced the footfalls of Dr. Livingstone via an outcropping of mulatto babies blossoming across the African savanna, Gerald's path through the Lower East Side could easily be followed because he'd spawned hundreds of miniature white chalk marks, drawn in a tiny scrawl, which detailed the rise and fall of these imaginary stock prices. Appearing where you'd least expect them, the numbers were tallied on telephone poles, at the bottoms of lampposts, along the crumbling facades of brick buildings, or on the warped and cracked pavements that carried their equally cracked and warped pedestrians. As my friend Slim once said while shaking his head: "There's no way that a guy like Gerald should be left to his own devices out on these mean streets."

In any case, during my noontime arrival Stanley could usually be found in his office next door. But now I was surprised to see him lingering at my desk, watching intently as Gerald tinkered with one of his sculptures in the trash can. Not only was Stanley firmly planted in place; a grave expression animated his pasty face.

"You don't look very chipper today, Stanley."

He stared at me for a moment, then appeared to be searching for the proper declarative sentence.

"I just received a call from Riverdale Community Living Program. One of their clients killed her roommate. Then she chopped the body into thirty-two pieces. Every network in town is broadcasting the story. I'm about to go over there again, to lend more support. It's a real zoo."

"Riverdale? But that's Olivia's program."

As the details trickled in, we learned that the murderer was a client named Celeste, who had recently applied for housing at our agency. My friend Bernie had also received Celeste's dossier from Manhattan Psychiatric Center, but after a brief interview he decided not to take her.

I'd rejected Celeste without even bothering to schedule an interview, because Bernie had once warned me about clients who suffered from command hallucinations from God. "If God orders you to do something," he said, "no matter how unpleasant, it may be difficult to resist."

In such circumstances the litmus test that Bernie administered was to ask a client what he or she would do if God issued a command. If the patient replied, "Of course, I'd obey," then Bernie rejected him. But if, instead, the client said: "I know that it's just a hallucination, so I ignore the voices," then Bernie might take a chance, accept the patient into his program, and offer him or her a place to live. But I remained unwilling to take such risks. Even if the clients claimed to ignore these commands, I knew that, just before they arrived for their interviews, they were often coached to answer this way by their case workers at the hospital.

Despite Olivia's prestigious social work degree, which she'd received from an Ivy League school, she'd never been trained in our more commonsensical approach. So she'd accepted Celeste with open arms. A few weeks later, God commanded Celeste to kill her roommate, Delia, while she was asleep. Then he told her to chop the corpse into thirty-two pieces, place the body parts into separate bags, and stack them in the basement, along with the refuse that a superintendent would normally toss into an incinerator.

But perhaps God's omniscience had been eclipsed while operating in the satanic regions of the Lower East Side. For the Lord had failed to consider the wits of a canny building superintendent, who'd grown suspicious over the inordinate number of bags that had emerged from a single flat. So he decided to take a peek. The first one contained a hand. The second, a foot. The rest, gentle reader, you can imagine for yourself. Except, that is, for the head.

As Alfred Hitchcock had once informed François Truffaut during their legendary interviews, "In all cases involving mutilation, the biggest problem for the police is to locate the head." And indeed, in this particular case, initially the hiding place of *la tête* posed a problem. But a detective finally found it: buried at the base of a potted plant in the far corner of the building's courtyard.

A few hours later Stanley called me into his office. His face was aglow with a curious motley of red and white splotches, which often appeared during moments of confusion or vexation. Prone to quicksilver moods, he now resembled a red pepper partially bleached by a recessive albino gene.

"What if something like that happens here," he asked, "and they discover that we don't have anyone on staff with a social work degree?"

In response, I told him about how Bernie and I had rejected Celeste based on common sense, and how Olivia, the one with the greatest qualifications and the most advanced degrees, was the only one foolish enough to be hoodwinked.

"Stanley, as any boy from Gravesend will tell you, pay careful attention to command hallucinations. They're guaranteed trouble."

Turning a deeper shade of red, he stuttered, "Well, just find someone, even for a case management position, who has a degree. It wouldn't hurt!"

* * *

As the agency gained wider recognition, I gradually developed a reputation for being a well-respected director. I was interviewed by a Swedish filmmaker for a documentary about mental health treatment around the world and quoted extensively in a book about the homeless mentally ill, which the producers subsequently published. Thus, I might have continued in this direction if not for the fact that, one day, Stanley's assistant Slim arrived at work with a copy of Nikos Kazantzakis' *Report to Greco* tucked under his arm.

Just like Stanley, Slim would occasionally regard me with a look of fascination: wondering if I was as mad as I seemed or if it was all just a playful hoax. But unlike Stanley, Slim decided to test the waters to see just how far into *harlequinerie* he might push me.

A petite Greek lad several years my junior, Slim was usually quiet and reserved. It was only after he'd been working there for a few months, stationed beside Stanley next door, that the rest of the staff even seemed to notice him. At first I didn't pay much attention to him either – that is, until he arrived with that explosive text in hand. Once we began to speak about the author of this magical Mediterranean adventure we gradually realized that we, too, were in desperate need of spiritual revival.

For we were each approaching a point in life where a fork appears in the road. To select either direction would mean becoming one person and not another: to sacrifice one thing in order to obtain something more vital. In our hearts we were restless, but we hadn't yet developed the temerity to assume the artist's mantle. Perhaps, if we hadn't met at precisely this moment I might never have had the courage to expatriate to Paris. And without me egging him on, Slim might still be a director of development, instead of pursuing his vocation as a musician.

He'd eventually form a band and zigzag across the country, performing in hundreds of shows and discovering America while I was exploring Europe.

After my relationship with Priscilla had fizzled, as if by counterpoint my friendship with Slim blossomed. While cruising the midnight tarmac and jabbering at bars and cafés in Lower Manhattan, a disenchantment over our fatuous roles continued to grow … until we resembled a pair of powder kegs primed to detonate at any moment.

* * *

Late one night we found ourselves seated inside an illegal speakeasy. A couple of Slim's musician friends had taken him there the previous weekend, but it was strictly confidential and "hush-hush." Located on Lower Broadway near Bleecker Street, the unmarked entrance featured a glass door that opened into a shadowy basement stairwell.

It was only after we'd begun to patronize this dive that Slim realized that we'd stumbled into a section of the original Pfaff's beer cellar, where Walt Whitman had once downed foaming drafts of ale and bemoaned the "failure" of *Leaves of Grass*. (In Walt's own words: "The vault at Pfaff's where the drinkers and laughers meet to eat and drink and carouse.") But that night, Slim appeared to be a bit frazzled at the edges and lacking his usual Whitmanesque buoyancy.

"You look green between the gills," I said. "What's eating you? Did the mistress up and leave?"

"Doctor, it's even worse than that. When I awoke this morning, I began to wonder about the meaning of life."

"You mean, the fourth dimension?"

"Well, of course! You, of all people, must realize that I've had numerous encounters with the dominion of the spirit. But in terms of an ultimate unifying force that provides *meaning*, I'm not sure anymore. You know, I grew up in barren times in a desperate, mean-spirited town. And I'm starting to feel as if I'm living in one now, as well. I thought that I still possessed a reservoir of optimism that would keep me afloat, but I'm beginning to wonder. I know all this sounds like nonsense; I'm using muddleheaded terms. But you get the picture: the ugliness and bitterness. And now, my grief is almost out of control – and I'm only in my twenties! But I feel as if I'm about to turn eighty …"

I stared at him in silence as he sipped his Scotch. "Anyway, the other night," he continued, "you said something that stayed with me. I forget the exact words, but it was to this effect: if someone suffers a terrible trauma, it tears a hole into the soul. And then a dark psychic force can enter through that hole and take on the shape of the wound – as if filling in a silhouette. I know I'm not doing it justice here. But in any case, I've thought about this quite a bit. I wonder if there could be a sort of free-floating evil that can enter someone who's emotionally damaged. Think of that chilling look that one sees in the eyes of a crazed street person: that zombie-like glare of the damned. Such constructs might work like viruses: always there, and generally not an issue, unless the system has been weakened in some fundamental way. But then they take root. Perhaps they can even be summoned by a third party, through the use of a destructive will power. But on the other hand, one might summon creative energies through prayer, or through an appeal to ancient thought-forms: so-called guardian angels or divinities. It's been proven that positive thought can accelerate the healing process. So perhaps there are also creative powers that can be invited into one's life."

After pausing for a moment to order another round, he continued: "Think of that mysterious force that one feels late at night while walking along a seashore. It's real, but it *transcends* man. We're part of it, yes. But we're not *it!* Or a tree, budding in spring, with those lovely light-green tips. How thrilling they are! Such things always inspire a mystical elevation in me: the uplifting appearance of the sprouting leaves; the profound awe one experiences on a star-dazzled night, with a palpable benevolence radiating from the heavens. Those feelings are *in* us, but what we feel is *beyond* us. I think I've always been in touch with this realm. I recall, as a child, being struck by such things, especially when the ambient light and atmosphere were just right. Once, when I was a teenager, I felt it sweep over me. The air crackled; it was that clear. But what is it? A connection that one feels in the very marrow, in the dynamo of the soul! Damn it, it's like being in love!"

He regarded me with a charming grin, then softly chuckled. "You know," he added, "it's often occurred to me that acid-heads and Christian Fundamentalists have something in common. We've all met someone who's tripping on LSD who just lays the truth on you: 'It's all in the *yellow*, man! It's the *yellow!* Just *open* yourself to it!" And you think, 'Yeah, sure, buddy; whatever you say.' But he feels that he's got the truth, or at least *some* version of it, and you're just not hip enough to get it. Jesus freaks are the same way; they're always tripping on Christ. 'He's the answer! Surrender to the Lord!' Come to think of it, whenever they lay that rap on you, they seem to have dilated pupils. If only they could administer that Christ thing on a *blotter!* But maybe that's what the *wafer* is all about ..."

"Careful now; you're treading on the Elysian Mysteries!"

"Maybe the Christian God secured a monopoly by floating junk bonds on a library in Alexandria. The library went under and got burned to a crisp, with no insurance. But then the deed was done. The Almighty made the grab, and, by the time he was finished, no investigator could touch him, because now he was too powerful."

"Don't piss him off, Slim. I hear that he's one crazy mother. He's even liable to *flood* the place."

"He's as crazy as a bedbug! But luckily, I still have your friendship to ground me. Sometimes, all this constant change can be a bit disorientating."

"Have you had any revelatory dreams? One can always request an omen from the netherworld."

"The other night I dreamed that leaves of grass were sprouting on my head. Not only grass, but white flowers, too. I was going to cut it, but I feared the consequences of spoiling such a splendid arrangement ... one that seemed to be carefully attended to by a gardener. But I couldn't go outside looking like that, so I stuffed the greenery and the little white flowers, which were bell shaped, under a baseball cap. I have so much fun while I sleep!"

"Perhaps it means that you know better than to cast your pearls – or your bell-shaped wonders – before the swine. It also suggests that your mind is resting on fertile ground."

"You mean to say that I'm full of *merde*?"

"Now, now, Slim, not at all the same thing!"

"What a relief!"

"Just imagine how Van Gogh would have portrayed you ..."

"Like a sunflower gone to seed!"

Crawling King Snake

I was seated at the terrace of the Dojo, sipping a bowl of miso soup and editing a manuscript, when a woman approached with a friendly smile.

"Do you mind if I sit here? It's the only empty chair, and I don't feel like being inside on such a nice day ..."

Wearing a Christian Dior designer dress and donning a pearl necklace, she seemed to be out of place on the most anarchistic block of the Lower East Side. Perhaps, I thought, she's a tourist, slumming it. With her blonde highlights and heavy, guttural speech, I imagined that she might be visiting from Germany.

"Where are you from?" I asked, gesturing for her to sit down. "You have a charming accent, but I can't quite place it."

"Can't you tell? The land of Gustav Klimt."

"Vienna? Lucky you. It's been my dream to live in Europe. I'm utterly exhausted by Manhattan."

"But it's such a lively city!"

"The sidewalks are like a treadmill, with people rushing from store to store, or from appointment to appointment ... and with very little in between to soothe the soul. What I really crave is history, beauty, and culture."

"It's true, Europe has all that, and a certain form of beauty that you just can't find here. But there's a regimentation in my country that I've grown to detest. Perhaps the grass is always greener elsewhere, but I'd rather live here, or in Paris, which is where I'll be headed next, than in Austria."

"Paris? But that's exactly where I want to be!"

With the subject of Europe on the table I was all ears, and

Dochma had a fascinating assortment of tales to tell. She said that, during the Second World War, her father was a calculating double agent who'd worked with the Russians as well as the Germans; yet somehow he'd managed to emerge unscathed. Years later, when she'd asked: "What exactly did you do during the Nazi regime?" he calmly replied, "The same thing that everyone else did."

"And what was that?"

"I tried to save my ass."

As much as she detested this reply – which she would hold up as "evidence" against him – I eventually came to realize that Dochma could be just as self-serving and duplicitous as her old man. But instead of surviving a world war, her mission was to do anything she could – no matter how unscrupulous – to avoid being hunkered down in a normal, salaried job.

When we first met she was milking her soon-to-be ex-husband, Kevin, for everything he was worth. I later learned that Kevin was a wealthy Austrian aristocrat, which was probably why she married him in the first place. It had long been her dream to form a tourism company, she said, and Kevin had agreed to finance it. But although the idea was hers, the sweat and blood – to manage it and make it work on a daily basis – had largely fallen upon Kevin's shoulders.

Her husband sounded like another wheeler-dealer, but he certainly didn't know how to handle Dochma. One day when they became embroiled in an argument over the direction of the company, she grabbed a steel-backed accountancy ledger and smashed it so hard over his head that the metal cover dented and reshaped itself along the curvature of his skull.

But despite such rage-filled dramas, Dochma's more tender side refused to be completely extinguished. Had she lacked this more humane quality, I would never have found her attractive. Eventually I attributed this benign aspect to her mother's influence. Dochma had dismissively characterized her as a sheepish, servile, dependent lady, adding that, before her parents had married, her mother had followed Dochma's father wherever he went, having concluded early on that her fate was inexorably tied to his.

According to Dochma, the only "heroic" event of her mother's life had occurred toward the end of the war, after her future husband had settled in West Germany. Not wanting to be separated from him in the East, she stole out after midnight and crawled through a dank, dangerous forest, braving enemy fire. But eventually she realized that she'd simply traced an enormous circle and had returned to precisely where she'd first started off. The following night, however, crawling on her belly once again, she found her way back to her future husband.

But was heroism only to be found in such high-pitched drama, I wondered. Besides, I was convinced that Dochma's mother possessed various other admirable traits that Dochma may have been incapable of seeing. It also didn't escape my attention that Dochma's search for self-affirmation had forced her to make a similar circuitous route through the existential underbrush of the world. And just like her mother, she often ended up right where she started.

As she searched for an adventure that might somehow define her identity, Dochma decided to leave Kevin and to travel – with his money, of course – to America. When we first met, she was winding down her American tour but postponing her return to Europe for as long as possible. She continually spoke about how she hated the rigidity of Austria, especially the strict, old-fashioned etiquette and endless rules and regulations.

"They behave like a bunch of robots!" she exclaimed with a *huff*, adding that she'd never live there again.

Rather than pursue a cosseted life of predictability, now she was obsessed with travel to foreign lands. And this fearlessness – or was it foolishness? – lent her a certain magnetism. But despite her loquacious manner, there was also something cold, hardened, and calculating about Dochma: a sort of hermetically sealed emotional life, which led me to lose interest in contacting her again. But a few days later, while walking along Lower Broadway, whom should I run into but Dochma.

She'd just attended a production at the Joseph Papp Public Theater, she said, and now she was on her way uptown, where she was subletting a small apartment.

"And what are *you* doing here?" Before I could reply, she added, "Would you like to go for a coffee?"

Against my better judgment, I accompanied her to the West Village. Although I'd initially decided to blow her off, this unexpected meeting seemed to be eerily serendipitous. After all, what were the chances of running into her again, especially in such a big city? As Knut Hamsun's protagonist sarcastically remarks in *Pan* – that novelistic testimony to the absurdity of love – "I don't know what to think. Maybe it was fate." But now, ignoring Hamsun's wry premonishment, I invited her to dinner.

* * *

I soon realized that I was an anomaly in Dochma's social life, for normally she'd pursue relationships only with men who could assist her in some direct, material fashion. Once she took a look at my flat, with its fifth-floor walk-up and monkish austerity – which featured little more than hundreds of paperbacks and a well-worn sofa that Drew and I had hauled from a nearby dumpster – it was clear that I was no sugar daddy. So she briefly distanced herself and disappeared.

But then it must have occurred to her that there was

something else I could offer: the dream of becoming a writer. For some inexplicable reason, Dochma believed that, if she could polish her language skills, she would reap a fortune by selling screenplays in Hollywood. The more she spoke about writing, the more she seemed to convince herself that only I could turn this magic key that would transform her into a world-renowned, fawned over, widely celebrated author.

At first I did all I could to dissuade her from such a plan; for the pursuit of a literary vocation wasn't at all what she'd imagined it to be. Time and again, I drummed it into her: "In the end, nothing may bear fruit. But one does it anyway, just for the sheer wonder of it, and never with any utilitarian goal. Otherwise, the Muse may revolt, and she may even sabotage you."

But Dochma would hear none of this. In her mind, the ideal artist was a proud, arrogant, boastful creature – a vainglorious preener who'd earned the right to lord it over everyone else.

As with so many things, our views were diametrically opposed. "No, Dochma, the authentic creator should be a *modest* fellow, especially once he realizes that such a gift transcends his personal control." But I might just as well have been speaking Swahili at a Mormon hootenanny.

The following week Drew decided to move back to Brooklyn, to live in his parent's basement in order to save some up some money. I was just barely getting by, but now I had a considerably larger rent to pay.

Enter, stage left, Dochma.

Upon learning of Drew's departure she offered what she referred to as a *simple business proposition*. She would move into my flat, and we'd split the bills until she left for Paris. But I could also accompany her there, where I would teach her to write and edit her scripts, in exchange for free room and board.

While elaborating upon her plan, her eyes widened and

seemed to glow with a naive enthusiasm. As I would later learn, she often assumed this expression whenever she began to concoct one of her more harebrained schemes.

"But what if we grow tired of each other," I asked, "and then I'm stuck without a centime on the Champs-Elysées?"

Throwing her hands up, she exclaimed, "But why are you so *pessimistic?*" Apparently, this wasn't the reaction she was expecting.

"Dochma, as a citizen of Europe, you can work there legally. But how will I support myself as an illegal immigrant in France?"

"You can teach English."

"Without knowing a word of French?"

"Of course! It's called English language *conversation*. Lots of expats earn a living that way. You just correct their grammar and help them to maintain, through practice, whatever skills they've already developed. Believe me, you'd be great at it! After all, you're a writer and an eclectic reader. I've already noticed that you can talk about almost any subject ..."

A few weeks later she moved into my flat and we set up house. But not surprisingly, it didn't take long for Dochma to grow restless. One morning, before we'd even finished our coffee, she blurted out:

"Artists need *inspiration!* Let's plan a trip. Pick a spot. Where would you like to go?"

I gazed up at an oversized world map that was tacked on a wall above my desk. At once, my eyes drifted to the contours of Venezuela.

* * *

From the moment that we stepped foot in Caracas there was trouble, most of it spawned by Dochma's unquenchable wanderlust.

We were booked into a palatial suite at the Sheraton, facing a nearby mountain. That night, from our bedroom window, I witnessed what appeared to be a joyous array of glittering lights, with the mountainside resembling a Christmas tree festooned with pinpoint bulbs.

But what had appeared so lovely at midnight bore a rather sinister face at dawn. The next morning we discovered that the lights were bare, incandescent bulbs hanging from mud shacks constructed of twigs and earth. A few of the luckier inhabitants slept under roofs composed of rusted sheets of corrugated tin. We later viewed these shacks up close, and I was horrified by the manner in which the peasants were forced to live.

Neither Dochma nor I were prepared for Venezuela's indigence – or for its dangers. Before departing from Manhattan, the only advice I'd received from my Venezuelan friends was not to drink the tap water. But while my comrades had emerged from the upper rungs of the social ladder, most of the country was stuck in abject poverty. As a trip on the Caracas metro quickly revealed, the middle class, composed mostly of office workers, was rather small. For the most part, the nation was divided between an elite of "haves" who dominated a burgeoning mass of "have-nots."

Checking into our hotel, I asked the manager – a blond-haired boy from Idaho – where we might promenade later that evening.

"Sir, you should go *nowhere*. Caracas isn't safe after sunset." Evincing a stiff, suspicious look in his pale-blue eyes, he inquired if we were Canadians.

"No, we're from Manhattan. Why? What's the problem with Canadians?"

His hardened expression now melted into a smile. Darting his eyes around the room, he leaned forward and whispered:

"They're *cheap!* They won't spend a *dime!* They refuse to shop at the local stores or contribute anything to the economy. Instead, they arrive with boxes of *canned food.* And they eat the rest of their meals in the cafeteria, where everything's already been paid for, with package deals!" It was the first time that I'd ever heard anyone making disparaging remarks about Canadians, and I was at a loss for words.

The following afternoon we were sipping coffee under an outdoor canopy when dozens of Quebecois tourists arrived en masse, for their scheduled meal. Afterward they splashed around in a swimming pool, then retreated back to their rooms. In the days ahead, this ritual was repeated like clockwork, three times a day.

The hotel had cordoned off a small section along the shore that featured powdery white sand and a lifeguard. Selecting an isolated spot, I unfolded a towel and reclined under a sizzling sun. But Dochma soon grew restless. Thanks to her ceaseless appetite for titillation, it seemed that relaxing on a beautiful beach just wasn't exciting enough.

"This scene is for *tourists,*" she groaned. "Tomorrow let's rent a car and drive through the jungle!" She was fascinated with untamed places, she said, because they served as a counterpoint to her own regimented upbringing. Having visited the African rain forests a few years earlier, now she wanted to explore the Venezuelan wilderness.

The next morning, while I was still asleep she rented a two-door sedan. But after thirty minutes of bouncing along a primitive road, I convinced her to turn around before the car bottomed out.

"If we're going to do this, at the very least we'll need a jeep. Otherwise, we'll be goners."

An hour later she returned with a brand-new Honda Land Rover, painted a shimmering tint of bronze.

My driver's license had already expired, so I was exiled to the passenger's seat. With Dochma regally stationed behind the wheel in her designer dress, and with me donning a faded jean jacket, shoulder-length hair, and an overflowing beard – now resembling Che Guevara more than Walt Whitman – we elicited plenty of unwanted attention as we embarked upon what would prove to be a most harrowing adventure.

Slowly ascending a towering mountain, from Caracas we headed east. Our plan was to follow the coast, then stop at a resort before sunset. For if Caracas was dangerous at night, I mused, I could only imagine what went on in the jungle.

Occasionally we'd pass a lonesome figure stationed on the shoulder of the road with a hot plate plugged into his car, selling drinks and homemade snacks. When we stopped to buy some coffee from one of these bare-chested entrepreneurs, he handed me a couple of paper cups filled with a rich, dark brew, but he refused to accept my bolivars. I remained puzzled when, no matter what I said or did, he waved the money aside. A deeply bronzed man with a proud, stoic bearing and wiry physique, he seemed to be preoccupied by something. After thanking him, we continued on.

"What do you make of that?" I wondered, still perplexed by his behavior.

"I don't know," Dochma frowned. "But he seemed to be awfully nervous about something."

A few hours later the tarmac was replaced by a dirt road, which zigzagged beneath a forest of staggering height. The foliage was so thick that it blotted out most of the light. And whenever we approached a hamlet, the road splintered into a several directions, making it difficult to see where it picked up again.

The settlements were composed of a handful of scattered

shacks. Though they were larger than the ones near our hotel, they were nearly as shabby. A dozen men wearing only shorts and sandals would be hard at work, hacking at banana stems with their gleaming machetes. No one smiled. Instead, with their glistening blades held upright, they glared at us. Perhaps, I thought, they were trying to decide whether to slice us into pieces, steal the car, and dump our bodies into a moldy pit.

When we first encountered one of these bone-rattling scenes, I told Dochma to stop the car about fifty feet before the hamlet and to keep the motor running. Pretending to be a laid-back tourist for whom glinting machetes were simply par for the course, I grabbed an oversized road map and sauntered up to the biggest, brawniest fellow. Behaving as uninhibited as possible and all the while maintaining a cordial, respectful manner, I pointed at the map – now unfolded like an accordion – and asked, in broken Spanish, *Where the fuck is that road?*

At first he just stood there, glaring at me. Then he glanced at the map as if it were a stinking piece of snake manure, unfolded his brawny arms, flexed his bicep, and pointed his shiny tool to the right.

Somberly muttering my thanks, I grimly nodded to each of his cohorts and gingerly backed away. As we drove off, they remained motionless – like a bevy of glassy-eyed iguanas – slowly blinking, silently contemplating their lost prey.

A few miles farther east, we stopped at a makeshift diner operating out of a back porch. Several tables were positioned under a plastic green canopy, facing a yard. As we sat down, an iridescent lizard stared at us, perched on a nearby boulder, while chickens and roosters cackled and hobbled round.

Three petite young ladies ran the joint. Native Americans, they possessed delicate features and an ethereal, otherworldly beauty. They regarded us with shiny ebony eyes as we silently communicated what we wanted in sign language, pointing to various dishes on the menu.

The youngest one, a slender girl dressed in a brightly striped red-and-yellow fabric, snatched a pair of chickens and sliced off their heads. Down to the last morsel, the meal was delectable.

Following several more confrontations with banana hackers – for each time we entered a village, the road seemed to peter out – panic set in.

"If this path doesn't turn into asphalt soon," I said, "we'll be in trouble. Once it gets dark, we'll be forced to sleep in this bloody jungle. And come dawn, I doubt that there'll be anything left of us." I figured that, at most, we had a couple of minutes left before the inky darkness completely enveloped us.

At the very last moment of dwindling light, just before I lost all hope, an asphalt ribbon suddenly appeared. The throbbing hum of rubber reverberating on solid tarmac had never sounded so sweet.

Allons! as Walt proclaims, *The road is before us!*

I was almost compelled to quote from his euphoric "Song of the Open Road" – "Henceforth I whimper no more, postpone no more, need nothing, done with indoor complaints, libraries, querulous criticisms, strong and content I travel the open road" – almost, but not quite. But there was one line that, had I remembered it, would have been chillingly appropriate:

> You road I enter upon and look around,
> I believe you are not all that is here,
> I believe that much unseen is also here.

* * *

Although our final destination was the coastal village of Cumana, I gradually realized that Dochma's actual goal was a flirtation with oblivion. Apparently she was a creature who never felt fully alive minus some colossal, death-defying rattle, despite the harm that it might cause those around her. And then, against all odds, if life wriggled out of death's maw once again, she'd repeat the gamble – or up the ante.

Emerging from the jungle, the road curved along the coast toward a resort village in Pueblo El Hatillo. From a distance we could see that it hosted one of those honeycomb-shaped hotels that had sprouted up throughout Venezuela in the late Seventies, often in the least likely of places, such as here. But more often than not, once they were halfway built they were abandoned. By the early Eighties the economy had taken a dive, and the financing for such projects had abruptly dried up.

Turning off the road, we entered a hotel parking lot that contained only a handful of cars. But when we approached the front desk, a clerk took one look at me, frowned, and announced that there weren't any vacancies. Following such a hair-raising escapade, I could hardly believe it.

Completely dispirited, we returned to the jeep and decided to drive a little farther east, to Puerto Piritu. When we arrived there, however, it was more of the same: hardly a vehicle in sight, yet "fully booked." But this time, the clerk took me aside and handed me a business card.

"This is my associate, Mr. Uribe. Perhaps he can help. He manages some private accommodations. Shall I give him a call?"

At this point I'd have accepted a mud shack, but I attempted to mask my despair.

"Sure," I replied lightheartedly, "Why not?"

Twenty minutes later a tall gangly shifty-eyed man sauntered in. Dressed in a dapper yet informal manner, Uribe could easily have played the part of a professional assassin.

He exchanged a few words in Spanish with the clerk, then turned to us with a crooked smile.

"Follow me in your car."

We drove along a side street, then ascended a coastal mountain. Twenty miles later we approached what appeared to be an armed barracks. A ten-foot-high concrete wall surrounded a compound. As we approached the front entrance, I spotted a guard with a machine gun positioned in a turret. He nodded to Uribe, then waved us inside.

The compound consisted of an interlocking series of buildings featuring elegant, well-appointed suites. The grounds were illuminated with brilliant floodlights, but there wasn't a soul in sight.

We followed Uribe into an elaborate apartment featuring sprawling bedrooms, a spacious living- and dining area, a sauna, and a commanding view of the foaming Atlantic on one side and the lush jungle on the other. But when he mentioned the price, I realized that, somehow, he'd mistaken us for millionaires.

As casually as possible, I replied that we really didn't want to spend that much. Upon hearing this his eyes narrowed, and he frowned. Confronted by his steely gaze, I realized that there was nothing to prevent him from slicing my throat, tossing me out the window, raping Dochma, and then paying the guard to dig a ditch and bury our corpses. What were we even doing there, I wondered, in the middle of nowhere, in a lavish compound more suitable for oil barons or powerful drug lords?

Then it dawned on me: They think we're *coke dealers!* And at once, everything fell into place. Me, with my Che Guevara beard, Dochma with her ostentatious jewelry and designer dress ... What else could we be? It also explained the awkward behavior of the fellow who'd offered us free coffee, the hotels that wouldn't dare book us, and the icy looks that we'd encountered almost everywhere.

Once we returned to the hotel, Uribe snapped at the clerk for having wasted his time. But he remained cordial with us, perhaps realizing that it was the clerk's error and not ours for sending us on a wild-goose chase.

Before we left, I asked the clerk for the name of the best hotel in the next town along the road.

As we approached Caicara, just as we entered the hotel parking lot, I turned to Dochma and said: "You go inside alone, while I stow away in the car."

The minute she approached the front desk we were immediately booked. I waited till she had the key in hand before daring to emerge from the jeep. When the clerk spotted me he grimaced, but now there was nothing he could do about it.

The next day we continued east. At every two-bit village along the way, whenever we entered a main street it was like being back in the 1950s. Standing in small groups on the pavements, the men wore their hair closely cropped and neatly parted on the side. As we drove by they'd stare at us as if we were narco-terrorists.

A few hours later we were pulled over at a military checkpoint and told to step out of the car. The captain, a petite man with a grim, haunted look, regarded me somberly and, once he realized that I didn't speak much Spanish, gestured for me to remove my jacket. First he pointed to his eye, then to mine, as if to say: "Watch everything I do so that afterward you can't claim that I planted drugs in your clothing."

I handed over my jacket, and he unrolled the sleeves and meticulously inspected every little crease and fold. Then he opened the hood of the car to search the engine. A half dozen soldiers stood behind him, glaring at us, their machine guns glinting under the harsh sunlight.

The captain was obviously the alpha male, and the look in his eyes seemed to be sharper and more keenly focused than that of his comrades. But he treated us fairly and, when he didn't find anything incriminating, waved us along. As we drove away, I turned to Dochma and said: "If only the cops in Manhattan were that civilized!"

The next town along the road was Barcelona, and we stopped there briefly for supplies. Dochma entered a grocery store to purchase some sandwiches while I waited in the car, studying a map.

Moments later a scrawny man staggered over to the jeep with a look of euphoria shining in his eyes. I figured that he was either drunk or a madman. Sticking his bony fingers through an open window, he touched my hair and stammered: "*Jesucristo!*" – convinced that I was the Savior himself. Just then, Dochma appeared and entered from the other side.

"What's he want?"

"He thinks I'm Christ."

"You must be joking."

"Listen, it's not the first time."

"What do you mean?"

"Never mind. Step on the gas, and get us the hell out of here."

Disembarking in the historic village of Cumana, we strolled at leisure and admired the whitewashed colonial architecture glaring under a midday sun. When we stopped for lunch at a diner, the proprietor said that Cumana had once hosted the earliest European settlement in North America. Then he proudly pointed out the window, at a long white banner that was hanging across a narrow lane, upon which was written: *Veinteaños de democracia* – twenty years of democracy.

We devoured a delicious spread of seafood that was served by his Native American wife, then we boarded a motorboat to travel to the opposite shore of the peninsula. A sign nailed to the side of the vessel said *No Smoking*. Several canisters of petrol rattled beside the stern, next to a pilot who was puffing away on a cigarette.

Observing this with increasing irritation, Dochma grew visibly annoyed. Just as she was about to say something, I told her to shut up. Besides not wanting to be pegged as a pushy gringo, I trusted this man with his steady grip on the tiller more than I did Dochma, whose hand on the wheel had never ceased to lead us directly into trouble.

From a distance the beach resembled an idyllic picture postcard. But as we approached, I noticed pungent oil slicks and raw sewage, which was flushed from rusty pipes emerging from sandy embankments. Now I understood why the resorts had featured their own swimming pools and why the Canadians rarely entered the ocean.

* * *

On our return trip, just as we ascended the tortuous road winding up the mountainside, a thunder-and-lightning storm broke out, and the roads were flooded.

We were driving on a narrow ribbon that abutted the edge of a precipice, minus any guardrail. Every few minutes structures resembling dog houses flashed by, some illuminated by flickering candles. Only gradually did I realize they were shrines to the dead: dedicated to those luckless travelers who had plummeted into an abyss – and vanished into nothingness. The wavering candlelight provided the only illumination on this dismal stretch, other than our own headlights. Every so often a truck would come barreling around a curve; and, from the way they were careening, I suspected that many of the drivers were drunk.

Just as we were approaching a hairpin turn, our jeep stalled.

Dochma managed to swerve onto a narrow shoulder, where we came to an abrupt halt. We couldn't have been positioned at a worse spot.

"We're probably stalling because of that cheap gasoline," she grumbled.

"Push the pedal very gently; try to restart it."

But despite her best efforts, it wouldn't turn over. Glancing round, I realized that we were stuck in a blind spot.

"If a truck comes speeding round that curve," I said, "it will slam right into us and toss us over the cliff."

Sounding uncustomarily sober, she sighed, "Maybe you'd better get out and keep an eye on the road while I keep trying."

As I unlocked the door, a pair of headlights flashed into our rearview mirror. A truck was coming to a stop about a hundred feet away.

"Either he's here to help us," I said, "or to slice our throats."

Just then the engine turned over, and we drove off. But as we approached another curve the car swerved on an oil slick. Spinning out of control, we slid right to the edge of the precipice. As we came to a halt, I gazed over a cliff and took a deep breath.

"Well, Dochma, you wanted an adventure. Here you are."

"Why must you always focus on the *negative* side of things?"

Upon hearing this I burst out laughing.

By now the rain was so heavy that it appeared to be coming down in sheets. How would we ever get out of this alive? Yet somehow, against all odds, we managed to creep back into Caucagua – about fifty miles east of Caracas – where we booked a room for the night. At dawn, we awoke under a clear sky.

* * *

By the time we rolled into Caracas my nerves were shot. I

told Dochma to park in front of the Sheridan so that we could make a beeline for the bar.

"Now, all I want from life is a stiff drink. Come and help me with the luggage."

"What are you doing?" she whined, as impatient as ever. "Just leave everything in the car. We'll get it later."

"Oh, no; I don't think so, Dochma. After what we've been through, I'm not taking any more chances."

With baggage in hand, I approached the bar deck and ordered a vodka for Dochma and a rum on the rocks for myself. Downing it in a flash, I immediately ordered another.

Suddenly remembering that my friends had warned me to avoid ice cubes for fear of hepatitis, I shouted at the bartender: "Hey, forget the ice!" Everywhere I turned, it was as if the hounds of hell were snipping at my heels, either via microbes or machetes.

Sipping my rum, I began to dream of simple pleasures such as donning a bathing suit and going for a swim. With this in mind, I paid for our drinks and turned to leave. But once we were outside, the jeep was nowhere to be seen.

In the twenty minutes that we'd been stationed at the bar, some enterprising thief had spirited it away – right in front of the hotel! Fortunately, I hadn't followed Dochma's advice about the luggage. The only thing I'd left behind was a cassette recording of John Lee Hooker's classic blues tune, "Crawling King Snake."

I continued to stare at the empty curb as I shook my head in disbelief. Bouncing along that reptile-ridden jungle, hour after hour, day after day, I'd blasted "Crawling King Snake" at an ear-deafening volume. All the while, I prayed that John Lee's words would somehow protect us, like the chant of a sacred mantra. But now, who – or what – would see us through the dawn?

"We survived the machetes, the military checkpoints, the explosive cans of petrol, the hazardous cliffs ... even the tainted ice cubes!" I exclaimed. "But we were no match for the street urchins of Caracas ..."

"I'd better call the car-rental company," Dochma sighed, "and tell them about the jeep."

Utterly exasperated, I returned to the bar for another rum while Dochma waited in the lobby for a sales rep. As soon as she explained what happened, he was convinced that we'd sold the car to a machete hacker. He just couldn't get over the fact that we were crazy enough to drive through that jungle at night. In fact, he didn't know what to believe. Maybe we hadn't traveled there at all but had simply delivered the vehicle to a thief around the corner.

He even called the president of the company, interrupting his sacred Saturday afternoon golf game. Now, instead of relaxing in a cart, the boss was forced to drop his balls and escort us to a local police station, to file a report.

"Not take *us*, Dochma. You're going there *alone!* If they take one look at me, I'll get the Che Guevara treatment all over again. And I'm *not* spending the night in a Venezuelan jail. In fact, I'm staying right here. While you're dealing with Mr. Rent-a-Car, I'll be studying the local talent as they ply their trade."

"The local talent?"

"Haven't you noticed? The hookers at the bar."

Seeing the logic in all this, she at once agreed.

Ordering another rum, I observed the comings and goings of several attractive young women dressed in bright orange mini-skirts, who were shuttling back and forth between the deck and the clients' rooms upstairs.

Meanwhile, Dochma was whisked away to the station. But once they arrived there, the desk sergeant couldn't be bothered. He remained sequestered with his colleagues in a back room, engrossed in a rerun of *Starsky and Hutch* – an American TV serial from the Seventies about a pair of "hip" LA cops.

It was only thanks to Dochma's insolence that they were finally roused from their torpor. Just as Starsky was handcuffing a dope dealer on the corner of Broadway and 23rd Street, Dochma stepped behind the front desk and banged on the back door.

Following a lengthy argument with the sergeant, during which Dochma continued to shout about how *appalled* she was to be treated like a *common criminal*, she at last agreed to be fingerprinted. Then everything went back to "normal," with the TV tuned to a rerun of that Robinson Crusoe-like comedy, *Gilligan's Island*.

Now that she was safe and sound and back at the Sheridan, it was time to get the hell out of Caracas. In the morning I insisted that we arrive at the airport several hours early: something that, normally, I'd never do, but I didn't want to tempt fate.

We exchanged our money; then we waited, first in line at the terminal. But at boarding time we were prevented from taking another step, because we'd failed to pay an "exit tax." *The final insult!* Now we were forced to rush back and forth to exchange dollars for bolivars, pay the tax at a bureau located at the opposite end of the airport, then scurry back to the boarding area. By the time we'd accomplished all this, the plane was already filled and idling on a sizzling tarmac, with the captain impatiently awaiting his last two passengers.

Frantically dashing to a boarding suite, I handed our passports to a gray-faced official who sat insouciantly behind a podium and lazily eyed them. Behaving as if we had all the time in the world, he slowly turned them round, casually flipped through the pages, scribbled a bit, yawned, scratched his nose, and did everything but check us out. Finally, I exploded:

"What the hell is wrong with you? If you don't step on it, we'll miss our flight!" Of course, he didn't understand a word, but the gist of it was crystal clear.

Following my outburst, a man seated nearby who was reading a newspaper suddenly stepped forward. He was an undercover agent of some sort; and, in perfect English, he politely asked what was wrong. When I spilled my guts, he listened carefully, nodded, then told the moron behind the desk to let us go.

Bolting to the end of a corridor, we were greeted by an unsmiling, stiff-lipped stewardess who sarcastically muttered: "*Welcome* aboard." Then we sheepishly entered a planeload of disgruntled passengers, with everyone eyeballing us angrily, well aware that they'd been forced to bake in the stifling heat because of our tardiness.

I slipped into a window seat, closed my eyes, and ignored Dochma for the rest of the ride.

As the Brazilian author Paulo Gomes writes in his novel, *Três mulheres*, "Never did a man owe so much annoyance to only one woman."

As I mentally reviewed the details of our trip, I realized that there were very few smiles to be seen on the land below. Even while promenading along the boardwalks of tourist towns that hosted bars, sandwich shops, and amusement rides, no matter where we ventured everything seemed to be enshrouded in lingering despair.

It wouldn't take long for the peasants to rise up and revolt. Twelve months later, over three thousand perished in the "Caracazo" riots, thanks to the iron-fisted rule of the Democratic Action government. And in 1993, after surviving two coups attempts, President Carlos Pérez was impeached for embezzlement. The sadness that we'd observed was real, and it was mixed with rage.

Shortly after we returned to the Lower East Side, I accompanied Dochma to the airport for her return trip to Paris, all the while wondering if this would be our final encounter.

Though I was touched by her teary farewell, I was relieved to be alone again. Returning to my flat, as I shut the door I sighed with contentment. At long last, I thought, the precarious adventure with the Fräulein was over! But then, I spotted a gift package sitting on my desk.

What could it be?

A copy of *Paris par arrondissement*, featuring maps of each *quartier* as well as an index of every street in Paris.

Dochma certainly knew which buttons to push. It was nothing less than a dare … and one that she suspected I would soon embrace.

The following week she called to say that she'd found a spacious apartment, located just a block north of Hôtel de Ville. "So, when are you arriving?"

She acted as if it were all a done deal, even though I hadn't reached any final decision about returning to Europe. But after speaking with my friend Slim, I realized that if I didn't move to Paris I'd probably regret it.

* * *

Six months before I expatriated I quit my job, hunkered down at my desk, and began to work on my novel about the Walt Whitman Asylum, attempting to weave the story of Jonah and the other lost souls who had inhabited that lugubrious dwelling named after America's greatest poet. After hauling in the day's catch, I'd amble outside to retrieve a cappuccino and to say hello to Bonzet.

That summer he'd positioned himself near the corner of First Avenue, seated regally in an aluminum-folding chair. According to Slim, this same spot had once hosted the southeast section of St. Mark's Cemetery: a nineteenth-century necropolis that was now paved over and largely forgotten.

Bonzet confided in me that, one by one, each of Freddie's cohorts had grown so fed up with his dictatorial nature that they'd abandoned the club. So now, Freddie ruled the roost like a solitary emperor – with no one to contradict, challenge, or disappoint him. Bonzet's post on the corner was a sort of public acknowledgment that even Freddie's congenial "wife" considered him to be so repugnant that "she" was more at peace on a lonesome street corner than in the shelter of the club. But lonely it was not, for every Tom, Dick, and Harry in the local Mafia would stop by and pay their respects as they chatted and laughed along with him.

Bonzet was an eminently discreet fellow, but one afternoon his curiosity got the better of him. With his baby-blue eyes looking me up and down and with a smile lingering at the corner of his mouth, he blurted out: "So, what are you doing with yourself these days?" When I replied that I'd arranged to collect unemployment so that I could work on my novel before moving to Paris, he broke into such guffaws that he nearly choked on his own hearty laughter.

"*Jeezus,*" he sputtered, "you have it better than a *made man!* You don't even have a *boss* to answer to!" Sizing me up with his widening saucer eyes and regarding me as if I were smarter than the most *capo di tutti i capi*, he added: "How did you ever manage to come up with such a *racket?*"

We'd carry on like this well into the fall, when the leaves from the trees in the school yard across the street began to rustle around his enormous feet. The shriveled foliage of Manhattan always seemed so unreal to me, painted with preternatural hues that shifted not only into flaring oranges and golden browns but also into deep shades of sulfuric black as the city's pollution welled up through the tree roots and deposited its poison into the elemental design of nature itself.

It was during one such autumn afternoon that Bonzet's corpse was discovered several days after he'd perished, when his disappearance had aroused suspicion. And by then, the neighbors had noticed the terrible smell. Blessed man that he was, he'd passed away suddenly, from a heart attack, while taking a bath.

His coffin was coated with polished copper, and it was the largest one that I'd ever seen. It could easily have accommodated a pair of normal-sized men, especially in girth. Instead of a casket it resembled a leviathan treasure chest.

All the local mobsters appeared at his wake, dressed in an impressive array of stolen suits and ties. But Freddie remained seated by himself in a far corner, and he kept his distance from the others – as if exiled because of his enduring mistreatment of the beloved Bonzet.

As soon as I entered the funeral parlor, Bonzet's younger brother Rocco spotted me and his eyes lit up. Grateful that I'd made an appearance, he took me by the crook of the elbow and escorted me directly to the catafalque. Rocco went to great lengths to describe how they'd found his brother's body rotting in a tub; how it had been too decomposed to do a decent embalming job; and how, instead, they'd just scooped everything up and dumped it into this goliath coffin. *And don't it look nice, with that beautiful copper sheen, and raised on that elegant berth?* From the way that Rocco spoke about his brother's remains being reassembled and served on this glittering dish, you might have imagined that he was sharing his recipe for baked ziti or chicken cacciatore.

It was all arranged at Fonzie's Funeral Home, just a few blocks south on First Avenue. Fonzie also owned a restaurant that was next door to De Sena's pastry shop. According to Slim, unless you were in the Mob, Fonzie intentionally served the most disgusting pasta imaginable, because they didn't want any civilians in there. Besides, who needed the hassle when, after all, it was simply a money-laundering joint? Slim loved to say that Fonzie flavored the tomato sauce with the formaldehyde left over from the embalming jobs – for that's how awful it tasted.

When the new attorney general for the Southern District of New York took office, he made certain to have the restaurant wired with plenty of surveillance mikes. Thanks to those hidden microphones in Fonzie's and next door, in De Sena's, many of those old time Mustache Pete's were now back at "school," doing time behind bars.

After paying my final respects to Bonzet, shortly after my thirty-second birthday I expatriated to Paris. I continued with the same routine: working on my novel in the morning, then sauntering along the street for a promenade in the afternoon. But now, with a bowl of espresso in one hand and an *International Herald Tribune* in the other, instead of approaching grimy First Avenue I was seated beside the bubbling fountains at Hôtel de Ville, focusing upon an endless parade of beauty. Despite a frosty December wind, *les parisiennes* continued to dress in flowing skirts and paisley-patterned stockings that highlighted their well-formed calves and thighs, for Paris was made for walking.

Draining my bowl of coffee I'd approach nearby Notre-Dame, whose bell towers were visible from our living room window if you stuck your head out and craned your neck south. Crossing the Seine and heading toward the Left Bank, I'd make a pit stop at the Robespierre bookshop to chat with the proprietor, borrow a novel, or flirt with the young women from Sweden, Tasmania, or Poland. And then, a picturesque descent along the well-worn stone steps at Pont au Double, to continue my leisurely amble upon the *quai*. Approaching Pont de la Tournelle, I'd sit beside the base of the bridge with a stack of books, remaining there till the sun circled over the flying buttresses of Notre-Dame. No doubt, the most corny, touristic view in all of France, yet I never ceased to be a sucker for it, and for good reason. Even now, I would trade all that America has to offer for just this one everlasting gem.

Intimately tied to it all was the steady flow of the Seine, swelling beside the embankment under the rustle of chestnut trees … and transited by fleets of rusty black barges sailing from distant ports. Some carried nothing but tons of sand; and sometimes, when I paused on the *pont* to watch the ships silently slip beneath me, I'd imagine leaping over the railings and falling into the powdery billows, secreting myself away there in order to travel to some forgotten part of France, where I'd continue to live incognito and become, in the vagabond tradition of the boy-poet Rimbaud, "somebody else." If things ever got to a point where I was so down and out that I could no longer survive in Lutèce, rather than tossing myself into the suicidal arms of the pea-green Seine as so many *parisiens* were said to do (at least, those who chose not to jump in front of a speeding metro; for Paris was not just about a tourist's evanescent joy or the soothing rustle of those iconic trees), I would take this leap into the arms of chance herself, come what may.

Year after year I promenaded along those magisterial bridges, especially when the summer winds caressed the topless sunbathers that flanked the cathedral like a divine halo. And I soon came to regard Notre-Dame as a sort of spiritual focal point, not because it was a place of worship but because of its cornucopia of aesthetic treasure.

The sights and sounds of Lutèce ingrained themselves within me through this incremental accrual of experience, until they formed the keynotes of a palette that I would later exploit in order to fashion some new creation. Whenever I returned to the States, however, this core part of my being would shut itself down and lock itself away, refusing to emerge from a self-imposed gaol.

To perceive even a glimpse of all this and then to have it slip away was the most unsettling experience of all.

Bienvenue à Paris

My first Parisian domicile dated back to the 1700s, and it featured those thick, roughly hewn crossbeams on the ceiling (*poutres*) that are often portrayed in paintings by Picasso. While sitting on a windowsill overlooking rue du Temple and sipping a bowl of espresso, sometimes I'd stare at these gnarly beams until imaginary figures emerged from the swirling knots, like ghosts from three centuries past imprinted in the timber. ("I can look at the knot in a piece of wood," says Blake, "until it frightens me.")

The other side of the apartment featured an anteroom that overlooked a well-lit courtyard. Seated there at my desk, I'd often notice, in an adjacent building across the way, a petite young man dressed in a red plaid skirt and starched white apron.

An olive-skinned lad in his early twenties, Adrian appeared to be far more juvenile; for he possessed fine, delicate features and was exceedingly small. He was the lover of our neighbor Louis, a slender businessman in his early thirties who, according to the neighbors, was a descendant of "fallen" aristocrats. What the coded term *fallen* actually meant, and what level of depravity it implied when uttered in such a susurrant tone was not immediately apparent, but we would learn soon enough.

Adrian hailed from Réunion, a French island east of Madagascar, and he'd met Louis while the latter was vacationing there. Louis was constantly on the prowl for adolescent-looking paramours, so he'd decided to set Adrian up as a sort of wife, even christening him with a feminine nickname: "Tandra."

Louis cut a dashing figure in his impeccably tailored suits and ties, but Adrian preferred to dress as a 1950s housewife. With a green feather duster in hand, "Tandra" would mime a French maid as he twirled round the apartment as if dancing in a Hollywood musical. Pirouetting like a delirious ballerina, he'd croon and karaoke with the singers on the radio. But sometimes he'd just hover there, immobile, poised with the duster held like a wand, entranced by his own ensorcellment.

When Dochma invited them over for lunch one afternoon, I turned to Adrian and asked: "So tell me, what do you want to do with your life?"

At first he merely sighed. But then, with a sweet resonant lilt that resembled an Indian flute trilling a haunting twilight melody, he cooed: "I want to be a *woman!*" And we all laughed along with him, for *of course* that's what Tandra wanted to be!

With the approach of summer Louis sublet his flat to a Chinese woman from California, a university student on holiday. Thus it came about that, one memorable afternoon in July, while seated at my desk and furiously typing away, suddenly I heard a deep, guttural moan.

Since it was a balmy day, the french windows were fully opened. I turned toward the sound and glanced outside, and there she was: sprawled naked on a futon positioned beside Louis' windowsill. With her legs spread apart and her ankles held aloft, her ample breasts were bouncing as if there were an earthquake afoot. Her rouged lips gleamed in the sun, and her gullet was opened like a robin redbreast about to pluck a wriggling worm.

Her companion was a broad shouldered, sturdy young man who was pummeling her with great gusto and abandon. To top it off, this gifted stallion possessed the largest member that I've ever seen.

But how can it be, I wondered, that such an unabashedly

pornographic scene is occurring right here, in broad daylight? It must have been about one o'clock, because I was still imbibing my espresso. Back then, I'd brew the highly caffeinated Café Noir brand, although eventually I switched to the superior flavor of Maison du Café, which also lent a greater mental clarity to my labor as I crouched over a keyboard and awaited the first utterance from the Muse. But now, as the reader may well imagine, this delicate, rather tenuous process was irrevocably ruptured.

I was so taken aback that all I could manage was to ask myself: "But am I actually *seeing* this? Or am I delusional? A luscious young lady is stark naked, and she's positioned her mattress so that everyone can watch. And Good Lord, what a gargantuan companion!"

All this flashed through my mind as I stared at the bottoms of her feet. They were making wavering curlicues, like a conductor's wand, while her hips were slapping away and the courtyard was echoing with a cacophonous rhythm of groans, grunts, and screams. For this was one talented boy! He knew exactly what to do with that cumbersome tool, and he played it with the finesse of a concert violinist. What a lucky young lady! As she wiggled, caterwauled, and squirmed like an eel, her high-pitched squeal came to resemble the gleeful trill of an operatic soprano:

> "Oh, I am getting screwed!" sang the nightingale,
> "so deeply and deliciously pounded!" And when
> the golden plum meets his ravenous lips he gasps
> with delight, for its juice tastes so sweet!

Or, as the dairymaid in Gilbert and Sullivan's opera, "Patience," has it:

Archibald! Is it possible? Why, let me look! It is! It
is! It must be! Oh, how happy I am! I thought we
should never meet again! And how you've *grown!*

Although it was her grandest performance, it wasn't the
only one. For she continued to treat us to this unusual *spectacle*
for a few more days ... until the normally tolerant French neighbors put an end to it.

Right after her debut, on the creaking spiral staircase, I ran
into an Algerian painter who rented a studio directly below us.
At once, Mohammed's eyes brightened as he exclaimed: "But
did you *see it?* Did you *hear it?* Can you *believe* it?" We were
each so dazzled and dumbstruck that now we behaved as if we
were old pals, united in this most elemental vision despite the
fact that we'd never before spoken more than a word of greeting to one another. It was as if we were relieved to know that
we hadn't lost our minds – that we didn't need to be carted
away to the Hôtel-Dieu insane asylum.

Mohammed even invited me into his flat to see his latest oil
paintings: enormous portraits of men who carried women
across their shoulders. *In imitatione Christi*, he said, holding up
his meaty palms, for the comely maidens were shaped into the
form of a crucifix. As I studied his passionate but deliberate
brushwork, he added – quite seriously, but with a roguish look
in his ebony eyes – "A man must carry his burden and bear his
woman like a cross, for he cannot escape his fate."

Several days before Louis and Tandra departed for their
holiday, Dochma invited them over for some roast duck. I don't
recall what, exactly, got Louis started on this nefarious subject;
perhaps it was his first glimpse of the main course, or maybe
when Dochma had noted her fondness for La Fontaine's children's tales, which often feature guileless ducks and other

personified woodland creatures, this had flipped a switch in his depraved, sinister psyche. For as we sat there savoring this delectable treat, Louis launched into a story about how, as a boy, he'd occasionally experience a *lust for ducks*. But the problem ("And isn't there *always* a problem!" Adrian whined, dramatically rolling his eyes and throwing his hands up in despair) was that Louis' mother would always catch him just as he was taking out his *zizi* and chasing the fowls round the lake.

"Oh, poor mother!" Tandra moaned.

By the time that Louis reached the end of this sordid tale, I decided that I didn't believe a word of it. I was convinced that he was merely trying to provoke us, but I played along anyway:

"Never mind *Maman*," I exclaimed, "what about those poor ducks, frenetically waddling away?" Out of the corner of my eye, I could see that, despite such admonishments, Louis was enjoying all this attention. And, in equal measure, Dochma was growing increasingly annoyed, as she was no longer the focus of admiration for having prepared such an exquisite meal. And imagine the effect this had upon her appetite!

I introduce this morsel only to illustrate how, despite such abysmal depravities, Louis, the quintessential haughty Frenchman, never hesitated to express his chauvinism and "cultural superiority." In early September, when he returned from whatever outlandish locale he'd traveled to – some third-world hellhole where no one could be bothered about his pedophiliac perversions – Dochma informed him about the venereal exploits of his tenant and her extraordinary paramour. But at first, he wouldn't hear of it. Instead, he brushed it aside with that "superior" French snicker – a hollow, sadistic guffaw – and he refused to allow Dochma to even finish her sentence.

"Ah, you puritanical Anglo-Saxons! Why are you so *pudique*?" Dochma's reaction to his bestial perversions had led him to regard us as prudes, so now he didn't believe us; he was certain that we were exaggerating. But the following week, when Louis and I passed each other in a corridor, he assumed an apologetic tone:

"I must say, you were absolutely right. I also spoke to Mohammed, and to several other neighbors, all of whom reported the same thing. She even came knocking at Mohammed's door, asking to borrow some *sugar*. Obviously, they were looking for participants. Extraordinary, what a *salope* she was! I had no idea ..."

* * *

In the early days, while Dochma was collecting alimony and I was teaching English to a few of our neighbors, neither of us worried much about money. But soon enough, the alimony ran out and the lessons dropped away as my clients disappeared on long summer holidays. All this was further complicated by the fact that I couldn't legally work there. One wrong move, and I'd be stuck on a plane and deported.

We were scratching our heads, trying to decide what to do, when Dochma suggested that I sell a few of my reviewer's books.

"There's a shop on the Left Bank, La Société Robespierre, run by an eccentric old American named Mr. Van Velsor. They say that he pays decent prices."

I selected a stack of books, carefully tucked them into my rucksack, and ambled past Notre-Dame, nodding respectfully, as I always did, to the limestone figures of the zodiac that adorn the western portal. No matter how frequently I visited this splendid cathedral, I knew that the source of its mystery would forever elude me. Entering the church, as you pass under a looming rose window and inhale the damp fragrance of ancient flagstones, and as you drift round the columns that rise up like tree trunks in a Druidic forest, everything else drops away and – *hush* – suddenly, there's no longer a modern world. But then, as your eyes refocus under flickering candlelight, you notice dozens of demoiselles scattered about with their pleated skirts pulled back as they kneel in prayer. Thus, "Our Lady" – Notre-Dame – will always stand as a monument to the divine feminine principle, engraved not just in stone but in the mystery of incarnation.

But now, I was headed for that den of thieves known as la Société Robespierre.

Upon entering the shop, I spotted Van Velsor seated at a front desk, staring into space with his beady eyes, and ignoring everyone around him. Known for his unusual appearance, that day he was dressed in a royal-blue velvet suit and a pink paisley tie, each of which were mottled with numerous food stains. His ash-gray beard was sprinkled with crumbs from a midday meal, and it was shaped into a point at the chin, lending him the appearance of a depraved leprechaun. He still possessed a full head of snow-white hair, which he trimmed by burning off the excess with a candle. Being the most frugal of men, he winced at the idea of paying someone to cut it. Though he was seventy-five he appeared to be in excellent shape, having spent so many years clambering up and down a worn wooden staircase that connected his fourth-floor flat to the shop on the ground floor.

"Excuse me, sir. I have some books for sale."

Annoyed that I'd snapped him out of his trance, Van bolted up in his chair and frenetically shook his head back and forth – as if being ripped from an opium dream.

"Well, then," he sputtered, "don't just stand there! Let's *see* them!"

I handed over several first-editions, each in pristine condition. But to my chagrin, one by one he slammed them facedown on the grimy surface of his desk, all the while behaving as if they were the most despicable trash he'd ever come across as a book vendor. *Irascible, wicked, rude,* and *evil* were a few of the adjectives that whirled through my mind like a tumbleweed.

All those years in Paris had done nothing to improve Van's manners. He didn't even bother to make eye contact as he churlishly barked: "And where did you get all this?"

With a growing sense of *annoyance, disbelief,* and *shock* over what a ridiculous *asshole* he was, I growled: *"I'm a book reviewer!"*

Swiveling his head round and finally making eye contact, he snarled: "And *who* do you work for?"

"Caritas magazine!" I shouted back at him.

Upon hearing this, his persona abruptly transformed into that of a *charming, ingratiating, sweet old man.*

"Caritas? Well, then, why didn't you *say* so?"

Turning to one of the starry-eyed travelers that Van had invited to sleep in his bedbug-infested shop in exchange for an hour of work each day, he shouted: *"Get this man a piña colada!"* With a crooked smile, and attempting to feign a benign regard, he grabbed my wrist with his long bony fingers and escorted me outside.

All around us, old wooden packing crates, now transformed into bookshelves, were stuffed to the gills with ripped, torn, stained, and molding paperbacks … and with everything shelved haphazardly, without rhyme or reason.

"Isn't it *wonderful* here! The most beautiful place in the *world!* Sit down, relax, and have a *drink!"* Gesturing toward an aluminum lounge chair – a rusty, dilapidated piece of rubbish that just barely held itself together – he positioned me under a beam of crisp, golden sunlight.

Moments later, an obsequious teenager shuffled outside with a chipped ceramic pitcher. Van grabbed it and poured me a bumper glass, the receptacle being a filthy, thumbprint stained former jelly jar. "Drink up!" he demanded, now treating me as if I were a visiting dignitary from some other flea-bitten empire across the great divide.

Once I finished my drink, Van returned to escort me upstairs, to personally introduce me to each of the travelers who were crashing there. He made a point emphasizing that I was a "highly accomplished American writer" who'd been published in "major literary magazines."

I soon discovered that the reason Van fawned over me during our initial encounter was due to the fact that *Caritas* – which I occasionally freelanced for, since they paid so well – had recently published a piece about him and his bookshop. This eulogistic, hagiographic article included a full-length photo of Van wearing that same pink paisley tie and royal-blue suit, with the lapels discolored by food stains from months before, and with Van staring into the lens with an impenetrable, enigmatic expression, as if secretly plotting his next great theft.

In the days ahead I noticed that he would often wear suits that were a bit too small, with the trousers cuffs running above his ankles or with the sleeves terminating just short of his wrists. Following a few more visits to this iniquitous hovel, I began to wonder where all these mismatched items of clothing came from. Eventually I learned that Van was a brazen thief who preyed upon his so-called guests, although *victims* is a more accurate term.

Working like a sleuth while piecing together various tales of misery and woe, I discovered that he'd been seen swapping the *vêtements* of his boarders at the local flea markets, exchanging brand-new American jeans – which sold for twice the price in Paris – for garishly colored French suits, many of them velvet, and for the other bits and bobs that comprised his uncoordinated accoutrements.

How fitting that *caritas* – a Latin term for the virtue of

"charity, benevolence, and love of humankind" – was the Open-Sesame term that had gained me entrée to this inverted, *Through the Looking Glass* version of "virtue" – one that exists only among thieves! And speaking of *Looking Glass*: besides cash, Van was obsessed with mirrors. They were installed in every available space in the shop and in the library upstairs: dusty antiques adorned with gilt-edged frames. Thus, in regal splendor, he could contemplate both himself and the lithe young figures of his gulls, many of them as parasitical as Van but who were now transformed into prey.

* * *

Throughout my years in France, Van never stopped treating me splendidly. Even when he caught me sleeping there one morning when I had nowhere else to turn, he wittily remarked: "Since you're the only gentleman in this place, you get to count the cash!" Then he handed me a plastic bag containing over twenty thousand francs.

Van was known to squirrel away his nuggets in nooks and crannies throughout the store rather than deposit his loot in a bank, where he'd be forced to pay those ridiculously high French taxes. But half the time he'd forget where he'd left it; and the kids who flopped there would uncover the plunder and pocket it themselves. They didn't just find it accidentally; they went searching for this buried treasure, just as Van would use every opportunity to steal it back from the guests that he'd so "graciously" offered to host.

Van's method, tried-and-true and, over the years, perfected to a fine art, consisted of temporarily kicking everyone out without notice, then locking all the rooms. Thus, he could rifle at leisure through their belongings: all those carefully packed trunks, knapsacks, and duffle bags. Not only would he abscond with cash and clothing; he even stole passports, which he'd sell at the *marchés aux puces*: the flea markets at Porte de Clignancourt and Porte de Vanves.

Besides stuffing his pockets with oodles of dough, Van loved to filch diaries and personal journals. Over the years, especially as he grew older, it developed into an enduring fetish. Sly old pervert that he was, he'd read them late at night, safely locked away in his bedroom. He'd also nick credit cards, prescription eyeglasses, fountain pens, and anything that might, at some distant point in the future, come in handy. Even after a card was cancelled, he'd use it to jimmy open the bolts on the doors whenever they became stuck.

That morning, while I was counting his filthy lucre, Van shouted, "Enough of that! Let's have breakfast!" – breakfast consisting of a bizarre concoction of pancakes slathered with a dark viscous goo of uncertain derivation. Since it resembled motor oil more than maple syrup, I attempted to politely decline, pouring only a trickle along the edge of my plate. But Van exploded: "No, that's not enough!" Grabbing the jar, he covered the pancakes with an oozing black puddle.

"Go to the kitchen! Top drawer on the right! Get us some forks!"

I pulled open a drawer as he barked, "No, not *that* one!" but it was too late. I'd accidentally uncovered a heap of prescription eyeglasses – about fifty pairs. They were almost brimming over the edge of the drawer: frames of every conceivable shape and color. God only knows why he took the trouble to steal them.

Retrieving some forks from the next drawer, I continued to behave as if nothing appeared to be out of the ordinary.

"Get some more napkins! Over there, in one of those bags!"

Walking to the opposite end of the room, I grabbed one of the plastic bags that were tossed in a corner and reached inside. But instead of napkins, I'd stumbled upon 100,000 francs. Once

I displayed this loot, which Van had completely forgotten about, he cackled: "*Ha!* No one even had the *initiative* to steal it! There's *honor* among thieves yet!" – well aware that everyone was fleecing him just as he was fleecing them back, tenfold. For, without a doubt, Van was the king of thieves.

All this became glaringly apparent the following month, after he'd locked everyone out to go pillaging upstairs. A few minutes later, when he was seated at the front desk, a girl from the Midwest – a slender blonde as fresh as a stalk of unripe corn – broke into a flood of tears. She'd worked so hard *all year*, she said, just to save 750 dollars for her trip to Paris, and now it was *gone!* She'd left it right *there*, inside her *backpack*, but *someone* had taken it! As she continued to babble beside the desk – crying uncontrollably and, in between sobs, informing Van of this calamity as if he might somehow *help* her – I witnessed something extraordinary:

A latently sane, latently normal, latently empathic glimmer appeared in Van's eye – a tiny sparkle that might otherwise have remained deeply buried within his psyche – which was followed by a nervous tick that rippled across his wrinkled, crabby face like an unexpected breeze. But then, just as suddenly, it vanished, subsumed by his fierce, psychopathic resolve. Then he continued to stare at the dusty windowpane, seemingly unperturbed by her copious weeping.

Besides attracting guests who were naive enough to be easily bamboozled, Van also possessed an uncanny ability to select the most self-absorbed narcissists, as if dramatizing the principle that like attracts like. Often, they were remarkably handsome, strikingly beautiful creatures, mostly in their late teens or early twenties. And they were never Black. Instead, he invited only the most comely Caucasian boys and girls. Occasionally, you might encounter a pale-skinned Asian, but this was the only racial exception.

There was a lingering rumor that, years ago, Van had forced himself upon one of his unlucky boarders and impregnated her. But he also had the hots for young men – perhaps even more so, especially after he'd reached a certain age. According to another rumor, in the Sixties he'd been caught screwing an adolescent who was the son of a cabinet minister: fittingly enough, the minister of finance. Fitting, because the one thing that Van really cared about was dough – despite that elaborately constructed persona of being a connoisseur of literature who was just a "hobo" at heart.

An American expat who often appeared to be staking out the joint from a park bench outside eventually informed me that Van had completed an MBA at the Harvard Business School. Sam claimed to have discovered this during a visit to the shop's hallway latrine. It was one of those "Turkish toilet" affairs, but it stank more than any other *toiletteà la turque* I've ever seen in France. (And if you know Paris, that's really saying something.) You literally had to pinch your nose as you entered this closet; it was that unspeakably foul. And that's where Sam had stumbled across Van's diploma: on a shelf behind a water tank, crumpled under a stack of molding *Paris Review*'s.

"Although Van uses eccentricity as his calling card," Sam groused, "he's simply a businessman pretending to be an eccentric. Essentially, he's a profiteer who's played on the concept of eccentricity for so long that even he's begun to believe it."

Once I befriended Sam, he filled me in on various other details of Van's underhanded adventurism. Apparently the thievery between the comely young travelers and the wizened old proprietor had spanned decades; but since Van's guests never remained there for long, they were rarely able to put the pieces together. It was only as a result of sharing my own suspicions with Sam – a retired detective who'd been observing

Van for so many years – that I came to learn the truth.

Sam added that many of these guttersnipes rivaled Van for conniving and duplicity. The fact that they were trying to get something for nothing was the most telling symptom behind this diabolical equation. It was a juicy bait that Van had ingeniously dangled; for, it was hardly even an hour of daily labor that was required in order to sleep there. They were basically flopping for free, Sam said, especially during the period before the fire: a catastrophe that Van had accidentally caused as a result of trying to save the cost of an electrician. He'd rewired the place in such a kooky fashion that it was only a matter of time before the flames would burst from the walls. A fireman was injured so badly in the blaze that he was placed inside a special red helicopter that landed in front of Notre-Dame, then flown to a burn unit in Lyons.

During this period there were at least twenty kids living there at any given moment, so there was hardly enough work for them all. It simply provided Van with a more bountiful selection of luggage to steal from. But once the fire came and went – and even the invincible bedbugs were roasted alive – he was forced to cool it a bit. The neighbors were vehemently complaining now, even threatening him with lawsuits. So he decided to maintain a low profile and to lessen the number of hooligans slamming doors and bustling up and down the stairs – a steady stream of *étrangers* from all over the world, whom the other tenants were convinced were to blame for the conflagration.

Despite these shenanigans Van still managed to get his shop prominently featured in most of the Parisian guidebooks. He even convinced some of the editors that he was a descendant of Walt Whitman. During my first visit there, after he poured my piña colada, he squinted at me and stated it boldly:

"You know, I'm the *illegitimate grandson* of Walt Whitman."

I found this to be rather amusing, especially since Walt, in order to camouflage his own homosexuality, had propagated much nonsense about how he'd fathered children while living in New Orleans. Studying a rapacious glint in Van's eye, I mildly admonished him: "But how could that be? At the very least, you'd have to be his *great-great*-grandson."

Winking back at me as if we were now in cahoots, after a muffled guffaw he concluded: "Well, after all, Walt was only adding to his legend. And here I am, in his footsteps, doing the same."

Attempting to change the subject, he pointed at the front window of the shop and added: "I've been searching for a couple of otters to install there, in a fountain. At first I thought that seals would be fascinating. But otters have such a fine sense of humor ..."

Now that Van regarded me as a "serious, successful writer," he began to hint that, one day, perhaps I might pen something truly remarkable about his legendary store, thus helping to extend his sticky web of illusion. All the while, he continued to pay me handsomely for my reviewer's copies. That first afternoon, for a handful of books worth far less, he handed me a crisp two-hundred franc note. As he did so – with a faux-sincere tilt of his head and utilizing that guileless tone that he could summon at will – he asked: "Are you sure that's enough?" Thus, during this precarious period, Van's largesse helped to keep us afloat. Meanwhile, Fräulein Dochma – Queen of Chaos and Diva of Drama – continued to scheme, plot, and connive in order to avoid succumbing to ordinary gainful employment.

While Dochma ran around in circles, I wondered how I could raise some more cash. Then it occurred to me that, since the Parisians hadn't yet been swept away by computers, perhaps I could eke out a living if I advertised carefully and began a word-processing business.

Soon, I was providing services for expats who were stranded in France without their bulky desktop computers and who needed their résumés to be continually revised and updated while searching for employment abroad. Ever fearful of change and of unnecessarily spending money, many native Parisians resisted such technology, especially since it sold for more than twice the price in France. And so, at the beginning, I advertised in both the French and English magazines, thus attracting a steady flow of clients. Since I was otherwise unemployed, it seemed like the perfect solution: to advise others on how to best present themselves for hire.

Of course, it didn't take long for Dochma to grow restless. We'd hardly been living there for a year when she decided to head back to the States. Upon completing her first screenplay, she grew convinced that only a relocation to Los Angeles would lead to success. *Hollywood was calling!*

"The future isn't in France," she announced one day with her chin held high, as if scanning a distant horizon. "Paris is *finished*."

"Dochma, I couldn't care less about what you call the future." I knew that I was right where I belonged, at least for the time being. And I was determined to remain there, even without a centime – which would often be the case in the months ahead.

But in any case, it was clear that the end of our affair was drawing near.

What made matters worse was that Dochma had recently been sucked into a nefarious religious cult. Once a week, she would submit herself to a so-called telekinetic healing. This involved lying on a couch while one of the guru's initiates passed his or her hands over her reclining figure, silently praying for a metaphysical harmonization … or an ectoplasmic realignment. Fortunately for Dochma, this grotesque ritual did not involve taking a good hard look at yourself in a mirror, that most painful but rewarding of spiritual exercises. Thus, it perfectly suited her hyper-extroverted temperament.

I later discovered that the cult had been placed on France's official blacklist of reprehensible organizations. But such information would have meant nothing to Dochma, who only believed in what was convenient. Apparently there were some wealthy members of the group who thought nothing of lending her the use of a provincial chateau for a weekend, including one with a maid and full butler service.

She even insisted that I join her there for a dinner party, but it was something I had no interest in, especially after eavesdropping on some of the more banal conversations that transpired between her nouveau riche acquaintances. I certainly had better things to do than to be stuck with such poseurs on a private tennis court in the middle of nowhere.

When I refused to accompany her, she blew a fuse. Like a diehard zealot out to change the world, she began to lecture me about my "spiritual evolution." She even demanded that I go for a "harmonization," adding that unless I did so I would never achieve my potential as a writer!

I found this last remark to be so infuriating – and even blasphemous – that I decided to leave her.

Imagine, a fundamentalist attempting to usurp the Muse!

The following weekend, while she was dallying at the chateau, I was seated at the base of Pont de la Tournelle with a translation of Céline's *Voyage au bout de la nuit*. That spring, Paris was blessed with clear skies and unseasonably warm weather. It was a delightfully balmy day, and the *quai* was lined with dozens of topless secretaries relaxing during their two-hour lunch break, lying in their panties beside equally bare tourists who were visiting from other parts of Europe. From my position at the *pont*, now and then I'd glance up from my book to revel in this receding line of undulating beauty that buttressed the nearby cathedral.

In the late afternoon, I noticed a woman at the far end of the *quai* in a flowing red dress. She steadily paced forward as it gently billowed, picked up the wind, tossed it aside, then grasped it again, all the while shimmering like a ruby. As she came closer her eyes appeared to be pinned to mine. "But what could she be staring at?" I wondered. "It's almost as if she's looking directly at me ..."

Bearing a friendly grin, she finally approached and knelt beside me.

"*Voulez-vous prendre un café?*"

When I replied in the affirmative – *Mais oui!* – she noticed my accent, and, switching to English, added: "You are an American? Ah, how charming, an American in Paris!"

"American? Not at all – I'm from Brooklyn."

"*Brooklynoise?*" she smiled. "*O la la!*"

"And you must be *la belle inconnue de la Seine.*"

Gathering up my belongings, I accompanied Florence across Pont de la Tournelle, a bridge featuring a remarkably panoramic view. For a moment we paused to watch the barges slip silently underfoot, the buttresses of Notre-Dame glowing like white gold, the horse-chestnut trees fluttering over a burgeoning verdure of ivy, the thick leafy vines cascading down the embankment and fanning out across the churning surface of the water. And the picture-postcard wonder of it all neatly camouflaging the venomous, vampiric, mendacious aspect of the City of Night. But with Florence by my side – and with the horrors of Céline's *Voyage* tucked neatly away – we merrily approached a café at the opposite end of the bridge.

"Or perhaps," she smiled, "you'd prefer to come up to my studio, and I can *make* you a coffee ..."

So now, walking past the café and cutting across Île Saint-Louis, we continued along rue Charlemagne. Turning at rue des Jardins Saint-Paul, we approached a crumbling wall of mortar and stone that ran perpendicular to a long rectangular yard.

According to Florence, this massive structure was all that remained of the medieval Wall of Philip Augustus, dating back to the twelfth century. She added that, in the sixteenth century, the writer Francois Rabelais had spent his final years in a house on this same street. He was later buried in a nearby cemetery. At the far end of the yard, lingering in purple shadows, a half dozen men were deeply engrossed in a game of *pétanque* – carefully tossing their heavy steel balls. For fun? No; as I also learned from Florence, substantial amounts of cash were gambled away with each toss.

Turning off the rue des Jardins, we continued into a labyrinthian passageway and entered the Village Saint-Paul.

"Have you ever been here before?"

"No, never!" I exclaimed, now completely enchanted. An interconnecting maze of narrow alleys ran through a courtyard like an ancient puzzle, with one arched passageway flowing into the next, flanked by the facades of renaissance-inspired architecture. Slender, diminutive buildings resembling doll-houses were covered with creeping ivy and featured wrought-iron balconies and wooden shutters. On the ground-floor, there were several softly lit antique shops with hand hewn timber crossbeams on the ceiling; as well as numerous *artisan* boutiques, *caves à vin*, and flea markets.

"Once, Saint-Paul was a separate village," Florence said, happy to share this tidbit of French history. "But after the seventeenth century, it was absorbed into the fourth *arrondissement*."

The crooked lanes and winding corridors were eerily reminiscent of a cubist *maquette*. The walls were set at delightfully bizarre angles, folding in and out of each other like a deck of collapsing and reassembling playing cards, and leaving you with that fluttering-in-the-air feeling that you get when you stare too long at a Braque or a Picasso from the Hermetic cubist period.

As we approached Florence's building, I spotted an ancient millstone lying in a corner of the yard. Such provincial charm, yet we were still in Paris! I ruefully mused over how such wondrous things do not exist in *Mannahatta*. Red petunias were planted in an indentation at its center, adding a patch of primary color to the pearl gray of the surrounding architecture.

Florence welcomed me into a modestly sized studio. Uncorking a bottle of wine, she invited me to sit beside her on a bed covered with a colorful quilt. And then, as if skinning an apple, she slowly peeled off her red dress to reveal a pulpy white fruit underneath.

Florence also had a Senegalese boyfriend, but she had no qualms about sharing herself between the two of us. When she eventually told him about her American *petit ami*, he wasn't too thrilled; but, this being France, we each assumed that such accommodations were simply the order of the day. And so, the coffee and croissants continued to flow.

Occasionally I'd linger on her windowsill and study the nearby dome of the Église Saint-Paul, which was so close and so large that I could view only a small portion of it as it peeked through the billowing clouds like a gilded seventeenth-century flying saucer. And then, sipping my *café noir*, I'd wonder: But how can I be living this dream? For now, I'm in *Paris* – and nothing else matters.

* * *

One thing that I admired about Dochma was the unhesitating boldness with which she approached life. But just like her father who had served as a double agent – working each side to his advantage, no matter what the cost – she often refused to play by the rules of human decency. As I'd soon discover, she thought nothing of gaining the trust of strangers, puffing up their egos while luring them into some mutual pursuit that seemed to glow with the candescence of an otherworldly splendor, then dropping them once she'd secured whatever it was she was after: usually, a financial loan that she never intended to repay.

Instead of that whirligig of drama which always seemed to hover about her every move, now all I wanted was a plain, simple, and sincere woman. If not a soul mate, then at least someone who greeted the day by taking the sun out of her pocket and shining. But when I tried to imagine such a creature, all I could muster was a pair of eyes as lucid as a freshly cut prism. Did such orbs even exist, I wondered.

Following a well-established Parisian tradition, with the arrival of winter Florence grew increasingly morose and withdrew into her shell. But perhaps it was more than just a seasonal depression; for she grew resentful when I failed to respond to her offer to move in and live with her. After being cooped up with Dochma, however, at that point what I needed most was my own freedom – or at least, a moment to catch my breath. In any case, when I phoned Florence one evening, she announced that she was now in "isolation from the world." Sadly, I pictured her ensconced in her pearl-gray dollhouse: a fable-princess stuck in an unbreachable tower.

But if not Florence, then who? Where would I find a suitable French mistress?

We would meet soon enough. Her name was Sophie Plaisant; and, in Sophie, I would find a gentle Frenchwoman who would offer me her heart, or at least what was left of it. And, since she asked for nothing, I felt compelled to give her everything. Or at least, to offer whatever I could manage.

*   *   *

Once Dochma and I had survived the sorrows of a breakup, perhaps because closure had been reached and the pressure to succeed was no longer there, she relaxed a bit and even permitted me to inject some dark humor into my assessment of her situation. When she lamented the fact that she still hadn't found a suitable lover, I replied: "But what do you expect? Ever since you arrived here, you've been chasing glamorous poseurs who are incapable of pursuing anything but the most superficial of affairs. Do you know what you really need? A truck driver!"

"You must be joking."

"Yes, a fellow who thinks nothing of hauling a heavy load! Or perhaps a milkman, who can at least offer you some authentic nourishment. Or maybe even a porter, who won't hesitate to haul your emotional baggage. Better yet, a gardener: someone who's used to shoveling *merde* and watching the flowers bloom after such an intensive labor ..."

I knew that she'd simply laugh off such remarks as if they were mere *blagues*, but I couldn't have been more serious. If only Dochma could have descended from her pedestal and joined the hoi polloi! But her obsessive drive to "get somewhere" meant that she would only join forces with someone who might help to "get her there" – no matter what.

"And what about you and me?" she asked with a plaintive tone.

I could see the sadness descend like a lowering cloud in her brooding gaze, but there was nothing I could do about it. For, fate had decreed that we would act more like catalysts than lovers – propelling each other in different directions while being transformed into new elements.

La bêtise de jeunesse!

Perhaps because I felt guilty about abandoning her, I decided to introduce Dochma to a Ukrainian artist named Alek: a modest, down-to-earth man who appeared to have little patience for pretension. A well-built, broad-shouldered expatriate, he resembled an auto mechanic more than one's traditional idea of a painter. And like any good mechanic, he always seemed to have his feet planted firmly on the ground; but just like many artists, he also seemed to be struggling with the murky silhouette of a shadowy inner demon.

A few months before we met, I'd befriended a capricious Frenchwoman named Claire, who was fluent in English and who often haunted the American bookshops on the Left Bank. Claire had recently broken up with Alek, but they still remained friends. One evening she invited me to his vernissage in a small gallery on the outskirts of Paris, which was how Alek and I first met.

After getting dumped by Claire, Alek had become a bit of a recluse, devoting himself day and night to his craft. Thus, after the vernissage, I saw him only infrequently. But we seemed to hit it off, perhaps because of the creative struggle that we each faced, which had so deeply shaped our respective lives. But as much as I enjoyed being with him, and as much as I would have enjoyed developing a closer camaraderie, Alek was a quintessential loner. Perhaps he was distracted by his demon: one that also served as a gatekeeper, past which few could travel.

In any case, one day it occurred to me that Alek might somehow embody a combination milkman, porter, and gardener. And while he might help to keep her emotionally grounded, Dochma might assist Alek in getting out of the house and approaching some art galleries.

At this point, he was merely subsisting in France. An émigré from the Seventies, he'd arrived in Paris with just a sketch pad and a duffel bag of clothing. Undeterred, he commandeered a spot in front of Notre-Dame – a place that one needed muscles to defend, such was the competition among buskers – and he began to sell charcoal portraits to the tourists. Those were the really lean years, he said, during which he'd barely managed to survive.

When Alek painted in his studio, he used mostly umbers and siennas, since many of the more colorful hues were too expensive. A tube of cadmium red or cobalt blue would last him several years, because he was careful to employ such exorbitantly priced pigments rather sparingly. Constantly scrimping and saving, he also didn't eat very well.

I was convinced that this austere, impoverished diet, which had lasted far too long, had affected both his physical and mental well-being. I also wondered if pandering to tourists and accommodating a pedestrian taste for "commercial" beauty had dulled his vision. Alek's latest paintings were based on photos of the bronze statutes in the Jardin du Luxembourg, and they captured only a surface realism that lacked any broader, deeper sweep of the imagination. After turning the photos into slides, he'd project the image upon a canvas, tracing the outlines of the statues to produce a verisimilitude that was surprisingly accurate. Anyone who studied the final result without knowing the process involved would assume that he was a magician who possessed miraculous hand-eye coordination. But while the streaked, iridescent surface of his portraits reflected a pleasing chromatic shimmer, there remained something lifeless and pro-saic as regards their content – just like the unremarkable munic-ipal sculptures in the park.

While we were talking about painting one day, Alek said that he considered Van Gogh to be "completely crazy" – a judg-ment based not on Vincent's biography but solely on his art-work, which Alek regarded as no more than the garishly colored daubs of a "lunatic." Picasso's Cubism fared just as poorly in his estimate; but, he added, at least there was the Blue Period and the neoclassical style.

Instead of being enraptured by modernism, Alek's aesthetic preferences dated further back in time, to things such as Jacques-Louis David's "Coronation of Napoleon." Perhaps this comparison isn't surprising, since David and his colleagues were said to have employed optical devices such as lenses and mirrors to achieve their ends, projecting the image of their models directly upon the canvas, just as Alek had done.

While Alek admired what he called the "realness" of classi-cism, he only approached the periphery of its alluring power. For although he was inspired by the photo, he was also trapped by its two-dimensional confines and fixed, deadening perspec-tive, which prevents a viewer's imagination from taking any greater leaps or bounds. While the camera's lens may be sharply focused, it's also deeply imprisoning. Ultimately, the photo fails to approach the richness of painting and its potential to unlock a world of multiple perspective.

But an oil painting is only a trigger point; the imagination of the spectator must be fully engaged in order to connect the dots and complete the task. If artistic talent is lacking, however, we end up right where we started, gaping at a superficial surface that leads nowhere.

When speaking with Alek, I was often tempted to quote one of my favorite dictums from Marcel Duchamp: "The painter who paints merely what he sees is stupid." Though I respected Alek too much to ever do so, I made it clear that, for me, men such as Picasso and Van Gogh were among the truly great sages of our time. But neither of us saw any point in arguing about such things; we simply accepted *la différence*.

After decades of living *en marge de la société*, Alek was finally beginning to have a few exhibitions; but they were usually in out-of-the-way places. By the time we met, he was convinced that he'd never be offered anything more serious in Paris simply because he was an outsider, an *étranger*. During his last exhibit, he was even forced to type a price list himself, since the gallery owner refused to lift a finger. Alek also had to pay the gallery's expensive electric bill, to cover the cost of lighting.

I found this out to be utterly outrageous, yet none of it was at all surprising. Gallery owners the world over had developed a reputation for being even more avaricious than lawyers – for who else would demand a cut of up to seventy-five percent? I'd even heard of one case in the States in which a gallery had offered a painter a show, but after the paintings were delivered, unsigned and *sans* contract, the proprietor had claimed that the artist in question had nothing to do with their creation. She refused to return them or to offer the painter a commission after they were sold.

Yes, things were really that bad.

With her native tendency to fearlessly rush into completely foreign terrain, Dochma sensed an opportunity to market this unappreciated artist, so she set about to change his life. Since Alek hardly spoke any English, Dochma convinced him to travel with her to Manhattan, where she might help to secure a better gallery. And, by some miracle, she actually accomplished this. Alek's first show, hosted in one of the more commercial, touristy galleries that were now sprouting up in Soho, brought him a profit of over 350,000 francs.

I was amazed by this latest development, because procuring an exhibit in a Manhattan gallery – even one dealing with touristic dreck aimed at the unsophisticated "bridge and tunnel" crowd – was no easy feat.

In keeping with a respectable French tradition of cheating on one's taxes, for a while Alek managed to hide the windfall profits from both the housing authorities and the tax bureau. But although he was pleased to have achieved such success, the unexpected arrival of all that cash had led him to become even more frugal. Rather than appearing to be more self-assured, I sensed an inexplicable emotional upheaval within Alek, which was now beginning to bubble to the surface.

Even before the money from the gallery was in his hands, Dochma was urging him to sink most of the cash into the purchase of a small chateau in the countryside. The building in question, a former monastery, dated back to the Middle Ages. It required plenty of repairs, but they decided that, once it was renovated, it would make for an ideal studio. And then Dochma, always with an eye out for an opportunity, could have her home away from home, just like any other respectably bourgeois *parisienne*. For didn't she deserve a pleasant little home in the countryside, where she could escape on weekends from the noise and hubbub of Paris just like any other well-heeled Madame? Such a hard life!

But there still remained the problem of repairs. Soon, they were covered from head to toe by a fine film of white powder, which descended as they sanded joint compound on freshly installed sheetrock.

While they were hard at work, perhaps as a means of thanking me for introducing him to Dochma, Alek said that for the next few months I could live rent-free at his flat in Créteil, on the outskirts of Paris. The apartment was registered in a state-sponsored program that provided low-cost housing for impoverished artist immigrants. All I had to do was cover the basics, such as heat and electricity.

* * *

Shortly after I moved to Créteil, Alek invited me to visit the chateau. Arriving at dusk, I demanded to be "introduced" to their pet: a shaggy-haired black bitch that was bearing its teeth and barking vociferously from the end of a long chain, tied to a pole in the yard.

When Alek had purchased the property, it came with this vicious, beady-eyed Maremma Sheepdog. At first he had no idea that it had nearly destroyed its previous owner, biting into his leg and not letting go. The poor fellow had to be flown by helicopter to a hospital, where he'd barely managed to avoid an amputation.

On the day that Alek and Dochma had moved in, a gnarly old Frenchman who owned an adjacent plot had knocked on their front door. Cordially introducing himself, he informed Alek about the incident, adding that the pet had turned against its owner because it was being abused. So he advised Alek to shoot the deranged creature, even offering to do so himself.

But Dochma insisted that this fellow couldn't be trusted. After all, they hadn't heard the "animal's side of the story" yet, had they? And if the former owner was abusive, then it wasn't the pet's fault for acting that way, now was it? Or perhaps this neighbor possessed some hidden, ulterior motive for wanting to destroy this unlucky critter. And could French neighbors – and peasants to boot – really be trusted? In any case, Dochma had gotten it into her thick skull that they should instead *rehabilitate* the hound and teach it to be a good, fun-loving, harmless companion.

When I first caught wind of this, I decided not to bet on Dochma's powers of persuasion to save the day. Therefore, within moments of my arrival, I selected a few blood sausages from their well-stocked refrigerator and, with Dochma and Alek by my side, I marched to the yard and approached the howling beast.

It was baring its fangs, growling, leaping, and snapping as I approached. Straining at the chain, it clawed frenetically at the earth as I knelt just a few feet beyond its reach and gingerly tossed over a juicy sausage. At once, it stopped barking and devoured the sacrificial offering. After a few more carefully tossed scraps of meat, it seemed as if we were becoming friends. So I felt a bit safer ... but only just a bit.

The next morning I was sleeping on a couch in the living room when the dog leapt over my reclining form, yapping and barking, but in a friendly manner now, with its tongue dripping and tail wagging. After a hearty breakfast, Dochma and Alek prepared to drive to the next town, to pick up supplies. They asked me to remain there to keep an eye on things.

I decided to amble around a swampy pond that flanked the chateau. So I strolled outside with the dog trotting beside me, still wagging its tail. Hoping to establish a deeper rapport, I spoke in low, resonant, friendly tones, evoking a melody that I hoped would soothe this savage beast.

We were tracing a wide circle around the stagnant, olive-green water. But at one point, as I ventured closer to the edge of the pond, the bitch slowly opened its mouth, bared its fangs, gingerly grabbed hold of my shirttail (which, fortunately, I'd neglected to tuck in), and pulled me back. In this manner, the animal let it be known that it certainly did not approve of me walking so close to the water. Once I changed direction it let go, and we continued our leisurely promenade. But as soon as Alek returned, I demanded to be driven back to the train station.

The next day I received a frantic call from Dochma. Alek had been playing with the dog, she said, tossing a stick and training it to retrieve. But eventually things got out of hand, and he must have tossed it a bit too aggressively. Suddenly Alek's right arm was clenched by its fangs, and it wouldn't release its grip. The teeth cut right through his flesh, almost to the bone. Not knowing what else to do, Alek leapt into the pond with the dog dangling from his arm, and only then did it release its grip. But the muck and mire of the swamp had filtered into Alek's wound, and his flesh soon turned gangrenous.

As she ranted on, I thought, "Here we go again – Dochma and her big ideas!"

To make matters worse, when he was operated on the physicians hadn't bothered to give Alek an appropriate regimen of antibiotics. Soon he was reinfected, and they had to operate all over again. But as it turned out, he was lucky. If the bite had been a millimeter to the left, it would have hit the median nerve, and he would have lost all use of his hand – and would never have been able to paint again. And the dog? While Alek was recuperating, he finally came to his senses and asked his neighbor to fire a bullet into its brain.

Despite the fact that Dochma's intransigence was the driving force behind this latest mishap, it came as no surprise that, of the three of us, she remained the least affected by this beast from hell. She'd been merrily daydreaming about canine rehabilitation while I'd stupidly wandered about with this dangerous force lurking beside me; and while Alek had nearly been crippled by it.

Not only had Dochma insisted on reeducating the hound; she'd also attempted to "rehabilitate" the soil surrounding the chateau. She refused to believe the wise old farmer, who had warned her not to plant anything there. The soil was permeated with clay, he said, so almost nothing could grow – especially anything requiring deeper roots.

But Dochma wouldn't listen. Instead, she convinced Alek to waste thousands of francs on all sorts of exotic trees and shrubs that soon withered and died. Dochma was forever attempting to bully the divine order, but it always backfired. With a stubborn resolve, she continued to plant things in places where they didn't belong: wasting time and energy while demanding that the universe reform itself according to the contours of her whims. But when it refused to do so, she grew enraged and resentful.

Of course, one could spend one's entire existence resenting reality instead of learning to adapt to it. Yet she remained incapable of realizing that only by paying careful attention to life's demands and nurturing them accordingly would anything grow and prosper. No wonder that Alek now referred to her as "Dogma."

Just like one of those exotic shrubs that had withered away, I began to wonder if perhaps she'd planted herself in a place where she really didn't belong.

* * *

An avid World War II buff, Alek possessed an impressive array of vintage helmets, medals, and weapons that had once belonged to French or German soldiers. His favorite item was a Luger pistol, which he'd occasionally fire into the pond. On the afternoon that I'd visited the chateau, Alek had pulled back the toggle-lock and handed it to me, fully loaded. But I refused to touch it. His dream, he said, was to own a tank: either a Panzer or a Sherman. Now that he had some land, he smiled grimly, perhaps it would be possible to store it here, along with a bazooka.

A pistol is a dangerous object to possess when your brain is not functioning at its maximum capability and when you suffer from a lingering, chronic form of depression. Even when Alek exhibited a droll sense of humor, it was often accompanied by an anxious look in his eyes. The cause of this irresolvable despair remained a mystery to me; for he wasn't the sort to open up and blithely discuss deeply personal matters. But in any case, ever since the disaster with the dog, Alek's mood was growing darker.

I also wondered if his grief was related to the tensions that had arisen between him and Dochma. I'd recently heard from Claire, his previous *amoureuse*, that Alek was a virile lover, in possession of great ardor and stamina. Yet Dochma had taken me aside one day to complain that, throughout their relationship, he'd remained impotent. Was there something about Dochma that he found overwhelming or intimidating? What obstacle, I wondered, was standing between him and his virility? But I never learned the cause of this reaction, or the cause of what would soon follow.

One day the farmer discovered Alek's corpse lying on the studio floor, with a bullet through his head. Alek was still gripping the Luger in his lifeless hand. When he'd slipped the gun into his mouth and pulled the trigger, his skull had blasted open, and his brains were spattered upon a freshly gessoed canvas leaning against a wall behind him.

It was his last act, a destructive rather than creative one.

Dochma didn't last much longer in Paris. After a brief stint in Hollywood, where she failed to sell her screenplay, she retreated to the nation that she most detested – her Austrian homeland. Taking pity on her, an aging "Uncle Heinie" had invited Dochma to move into his cottage.

The way that I learned of Alek's demise was rather unsettling. In a missive that arrived via post, Dochma's final words to me were:

"Despite your material struggles, you were the one who possessed more fortitude, resilience, and courage. Not to mention creative stamina."

Naturally, I took great offense at this blasphemous utterance. What in heaven's name did she think this was – a perverse sort of Olympian competition? Was this all she could think of in conjuring Alek's troubled spirit?

I refused to answer. At that moment it was Dochma, not Alek, who had died for me. But there was more to come.

Like a snowbound Icarus, Dochma would later perish while attempting a dangerous ski jump on the powdery hills of Innsbruck. When I received word of this unfortunate news from a mutual friend, I thought that, at last, Dochma had completed the adventure she was always unwittingly pursuing.

Meeting Ray Bradbury

Now that I'd managed to procure a steady source of income – barely enough to survive, but steady nonetheless – I set off to find a cold-water garret, or as the French say, *une chambre de bonne* (a room formerly occupied by French maids or *domestiques*).

As I began my search, I remained fearful that I'd end up homeless in the City of Light. With such gloomy specters looming overhead like gargoyles, one morning I received an unsettling missive from my friend Slim, who was still hunkered down in the Lower East Side.

I'd often watch Slim perform in one of the local dives, particularly in a restaurant fittingly called the Apocalypse Café. Now, as I scanned his letter, I could feel the denizens of the deep closing in. His haunting portrayal of what I'd just barely managed to escape from sent a shiver along my spine:

"Remember that junkie girl," he asked, "who was treated so rudely by the staff at the Apocalypse? She offered to draw your picture for a buck one night, while we were seated outside. If I recall correctly, there was something tragic about her that you found sympathetic.

Well, for some time now, she's become a fixture in the local neighborhood. As the months passed, she'd look a little worse for wear each day – more worn and sunken. Then I noticed that her hair was turning gray, along with her face. Her moments of derangement soon supplanted those of lucidity.

She was slipping away, right before my eyes. I'm sure that everyone else in this so-called neighborhood realized it as well. Besides being charming, she was also a pest, so she was someone that you'd notice. But then, one day – and it did seem to happen suddenly – when I passed her on the street she looked as if she were sixty. Hunched over, ashen, withered. A week later, all her hair was cut off. Lice, I suppose, because all she would do is walk around scratching her head with a pen. Perhaps, the same one that she once used to draw portraits.

That's all she does now; you wouldn't recognize her. She no longer speaks ... or even looks at anyone. I often see her facing a wall or standing in a doorway with her back to the street, scratching her scalp, which is covered with big, bloody scabs.

She's gone mad, of course. But no one's lifted a finger to help her, and perhaps no one ever will, myself included. Instead, we'll just watch another person go to waste.

'Some kind of moral in all this,' one might say in a rare moment of reflection. 'The price you pay for trying to feel good. Another casualty of the war ...'"

Studying Slim's note as if it were freshly penned by the Delphic Oracle, at once I decided to take action. Instead of waiting on another long, dreary line with dozens of other waifs and strays who were summoned en masse to meet with a prospective landlord, I created my own ad in a newspaper that was freely distributed in the *boulangeries*. I simply stated that I was an American writer in search of a *chambre de bonne* to use as a work space, where I could quietly pursue my craft.

As soon as it was published, I received a deluge of calls. What I hadn't realized was that I'd accidentally tapped into a principal French obsession: to avoid paying taxes. All across Paris, there were thousands of empty garrets that remained unrented simply because the owners were afraid that if they placed an ad it could later be used as proof that they were accruing an unclaimed income. They were also afraid that if a French tenant moved in – someone who knew exactly how things worked there – he might stop paying rent and instead demand to live rent-free for another six months. Otherwise, he'd threaten to inform the authorities. But an American probably wouldn't know about such things; hence, he or she might make an "ideal" tenant.

My first *chambre de bonne* was located on the inauspiciously named rue Chapon (from the word *capon*: a castrated male chicken). The rent was 1500 francs a month – about three-hundred American dollars. But there was a catch: it was only a temporary arrangement, for summer and winter. I'd have to move again before the following spring. Nevertheless, I didn't hesitate to grab it, as such accommodations, despite their modest attributes, were becoming increasingly more difficult to find at such a price. And its location in the third *arrondissement* was a good one: just a few blocks north of Centre Pompidou, and an easy jaunt across the river to Notre-Dame.

That fall, I happened to wander into a bookshop where a big jovial man with an oversized head was seated at a front desk, signing autographs. He seemed to enjoy the attention he was receiving; his booming laughter and raucous remarks echoed like thunderclaps. Silver haired and wearing black-rimmed glasses, he was dressed like an adolescent, with a blue baseball jacket, white tennis shorts and sneakers, and white athletic socks that were pulled up to his knees. The fact that he was seventy years old and weighed over two-hundred pounds made this outfit appear all the more absurd, especially since his body was shaped into an enormous egg.

Back then, adults donning sneakers in Paris were usually Americans. And so, even before I heard him speak, I decided that he must be from the States. But *who* was he? When I turned to a woman standing beside me and asked, she reverentially whispered: "Ray Bradbury."

Cutting through a gaggle of admirers surrounding the desk, I stepped forward and introduced myself. "I'm a writer with the *Bloomsbury Review*, and we'd love to interview you."

"Sure! Contact my publisher, Denoël. Work out the details with them," he exclaimed, "then I'll tell you about all the problems I'm having!"

A pervasive scent of wine hung in the air between us. Upon closer inspection, I noticed that Ray's bulbous nose was finely veined and tinted the color of Beaujolais Nouveau. I later learned that, while promenading along rue Saint-Jacques, he'd stopped at nearly every pub along the way, to sample numerous glasses of Burgundy and Bordeaux.

Ray probably had no idea how difficult it was to get past a French secretary, especially one in a publishing company as prestigious as Denoël. As my Parisian students had taught me so well, a receptionist's main task was to practice *blocage*, the goal being to protect their boss's solitude so that he or she could work – or dream – the day away, with only the most minor of interruptions.

But I'd fashioned a little trick to deal with all this, something I'd stumbled upon quite accidentally. Since the average receptionist didn't speak English (or rather, didn't *dare* to, out of fear of being ridiculed, since this was how Parisians often treated foreigners who spoke French), when I picked up the phone, after mouthing an obligatory *bonjour* (without which no further progress could be made), I spoke *only* in English. As expected, this had the effect of turning the tables. Both frustrated by her limited English skills and wary that the caller might be someone too important to blow off, the receptionist would usually surrender and pass me further up the line. Thus, I was soon speaking with a senior editor at Denoël whose English was impeccable.

"Monsieur Bradbury has asked me to contact you," I said, "to schedule an interview. I'm with the *Bloomsbury Review* in the States, but right now I'm in Paris."

"I see. *Alors*, give me your number. We'll have Mr. Bradbury call you in the next few days ..."

Of course, he had no idea that, despite the fine work that *Bloomsbury* produced, it was a small-press paper operating on a shoestring, and I hadn't even bothered to ask if they were interested. The phenomenon of small press publishers and little magazines (there were at least 5,000 in the U.S. at that time) hardly existed in France in the Nineties. Instead, it was assumed that if you published with a literary journal you must be a rather important chap.

And little did he realize that I was also operating on a shoestring and living in that most humble of nests, *une chambre de bonne* – one accessible only by climbing five steep flights of worn wooden stairs, discreetly tucked away in the back of a building.

I spent the next few days scurrying about the English-language bookshops and libraries, attempting to read as much as I could of Bradbury's prodigious oeuvre. I really had no idea how to proceed, for I'd never before attempted an interview. But the opportunity seemed too good to pass over, and only in Paris would it have been so easy to arrange. Spring and fall in Lutèce hosted those magical months during which foreigners descended along the *trottoirs* and let their guards down. Overwhelmed by the architectural beauty as well as feeling linguistically isolated, even celebrities such as Bradbury were more likely to embrace an overture from a fellow American in Paris than they might have been back at home.

Sci-fi had never interested me as an adult, but I'd attended a class in high school devoted to the subject, where we read

Fahrenheit 451, The Martian Chronicles, and a handful of Ray's other stories. Having come of age in the Seventies, I'd always assumed that the book-burning episodes in *Fahrenheit 451* were a warning about the threat of totalitarianism in the United States, where books had indeed been burned by right-wing reactionaries. U. S. Postal Inspector Anthony Comstock was all too proud to admit that, under the aegis of Victorian institutions such as the New York Society for the Suppression of Vice, he'd arranged for the liquidation of fifteen tons of books, over a quarter of a million pounds of printer's plates, and four million pictures that were deemed "obscene." There was even a phrase coined after Comstock and his vile actions – "comstockery" – minted at the turn of the century by the *New York Times* and later immortalized, in 1905, by none other than George Bernard Shaw.

When "Nanny" Comstock tried to arrange for the arrest of the famous dramatist over the production of his play, "Mrs. Warren's Profession," Shaw called *comstockery* "the world's standing joke at the expense of the United States. Europe likes to hear of such things. It confirms the deep-seated conviction of the Old World that America is a provincial place, a second-rate country-town civilization after all." But book burning wasn't always so "official." Decades later, in 1964, bonfires in the South were fueled by copies of *Tropic of Cancer* after Grove Press had managed to win a historic Supreme Court censorship trial.

I'd also read that Ray had joined in protests against the Vietnam War, so I'd assumed that, surely, in all these matters, he must have been on "our" side – a fellow progressive.

* * *

I was immersed in a deep sleep one morning when the phone rang and my answering machine clicked on to record a message. Not wanting to miss a call from Ray, I'd left the volume on, full blast.

"Hello, this is Ray Bradbury." For a moment, it sounded like the opening of a television serial. The voice was sonorous, authoritative, and self-assured. Very very very self-assured, as I would soon discover.

Snatching the receiver, I groggily replied, "Hello, Mr. Bradbury. Thanks so much for getting back to me."

"If you're available, we can meet at the lobby of the Hotel Normandie. That's where my wife and I are staying, right beside the Palais Royal. How about eleven o'clock?"

Once we arranged the details, I took a "bath" by standing in front of the sink, running a cold stream of water into a tin pot, spilling it over my head, and splashing it across my shivering body. Then I dressed and entered a nearby metro station.

When I arrived at the hotel lobby, I immediately spotted the hulking figure of the famous author. Seated at a bistro table, Ray was tucked into a plush Louis XIV-style *fauteuil*, which barely contained his impressive girth. Still dressed in white shorts and socks, he resembled a luminous flying saucer trapped in an ornate red-velvet chair, with the gilt molding of the salon glittering overhead as if from a distant constellation. Gripping a tiny mug of espresso in his sausage-sized fingers, he assumed the pose of *le grand bon-homme*.

I did my best to hide my growing anxiety, for I could scarcely believe that I'd pulled off such a coup. Here I was, a struggling, unknown writer, seated beside this widely cele-brated author. Even the Apollo astronauts, when they'd first landed on the moon, had paid Ray homage by naming the Dandelion Crater after his novel, *Dandelion Wine*. Perhaps even more impressive, in 1966 François Truffaut had adopted *Fahrenheit 451* into a major art film. But as I took a seat at the table Ray's friendly manner put me at ease, and we fell right into conversation.

Though I hadn't managed to read very much in such a brief period, I was favorably impressed by one of his short stories, so my first question concerned this memorable tale:

"I'm curious about your vision of the future. I'm thinking now of a story that first appeared in the early 1950s, 'The Pedestrian.' In this rather paranoid vision of the future, a Mr. Meade is arrested and sent to a psychiatric center for having committed the transgression of walking, without a purpose, through the streets at night. It's a world in which magazines and books don't sell anymore, and people sit in rooms mesmerized by television sets. In many ways, this tale epitomized a very dark undercurrent of the 1950s. Yet there are forces at work in the world today that are not that dissimilar. What's your personal vision of the future, especially the political future?"

"It's very optimistic," Ray replied with a stentorian tone and grave expression. "Look at what's happened in the last eight months. Because America stood firm, and helped form NATO, and just stayed quietly there, finally, the Communists gave up. They *were* an evil empire; President Reagan was absolutely right. And they partially still are, because they haven't finished disarming."

Could I believe my ears? Ronald Reagan, his hero? Was Ray a right-winger now? And what's this about an evil empire? I could hardly restrain myself from either laughing in his face or mounting a full-throttle attack. *Steady, steady as she goes!* I silently admonished myself. *We're at the very beginning; don't blow it out of the water! Just try to gently change the subject ...*

"How about the opening of the East Bloc? How will that affect science-fiction writing?"

"I don't think it will affect it much, because we're running ahead of all that. We've always talked about freedom; we've always talked about totalitarian governments. After all, *Fahrenheit 451* is all about Russia, and all about China, isn't it? It's all about the totalitarians anywhere: either left or right, doesn't matter where they are; they're book burners, all of them. And so, *Fahrenheit* will continue to be a book read by people all over the world. Because there are still totalitarian governments. And book burners. So, as long as that's true, or if the threat is true, the book will be read."

Still no mention of our own evil empire. Bradbury seemed to believe that the American government was as pure as the freshly driven snow. As I focused on his latest harangue about the Chinese and Russians – *dirty Commies!* – I realized that his additional remarks were proving to be even more bizarre:

"And they have very few telephones, because they don't believe in communication. That's a freedom. We have a telephone for every person in the country in America. There are no automobiles in Russia. It has yet to be invented ..."

This last remark was so off the rails that I didn't know where to begin. Did Ray really believe all this? How did he ever become so deeply indoctrinated?

I later made a point of doing some research and discovered that, not surprisingly, automotive production was a thriving industry in both Russia and, later on, the Soviet Union. An automobile with a petrol engine was manufactured in St. Petersburg as early as 1896. Three years later, a Russian inventor named Romanov created an electric car, followed by a battery-powered bus. By the time the USSR was dissolved – about a year after our interview – it was already producing over two million buses, trucks, and cars per year, ranking sixth in global production.

But now, as my temper began its slow boil, I was totally unprepared for this dire turn of events. On the one hand, I knew that I'd been handed a golden opportunity. A successfully completed dialogue with Bradbury would make it that much easier to approach other authors and to build a solid list of interviews. But on the other hand, I couldn't just sit there and remain silent as he spouted such nonsense.

I decided there was only one solution. I'd have to contain my temper but, at the same time, confront him in the most subtle, diplomatic fashion. But diplomacy was something I knew even less about than interviewing famous authors.

Taking advantage of a lull in his long-winded monologue, I leaned across the table and gently intoned: "Now, a moment ago, you said that we have a telephone for every person in America. But that's only for those who can afford them, right?"

He regarded me with a genuine expression of confusion. "Huh?"

"You said we have a telephone for everyone in the country. Everyone who can *afford* a telephone."

"Everyone has a telephone, whether they can afford it or not. It's one of those things that people have, regardless of their income. There are some things that all poor people have, automatically. They have TV ..."

I flashed back to the four years that I'd spent working as an advocate for the homeless mentally ill in Manhattan. "Mr. Bradbury, how about a homeless person in New York?"

But he remained adamant: "Well, no, that's another problem entirely, which has to do with our emptying the lunatic asylums twenty-five years ago. It was a big liberal movement, and a conservative movement, too, because we hated lunatic asylums. We hated the idea of them, and we had medicines which we thought were going to work, right? It was an honorable experiment, but it didn't work. So, those people are out there. Now we have to take them off the streets; we cannot leave them out there."

"For several years," I replied, "I worked in a program in New York that was involved with trying to find jobs and housing for the homeless mentally ill. It was one of the few programs set up to solve this problem. And I did encounter many people who barely got by, who had an apartment but couldn't afford a telephone, or couldn't afford clothing or other things that we take for granted. And what I'm getting at is ... you're talking a lot about the Soviet Union. I'm wondering about your feelings about totalitarian strains within the United States."

"There are none."

"None whatsoever?"

"No. Of course not. Never have been. We're a free society. We've got television. We have radio. We have newspapers. We have the videocassette, which is coming into play. These are new freedoms."

We have the videocassette! Incredulous, I could barely stop myself from laughing. "How about right-wing reactionary forces such as the Klan? Wouldn't you say that's a totalitarian strain?"

"No," he shook his massive forehead back and forth. "Those things exist on both sides. The left wing wants to burn certain books, too, but they don't. We don't allow them to."

"When I first read 'The Pedestrian,'" I continued, "I thought it was such a wonderful story because I thought it was *universal*. It was something that wasn't specifically about China or the Soviet Union, but it was about totalitarian forces that may exist within any individual."

"Oh, yeah," he nodded, "Every single individual is that same thing. You are; I am. And we have to make sure that we don't misbehave. Look at what happened with the French

Revolution. It started out honorably, but then it passed into the hands of the mob. And so, they decided to have revenge, and everyone got killed. They devoured themselves, which is neither left nor right; it's just destruction."

"So then, your stories *do* speak to these totalitarian strains that may exist within *any* individual." At last, his mind appeared to be opening a tiny sliver past its narrow, bunker-like embrasure.

"Oh, everywhere. Us ... but our record is clean compared to what's ... I mean, China has burned millions of books in the last twenty years."

"How about our record not just domestically but regarding some of our questionable policies in South America over the last hundred years? Do you really think it's that clean?" After all, I knew a thing or two about Henry Kissinger's Nazi-inspired goons running torture chambers south of the border.

"We recognized that. I think most people have discussed it, and here and there we're trying to do something about it so we erase the memory of that. But it's not totalitarian in the sense of what Russia has done when they invade a country and kill millions of people. We haven't done that."

Perhaps Ray had forgotten about the atrocities of the Vietnam War, or the heinous acts committed by the CIA the world over, including the overthrow of democratically elected governments, all of which resulted in the deaths of millions of innocent people in violation of the basic precepts of the Nuremberg Code. But I simply replied: "Do we want to erase the record, or do we want to face the record?"

"I think we've faced it. We've got plenty of books on it. Our libraries are full of them. And plenty of newspapers to remind us of that."

Somehow, I'd managed not to lose my temper. Having made my point, I decided to let him blabber on.

By the time we were finished our rapport remained as warm and cordial as it had been from the start. This was one thing that I admired about Ray: he didn't demonize those who disagreed with him. Perhaps because of his impregnable self-assurance, he seemed to take it all in stride. This was also a trait that was widely practiced – and polished to perfection – among the more educated classes in France. While a Parisian dinner table might serve as an arena for clashing ideas and opinions, by the time dessert was served even the most acrimonious of assaults were forgotten and the conversation returned to normal. Unfortunately, in America things were rapidly moving in the opposite direction.

The diplomacy that I'd managed to extend to Ray that afternoon continued to pay off; for never have I gained so much mileage out of a single piece of writing. Though the editor of *Bloomsbury* wasn't interested, fearful that it was too confrontational, I immediately published an excerpt in the *Paris Voice*, a newspaper edited in the basement of the American Church in Paris.

Like many small-press endeavors, though it was a modest operation it was largely written by an in-house staff and, therefore, remained rather difficult to break into. But the editor, who was a longtime American expat and Sixties aficionado, was delighted to have it; and he continued to publish more of my work in the months ahead. He even invited me to join the editorial staff, which I agreed to, because it gave me more control over how my own essays would be presented. Thus, I managed to establish a literary presence in Paris via the *Voice*, which was distributed to all the Anglo-Saxon cafés.

The following spring I published another excerpt in *Quantum: Science Fiction & Fantasy Review*, a magazine produced in Maryland. Twelve years later I was contacted by the editor of a grammar textbook published by Nelson Thornes, which was widely used in schools in England. They asked for an excerpt that dealt with the creative process, which featured some of Ray's more insightful remarks. When I asked him: "Do you have any sort of daily ritual that serves as a preparation to writing, or do you just sit down every day at a certain time and begin?" Ray replied:

> Well, the ritual is waking up, number one, then lying in bed and listening to my voices. I call it my morning theater; it's inside my head. My characters talk to one another, and when it reaches a certain pitch of excitement I jump out of bed and run and trap them before they are gone. So, I never have to worry about a routine; they're always in there, talking.

A few years later an editor named Steven Aggelis, who was assembling *Conversations with Ray Bradbury* for the prestigious University Press of Mississippi, asked for permission to publish the complete interview, minus any edits.

"How did you get him to say all this stuff?" Aggelis asked, sounding utterly flabbergasted when we finally arranged to speak on the phone. "He almost never talks about politics!"

"That's probably the fault of those straight-jacketed mainstream editors. But since I'm a freelancer I don't have to answer to anyone, and I can ask whatever I like." Aggelis said that he'd combed through more than two hundred interviews with Bradbury and that mine would be among the twenty-one that would be featured in the book.

By now the Internet was devouring everyone's time and attention, and after I posted the piece online both Aggelis and Nelson Thornes had easily managed to find me. The publication of Aggelis' book in 2004 brought further attention, and journals such as *Senses of Cinema* and the *California Literary Review* cited our conversation. After Bradbury died at the age of ninety-one, both the *Chicago Reader* and *Archdaily* (an online venue for the magazine *Architectural Digest*) quoted from the piece. All this made it easier for me to embark upon a variety of interviews with celebrated novelists, biographers, and artists.

And then, in 2015, a journalist published an essay in the *New York Times* titled "Reclaiming the Age-old Art of Getting Lost" in which she quoted from our conversation:

> "We travel for romance, we travel for architecture, and we travel to be lost," the writer Ray Bradbury said in a 1990 interview with Rob Couteau. "There's nothing better than to walk around Paris and not know where in hell you are."

Ray was certainly right about that. Although his political views were uninspiring, his insights about architecture and science fiction were engaging. When I asked, "When did you first become intrigued with cities?" he replied:

> When I was eight years old and saw the covers of the science-fiction magazines. They're all architectural. We love science fiction because it's architectural. All the big science-fiction films of the last twenty years are architectural. In the film *2001*, when you see the rocket ship flying through the air, it's a city; it's a big city up there. And in *Close Encounters of the Third Kind*, when the mother ship descends, it's not a ship; it's a city ... And when the aliens come out of the ship, you want to go back in with them and go away forever. And

when one of the characters does, your heart goes with him. So we love architecture; we love the romances of places.

Thus, "The Romance of Places" served as a perfect title for our interview.

* * *

A few years before Ray died, one of his assistants contacted me, hoping to obtain a copy of the original *Voice* article for a Ray Bradbury museum in California. By then Bradbury had received a considerable amount of flak, even on his own website, from fans who were perplexed, nonplussed, or offended by some of the remarks he'd made during our talk. So I wondered if he might have grown annoyed with me. But when I asked his assistant to give him my regards, Ray passed along a note that said: "Send him my love!"

One of the strangest things to come out of all this occurred on the day that Bradbury died, on 5 June 2012. That afternoon I was contacted by Monocle 24, an international media conglomerate located in London.

"We're like the CNN of Europe," a young man on the phone announced with a certain bubbly pride. "And since you're an expert on Ray Bradbury, we'd like to interview you for our broadcast tomorrow." Rather than informing him that I was by no means an "expert," I played along and we scheduled a time to speak.

Though I was impressed by Ray's ability to climb out of obscurity in Waukegan, Illinois and rise to such notable heights, my admiration wasn't really based on his literary skill, which was fashioned more for an adolescent taste than for serious literati. So I did my best to tip my hat to his accomplishment but without sounding like a naive acolyte. When asked about his place in the literary canon, I unhesitatingly replied:

"To be honest, I don't think that, a hundred years from now, Ray Bradbury will be remembered as a great literary author. But there was a time in the Fifties, when science fiction was still relatively new, when he did something that no other sci-fi author did, which was to bring certain elements of high art and literature into what was basically a commercial genre at that point. A more human quality, and things that you'd typically find in a novel in terms of human interaction, and emotion, and things like that.

"There's something about Ray's work that appeals to adolescents or to readers of a certain age. If your thing is high literature, I don't think that you're going to go back to him when you're fifty years old. But there's a *spirit* in Ray Bradbury that is just wonderful, and unique, and that radiated from his personality. Even if you didn't agree with some of his more farfetched ideas or political opinions, still, you *liked* him. He resembled that eccentric uncle that you'd visit every now and then, who would just sit there and hold forth but who would connect with you on a human level. One reason that I connected with Ray is that we both had a great love, as outsiders, for Paris."

The last time I heard from Ray – via email – he said that ever since he was wheelchair bound, what he missed most was wandering without plan or goal through the lovely streets of Paris.

Rue Claude Lorrain

A month before my lease ran out I placed a classified ad saying that I was an American writer in search of a quiet place to work. A few days later I received a message on my answering machine from a woman named Monique Ventanas, who lived in the posh *seizième arrondissement*.

When I returned her call, Monique said that she was intrigued by my ad because she was also a lover of literature. She'd recently translated several works of fiction for a small publishing house in Quebec, which featured young aspiring novelists. Upon noticing my *petite annonce*, it occurred to her that she might rent the downstairs *chambre*; something she'd never done before, but why not? And what a delightful idea, to offer it to an *écrivain américain!*

The following afternoon, she greeted me in the lobby of her building. I was immediately taken by her warm gentle manner and kind regard: qualities that were rarely displayed to strangers in a city known for its legendary coldness.

Monique was Spanish on her father's side and possessed dark, brooding, heavily lidded eyes. They glimmered with such a powerful, soulful beauty that it was difficult to directly confront her gaze. Though she was a couple of years my senior, Monique still possessed a youthful spirit and charm. She also exuded an eminently "correct," sophisticated manner that she'd inherited from her aristocratic French mother.

I soon learned that Monique was the only child of this Spanish entrepreneur, who had amassed a fortune in the food supply business, and of his prim, proper, and stiff-backed wife, who often looked as if she'd just swallowed their bright-green parrot. When I first entered their living room, the bird babbled, screeched, and squawked *"Alors!"* from a gilded cage that stood in a far corner of their well-appointed digs.

Besides being lucky enough to have such a hospitable land-lady, the *chambre* was an exceptional find. It was a standard ten-square-meter affair; but because the building was constructed in the 1950s, it had an *ascenseur* (elevator) that brought you directly to the flat. (Most unusual for a *chambre de bonne*, as normally you'd have to stagger up five or six steep flights.) And the rooms were located just below the ground floor, so they were also easily accessible by foot. The well-lit corridor was spic-and-span clean, with marble floor tiles instead of the usual raw wooden planks leading to poorly lit, dusty, eighteenth-century hovels. The latter often featured crumbling walls with paint peeling into prodigious flakes, the plaster imbued with a mortuary smell, and hallway latrines – rank Turkish toilets – stinking to the high heavens and sulfuric hells.

Despite the dearth of sunlight in Paris, the building was located on a small side street named after a renowned French landscape painter, Claude Lorrain, whose works, Constable declared, shimmer with the "calm sunshine of the heart." The address to my *chambre* included the phrase *rez-de-chaussée bas*, meaning one flight below street level. The *chambres de bonnes* that faced the front of the building were partially submerged, with their windows overlooking a sunken garden. But since the back of the building was set upon a decline, the ones at the rear (such as Monique's) were actually at ground level, and they featured a picturesque view of an adjacent Polish churchyard.

Between the window and the yard ran a cement ramp where a hard working Portuguese concierge – a statuesque woman with elegant features and a graceful manner – or one of her daughters could be seen padding up and down, insouciantly grinding their muscular derrieres as they carted bulky green garbage bins to and fro. At midday, when I'd open the metal shutters, sit beside the casement, and type away, I'd watch the girls with a mixture of admiration and curiosity, for I'd never before encountered such poker-faced teenagers.

If their father was scrubbing floors inside the building while their mother was alone outside, Madame Concierge would glance at my window to see if I was there. If she caught my eye, a broad smile would bloom across her florid cheeks as she whispered a coquettish *bonjour*. But if the husband happened to be nearby, she wouldn't dare to acknowledge my existence. Once, I'd made the mistake of nodding at her while he was puttering around outside, and she quickly turned away as her husband stepped into view and regarded me with a murderous glare.

All this for a mere fifteen-hundred francs a month: about three hundred American dollars to live in a neighborhood that rivaled the opulence of Park Avenue.

*   *   *

I soon came to realize that Monique was split between the cobwebbed mindset of her mossback mother and the laid-back attitude of her ever-mellow father, a gentleman who always impressed me as being *colossally* relaxed, exuding the contentment of a Titan in repose.

Whenever she spoke of her paterfamilias and shared her admiration for him, I'd envision Rabelais' literary character "Gargantua," whose tremendous feet had once been planted atop the bell towers of Notre-Dame as if they were footpads flanking a Turkish toilet. According to Rabelais, who first published this tale circa 1532, from this magisterial position Gargantua had pissed upon the place du parvis Notre-Dame, an act described in loving detail. On page forty-two of *Gargantua and Pantagruel* the author says that, as a result of this *spectacle,* one may conclude that *les parisiens* are inveterate *gapers*, *gawkers*, and *voyeurs*. For they gathered there en masse, transfixed as they witnessed this extraordinary unloading of a steaming bladder upon the very center of Paris. Indeed, the *parvis* is officially designated as "kilometer zero" – a Parisian Archimedean point from which everything else is measured.

In a similar nonchalant, unfettered fashion, with his feet propped upon a stool, Monique's father would hunker down in his capacious *de luxe* armchair (with Madame's lace brocade carefully pinned to the armrests) while he calmly scanned his Spanish newspapers or drank his Spanish coffee, unperturbed and seemingly at peace with his legumes, his fruit-and-vegetable business now thriving and supplying a great swath of Parisian markets, restaurants, and supply chains. As he dozed upon this velvety throne, his wife would gracefully but frenetically – if one can imagine what I mean – scurry about: in and out of the kitchen, bedroom, living room, and dining room, straightening everything out, even though things could not be any straighter, all the while holding her back stiffer than the stiffest *planche à repasser*, or ironing board.

Monique's visibly strained relationship with *Maman* was revealed to me one day while we were seated on a bench in Boulogne-Billancourt, in the nearby Jardin des Serres d'Auteuil. As we observed the puffy Parisian clouds billow over rue Claude Lorrain, suddenly, unexpectedly, Madame Ventanas strolled past, now appearing even more rigid and gray faced than usual. Gliding along in that graceful but frightfully stoic manner of hers, at once she called to mind the disembodied spirit of a vanquished Spartan warrior.

Then I noticed a subtle, gossamer, nearly imperceptible communication rise up between Monique and her mother. It registered only because I'd been living in Paris just long enough to detect such fine, delicate, microscopic vibrations that are often exchanged between the natives with gestures and intonations of such infinitesimal density that one can find their equivalent only in the realm of quantum physics: subatomic quarks, bosons, or fermions of "attitude" that, nonetheless, indicate major seismic activity.

As if to confirm all this, Monique even went that extra step of making a disparaging remark about how difficult it had been to grow up under the constant scrutiny and gimlet-eyed surveillance of this staid, severe, tradition-bound matriarch. Of course, she never used those exact words; the language employed was far more encoded and reserved. Yet, in a "French context," it was remarkably *direct*. Even to an *inculte* imbecile such as myself – one who, at that early date, knew next to nothing about the vast complexities of French culture – the message was clear.

After Madame disappeared around a corner, Monique continued to speak even more directly (*franchement!*) about how frustrating it had been to remain at home and passively observe the unfolding events of May 1968: that historic fulcrum point in France when – "suddenly" – everything exploded. But in fact, such mounting unrest had been brewing beneath the calm, sober, "correct," surface reality of things for quite some time.

As is often the case in French history, such an "explosion" is engineered incrementally; and, whether it takes decades or centuries, eventually it ignites. And then that most fearful of things for the French – *change* – rears its terrifying, Medusa-like head. As one of my students would later explain to me, until May 1968 the word *changement* almost always connoted something *pejorative*. It was rarely used in a positive sense until *after* the uprising of '68, when *"Peut-être! peut-être! peut-être!"* he added, "it *might* be positive." And so, one can well imagine how enervating all this was for poor Monique, living in that mausoleum of a "living" room and stuck beside an icebox of a mother whose mentality remained closer to May 1668.

We were seated upon this freshly painted bench in an otherwise empty park when it occurred to me that, oddly enough, Monique and I – so removed from each other in culture and upbringing as well as in time and space – somehow shared a fundamental link. For her story reminded me of how, when I was a mere adolescent, I had witnessed, largely through television, the derangement of the entire cultural and political landscape – and how I'd yearned to participate in all that.

During our camping trips each summer, with our family packed into my father's secondhand Impala, we'd occasionally pass the shaggy-haired hippies and their beatific, doe-eyed girlfriends hitching on the interstate. But during one such trip in the late Sixties, while we were in the midst of a long, tedious haul to New England *sans* air-conditioning, I spotted a truckload of soldiers dressed in battle fatigues, their muddy boots dangling over the rear bumper as they rumbled past us on the highway. They were being transported farther north, perhaps to a camp from which they'd be shipped off to die in Vietnam. They appeared to be exhausted as well as forlorn as they held their rifles in the most lackluster fashion and stared at us from beneath their cumbersome green helmets.

As the truck gradually accelerated ahead of my father's slow-motion trajectory – forever trailing behind everyone else in the right-hand lane – my brother and I flashed them a "peace sign," with our index and middle fingers upraised. At first, they continued to regard us like zombies. But then, a blue-eyed boy seated in the left-hand corner slowly raised his hand and returned the gesture. And he held it there; he didn't just momentarily flash it, but he held it as if he wanted to make certain that we could see it. Then the truck accelerated, vanishing in the distance. But I never forgot that boy; and, in the years ahead, I'd occasionally wonder what had happened to him and whether he'd survived the war.

In any case, Monique and I had wanted so badly to be a part of this unique cultural transformation. How painful it is for an adolescent to observe the stream of life bursting forth and burgeoning all around – and such an extraordinary flowering of life, at that time – and to be deprived of fully participating in it. Although Madame Ventanas had forbidden Monique to go anywhere near the protests and demonstrations, now she wished that she hadn't obeyed. Most of all, she said, she regretted being that good little girl who always listened to this severe martinet.

And now, she was still living at home, and she realized that, even by French standards, she was too old to remain there. All along, she'd wanted to create her *own* life – with a loving family, or at least a *boyfriend* – but she'd never gotten past her parents' front doorstep. Instead, she lived a sheltered, protected, make-believe existence: one from which she didn't know how to escape.

But I could sense that it was reaching a breaking point; and, like all great French revolutions, it too would "suddenly" explode. Then she would finally set out to accomplish something: to find a lover at least, or to live something uniquely her own.

Just before I left this sweet little room with its enticing view of Madame Concierge's curvaceous rump rising and falling to the cancan beat of her garbage-bin promenade, Monique informed me that she was now dating an Englishman who worked as a language teacher at a school in Paris. This revelation struck me as both unexpected and shocking. The British were often light years away from comprehending the nuances of a traditional French mindset, especially an aristocratic French mindset, just as the French were often incapable of grasping what they called *le bœuf*, or "roast beef" (a term derived from the ruddy tint of an Englishman's skin). But there it was. And I thought: If a middle-class Englishman is good enough for Monique, then even *I* might have stood a chance despite my abysmal lack of French culture, history, and etiquette, not to mention my rather modest bank account.

But even if I might have overcome such hurdles, I'd placed Monique on a pedestal, and I would never have dared to approach her with such a proposition. Nonetheless, she never appeared to be annoyed by my frequent *maladroits* and, instead, often appeared to be charmed by them.

Shortly after I'd moved in, one afternoon she invited me upstairs and treated me – along with several of her friends – to crêpes dabbed with exotic creams and jellies. She explained that they were celebrating *Fête de la musique*: a day when the *citoyens* of Paris unpack their musical instruments, which are gathering dust in storage units or *caves* (pronounced "cahvs") and parade along the street singing and performing, usually noticeably off-key.

And so, after she prepared the crêpes, she asked if I'd prefer *la crème* or *la gelée* – the raspberry or the marmalade, the peach or the pear jam – and I replied, only half-joking, *Well, why not give me a dollop of each, and we'll mix them all together?*

Monique was so taken aback by this that she even wondered if she'd misunderstood me. Almost stuttering, she again inquired: "But *what*, exactly, would you like?" When I made myself perfectly clear, she replied, "*Alors*. I'm not really sure if I understand. Here ..." (handing me the silver serving tray), "why not just help yourself?" And I did.

At first she appeared to be bewildered. But once she regained her composure, she burst out laughing. But not in that typically patronizing manner of *les parisiens* who know least of all how to laugh good-naturedly. ("Laughing mirthlessly" is how the author Edmund White characterizes it in his own Parisian memoir.) Instead, it was simply a delightful expression of her amusement upon witnessing this eminently *un-French* thing. I regarded it as a robust effusion of her Spanish soul, which never completely fit into *la mentalité française*.

Perhaps Monique experienced a certain kinship with me because I, too, didn't really fit in there. I was no longer American, but, despite my French ancestry, I'd never become an official Frenchman either. Though I'd attempted to acclimate myself and to adopt a variety of Gallic mannerisms, eventually the idea of emulating a Parisian grew to be something I abhorred. Clearly, it would be a nightmare to be stuck in such a nineteenth-century straightjacket. As a result, I became not only an exile but also a *cultural orphan*. And maybe Monique felt something similar.

* * *

In her adolescent years, my atypical *chambre* had served as Monique's playroom. While she was still a teenager, she said, she'd commandeered the flat as a "get away from mommy and daddy space," utilizing it as a private hideaway or bunker. I often imagined her being happily sequestered there in the early Sixties: playing pop-music records on a small turntable as she daydreamed about what life held in store, all the while enjoying the solitude of this peaceful little space as the sparrows chirped on the boughs in the adjacent churchyard.

During spring and summer, the leaves would occasionally be dappled with that rarest of Parisian commodities: sunlight. As Ernest Hemingway says in the very first sentence of *A Moveable Feast*, "And then there was the bad weather." *La pluie!* (The rain.) *Il pleut!* (It rains.) I learned those phrases rather quickly. But on such joyfully illuminated days, when you opened the squeaky metal shutters, you could almost imagine that you were living in Provence.

And not only was it a room with a view. Rather rare for a *chambre de bonne*, it also featured a square bathtub, three-feet high by three-feet wide, where the maid had once washed the clothing. And, wonder of wonders, there was also *hot water!*

Perhaps you're perplexed by this shock and awe over such basic trifles, such commonplace necessities. No doubt, you're wondering why I'm waxing poetic over these various and sundry banalities. But anyone who's ever managed to attain a tenuous foothold in Paris – living there *sans papiers*, unofficially and thus illegally, and therefore unable to seek gainful employment, and reduced to the penury of menial, under-the-table jobs, and forced to live in a shabby sixth-floor walk-up with colossal wads of paint peeling from the ceiling and the incessant noise of your neighbors coughing, moaning, and groaning behind paper-thin walls – will understand and vicariously rejoice in landing such a deal.

I myself had witnessed so many otherwise sane, normal, healthy Americans descend into Paris and slowly but surely develop this peculiar third-world mentality: waxing lyrically over a hot-water spigot, for example, or bragging that their walk-up is only four flights instead of the usual five or six. And since they can't officially work in France, their diploma is worthless. It doesn't matter that, once, you were a schoolteacher in Minnesota or a pharmacist in Nebraska, because now you're reduced to being babysitter or a language tutor, all off the books of course. But you do it anyway, for the simple reason that, when you open your shutters in the morning, there it is – *Paris*.

And despite the fact that France is no longer the center of the universe, even the most mundane interactions there are often presented as earth-shattering events. When a *boulanger* offers you a baguette, it's presented with a stupendous flair: a histrionic performance of such peacock-feather fluttering, over-the-countertop drama that one would imagine he's handing you a solid gold bar. *"Voilà!"* – the baguette is thrust forward with a snap of the wrist that's been rehearsed for countless decades. And if you settle upon a *terrasse* and order a *café*, expect it to arrive with the same Oscar winning, heel-clicking crescendo. Where else in the world can one encounter waiters who become so entranced by their role? Or who stand with backs held so straight and rigid, with chests puffed like helium balloons, and with noses contemptuously sniffing at the air as they hover beside your table and impatiently await a tip? *Voilà!* the *café noir*. *Voilà!* the metro *billet*. *Voilà!* the summons a policeman hands you when you're caught leaping over a turnstile.

And it's been like this ever since Louis XIV, the Sun King. Every Frenchman has learned to model himself after Louis, who once proclaimed: *I am the center of the universe; hence, all rays emit and shine forth from me – and then fall upon you.* And so, if you're lucky enough to receive from Louis a divine baker ray, henceforth, as a *boulanger*, you will incarnate this baker-god emanation and transform yourself into a local baking deity. Haughtily displaying your prowess, you will lord it over everyone else because now it's *your moment to shine forth.* As the customers shuffle along a barely moving line they will passively absorb, like mere satellites, such exquisite baker rays as they hold out their palms and the *boulanger* proclaims *Voilà!* – bestowing upon each client a scintilla of this sacred radiance, the baguette itself.

But if, on the other hand, you're a clerk at a metro station and safely ensconced behind a thick wall of bulletproof glass, then you'll revel in the fact that, no matter how rude you are to your customers, they cannot can harm you as you regard them with an insolent display of disdain: one that a Parisian learns to master to perfection. Indeed, it's the one thing they excel at. And this is precisely why they are so cherished and beloved the world over.

And yet, what would France be without all this? The very

things that I grew to detest were implacably twined with all that I came to miss – and even cherish – upon my departure from Lutèce.

*   *   *

After two years of living on rue Claude Lorrain, when I finally decided to move I didn't have the heart to say goodbye to Monique. So I slipped a note under her door and skedaddled. But a few days later, she wrote me care of my previous address:

"Wherever you end up in this big world, think of me; and if you have a moment, stay in touch!"

Such elegance!

Monique, I shall always remember you with an everlasting fondness. I preserve your memory like an eternal dollop of pear jam savored on lips singing songs of joy on Fête de la musique, Paris 1990.

Êtes vous paranoiaque?

Operating a small word-processing business meant that I'd have to open my dwelling to strangers, a prospect that was unsettling since I considered myself to be a rather private person. Yet I adapted to this practice relatively quickly, especially since my livelihood – and thus my ability to remain in Paris – depended on it.

But this also helped me to develop a more diplomatic manner. Since I was working there illegally, one phone call from an irate client to the proper authorities would result in being frog-marched to the airport and forced to board a plane back to the States. At that time, Americans were allowed to remain in France only three months at a stretch. You could reenter and remain for another three months, but the maximum stay was no more than six months per annum.

If you didn't have any run-ins with *les flics*, however, staying there year-round rarely posed a problem. The prevalent notion seemed to be that an American wouldn't remain in France forever, since there were better opportunities back home, *n'est pas?* And so, I was rarely questioned as I made a beeline through French customs when returning from a visit to the States.

But I'd heard some disturbing stories. For example, there was an American who'd made the mistake of strolling into the Préfecture de police to inquire about what she should do, since she'd accidentally overstayed her visit by a few days. The cops took one look at her passport, escorted her back to her flat, threw her belongings into a duffle bag, and stuck her on a plane at Orly. Since it was an enforced flight, the ticket was paid for by the French government.

An enterprising lad who'd heard about her unfortunate plight decided to use it to his advantage. The reason that *he* walked into police headquarters after purposely overstaying his visit was that he was broke and wanted a free flight home! And he wasn't disappointed. They packed him up and shipped him off to Chicago, *gratis*.

Bearing this in mind, I was always careful to be exceedingly courteous, pleasant, and polite to my clients. Thus, I rarely had any problems as I interacted with a steady flow of Parisians seeking either a résumé-typing service or a series of English lessons. But every once in a while, something unexpected would occur while encountering such *étrangers*.

One day I received a call from a Frenchman in his early twenties who spoke fluent English but in a halting, cautious manner. When he said that he needed a curriculum vitae, I instructed him to phone from a *cabine* in the metro once he arrived. Since the entrance to my building was locked and there weren't any buzzers for those of us living in the basement, after I received a call I'd wait for my customers outside. Although there was a door code to unlock the main entrance, some of my clients had such a bad sense of direction that they'd wander through the building for half an hour before finding me. Thus, in order to keep to my schedule, instead of giving out the code I'd insist on personally escorting them to my flat. But unbeknownst to me, this seemingly innocuous ritual had produced an unsettling effect upon my new client's equilibrium.

From the moment he arrived, he behaved erratically. As I sat at my desk and prepared his CV, instead of remaining seated beside me he hopped from his chair and nervously paced back and forth – a rather difficult task to perform in a tiny, ten-square meter room.

I attempt to put him at ease … we start talking … he slowly

relaxes ... Finally, he feels he can trust me. Then he reveals that he has information that *World War III is imminent ...*

It doesn't take long for me to realize that this poor fellow is more than just a bit schizoid. But since he's on the paranoid end of the spectrum, I agree with whatever he says, this being the only way of not getting grouped into the wrong side of the "us-versus-them" mentality that seems to plague him.

"Yes," I reply, "I believe that you're right!"

"*Believe?* Oh, no! It's not a matter of *belief.* It *will* happen – there's *no doubt* about it!"

I correct myself: "Of course, you're *absolutely* right!" The more deeply conspiratorial he becomes, the more wholeheartedly I endorse his ideas.

After several more exchanges like this, he's convinced that he's encountered a rare, kindred spirit. Now, he can barely contain himself ... he's ranting about Freemasonry, the Knights Templar, and God knows what else. In France, even the conspiracy theories are antiques!

Hovering beside me, suddenly he sinks back into a chair, drills his eyes into mine, and speaks in a soft, whispery tone:

"What a *shame* that it's so *difficult* to meet those who can *see the light!* But perhaps, between the two of us, we'll discover a means of *finding* them."

With a euphoric glow in his eyes, he reaches for his wallet, offering me some "extra money" just for speaking with him. But I say no, really, it's not necessary; it's a pleasure. Then he leans forward and adds:

"By the way, I hope you don't mind me asking ... but ... are you *paranoid?*"

"Why do you ask?"

"Well," he murmurs, swiveling his head back and forth between my desk and the window that opens into the courtyard, "I see that you make people call from the metro before you give out your address." As he continues to whisper, I glance at the cover of a magazine that he has cradled under his arm. It's *Le Nouvel Observateur*, and the headline reads: *Êtes vous paranoiaque?*

While preparing his résumé, I notice that he's worked for *Le Front National*: an anti-immigration, right-wing party that was gaining ascendancy in France. In just a few more years, the NF would garner fifteen-percent of the vote in presidential elections, and it would eventually become the third most powerful political force in the nation.

As I type this particular detail of his employment history, he feels compelled to reassure me of his innocence: "I hope you don't think I'm like this" – he leaps up, clicks his heels, and raises an arm in Nazi salute – "just because I worked for *Le Front National!* I did that only because I wanted to know what *really goes on there*. As you can see here" – pointing to the next line of his résumé – "I also worked for the *Socialists*. Yes, I believe in getting in, behind the scenes, just to see how things *really work*."

I print out a final version of his résumé, and he plops a rather large tip on my table. Thanking me profusely, he smiles nervously, quickly gathers up his papers, and prepares to exit.

I escort him to the door, where we silently shake hands. But once he's out in the hall, approaching the stairs, he just can't help himself:

He peers round, over his shoulder, staring at me with one last look of lingering *suspicion*.

* * *

On sunny days, I'd pack my manuscripts into a knapsack and travel to one of the celebrated Parisian parks, to work outside. My favorite was Parc Montsouris, a landscape redolent with such seductive tranquility that I could easily dream away an entire afternoon while reading my books, editing, or admiring the young *au pairs* gliding along with shiny chrome baby strollers in hand.

One afternoon while I was seated there on a bench and rereading *Last Exit to Brooklyn* – hoping to somehow emulate the raw, brutal, violent tenor of Hubert Selby's maniacal prose – suddenly I heard a child sobbing, followed by series of *smacks*.

A baby, just an infant, a tiny little thing swaddled in a woolen blanket in a stroller, was screaming. Seated beside me was a heavyset young woman with an ugly grimace on her doughy face. Obviously an *au pair*, she was cursing in German and smacking this infant on the face, simply because it had started to whimper, causing it scream even louder.

I slammed *Last Exit* on the bench and confronted her with a glare of such homicidal rage that it would have terrified even one of Hubert Selby's psychopathic figures. Absorbing my menacing leer, she leapt up, whisked the stroller away, and scampered over a nearby hilltop.

As I digested this traumatic event I suspected that, although her actions were utterly inexcusable, it probably wasn't only the baby's cries that had pushed her over the edge. More often than not, after these inexperienced, gullible young girls receive a job offer in Paris and travel a great distance from their native land to settle in some woebegone *chambre de bonne*, their French employers will plot and scheme, adding additional tasks to their already burdensome schedule – and without ever raising their salary. Indeed, I'd heard of such stories on numerous occasions. Instead of sticking to the initial agreement, the family would squeeze more and more out of these harried young ladies. Treated like veritable slaves, they were stretched to a breaking point.

I, too, had my own experiences and, as a result, I learned the hard way how business was often conducted there. One day, hoping to eke out a few more francs, I advertised for French résumé preparation with a carefully worded ad that offered a "bilingual" curriculum vitae prepared by a "native New Yorker." Little did I suspect that I'd receive such a flurry of calls; for, once again, I'd naively stumbled upon something. Many of my French clients were afraid to prepare their résumés with a native Parisian typist, because – as one of them explained with a subdued tone – what if the typist knows someone who knows someone who *knows someone who is acquainted with their employer?* Word might get back that they were searching for a job! So instead, they'd call me, a complete outsider, an American.

But what a colossal headache! As soon as I'd prepare the text, correct it, and print it out – now patiently waiting to be paid – inevitably a drama would ensue: one that illustrates a keynote in the traditional French mindset:

"Ah, Robere!" (pronouncing my name the French way, *row-BEAR*, as they usually did unless they used the more familiar *row-BUH*), *"C'est splendide! Magnifique! Merveilleux! Mais* … if you don't mind … *peut-être* … we can change this period… to a *comma.* Then it will be *parfait. Parfait!"* Over the years, I met so many Parisians who were obsessed with this notion of *perfectionnement*; because, heaven forbid, what if there was a crease on your lapel? Then, surely, someone might suspect you of being an ax murderer! A child molester! A communard! So now, instead, we must transform this comma … into a semicolon. And then: "Ah, now we're getting somewhere. *C'est bonne. Voilà."* But then … another pause … which might last for two or three hours if you let them indulge in it.

And if you find this hard to believe, let's have a look at how Olivia de Havilland, that glamorous film star from Hollywood's golden era, describes her own travails in a memoir about life in

Lutèce published thirty years before, in 1962. Olivia says that, after a series of nearly insurmountable difficulties with her Parisian *ouvriers*, who fail to follow even the simplest of instructions (painting the kitchen gray, for instance, when she'd specifically requested *blue* paint), Olivia finally experiences her own version of satori in Paris:

> It came to me what, to a Frenchman, the true function of a plan is.... Of course a plan is something to be *changed*.... Furthermore, it is the keenest possible challenge to Gallic ingenuity to ring in as *many* changes on it as it can.

In other words, the only sort of change that wasn't feared was changing the terms of agreement – in order to make one's life easier!

"Ah, Robere, I've just realized something. This paragraph ... it seems rather lengthy, don't you agree? It's so dense that it almost hurts the eyes! It's ... how do you say ... *unharmonious*. Yes, lacking in *balance*, verging on the *asymmetrical*. *Alors, en effet*, a harmonization is needed! So, what do you think? Is it possible to add *une pause*? *Un espace*? Something that will allow the eye to relax until it moves on, to the next challenge? A moment to *décontractée*, as we say in France. A rest stop, such as you have on those extraordinary American highways that zigzag across that monstrosity of a country of yours. For, otherwise, a prospective employer, upon seeing this, might grow *fatigué ... angoissée ... et déprimé.*"

Wherever I traveled in Paris, eventually I'd encounter those three most telling phrases: the real Holy Trinity of France! Not *liberté, égalité, fraternité*, but *tired, anxious,* and *depressed!* A pharmacy around the corner from my flat on rue Claude Lorrain had even displayed a tricolor poster in the traditional *bleu, blanc, et rouge* of the French flag, embossed with the words: *Fatigué? Angoissée? Déprimé?* And beneath each phrase, in identically tinted blue, white, and red bowls, was a glittering heap of pharmaceutical pills, each pill dyed to match these *raisonnable*, relaxing colors. Indeed, it was an impressionist tricolor – a sky blue, a dove white, a lavender pink – and one light-years away from the jarring hues of a Picasso, say, or even a Van Gogh. Instead, these "civilized" tones were guaranteed to attract the attention of all those poor souls who were so terribly *fatigued*, *anguished*, and *distraught*, and forced to labor under a considerable burden. That is, the *curse of earning a living*.

Perhaps even Adam himself had been a Frenchman; for the trauma of the Garden of Eden reflects a fundamental nightmare ever-brewing in the Gallic psyche: of being cast from paradise into a workaday world – a plot that would make even the most level-headed Cartesian *paranoiaque*.

Hubert Selby

A few years after encountering the Teutonic beast who smacked that poor little infant while I was reading *Last Exit to Brooklyn*, I actually found myself standing before the author himself – Mr. Hubert Selby.

Selby had published one of the most important novels to ever breach the strictures of Anglo-Saxon censorship. First released by Grove Press in 1964, two years later the British publication of *Last Exit* resulted in a court trial in London, where it was defended against charges of obscenity by Selby's courageous publishers, John Calder and Marion Boyars. At first, it seemed to be a case of David versus Goliath. But regardless of the massive legal team assembled by the state, the publishers' noble defense of liberty won the case on appeal in the summer of 1968, embarrassing the British Empire and its rearguard, nanny-like mentality.

Now, decades later, Selby was seated at a small wooden table in a bookshop in Saint-Germain-des-Prés, hunkered down for a book signing. In 1970 Editions Albin Michel had issued *Last Exit* in French translation, but there were still plenty of unsold copies stacked on the shelves behind him.

When I entered the shop there were only two other customers who had arrived for the event: a young French couple. Charmed by their attention and adoration, the author was chatting with them at length as they struggled with their broken English.

I was hardly surprised by the shortness of the line. By now, this Brooklyn-born author had been largely forgotten in the publishing world despite the powerful prose that he'd managed to incarnate in subsequent novels such as *The Room, The Demon,* and *Requiem for a Dream.* He was also in fragile physical condition, suffering from chronic respiratory problems that dated back to his early years.

While working as a nineteen-year-old merchant seaman, Selby had contacted tuberculosis. By the time he was diagnosed it was already in its advanced stages. During his surgery, one lung had collapsed and part of his other lung was removed, along with several ribs. An experimental drug treatment wreaked havoc on his immune system, and the doctors gave him only three months to live. But Selby proved them wrong; largely, I believe, through the sheer force of will. All these challenges, combined with years of battling drug addiction (for nothing else could relieve his pain) had taken their toll.

An independent Parisian film company had just produced a documentary on Selby that would be screened the following evening. Over the years, this same company had employed me to do English language voice-overs, mostly for industrial films that were being rereleased to Anglo audiences. Shortly before I'd arrived at the bookshop, the producer had called to ask if I'd be interested in doing a voice-over for this new film: an offer that nearly floored me, because I regarded Selby as one of the literary giants who had helped to shape and influence my prose during my long struggle to become a writer.

"I see that you've published a review of two of Mr. Selby's novels," he continued. "Are you aware that he's in Paris right now?"

Surprised that this earth-shattering event hadn't received any publicity in the expatriate press, I asked, "But *where* in Paris?"

"He's signing books in a *magasin* near Odéon."

I took down the address, hailed a cab, and sped over to Saint-Germain-des-Prés, hoping to arrive before closing time.

During my first year in Paris, Marion Boyars had sent me a large box of hardcovers for review, along with a personal note. Included in that shipment from London were Selby's *The Demon* and *The Room*, neither of which I'd read before. Now I handed Selby a copy of my combined review of the two novels, introduced myself, and requested an interview.

His gentle pale-blue eyes seemed to be gazing at something far away: a distant memory that would always remain private. His gaze also reflected a lingering sense of world-weariness, balanced with an admixture of stubborn persistence. Then he glanced at the clipping as if it were an advertisement for shoe polish. Slowly unfolding it, he paused to read the following:

> In every superbly constructed line of Selby's shockingly brilliant prose, a grisly irony informs us not only of hopelessness but of how, when things have become so hopeless, they must go even more wrong before they may be righted. Selby doesn't advocate brutality so much as portray it; he records the violence of contemporary life. Yet he also seems to hint at something within us that clamors for a transcendence of our existential condition.
>
> Perhaps that's hard to see in a "typical" Selby sentence such as: "He could feel the sooty grayness crawl under his skin as he looked at the scummy walls and floor, and felt the gritty sheets as their foul stench reamed his nostrils." Yet the authorial presence that recognizes such ugliness (through the character of Harry) does so in such a pointed manner only when there's an implicit yearning for something beyond that gross, mundane realty. Perhaps, that's what's most shocking

in Selby: his ability to inform the reader of a tender vision lurking beneath the prose, and this tenderness is the very thing proclaiming – in such harsh and brilliant tones – the abject condition of our world.

Nodding his head, he slipped the article into a manila folder and scribbled his name and phone number on a small square of paper. He suggested that I give him a call after he returned from his European tour.

"And would you mind signing this?" I handed him a French translation of *Last Exit*, in which he wrote: "With love, Cubby" – a nickname from long ago.

When I finally called Cubby, he almost didn't pick up the phone. Too poor to rely on a secretary, he still screened his calls with an old answering machine. But I suspected he was there, somewhere in the background, hoping that I would just go away. Instead of giving up, I continued to babble into the machine – increasing, with each syllable, my tone of obsequiousness. By the end of the monologue I must have sounded utterly pathetic. Perhaps I was hoping that he might take pity on a fellow victim of literature.

As I later learned, he was in the midst of a painful day. And while at first he'd avoided the call, by the end of our conversation – which lasted almost three hours – I'd helped to distract him from his discomfort.

Before we said goodbye, he added: "You asked some very interesting questions."

And that made it all worthwhile.

* * *

One of the reasons I felt so strongly about Selby's work is that he'd successfully transmuted his own personal crucifixion into the soul of his literary characters. It wasn't just the physical agony that he'd captured; the psychological and emotional nightmares that he'd ridden throughout his life were impressed deeply upon the fabric of these figures. His narratives are fueled by an emotional tension that remains raw, up front, and unmitigated: a desperate, driving, hypnotic force that propels and transfixes the reader.

But sentimentality plays no part in any of this. Instead, it's an acerbic voice that cuts directly to the marrow and leaves you wounded, yet grateful – because it conjures a landscape that the average publisher not only disdains but also forbids.

Fortunately, as a younger man, Selby was working during a period of remarkable independent publishing, as exemplified not only by Calder and Boyars but also by Richard Seaver, then editor in chief at Grove, who helped Selby to shape *Last Exit* into its final form.

When I'd first expatriated to Paris I was in the midst of rereading *Last Exit*, and, thanks to Boyars, I later dipped into his subsequent work. The immediacy of his prose impressed and inspired me, but there was also another dimension to his artistry that made novels such as *Last Exit* special. They were set in a Brooklyn I knew only too well. A place where, instead of beauty for beauty's sake, violence for violence's sake often reigned as the highest value. I suspect this is the real reason why *Last Exit* was banned. Sex or violence as portrayed in a banal, Hollywood fashion was never a problem. The masses could be expected to feed off it like a cheap, mind-numbing drug: one that would divert their attention from more important things. But Selby had committed the greatest offence of all, because somehow he'd managed to depict aggression and obscenity with the palette of high poetry.

This was also why, after the publicity triggered by the trial had died down, Selby's audience would remain a small one. That is to say, his *authentic* audience. During a censorship trial millions might flock to purchase something labeled as "obscene," but only a handful could appreciate its true literary value.

"In any age," says Picasso, "only a handful can truly *see*."

Selby's gentleness as a human being – if not as a narrator – was apparent during the hours we spoke on the phone. And linked to his empathy was a modesty that was more than just endearing. For here was a modern master who'd struggled for six years to write *Last Exit*, then another six to complete his second novel, the moving tale of *The Room*, with both books receiving significant critical acclaim. And yet, this is how he chose to view himself and the question of his own inherent ability:

When I asked, "What is the price you pay for carrying the demon within you and giving it a voice?" he replied:

> I have no natural talents or abilities in any area of life. I'm not a natural writer or a natural reader; I'm not an exceptional mechanic; I'm not an exceptional athlete; I'm not a draftsman at all; I can't draw or ... Absolutely no natural talent. But I had an obsession to do something with my life before I died. And I just sat in front of that typewriter every day for six years until I learned how to write. Now, I can't say that the ability wasn't there, obviously. I guess it was there, and I just had to fight like hell to activate it, to animate it, to nurture it, to love it ... I just know that it was a lot of work.

It was also from my interaction with Selby that I learned to distinguish between an author and the narrative voice that shapes his creation. (Or perhaps I should say: the voice that *chooses* him.) While reading a text by a beloved novelist, one may develop unrealistic notions about who and what that author really is. The art of the interview poses a unique challenge: to balance this subjective expectation with the actual person who's now speaking in an intense, probing, creative conversation that we call an interview. After a mere hour or two, an entirely new figure may emerge – as if the novel itself has engendered a fresh character. And in the best of interviews, one begins to view the narrative through the eyes of the creator himself.

If I hadn't remained in Paris, I doubt I would have been given the opportunity to meet Hubert Selby. And I probably would never have attempted to interview him, as I had no idea that he was so accessible. Unfortunately, part of this accessibility was due to the fact that he'd become so professionally marginalized.

In the year 2000 director Darren Aronofsky released a film version of *Requiem for a Dream*, and he gave Selby a part in the movie, as a prison guard. This resulted in a small bump of publicity that brought the author some new readers, but he remained far from being a household name. When Selby died in 2004, although he was still regarded as a literary castaway, his obituary was featured throughout the major media. And his hometown paper, the *New York Times*, published a lengthy in-depth article. He continued to accrue some new followers, but in the hallowed tradition of so many great American artists he passed his final days living in relative obscurity.

La Belle Noiseuse

By the late 1990s a fear and loathing of *l'étranger* – a word that means both "foreigner" and "stranger" – continued to roil throughout France. Hosting the seventh-largest number of immigrants in the world, many of *les français* remained proud of their tradition of welcoming newcomers, although an increasing number were fed up with the escalating tensions that resulted from this inevitable clash of culture and mindset.

In my daily life as a language tutor, in conversations with *citoyens* from every political persuasion and walk of life, I listened to story after story chronicling such affairs. But perhaps the most peculiar tale to unfold at my table was that of Domenico Mazzucco, an immigrant from Northern Italy, and his cousin Alfredo, a Milanese who had settled in Provence with a native *parisienne*. Although they would never think of renouncing their Italian heritage, Domenico and Alfredo considered themselves to be fully integrated citizens of France.

When Domenico phoned one day to inquire about my *cours d'anglais*, he said that he needed to improve his English due to an increasing demand to interact with international business clients, who were adopting English as the new *lingua franca*. But his responsibilities left him with little time, so he wasn't sure if he could commit himself to a weekly schedule.

As I learned during our first encounter, Domenico also lacked the time to pursue any romantic interests. Thus, at the age of thirty-five, he was still a *célibataire*. And though he was a chief executive, he considered himself to be a mere "pauper" as far as relations with the "fair sex" were concerned.

I found this to be understandable but also puzzling. Besides being a cultured, skillful conversationalist who exuded an abundance of intelligence, discretion, and charm, Domenico also possessed a buccaneer's swashbuckling good looks. He was graced with a thick crop of coal-black hair, an olive complexion, and a dark pair of riveting eyes set in a beautifully formed physiognomy. Why should it be so difficult for such a chap to find a suitable mate? There seemed to be a missing piece to this puzzle, and I wondered if lack of time was the only obstacle that he faced.

As was often the case with my European students who were successful lawyers, bureaucrats, or entrepreneurs, despite being deeply committed to his work, Domenico rarely mentioned his daily labor. Instead, he preferred to speak about artistic or cultural events. I never failed to be impressed by how these Continental "company men" took an enormous pride in recounting their recent trips to art exhibits, or discussing the novels they were reading, or remarking upon how lovely the Luxembourg Garden appears at sunset. *And have you visited Parc Montsouris, with its 345 varieties of roses?* So unlike their American counterparts who could babble endlessly about stock portfolios and retirement pensions and who concerned themselves almost exclusively with finance, profit, and the so-called bottom line.

But Domenico differed from the typical French Cartesian in one significant aspect. Instead of continually attempting to exhibit an intellectual prowess, he didn't hesitate to communicate his deeper *feelings*, which often appeared to shine through his lively ebony eyes: honing in to the person seated before him with the tentacular reach of his native empathy. Indeed, he was a man of the heart and proud of it. And he wasn't at all embarrassed to "tear up" one day as he related a sad, uncanny, and surrealistic event that had shaken him to the core:

With his voice trembling with affection, Domenico said that he had a cousin named Alfredo, whom he always regarded as a beloved brother. Domenico's gaze assumed a troubling cast of melancholy as he added that Alfredo had married an "attractive Parisian director of communication" who was known for her elegant taste and chic, stylish manner. By all accounts, they'd led a most blissful life in the south, living for the last ten years in Provence. Everything seemed to be hunky-dory, and life was gliding along splendidly; but then, one day, a stranger – an *étrangère* – knocked unexpectedly on Alfredo's door.

Standing at the threshold was a smartly dressed business-woman who smiled invitingly as she explained that her car had broken down, right outside Alfredo's house on the road to Montpellier. And so, she wondered if she might use his telephone.

Without hesitation, Alfredo offered to assist her and invited her inside. Though she bore an uncanny resemblance to his wife, Alfredo doubted that this woman was French, for her accent was difficult to place. She spoke fluently, and with a grasp of the language that was as impeccable as any native, but her intonation resonated with the hint of a foreign tongue.

Speaking with a slightly wavering tone, Domenico said that shortly after she completed her call, another stranger appeared with a tow truck. And this repairman, with the woman standing beside him, fiddled around beneath the hood of her car. But when the engine still wouldn't turn over, they decided to tow it.

Just before she left, she approached Alfredo and stared at him intently. Then she grinned in an odd manner. When Domenico asked Alfredo what he meant by all this, Alfredo said that her lips had curled into a smirk that was at once menacing and cruel. "A sort of superior, mocking, patronizing smile," Alfredo replied with a grim expression, "and one meant to communicate something threatening and dangerous."

Alfredo added that, upon vanishing with the truck, this strange lady had also disappeared with something rather precious. For the real purpose of her visit was to take possession of Alfredo's heart, mind, and soul. Not in any romantic manner but in a devious, evil fashion. Indeed, muttered Domenico, his eyes now widening into a look of utter despair, his poor dear Alfredo was never the same again.

Alfredo believed that *l'étrange dame* was from *another planet* and that she'd *hypnotized* him to gain control over his entire being. While they were awaiting the tow truck, he said, she had penetrated into his psyche and *fiddled around*, just as the mechanic had fiddled with the engine. Alfredo had also deduced that this so-called repairman was a key principal in the plot. For, clearly, he too had come from somewhere very far away. Perhaps he was an *étranger* from Mars or from whatever planet the woman had originally hailed from.

To thank Alfredo for his assistance, the following day the strange lady sent a deluxe box of chocolates to his house via special delivery. But Alfredo refused to eat them; and he warned his wife, who was now growing desperate over this entire turn of events, not to touch them but, instead, to dispose of the box.

"Not long afterward," Domenico sighed, "this glamorous wife, the so-called director of communication who had seemed so lovely when they first married, lost her patience and decided to divorce." Then she, too, vanished, never to return.

As a result, Alfredo barricaded himself into his house and refused to let anyone in except for Domenico, who pleaded with him to seek professional help. But Alfredo wouldn't hear of it. As far as he was concerned, this was obviously a problem that transcended any medical or psychiatric situation.

When Domenico reached this poignant part of the tale, he nearly broke down. His tears welled up, but he struggled to control himself: gripping his fists together till the knuckles were glowing. Not one drop spilled over the rim of his reddened eyelids, and his cheeks remained dry and unstained. But I felt as if his upset was just as profound as it would have been if he'd sobbed uncontrollably.

Clenching his jaw, Domenico glanced over my head, and his attention now shifted to a painting hanging on a wall behind me. During each of his previous visits I'd noticed that Domenico's gaze would eventually drift to this far corner and remain there, like a butterfly pinned to a lepidopterist's specimen card. For a moment I imagined that, instead of a portrait of a nude seated upon a divan, there was an actual woman hovering there, beckoning Domenico to surrender his professional responsibilities and to submit himself to her every whim.

Glancing back and forth between me and the portrait, he added that perhaps this trouble of finding a suitable mate was genetically rooted to his family tree. For just like Alfredo, he too was alone, without any imminent prospects of finding a romantic companion; while his cousin was not only isolated but now rendered incapable of pursuing any sort of human interaction.

*   *   *

When we met the following week, Domenico gestured to the painting and, speaking with a subdued, almost entranced tone, remarked that he greatly admired it.

Composed on a sheet of masonite, it portrayed a *parisienne* named Sabrina: a model who, like Alfredo, had also experienced a loss of soul. For Sabrina was a victim of pathological narcissism: something that had slipped beneath my radar at first. When she'd answered my ad to pose for a painting, she had just turned eighteen, so I'd assumed that her self-centeredness was merely a reflection of her youth, which she'd eventually outgrow. A normal narcissism, so to speak; which, as it turned out, was a serious error in judgment. For I soon discovered that she was a precocious sadist who reveled in tales of cruelty that were delivered with a sort of professional coquetry that was entirely unsettling. A sort of composite, one might say, of Lolita and the Marquis de Sade. And the more I absorbed all this, the less I was able to concentrate on my work.

Once I realized how dangerously ill she was, I refused to hire her again or to return her calls. So now, all that was left was this image of a young woman staring at the viewer with a secret in her eyes – since I'd completed the painting before learning of her darker side. Hence, I'd christened it *La Belle Noiseuse* – "The Beautiful Troublemaker."

As Domenico studied Sabrina's likeness, he appeared to grow increasingly enraptured. Her icy-blue orbs seemed to bore into his soul, leaving him frozen on the spot. While his eyes widened, I began to wonder if he was right – maybe there *was* an abnormal genetic marker lurking in his ancestral makeup: something that attracted the male descendants in his line to such ominous predicaments.

Now, instead of tearing up, his eyes were glazing over. Perhaps, I thought, he was suffering from what the French call *amour fou* or *aimer la folie*: "crazy love" or "love madness." And since the portrait featured such a realistic likeness, I imagined that if Domenico were to encounter Sabrina in the flesh the gravitational pull would be that much stronger – and more fatal.

As our conversation drew to a close, he turned to me with a smile and asked if it would be possible for him to purchase the painting. Since it was over four-feet long and two-feet wide, I knew that it would be problematic to depart with it on a plane if I ever decided to leave France, so I decided to offer it to him as a gift.

Domenico appeared to be surprised as well as delighted, and he again volunteered to recompense me. But despite the fact that I was merely subsisting in France, I refused to take anything. In fact, I was glad to be rid of it.

After paying for his lesson, he assumed a grave expression: as if a weighty responsibility had been thrust upon him. Gripping the masonite beneath his suit-jacketed arm, he somberly marched to the front door where he turned, paused, and nodded. Though the look in his eyes was a peculiar one, at first I didn't attempt to fathom its significance. But in retrospect, he appeared to be sizing me up one last time: snapping a photographic souvenir, which he might later study if he ever wished to contemplate the creator of his beloved painting.

Once he closed the door, he never again returned.

At a loss over how to explain his disappearance, I wondered if Domenico had suffered a similar sort of abduction as that of his cousin – but via the painting itself. Perhaps he'd arranged a semiwithdrawal from society, content to merely gaze upon Sabrina's enigmatic facade. By now, I mused, it was probably mounted in an expensive frame and prominently displayed so he could more easily commune with her image as he padded back and forth in his capacious flat.

But I finally conjectured that the simplest explanation might be the most fitting one. From the very beginning, Domenico had underscored his inability to commit to a weekly language lesson, yet he'd never once missed an appointment. Furthermore, during each of our encounters, his eyes never failed to rest upon that same spot on the wall where his "mistress" was poised like a damsel patiently biding her time as he plotted her rescue.

So I concluded that, once Domenico had gained possession of his treasure and achieved his goal, it was pointless to return.

Just as Alfredo had fallen headfirst into the mystery of the "stranger" and had been swallowed whole, so too had Domenico. But one man had been destroyed, while the other was seemingly revived.

François and Sophie

François was a young French aristocrat who wore gold-rimmed spectacles and shoes that were polished to a luminous sheen. He took a shine to me as well, amused by the fact that, in his eyes, I was an "American intellectual" – "Something one doesn't chance upon every day," he said – and a writer to boot. As if paying homage to an exotic effigy, while handing me a handwritten copy of his curriculum vitae he also handed me an invaluable key:

"In America," he proclaimed, "the taboo is *sex*. But here, it's *money*. We never speak openly about it, but we constantly think of it. Almost all the bickering in French families centers round this theme. It's such a taboo," François laughed, "that one doesn't even ask one's own *brother* what his salary is! *En fait*, once, I attempted to break this taboo. I asked my older brother what he was paid; but I did so only because we were pursuing the same vocation. Therefore, I thought it might be *raisonnable* to inquire, since I was attempting to determine what sort of salary to expect. So I carefully explained all this to Pascal in the most circumspect, diplomatic fashion before broaching this delicate question. But of course, he refused to answer.

"So you see, Robere," he concluded, now smiling indulgently, "we French often make fun of you Americans for speaking so unapologetically about *argent*. So shamelessly, and without inhibition! But not only do we constantly think of it; we also speak of it, but in a more encoded fashion. That is, we employ the term *sécurité*. Which is merely a polite, roundabout manner of referring to exactly the same thing." To properly emphasize his point, Francois leaned across the table and raised his index finger in didactic Cartesian glory. As if making ready to hand over a precious commodity, his voice dropped as he whispered: "Never forget! In France, money is *le roi*. The king!"

According to his curriculum vitae, François was also a certified pilot; a few years earlier, he said, he'd learned to operate a Cessna. In order to maintain his license, he was required ("*Il est obligatoire!*") to fly a certain number of hours each month. As I printed a final draft of his résumé, he invited me to accompany him on his next flight.

I casually mentioned all this to Monique, who responded by exclaiming: "Oh, this has always been my dream – to fly in a small plane!" Since François was the consummate gentleman, when I asked if Monique might accompany us he smiled and replied: "What Frenchman would refuse the opportunity to fly with such a cultivated woman?"

The following weekend, seated beside me in the back seat, Monique could barely contain her enthusiasm. The little plane rolled across a grassy meadow – vibrating like a tin can as we bounced upon the field – until we finally took off. As we ascended toward the clouds, François' supervisor instructed him to kill the engine and glide. This produced a peculiar sensation, as if we were bobbing in a hot-air balloon while hovering over a placid French landscape. At once I thought of the garishly colored nineteenth-century prints of balloonists that the *bouquinistes* dangle on wooden clothespins and sell along the embankments of the Seine.

After retiring to Monique's flat, we were treated to a serving of delectable crêpes, and Francois invited her to accompany him on a flight scheduled for the following month.

Although we soon lost touch, his sage advice concerning the true "king" of France would come in handy in the years ahead.

* * *

Hoping to increase my meager income, I began to advertise for lessons for the *perfectionnement d'anglais*. That is, to pursue the slightly more remunerative task of sitting there, bored beyond measure, and correcting the minor grammatical mistakes made by impeccably dressed executives, stodgy *fonctionnaires*, and bright-eyed *lycéens* preparing for the *baccalauréat*. And, come spring, travelers planning for their first trip to *Les États-Unis*.

Despite such leaden boredom, it remained an easier task than word processing and provided a steadier form of income, especially since the French school system continued to offer such sketchy, outdated versions of the Queen's English. Even major book publishers in Paris produced bilingual dictionaries that were edited only by *les français*; and, as I mentioned to one of my students, despite their prestigious degrees from elite universities the professors who produced these tomes always made outrageous mistakes. If only those renowned publishers had paid an American teenager living in a garret a minimum wage, they might have entered into a much higher level of *perfectionnement*!

At first I assumed that offering a course in "English conversation" would be a relatively simple task, since I worked only with those who were nearly fluent. For the most part, they simply wanted to retain whatever language skills they possessed and to pick up a few extra words here or there while sipping an espresso and relaxing after a grueling day of work.

But I soon learned that to be engaged in an actual conversation with an *étranger* in France was a frightening prospect for the average Parisian, who feared that to reveal what one *really* thought, or how one *actually* felt, could lead to a *catastrophe* or even – heaven forbid! – a *scandale!* Eventually I discovered that some of my students rarely conversed uninhibitedly even with their own wives or husbands. *For, Robere, whom can one trust these days?* Thus, our dialogue would often range – or perhaps I should say *skitter* – across a remarkably superficial linguistic landscape.

One of my more memorable students was a statuesque *fonctionnaire* in her late twenties who'd developed the art of the Parisian poker face to a masterly level. But there remained a devious sparkle in her eye that, try as she might, she could never completely disguise.

Once a week over the next two years she'd arrive promptly for her *cours d'anglais*, never once veering away from the most drudging and guarded of "dialogues." Month after month she pontificated about such tedious topics as French politics, and in a manner that was so "abstracted" and emotionally detached that it was utterly frightening. Therefore, in growing desperation, one day I looked her square in the eye and, though I'd lived there long enough to know that one should never ask such a question, I did so anyway. I deliberately broke the rule and boldly inquired: "Now tell me, Marie-Rose, do you have a *boyfriend?*"

Stammering incoherently, Marie began to blush until she finally managed to mutter: *"Mais, vous êtes très curieux!"* In France, telling someone they were "very curious" was a polite way of saying that you should mind your own business, for curiosity had killed the cat. Nonetheless, I persisted:

"But I really want to know! After all, we've been speaking for over two years, yet I hardly know a thing about you. I mean, on a more personal level. And I assure you, I do not work for the CIA or the DGSE; this is purely a matter of my own interest. For, at some point, we must broaden the trajectory of our *interpersonal intercourse*, if one might phrase it that way. And so, do you or do you not have a *petit ami?*"

Sputtering like a sprinkler that's been triggered upon detecting a significant rise in room temperature, Marie-Rose exclaimed: "Actually, Robere, I have *two* boyfriends." And I thought: *Ah ha. Now, we are getting somewhere.*

"And how did you meet these lucky paramours?"

"*Sur la quai de le métro.*"

"But what on earth did they say to you while you were standing on a metro platform that could possibly have been so interesting?"

"They each said the same thing: '*Vous êtes belle.*'"

"And *that* was so interesting?"

By now, Marie had regained her composure. Like a professor correcting a wayward, thickheaded young lout, she exclaimed: "*Mais oui!* What could be more interesting than *that?*"

And I thought: "Perhaps, she has a point."

With Marie and with a handful of others, I succeeded in breaking through this formal boundary only because, all the while, I would share personal anecdotes about my own life, but couched in that witty, urbane, sophisticated manner that makes such a confession not only forgivable but also entertaining to the well-bred *parisienne*. As a result, with a little prodding they'd incrementally divulge some amusing detail about themselves, perhaps as a means of not appearing to be defeated in such a competition of wit.

By this time I'd long since fired most of my male students. I reasoned that it was pointless to continue with the Frenchmen since the women were usually far more intriguing. Once these demoiselles relaxed and lost any lingering fear of causing a scandal, gradually their dialogues became less abstruse and cerebral. In dire contrast, the men could wax poetic about the most ridiculous rubbish imaginable. I mean, who cares whether their president, François Mitterrand, screwed his cleaning lady (a persistent rumor at the time) or whether he was a true socialist or instead a wolf in lamb's clothing? I'd rather hear about Marie-Rose and her two boyfriends, each wondering if the other possessed a larger tool – something I eventually managed to glean by asking, point-blank, if this were the case.

"Well, *of course!*" she exclaimed. "What *else* do men think about?"

I continued to flirt and parry with these tight-lipped *parisiennes* who returned week after week, hoping to *décontractée* and to take a break from fretting over their wearisome employment, unfaithful lovers, or high taxes – *seventy percent in most cases, Robere!* – which insured that they'd never transcend a certain predetermined position on the socioeconomic ladder. As I learned from numerous students from every walk of life, in France there was rarely even a dream of upward mobility. Instead, it was a nightmare – a *cauchemar!* – of horizontal stasis and stability. Where you were going was indelibly stamped upon your forehead as soon as you took the *baccalauréat*, the French equivalent of the American SAT: a test that we briefly endured in high school but then completely forgot about. In the States, it simply determined which university would accept you. But in France it meant that by the age of eighteen at the latest, your professional station on earth had been fixed forever. If you didn't ace the *bac*, you were doomed; you could never attain your goal. There was never a question of waking up one day and deciding that now you'll start afresh and pursue a vastly different career track. No, it was all settled by the time you were an adolescent. Even my fifteen-year-old students could tell you the precise year, month, day, and hour that they'd retire; their lives were that well planned in advance.

A quick perusal of the classified ads reflected this phenomenon in microcosm, like a set of cameo portraits laid upon a table: *Young Parisian boy, 35, handsome, intelligent, refined, bac 16,*

Nanterre, seeks charming Parisian girlfriend – listing their *bac* scores so that it would be crystal clear what you were getting yourself into! *French girl, 37, bac 14, Lyons*, and so on. (Yes, in France, it's the norm to call yourself a "boy" or "girl" until the age of forty, reflecting a strange mixture of vanity and modesty.) Imagine including one's high school test results in a personal ad in a Manhattan newspaper! Readers would assume that you were either a madman or a prankster! But in Paris, it was a tattoo rendered with permanent ink.

Following this *raisonnable* reasoning, you marry at your proper station, but only after infinite precaution. And one never hopes for anything more than that, for even hope itself – wearing a perfumed *perruque* and high-collared frock coat – had escaped from Pandora's gilt-encrusted box sometime during the Enlightenment.

All this was directly connected to the well-honored tradition of building moats – also called *sécurité* – around your implacable station in life. The average citizen subscribed to as many life-insurance policies as possible as well as to an impressive variety of other forms of insurance, too plentiful to mention here and nearly impossible to translate into English, since their premise is so farfetched. There's even an insurance policy for the bad weather that might erupt during your sacred five-week holiday! All this in a vain attempt to erect as many obstacles as possible in order to forestall the inevitable calamities that life will surely toss at you.

* * *

A few days after my last encounter with Francois, I received a call from a cheerful-sounding woman named Sophie Plaisant, who lived near Métro Nation, on the other side of Paris. Though I warned Sophie about the subway ride of nearly an hour, she insisted on coming because of my discount rate.

At the appointed hour, standing under the tenuous rays of faint September sunlight, I was delighted to behold a woman with wavy blonde hair, piercing green eyes, and a warm but nervous smile. Dressed in white slacks with a matching low-cut blouse, both her clothing and her manner reflected an understated elegance. Unlike the typical *parisienne*, instead of acting aloof she exuded an openness ... and even a childlike spontaneity. Gazing into her sea-green eyes, I thought of a mermaid. But where would this *sirène* lead me?

As I prepared her résumé, Sophie glanced at the wall behind my table and studied the picture postcards and photos that were displayed there, some of which I'd collected while traveling across Europe and visiting various monuments, castles, and cathedrals. Forced to remain indoors to eke out a subsistence during so many glorious afternoons, these images served as my "portals" to the outside world and allowed me to mentally escape from my confining ten-square meters. But I had no choice but to remain there, for if I failed to raise enough dough who would pay the rent?

So now, seated beside me, Sophie gazed with bemused curiosity at this motley collection of images tacked and taped upon the wall. Her eyes finally rested upon a glossy eight-by-ten photo of the rock star Jim Morrison – the Lizard King himself – standing before the entrance of a building on place Tristan Bernard, in Paris.

Of course, it's always a mistake to read too much into a single photograph. As Renoir says, a photo is a lie. And not even "a lie that tells the truth," as Picasso would have it, but simply an outright deception. Nonetheless, one can still *imagine*. And so, as we inspect this image plucked from the ether by a photographer named Gilles Yepremian, we notice that Jim lingers *dans la rue* before a gloomy Parisian doorway. His face appears to be a bit puffy, no doubt from drinking too much, and his doughy mug is unshaven, bearing a day or two of stubble. With his sensual locks spilling across his broad shoulders, and with his hands folded and resting upon his abdomen, he assumes an almost saintly pose. But instead of clasping a gilded crucifix, an angelic wand, or a silver staff pointed to the heavens, it's a rolled up newspaper that he grips: held vertically, just as a Frenchman might grasp a baguette. Instead of a fallen rock star gone to seed, Jim might now be mistaken for a bookie about to inspect the daily racetrack results.

Jim is portrayed at the center of the photo while his willowy junkie girlfriend, Pamela Courson, is standing in profile on the left. Her fine silky hair covers most of her face, so you can catch only a glimpse of her delicate features. On the right we espy the gnomish figure of Hervé Muller, a bespectacled German hippie with an aquiline nose and slight, diminutive build. His stringy hair and ratty mustache comprise his principal features. Also standing in profile, he stares at Jim with a tight-lipped, pensive regard.

The more you study the image, the more you wonder why they all look so serious – as if somberly considering something that's being said. But then you realize that, besides the photographer, there's also a fourth figure. You can barely see his outstretched hands, but they're captured at the bottom right-hand corner. That's what Jim is gazing at with such concentration: whatever this man is holding in his bony fingers. Of course, one wonders if it's a drug or some other forbidden object that he's clutching, but I doubt it. As insane as he was, Jim probably wouldn't be enacting a dope deal in public, standing in plain view on place Tristan Bernard. More likely, it's something innocuous, and Yepremian just happened to click the shutter at this random moment. After all, this was Jim Morrison, one of the biggest rock stars ever, just months before – like all good

Americans – he would perish in Paris and be forever entombed there.

Jim's grave at Père Lachaise marks the culmination of an oddball pilgrimage: a cultish memorial for waifs and strays who have yet to figure out who or what they really are; as well as for those lost souls who have jettisoned whatever nascent talents that they possess to instead pursue dope or prostitution, as if hoping to be consumed by the same hobgoblins that had once swallowed the Lizard King. For, without a doubt, Jim pissed it all away, and that's what he symbolizes for so many: wandering, lost, on a deviant path. From all around the world, they fly into the cemetery like mosquitoes hypnotized by a Day-Glo light. Though he's been dead for decades, his fans still appear to be sucking some vital essence from his remains. In their wake they leave behind a heap of empty whisky bottles, sticks of burning incense, and oozing puddles of candle wax. Not to mention necklaces, panties, and bundles of wilted flowers.

In the center of this chaotic jumble is a bronze plaque that reads ΚΑΤΑ ΤΟΝ ΔΑΙΜΟΝΑ ΕΑΥΤΟΥ. Meaning: *In accord with his inner daemon*; although it might just as well have read *In utter discord with his daemon, but in remarkable consonance with his Jack Daniels.*

Sophie turned to me with a smile and asked, "So, why did Jim come to France?"

"I believe he was fulfilling a prediction of Oscar Wilde's, who once remarked: 'When good Americans die, they go to Paris.'"

Nervously laughing, she continued, "I see! But why are *you* here?"

"Now, it's my turn."

But I might have answered her in a dozen different ways. For a moment I pictured the churning of the Seine at midnight, and how your soul yearns to be swept along with it. But there were other, more mundane images that also hovered across my mind's eye, such as the lugubrious corridors of the all-night post office, manned by sleepy owls who religiously vote for socialism ... The cigarette-puffing *lycéennes* with their dreamy young eyes and moleskin *agendas*, chattering at noisy tables in smoke-filled *tabacs* ... The amber-tinted streetlamps that cast the boulevards in such a dreamlike glow ... The Payne's-gray rooftops set at such delightfully cubist angles ... The trilling, flutelike tenor of a Frenchwoman's voice as she says *bonjour* and kisses your cheek.

No matter how much I complained – like any good Frenchman – about the quotidian difficulties of living there I never wanted to say *adieu*, because escaping the deadening clutches of America had remained my primary goal. That, and to live this over and over ... all the little details and overblown dramas, as long as it occurred in Paris. What was my greatest desire? To eventually die there, my corpse tossed into the welcoming arms of the rat-infested Seine. And poverty seemed like such a small price to pay for all this.

As I tapped on my keyboard, Sophie regarded me with an inviting smile. "I have a film about Jim," she said. "Perhaps you'd like to see it."

"*Bien sûr.*"

"*Alors*, when can you come?"

"Whenever you'd like."

"What about tonight?"

Turning round, I studied her gentle expression. And then I noticed a haunted look that emerged from deep within her moody green eyes.

Street of Bullets

Sophie lived in a charming little studio on rue des Boulets, which runs diagonally across boulevard Voltaire in the eleventh *arrondissement*. I later learned that "Boulets" means *bullets* and that upon this otherwise unremarkable lane the largest number of projectiles had once flown during the Franco-Prussian War: an event that seemed to occur "only yesterday" in the minds of so many Parisians.

During our first evening together, I told Sophie about my one American friend in Paris, Danielle, who'd spent over three years at Père Lachaise photographing the strays who congregate around Jim's grave. Danielle also collected their stories. Many of these lost souls would ogle at the gravestone for hours, as if they were too young to comprehend death and were utterly bewildered by it. Others would dump tumblers of Jack Daniel's over the soiled plaque or scribble love poems or suicide notes. As if cured by a trip to Lourdes, an Italian soldier had left behind his official "leave of absence papers": excused from military service because of "depression." And the splendid dialogue that one occasionally overhears there! *"I don't dig the girls dressed in black, who leave vials of blood, but that old wino who sells postcards is cool ..."*

Danielle said that the *fonctionnaires* had finally lost their patience with the carnival atmosphere that had overtaken the cemetery, especially because it meant so much extra work: sorting through the interminable refuse and dealing with complaints from the aristocratic families who maintained plots nearby. Until recently, the small gatherings at the grave had remained more or less civilized, with no more than a dozen visitors at a time. But after the director Oliver Stone had released a film about Jim that included a scene at the cemetery, the tourists arrived in droves. Now there were about two hundred kids crowding round the tomb at any given moment, constantly coming and going. As a result, the administration had installed a surveillance camera on a pole overlooking the site, which was wired to a computer in the main office. Every few minutes an image would be copied from the video and printed.

A cardboard box was positioned directly beneath the printer, and the police would carefully study the results: searching for runaways or for evidence of drug dealing, pimping, and whoring. In this typically plodding French manner of proceeding at a snail's pace, eventually they constructed an elaborate, byzantine file: one of those labyrinthian *dossiers* that the Préfecture de police specialize in. One can still read about such things in Emile Zola, especially in his *Belly of Paris*. At first, *les flics* will stand back and passively allow the criminals to operate, thus further incriminating themselves. Then they'll circle round and tighten the noose. And *voilà*; now, you must turn state's evidence and rat on your pals, *and then we'll screw the whole lot of you, s'il vous plaît!* And that's precisely what they were hoping to accomplish at this crossroad of vice and debauchery at Jim's final resting place.

Wherever you wandered in the Victorian necropolis with its gently rolling hills, thick verdant foliage, and ornately sculpted mausoleums, you'd eventually encounter graffiti pointing you in the right direction: JIM→ or ←LIZARD KING or ↑MORRISON HOTEL or ↓NO ONE HERE GETS OUT ALIVE. Though the working-class gravediggers just shrugged their shoulders about such vandalism, the clients of the cemetery, the well-to-do *aristos*, were growing furious. When they arrived each November First for *Toussaint* (All Saints' Day) with bundles of white chrysanthemums in hand (the "appropriate" flower of mourning, which marginal characters would sell on street corners under the November boughs), they were visibly appalled, their faces blanching as they absorbed the circus-like antics. But the poor devils who had the misfortune to be buried right beside Morrison suffered the worst fate of all. The facades of their mausoleums were covered by what appeared to be a millennium of chicken scrawl: an overlapping crosshatch of graffiti etched into stone such as one might discover at an ancient Roman crossroad. So now, the cemetery officials were threatening to exhume Jim's coffin and ship his rotted remains back to sunny California.

Jim's elderly parents, Clara Clarke and Navy Rear Admiral George Morrison, had been forced to purchase expensive graffiti-cleaning equipment; to erect this classy brass plaque; and to engage in a number of other mollifying gestures that they hoped the French courts would regard as a serious attempt to assist in the reparation of this colossal mess. But meanwhile the surveillance prints continued to flutter into the cardboard box. And Danielle, who was friendly with every *gardien*, grave-digger, and bureaucrat who worked there, said that when she'd stopped for a drink at Café de la Renaissance one morning – a grungy establishment located near a side entrance to the ceme-tery, on the appropriately named rue du Repos – she'd bumped into the clerk in charge of gathering the surveillance prints. Clearly distraught, the poor woman had remarked:

"Oh, Danielle, you won't believe what happened last night! An American couple broke into the cemetery, and, oh, *mon Dieu*, the things they did at poor Mr. Morrison's grave!" For they'd stripped naked and screwed the night away, right on top of the headstone.

Ignoring Madame's nuanced gestures that indicated that one should not to proceed any further, Danielle attempted to press for additional details. But all Madame would say was: "What did they do? *A proximité de tout imaginable*" – everything imaginable!

The following week I brought Sophie to Père Lachaise and introduced her to Danielle, who was visibly moved by her physical beauty. Danielle photographed Sophie prancing round the graves; then she arranged a shot of her leering into the camera with a playful lusty grin as she runs her fingers over the bronzed "erection" of Victor Noir's statue.

Noir, a great-grandnephew of Napoleon, had perished in a gun duel over a woman; and a reclining bronze statue portrays him lying there, dying, with a bullet hole in his vest – and a manly bulge swelling beneath his baggy, nineteenth-century trousers. Danielle said that the statue had become a fetish object, and women from all over France would travel there to mount it. (In the words of Holden Caulfield: "Who wants flowers when you're dead?") And in fact, the boots, crotch, and face were polished to a golden sheen, in marked contrast to the rest of the figure which remained a dull, oxidized green. *La petite mort* indeed!

Later that day we received a warm welcome from the degenerate *marginales* – the pimps, prostitutes, and hoodlums who gather at the Café de la Renaissance – who were all bosom buddies of Danielle's. The alpha boys of this guttersnipe contingent were named Jacques and Didier. Jacques, the leader, was a *maquereau* or pimp; Didier was a dope dealer whose *spécialisation* was heroin. They were each rather short, but they were as strong as bulldogs. Warning me to tread carefully, Danielle said that she'd once seen Jacques beat the living daylights out of a man twice his size.

As with every other level of French society, even there, in the gutter, a personal introduction meant everything. As soon as it was established that Sophie and I were Danielle's boon companions, we were "in." During our first appearance, even the proprietor came out from a back room to greet us. Introducing himself with a crooked grin, he offered Sophie a free carafe of wine. When he went to retrieve it, Danielle said that this was something she'd never witnessed before: "Not only did you get something for *free*, Sophie," she cackled, "but you also made him *smile!*"

*   *   *

A few days after we met, I began to suspect that there were some pieces missing from the Sophie puzzle. We were seated at a restaurant near the traffic circle at Porte de Saint-Cloud when she began to unburden herself and to share certain secrets about her ill-fated history.

Her former husband was a huckster from the Midwest, she said; and, like Sophie, he'd worked as a catalog model in Spain. He was the father of two children, but his wife had flown the coop. Once he was left in the lurch with these kids, he didn't know how to care for them.

"When we first met in Madrid, he was looking for a wife. And then, shortly after we became involved, I gave birth to our first child, a boy."

From the sound of it this fellow was an expert manipulator who'd attempted to turn her into a sort of domestic robot. And if Sophie disobeyed, there would often be dire consequences.

One day while we were arguing about something inconsequential and I was growing a bit frustrated, I raised my finger and waved it harmlessly in the air to make a point. But as soon as I began to gesture, Sophie cringed: covering her face as if readying herself for a blow.

I froze in place and asked, "But what's wrong? What is it?

Did that bastard hit you?" And she nodded and murmured, "*Oui!*"

As a result of all this, Sophie didn't understand that couples need to argue once in a while – that it was a symptom of a healthy relationship. For, in the company of this fiend, there was only his way or the highway. And if she dared to protest, the result might be an argument that turned into more than a simple disagreement: it might be an invitation to injury, to physical harm.

Now, seated in a booth at the restaurant, when I asked about her friends in Paris, Sophie lowered her head and said that she didn't have any.

"Not even one?" I asked, incredulous.

"No," she shook her head, "I'm all alone here." And then I wondered: but how is it possible that such a kind attractive woman is so isolated in a city where it's remarkably easy to socialize?

"But what about casual acquaintances? Surely, you must have some companions with whom you spend some time."

"*Non.* No one."

As Sophie continued to reveal the details of her past I realized that, besides being marked by tragedy, hers was also a miraculous life. Miraculous, because somehow she'd survived all this, although not exactly intact. But she never lost her empathy or tenderness, though it was interwoven with a stubborn, dreadful paranoia. Her constant companions were fear and worry; spawned, no doubt, by the prospect of being further wounded.

The disquietude this had engendered within her might spring up when least expected. I might utter something innocuous or gesture in the most harmless fashion, but then the switches in her febrile brain would make misguided connections because something I said or did had resonated with a

malefic event from the past. An ancient but enduring disso-
nance would resurrect itself, and then Sophie would grow
temporarily disabled. Her emotions would leap like alley cats,
scrambling to regain control, and her eyes would change color,
flickering into nefarious octaves of phthalo emerald. But then,
gradually, I'd manage to navigate her back to safety.

Eventually I learned that she was born out of wedlock, a so-
called unwanted child. Her mother, a countrywoman who
hailed from Haute-Savoie, was only eighteen years old when a
man from Eastern Europe had impregnated her. After giving
birth to Sophie, the mother saddled her own parents with raising her: Sophie's French grandmother and Italian grandfather, a
fellow who was always smiling in the photos that I later studied
of him. Like Sophie, he was fair-haired and possessed high
cheekbones and light-green eyes; and it was from him that
she'd inherited her beauty. I immediately noticed that he bore a
striking resemblance to that great Provincial writer, Jean Giono,
author of *Joy of Man's Desiring*, who was also of Italian descent.

The link to Giono is rather fitting. Of humble origins – the
son of a laundry woman and a cobbler – Giono had lived most
of his life in Manosque, where he'd cobbled together dozens of
novels about a way of life that was now forever lost but that,
once upon a time, had been celebrated in villages and hamlets
all throughout France. A world where peasants were really
peasants, which is to say creatures of the soil and of that unfathomable essence that we call *nature*. I mention this because, for a
time, living with her kind, doting grandparents, Sophie had experienced firsthand this more natural, Jean Gionoesque lifestyle,
and it set her apart from the typical street-smart Parisian.

But apparently the problem of being an outsider went all the
way back to when she was just a little girl. One of Sophie's
earliest memories was of her first day at school, when the other
children beat her. She said they sensed her vulnerability, her

lack of independence. From then on, her mother was forced to retrieve her after school. It was one of many things that had sowed evil seeds of self-hatred: a *maladie* she continued to suffer from. Although she never fit into that provincial little town in Haute-Savoie, Sophie said that she didn't belong in Paris, either, among such "sophisticated monsters."

Much to Sophie's chagrin, her mother eventually married a gruff, ill-mannered, cantankerous fisherman: an embittered local fellow whose previous wife had died, leaving him with a bevy of sons and daughters. Judging from the way that Sophie related all this, it appeared to be a marriage of convenience. Since they each had children – so went the reasoning – why not join forces?

With his creaking wooden rowboat, this hardened character followed in the watery footsteps of his fisherman father, fisherman grandfather, and who knows how long into the whirlpool of the past those ghostly fishermen – like a never-ending spool of tackle – went reeling into the shadows of Lake Geneva. But unlike his forebears, slowly, stubbornly, incrementally, he built up his business year after year, selling a hard-earned catch of perch, whitefish, and crayfish to the local markets, until finally opening a restaurant beside this idyllic, swan-festooned lake.

A fiercely independent fellow, he once proudly informed me that Haute-Savoie was the last mainland department to join France, as late as 1860. He added that the population was known for its mix of Swiss and Italian blood and for proudly maintaining its autonomy. The shores of the lake were dotted with houses flying these various national flags: something that one rarely encounters in France. *Normalement*, only government buildings display a tricolor. Unlike in America, the idea of placing one's "patriotism" on public display would be considered rather tacky and boorish, and rightly so.

Once he was financially prosperous, Sophie's stepfather declared himself to be no longer a communist. Now, he enrolled in the right-of-center Gaullist party; for things were good. Everything seemed to be hunky-dory ... except for the fact that Sophie despised him.

How she hated to be forced to sit beside his children on the muddy embankment and clean those stinking fish! Instead, she wanted to pursue an artistic career. And I always encouraged her to do so, for she certainly possessed the talent. In the handful of pencil sketches and watercolors that she shared with me, it was plain to see that Sophie had acquired a compelling, original style for drawing and painting the figure. But most of all, she wanted to escape from the banal routine of that bucolic lifestyle and to travel somewhere exciting, such as Paris. But her parents wouldn't hear of it, not as long as there were fish to fry.

Though I continued to dig deeper into Sophie's past, I was never certain about how her psychic disorder had first taken root. Was it the result of being ripped from that easygoing lifestyle with her kindly grandparents and having to put up with this Billy Goat Gruff of a stepfather – that gnarly, hard-boiled egg – or from some other calamity? During each of our encounters he never smiled. Instead, he often appeared to be seething with a silent rage. He also bore an uncanny resemblance to that great literary stylist and xenophobic miscreant, Louis-Ferdinand Céline. They were each endowed with a darkly brooding, arched forehead: one that seemed ever ready to boil over, into unremitting anger – or even violence. Once, when Sophie was a teenager, he gave her a hard smack on the face after she stayed out late one night, claiming that she "behaved like a whore."

Of course, it's possible that her fundamental problems stemmed from something else entirely: an unspoken tragedy that had befallen her as a little girl, perhaps even something she could no longer recall. But whatever it was, she was unhinged.

By the time we met, she'd been pushed over the edge by the disappearance of her children and by the constant worry over what had happened to them. She continually wondered whether they were dead or alive. When she was still living in Los Angeles, after reaching a breaking point with her abusive husband, she ran out of the house while he was visiting a friend, phoned her mother, and begged her to book a flight back to France. Then she spent the night sleeping in a bathroom stall at the airport. She wanted to escape with her children, she said, but without passports it was impossible. So she decided that she'd attempt to unite with them later on.

After she returned to Haute-Savoie, they eventually made arrangements for the husband to visit, along with the children. Sophie's parents gave him some funds for support; but after a while her tightfisted stepfather refused to offer any additional help. As a result, once her husband had returned to LA with the kids, he decided to sever his ties with France. He never called or corresponded; and now, no one knew where they were. They disappeared without a trace.

* * *

About ten days into our affair, one morning Sophie awoke with a troubled expression. It was *dimanche*: a day traditionally reserved for promenading. All throughout France one could witness the wan, *mélancolique* facades; for, within twenty-four hours, one would have to return once again to *work*: a phrase that one was never supposed to utilize once the workday was over. *Travailler*, that most dreadful verb! But instead of preparing for a promenade, now Sophie was sweating bullets – more than had ever been fired along rue des Boulets – as she contemplated the looming specter of *lundi*, or Monday.

I should add that I'd accidentally discovered that the word for "work," *travailler*, is derived from *trepālium*, which in Late Latin means "an instrument of torture." When I later shared this gem with Sophie's stepfather, he nodded, smirked, and replied, *"Voilà! C'est ça!" It is torture!* he exclaimed, with a subtle, curl-of-the-lip approval. Thus, Sophie's apprehension wasn't completely unheard of; it was just far more pronounced in her than it was in the average Frenchman.

But now she turned to me and confessed that she *dreaded*, absolutely *abhorred* the train ride to the gulag each day. An interminable haul on the RER, she said, all the way to the suburbs. When I asked why she felt this way, she added: "Because everyone *stares* at me. And they're thinking *bad thoughts*. I can *feel* it. In their minds, they're *criticizing* and *making fun of me!*"

Beads of sweat continued to trickle along her pale gleaming forehead until I replied, "Well, then, let's you and I travel there together, and we'll see what this is all about."

Upon hearing this Sophie grew nearly ecstatic. What a gift, that someone would actually accompany her into that pernicious vale of tears, that "hellish" commute into Boulogne where she was employed each day as a *hôtesse d'accueil*. That is, a *welcoming hostess* who sits at a reception desk at a ground-floor lobby smiling magnanimously, occasionally saying *Bonjour*, and nodding reassuringly at the workers as they stream back and forth like ants over a teeming anthill, their facades riddled with despair.

Sophie added that many of these embittered office workers would linger beside a water cooler for the first ninety minutes of each day, gossiping and maligning all the other employees who might not be present at this shining moment. Thanks to her native paranoia, this event served to rattle Sophie to no end. I was also told by several of my students that, in business offices throughout the land, this daily ritual was a well-established tradition; and no boss in his right mind would possess the courage to object and incur the wrath of those powerful French labor unions. The remainder of the day was spent stationed behind a desk, shuffling papers back and forth, then forth and back, while pretending to accomplish something.

En effet, un spectacle!

Upon absorbing all this, I began to suspect that the *République française* would long since have gone *kaput* if not for their so-called former French colonies. But if you followed the money trail, it was plain to see that they were *still* French colonies – subservient nations all across the "Dark Continent" – where France exercised Machiavellian control: secretly assassinating nationalist leaders and instead placing their own puppets in presidential offices. When I first introduced this subject to one of my atypically talkative students – an Italian native named Ernesto, who ran one of the largest telecom companies in France – he revealed that one of his friends was a paratrooper who worked for the DGSE (the French equivalent of the CIA), and that he was often parachuted into such places.

And, Robere, he added with a dramatic tone and grave expression as he opened his impeccable suit jacket and pointed at a custom label woven inside, *Even the labels are removed. They drop in with no identification whatsoever, and with the understanding that, if they're caught, they'll be killed. Then, no one is the wiser.* A policy, he said, of ultimate deniability. Once the French regained control over these countries, the puppeteers would force the new puppets to sign blank sheets of paper. A *page blanche,* he called it, upon which the masters would inscribe all the new laws and policies that they wished to impose. *And that's precisely how such nations are governed,* he whispered, *for they remain under the iron eighteenth-century fist of the French empire.*

According to Ernesto, if not for these so-called protectorates and "former" colonies, the French economy would be in dire straits. But instead, the Parisians fed off them like parasites, he said, like maggots on a corpse. Ernesto added that the construction projects in these faraway places were all managed by a single French corporation, Bouygues. And all the energy was provided by a state controlled French electric company, Électricité de France, or "EDF": a nationalized corporation that provided some of the most expensive electricity in the world, even in Paris (as I knew all too well from my electric bill!). Although it was state owned, you still had to pay taxes on your final bill; and, by some clever and arcane accounting system, even the taxes were further taxed. The "former" colonies were also saddled with a notoriously expensive telephone company, France Telecom, which was another monopoly in France. The list went on and on. Therefore, while safely ensconced in Paris, a Frenchman could sit back at his desk and daydream all he wanted and, no worries, went the reasoning, the nation would still survive.

I trusted this telecom fellow *implicitly* (as the French are so fond of saying, ever fearful of being too *explicit*), because, several weeks before Paris awoke to the sound of handmade bombs exploding along the Champs-Elysées and in the traditionally left-wing Latin Quarter, while we were seated at my table and conducting our English lesson, Ernesto said: *Robere, take special care! Proceed with caution, for terrorist attacks are imminent. And please, be extra careful on the metro. Soon, you will notice many more policemen on the subway platform, for they've been alerted. I have the word directly from the mouth of my friend, the DGSE man ...*

Although there wasn't a peep about it in the newspapers or on TV, the following week there they were; the gendarmes were out in force. Even now I call them *gendarmes* simply because I love the sound of this word, but in fact it was a combination of various paramilitary forces, and mostly composed of the dreadful Companies Republicans de Sécurité, or CRS: a brutal bunch of muscle-bound goons and right-wing maniacs. Until recently the CRS had refused to induct anyone above a certain IQ level; they also regarded those who'd been orphaned with a special fondness, since such candidates can easily be reprogrammed via surrogate father figures. Legendary for its wanton cruelty, the CRS rivaled even their American counterparts when it comes to violence.

One particular story that I'd stumbled upon in the chronicles of the author Mavis Gallant illustrates this point quite well. According to Gallant's account, during the revolts of 1968, the CRS rounded up hundreds of naive student protestors, beating them so severely that one boy was seen stumbling across a police courtyard with his entrails streaming behind him. He was gripping the filaments, strings, and fleshy cords of his frayed genitals in his hands – for he'd been torn apart. A girl who was imprisoned in a cell with a barred window that faced the courtyard witnessed him stumbling and gushing blood as he tried, in vain, to hold himself together – all the while emitting a horrifying scream. And that's what always happens when France experiences its perennial upheaval: the Cartesian god is unseated, and then all hell breaks loose.

When the bombs at Saint-Michel burst into a shower of shrapnel, injuring over eighty subway passengers and killing eight, some of the students that I'd attempted to warn (for I'd discreetly passed along Ernesto's message) were now convinced that I worked for the CIA. One of them even asked me point-blank: "But how else could you, as an underpaid *professeur américain*, afford such expensive computers?"

I replied that it was really no mystery; they were half the price in Manhattan as compared to Paris. Before I'd embark upon my annual visit to the States, I'd sell my computer in Paris for the same amount of money that I'd originally purchased it for. Then I'd shop for the latest model in New York. Thus, like a perpetual-motion machine once spun into action, after my initial purchase the equipment cost me nothing.

But she refused to believe me. For the notion of an American expatriate – especially a long-term expat, such as myself – really being an intel agent wasn't even an original idea; it was a veritable tradition. Harry Mathews, an American author who'd lived in France for over fifty years, had this accusation cast at him so frequently that he did what any good writer would do: he wrote a novel called *My Life in the CIA*. And his neighbors probably took this as further evidence that he worked for the Agency, since they would never have bothered to read anything more than the title and would then have exclaimed, *Voilà, c'est ça!* – "There, I knew it all along!"

All this passed through my mind as Sophie and I boarded a crowded RER headed for Boulogne. By now the poor woman was a bundle of anxiety. Her nerves were frazzled, and all this at only 7:17 a.m.

We settled upon a pair of *strapontins* (the folding seats located at the far end of each car), and she glanced up and nervously made eye contact with each of the other passengers seated around us. As she did so, she smiled with an exaggerated grin. She ended this ritual with a series of nods: obsequiously acknowledging the presence of each and every commuter with an awkward shake of her head.

Of course, they stared right back, disturbed that not only was someone smiling (something that, according to one of my French students, "Only the insane, the mentally retarded, the childish, or the *vicieux* merchant about to shortchange you will do in public") but that she was grinning in such a frenzied manner as the sweat continued to ooze from her brow.

Trying to snap her out of it, I whispered: "Sophie, look at me. And listen carefully. They're staring only because, in Paris, you do *not* make eye contact with strangers on a train. Instead, you must assume a completely impassive, disinterested *metro face.*"

"A what?"

I held her hand and squeezed it reassuringly. "*Ma chère*, a metro face! You concoct a blasé expression, stare into deep space, and force your eyeballs to glaze – like an *éclair au chocolat* or *tarter aux fraises* covered with an opaque syrup, just like the ones for sale in the *patisserie*. Or else you pin your eyes to the floor and study the linoleum tiles as if you're examining a fascinating article in *Le Monde* ... an analysis of the Dreyfus Affair conducted by the esteemed journalist, Babillard Bavard. Or instead you gaze within, feigning a prolonged meditation upon the holy trinity of *vin rouge, pain au chocolat*, and *café noir!* And if you really want to reach for the stars, imagine that you've just returned from your day of *torture* and are now sinking your teeth into a slimy rind of a Gruyere. But whatever you do, one must never smile at a stranger in public. Remember, this is Devil's Island, and sooner or later such a gesture will land you in *merde profonde ...*"

By now her look of horror had transformed into a broad, amused grin. How fortunate that, when all was said and done, she could still laugh at herself. In fact, it was her saving grace. For, there was a part of Sophie that realized it was pointless to harbor such overwhelming anxiety: that life was absurd, that nothing was more ridiculous than a human being. So, why not surrender to mirth and give up the ghost? Indeed, her self-effacing laughter was the one thing that prevented Sophie from really losing it.

For the remainder of the ride, as I coaxed and encouraged her along, she attempted to master the intricacies of the metro face. By the time we arrived at Boulogne, the opaqueness of her persona had gelled into an unmistakable mask of Gallic indifference.

Perfectionnement!

* * *

We were devouring a lavish spread that Sophie had prepared for breakfast one morning as I silently turned the pages of an oversized art book until I came upon a brightly colored print. Gesturing from across the table, she said, "I know what that is. That's by Max Ernst, isn't it?" Then she removed her ear plugs, which she'd normally wear for an hour or two after waking: something I hadn't noticed at the beginning. We must have lived together for several months before I realized that the reason she just smiled and nodded for the first few hours of each day was that she couldn't hear a word I was saying. As far as Sophie was concerned, it was ludicrous to chatter so early in the morning. In fact, she didn't see the point in much of what normally passes for "conversation." Instead, she found it exhausting. She communicated more through smiles or frowns, by relaxing or tensing her sensual lips, by adjusting the luminosity of her viridian gaze, or by a subtle form of body language that I learned to decipher like an ancient papyrus. In any case, as I thumbed through my art book, I casually replied, "Yes, Sophie, it certainly is." Then we lapsed into silence and continued to enjoy breakfast.

Finishing her *tisane*, she added: "He's like Salvatore Dali, a surrealist, right?"

"That's right ..."

"*Oui*, I thought so." And then, following a long pause: "You know, I had dinner with him once."

"You had dinner with Max Ernst?"

"No," she laughed, "with Salvatore Dali."

After gathering her thoughts, Sophie said that while she was working as a model in Spain, a young god – for that's how I conceive of him now: a majestically proportioned Nordic boy from Sweden, a gay athlete with one of those magnificently sculpted physiques – was hired by Dali to pose as a model. But he was afraid that Dali might attempt to molest him, so he'd asked Sophie to trail along and pretend that she was his girlfriend.

Shortly after they arrived, Dali positioned the Swedish boy at the edge of his Olympic-sized swimming pool, beside a long winding sculpture of a glittering silver snake. And several hours later, Dali, his wife Gala, the Nordic god, and Sophie all retired to an expensive Spanish restaurant, where they dined together at the invitation of the half-mad millionaire painter.

As the months rolled by and we shared our life together in that cramped little studio – hardly ever arguing and mostly just enjoying each other's company – I gradually realized that, finally, I'd found a pleasant and tender companion. *At last,* I thought, *no more teeth gnashing, blood curdling, drama-driven Dochma's!* Instead of such hair-raising, death-defying spectacles, Sophie enjoyed the simple things in life. At night, for entertainment, we'd promenade through Saint-Michel, perhaps patronizing one of the revival houses to watch black-and-white films from the Thirties or Forties. There was even a theater exclusively devoted to the Marx Brothers, and, for several years, they showed nothing else. Many of these cinemas were state funded, so it didn't matter whether anyone showed up for such events.

Though I rarely patronized any American films, one evening, simply out of curiosity, we entered this nearly empty Marx Brothers theater. But more amusing than anything occurring in the film was the heroic attempt to translate Groucho's interminable rants and stellar raves into a series of suitable French subtitles. We entered the theater just as he was in the midst of one such rambling monologue, sprinkled with a plethora of double entendre (or, as the French actually say, *double sens*). It went on and on as he rolled his eyes, precariously balanced a cigar on the edge of his lip, and jabbed an index finger at the heavens – waving it like a wand that might draw down his inspired, effusive babble. As I say, the French, God bless them (although, since the Enlightenment, God no longer exists in France), had painstakingly attempted to render this harangue into a logical set of idioms. As the Parisians themselves are so fond of saying, *Quel spectacle!* For the translation filled *three-quarters of the screen*. In a vain attempt to keep up with Groucho, the sentences rolled by so fast that even the most speed-reading Frenchman could never have grasped them. And God only knows how they rendered Groucho's legendary *jeu de mots*: "*Viaduct?* Why a duck, and not a chicken?"

On the way home, Sophie said that while she was living in Los Angeles she'd appeared as an extra in a tragic Hollywood drama about the actress Frances Farmer. And then, shortly afterward, she'd chanced upon an ad in *Billboard* announcing an open casting for a minor part in Francis Ford Coppola's next production.

As I soon came to realize, Sophie was occasionally blessed with a golden nugget, just as she was forever trailed by a lowering cloud of *catastrophe*. As fate would have it, when she appeared at the casting lot, the chic young lady seated at the application desk was a native *parisienne*, so she bumped Sophie up to the front. And rather miraculously, she was given the part that all these hundreds of actresses were competing for: she was to play a "Dream Girl." And I mean, what could be more suitable? Sophie would portray a demoiselle that the protagonist sees *only in a dream*. But perhaps the very thing that made her so perfect for such a disembodied role had also doomed Sophie; for hers was also a dream that must never come true … perhaps because she didn't really belong in the world of the finite, the carnate, the manifest, or the mundane.

When she first entered the film studio, Sophie was wearing a bra that was two sizes larger than her actual breast size: one filled with a bouncy, gelatin-like substance. But just before they began to film, she was handed a semitransparent nightgown and told to change into it. So now, minus the stuffed bra, she was modestly sized again.

Sophie wasn't certain if this was the misstep that had turned the tide or if, instead, the scene was scrapped simply as a result of Coppola's habit of constantly revising and then discarding so much of what he'd produced. In any case, a few days later, she was called back to the studio. Accompanied by one of Coppola's top assistants, Sophie was taken on a long, circuitous route, finally landing outside the *sanctum sanctorum*: Coppola's trailer. And she was told to enter, alone.

Suddenly she was seated beside the legendary director, who spoke softly and with a palpable affection, almost as a loving grandfather might commune with his favorite granddaughter. Apologizing profusely, he said that they'd decided not to use the "Dream Girl" sequence and that the film was rewritten minus this episode.

"So now, Sophie," he continued, "you must imagine that it never occurred. That it was never shot, that it never happened. Just continue on with your life and regard it as no more than a minor wrinkle, an inconsequential detail. For life must go on!"

He stood up, embraced her, and exclaimed: "*Allez, avoir!*"

Which was perhaps for the best. For if Sophie had achieved "success," the cutthroats of Hollywood might have destroyed her. I could easily imagine her being lured into a ruinous life of excess. I was certain that she was far better off hunkered down in her modest flat on rue des Boulets.

A few months later, when my friend Sally Osgood asked Sophie about her adventure with Coppola, she replied:

"I was supposed to be a girl in a dream, but at the last minute Francis Ford Coppola decided that he didn't want to have a dream. But he was very nice. He invited me to his cabin and personally apologized for taking away the dream. But that was alright, because then they called me for a music video ..."

* * *

Since Sophie was so isolated, I decided to introduce her to Pete and Sally Osgood, my only British comrades in Paris. A highly skilled jazz saxophonist, Pete occasionally worked as a studio musician for well-known pop bands. On stage he resembled a colossus. Six-foot-four and barrel-chested, he easily overshadowed the other musicians in the quintet that he would tour with each summer, when work at the studios was scarce. But at heart Pete was a gentle giant who loved nothing more than to imbibe good French wine, bottle after bottle, and drink everyone around him – the entire bar, if necessary – right under the table.

Sally was Pete's rock of Gibraltar: his constant support and the woman who kept him grounded. When he wasn't performing they would laugh, drink, and enjoy the remarkably un-British atmosphere of Lutèce. According to Pete, this was the principal reason they'd expatriated; for the pursuit of *la joie de vivre* was well understood in Paris; whereas, in England, they were constantly viewed as eccentrics. Though Paris was filled with even more pretense and overflowing with poseurs, he said that at least in France you were always an outsider looking in. Thus, laughing at it all remained that much easier. Thanks to this laid-back Latin appreciation of life's pleasures, you could relax and enjoy yourself while seated on a *terrasse* while downing your bottle of Beaujolais or Burgundy, and who would bat an eye? *C'est la vie!*

Pete's only real complaint was that there was a remarkable lack of professionalism in the French music studios. For example, in order to play in time with each other, they'd have to count down to four. But when they hit "four" ... someone would say *Un, deux, trois, quatre* ... they'd each begin to play at a different moment, and they'd have to start all over again.

"I've never seen anything like it," he added, wistfully shaking his head.

One evening Pete invited us to an "elite" club where he was performing with his quintet: one of the only times that I ever ventured into such a hellhole. The cigarette smoke was denser and more opaque than the clouds that brood over Paris, and there was hardly a soul in there that you'd want to converse with. For the most part it appeared to be a den of preening narcissists showing off their latest fashionable accoutrements – their gold cigarette lighters and Rolex watches. Even in the late Nineties, they still dressed mostly in black, as if reenacting a scene from a film noir set.

Whenever Pete took a break from playing on stage, he'd nearly be mauled by the women in the audience, regardless of whether Sally was seated beside him. With a lustful glimmer in their eyes and a gelatinous *frisson* in their quivering thighs, *les demoiselles* were constantly on the prowl, especially when they saw him perform in such a virile, action-packed manner. Pete and his fawning females! They lasciviously trailed, they seductively cooed, they continually ogled while spasmodically wriggling in their chairs. Until finally circling round him at the bar deck as he stood there like a sentry, chasing down expensive glasses of Burgundy as if they were shots of whisky, and instructing everyone to *Drink up, mate! Drink up!*

Yet, despite all this, to my great admiration Pete never once cheated on Sally, whose warm smile and playful sense of humor made her attractive in her own unique way. Their fidelity toward each other, especially in a place such as Paris, was endearing.

One night when I made the mistake of attempting to keep up with Pete, he managed to get me so tanked that, without realizing what I was doing, I reached behind Sally and squeezed her bottom. In response, she turned to me with a broad smile and said, *Oh, dear!* – and burst out laughing. We were sandwiched together in a crowded pub at the Contrescarpe; and, since I'd managed all this with utmost discretion, Pete had no idea that I was mauling his wife. But I'm certain that he, too, would have laughed it off as merely a whimsical display of camaraderie.

I sensed that Pete wondered what I was doing with Sophie, but he was too much of a gentleman to utter a word about it. He suspected that Sophie faced some unnerving challenges, but he would never directly broach the subject. But from the moment they first met, Sally fawned over Sophie as if she were her own daughter. She even said that Sophie was the *best of all*, meaning that she preferred her to the rest of my female companions.

* * *

In the mid-Nineties Pete and Sally lived in Ernest Hemingway's former residence on the Contrescarpe. In one of his novels Hemingway describes the view from the kitchen window overlooking rue Descartes. Unlike a typically meandering Parisian lane, the rue Descartes is laid out straight and narrow, like a perspective drawing neatly receding to a vanishing point. As I stood by the casement and gazed down at the street, I imagined that this was why it was named after such a linear-minded philosopher, who, figuratively speaking, abhorred anything *curvilinear*.

Following a night of Olympian drinking, while standing beside this same northern window, Pete and Sally would entertain themselves by watching me zigzag along rue Descartes as I headed home. *Here's one for you, mate!* Pete would shout, holding up his wine glass while his words echoed in a baritone across the empty Contrescarpe. And Sally would chime in: *Take care, love!*

As they stood there waving goodbye, I often imagined that my wobbling transit was causing great consternation and confusion upon this *rue* that, *normalement*, did not abide any wavering lines.

Il fait un zigzag!

And eventually the cobblestones would ascend to reveal a panoramic view of the leafy arbors and zinc rooftops that buttress the Seine: a river that possesses a bigger heart than most Parisians do.

One evening Sally went to bed a bit earlier than usual, while Pete and I continued to linger on the pavement just below his flat. For no particular reason I began to wonder what his life was like in the early days, before he'd met Sally.

"I can easily imagine you as a carefree bachelor," I said, "bounding from one gorgeous female to the next!"

Upon hearing this Pete screwed his face into a serious expression: one that he normally reserved for the most personal of revelations. Pausing to gather his thoughts, he finally replied, "Mate, did I ever tell you about the cruise ship with the Danish model and her girlfriends?" And then, in intimate detail, he described how, at the beginning of his career, he'd been hired to perform on a ship that was equipped with a full band, including a singer named Billy Joel, who would later achieve success as a pop star. Five young models were also on board, and they were celebrating because they'd just graduated from high school and were now embarking upon a successful career.

The first night he performed, after the show was over and he was packing his equipment, one of the models approached and invited him back to their table. Then they invited him to their cabin, where he slept with all five of them: all together and all at once.

"But how on earth did you manage to keep all those women entertained simultaneously?" I asked – as if such pressing concerns were now looming overhead, about to crash through the skylights that dot the rooftops of the Contrescarpe.

"Mate, always remember: stay in the center! Dead smack at the hub!" It was as if Pete were positioning me at the *axis mundi* that runs through a cosmic mandala and connects the subterranean, mundane, and celestial levels of existence. "Just let the *women* decide what to do! Let *them* figure it out!" So, I made a mental note of all this while he continued to relate his rather incendiary tale.

Pete said that the following night, the Danish model – "a shapely blonde with lips the color of cherries, and hair that glowed like sun-dappled honey" – returned to his room alone. They were inseparable for three next three weeks, and never in his life had he achieved such bliss. Shaking his head and smiling, all he could mutter was, "It was *heavenly*, mate."

But then, his gaze narrowed, as if once and for all burying this illicit treasure trove of memories; and with a soft, whispery tone, he added: "But now, I have this."

And rather nonchalantly, he gestured up at his flat where his wife was preparing to go to bed.

Pete communicated all this in a humble, matter-of-fact,

almost pious manner. He was implying that, like an everlasting responsibility, he had this sacred bond to protect. For they were committed partners who, together, would embark upon life's hazardous journey, come what may.

Au revoir

As much as Pete and Sally loved Paris, they often grew frustrated by the lack of opportunity. This residual discontent formed a keynote that resonated between us. There were many times when, experiencing my own vexation and dismay, I'd say: "Pete, sometimes I wonder if I should just pack it in and return to the States." But he'd always go out of his way – really putting his heart and soul into it – to convince me to remain there. "No, mate, you mustn't *ever* go back. This is where you belong!"

Though they were enraptured by the enchantments of Lutèce – which, by now, had permeated our every fiber – eventually they changed course and abandoned Paris for London. Sally said that the subsistence lifestyle had finally gotten to them. They were getting on in years, and the future was beginning to look bleak. When she broke her eyeglasses one day and couldn't afford a visit to an optometrist, she insisted that it was time to leave.

The last time I saw them they were living in a more modestly sized flat. Just a bit larger than a *chambre de bonne*, it featured a small bedroom with an adjoining kitchenette and bathroom. Instead of a bedframe, there was a sunken mattress lying on the floor, covered by a threadbare sheet. It was positioned directly under a bare bulb that was screwed into a fixture on a peeling plaster ceiling.

The flat was halfway down the hill from the Contrescarpe, on a side street running off rue Mouffetard. Though it was just a few blocks away from that lovely hilltop circle where a fountain gurgles so pleasantly, its dismal interior reminded me of a woebegone cold-water flat in Hoboken.

Standing beneath that glaring light bulb, Pete said that, even after all those years of professional experience, and despite his consummate skill, the music studios would only book him if a French musician called in sick at the very last moment.

"No matter what, mate," he said, now speaking in a forlorn, dispirited, uncustomarily embittered tone, "we'll always remain foreigners here. *Étrangers*." He looked me in the eye and added, "You know, you can't just live off the architecture."

His parting words resonated like an unresolved chord at the end of an orchestral performance. And this disquieting conclusion, reached at the very end of our rainbow, struck home. "The naked truth at last," I thought, as we lingered under that bare bulb.

A few weeks later they jumped ship and returned to England. And then, an unexpected tragedy – my mother's sudden death – forced me back to the States. But I knew that, sooner or later, I'd have to return. For Europe had claimed my soul, and what was there in America? Nothing but irrelevant memories.

Pete and I often complained about being outcasts, but it was precisely this outsider status that had made Paris so special in the first place. It wasn't until many years later that I would come to see this more clearly. Eventually I realized that being an "outsider looking in" was precisely what had fascinated me about life abroad.

* * *

As restaurateurs, Sophie's parents were often paid in cash, and they avidly participated in the national sport of avoiding taxes. According to Sophie's stepfather, playing games with the Ministry of Finance was not only *obligatoire*; it was a mark of honor.

In the mid-1990s he purchased an investment property in a high-rise, near the traffic circle at Place de la Nation. A deal was cut with the previous owner whereby, in exchange for a deduction, he was largely paid under the table. Thus, the tax assessment for the property would remain minimized, and Sophie's stepfather wouldn't have to explain where all that unclaimed loot had come from. Sophie would occupy this spacious modern suite while I was to rent the studio at rue de Boulets, paying a reasonable sum, also in cash, to her family.

Not long after we'd settled into our respective abodes, Sophie left a message on my answering machine that I had to play several times to fully digest. With a tone of growing excitement, she said that her ex-husband had died and that her children had finally tracked her down. She'd received a call from them that very morning. And she saved the best part for last. Soon, they were coming to visit.

The following month I joined her and her children at her flat; then we invited them to our local café.

I was immediately struck by how exceedingly American they behaved. There was no hint that either of them might have been engendered by a European parent. The oldest one, Laurent, who sported a thick crop of red hair, resembled his father in physical appearance as well as in temperament; for he exuded a certain calculating quality. He regarded me with eyes that seemed to take everything in and weight it carefully – like a prospector keenly observing the scales as he unloaded precious bullion. But judging from some of his remarks, he was also aware of his father's shortcomings and was careful not to intentionally model himself upon them.

The younger one, Genevieve, was endowed with Sophie's glowing flaxen hair and lively emerald eyes. She seemed to possess none of the older lad's craftiness and, instead, possessed an artless, childlike openness, reminiscent of Sophie herself. While Sophie bonded more strongly with the boy, I developed an affectionate rapport with his sister, probably because she reminded me so much of her mother.

Once we were seated at the café, Laurent remarked that he was interested in the tourism industry, and he was considering a career in Paris. But Genevieve, who was a junior in high school, still wasn't certain about what career to pursue. As I listened to them cheerfully describe their hopes and dreams, I glanced repeatedly at Sophie, who was beaming as I'd never seen her beam before.

But perhaps it's pointless to attempt to put words to all this; for what can anyone tell you about the heart of a woman whose children were lost and now, all of a sudden, were found?

Sipping my *noisette* (an espresso mixed with a dash of cream, lending it a hue of "noisette," or hazelnut), I silently recalled a conversation I'd had with Sophie at the very beginning of our affair:

After finishing work one day, she called and asked me to meet her at a restaurant in Les Halles. When I arrived, she was seated in a dimly lit corner, and she appeared to be crestfallen.

"I feel so consumed with self-hatred," she said, adding that the uncertainty of her children's whereabouts had caused her not to care enough about life. She lowered her gaze and stared at her plate with an anguished expression. "Mainly," she sighed, "I suffer from a sense of pointlessness."

Tenderly holding her hand, I replied: "Apathy is a form of suicide. One must avoid it, reject it. Instead of looking for life's meaning, you must accept the fact that life is the *reason* for life."

"But what exactly do you mean?"

"I mean that when all is said and done, nothing is more precious than life."

Although she patiently absorbed my words, she maintained a morose silence.

But now, as I watched her rejoice in this miraculous reunion, I was once again confronted by the limitation of words. Yes, life is the reason for life; but without a palpable connection to the lives of her children it had been nearly impossible for her to sustain herself.

* * *

In the spring of 1991 I had several dreams that portrayed the death of my mother. They arrived like portraits commissioned from a distant realm, composed in a language at once hermetic and universal.

The first was the most prophetic:

> I'm standing on the back porch in Brooklyn. My father says that, when I was born, mother spent the afternoon *planting flowers in the garden*.
>
> Then another dream, of mother dead. In the dream, I regret that I didn't spend more time with her – even doing simple things, such as sitting at the kitchen table and talking. Afterward, I'm left alone with Arthur. She passed away quickly (overnight).

This was exactly as it would come to pass. Ten years later, Bridget died of a stroke at night and was survived by my father. And this was the tragedy that made me return at last, to offer whatever support I could to Arthur during those difficult days ahead.

The flower – with its delicate, ephemeral nature – is a

well-known symbol of the soul. Thus, the dream lent me the precious insight that *Women plant souls in the garden of the world*.

The following month I dreamed that there was a cemetery adjacent to our house in Brooklyn, where the backyards would normally be:

> I peer through a picket fence at a row of tombstones, which are engraved with images of human figures and crumpled, dehydrated plants. The images are superimposed on one another. As I study them more carefully, I notice that the human figures are twisted and shriveled like the stems and leaves of the dried plants, and that they're crying out in *strange expressions of agony*. They depict something horrific, yet they remain strangely beautiful.

The most memorable dream occurred just three days before Bridget's actual demise. A rather peculiar dream, in that it was silent: nothing was verbally expressed. We were standing in the living room – the entire family, minus Bridget – positioned in a semicircle and gazing down at the floor. An antique porcelain vase had fallen off a mantelpiece, and it was shattered into so many pieces that it was irreparable. Our shock over the loss of this priceless heirloom left us speechless. We just stood there – my father, my brother, and I – staring at the glittering shards that were spread across the parquet floor – as if the vase had been reduced to its merest atoms.

I awoke with a sense of dread and immediately phoned my parents. When Arthur answered, as casually as possible I asked: "Is everything OK?" But he sounded fine – even happier than usual. It was a sunny day, he said, and they were seated outside, on the lawn.

"We're enjoying every bit of it!"

"I had a strange dream," I continued, "and I wanted to see if you were all right."

Bridget picked up the receiver and, sounding equally cheerful, asked, "So, how's life in Paris?" By now she'd begun to vicariously live through my various adventures abroad. Sometimes she'd even laugh and say: "You're living the good life; you're a free man in Paris!"

Relieved to hear her sweet, melodic voice, I began to tell her about a trip I'd scheduled for the following week, to visit a chateau in Vallauris where Picasso had painted his famous mural, *War and Peace*. (Little did I realize that it was a trip I would never take.) But then she exclaimed, "Oh, your brother's just arrived with his children; I'd better go!"

Bridget displayed such bountiful love for her grandchildren that it often left me feeling a bit jealous. They had largely replaced me as the object of her affection, especially since I lived so far away from the rest of the family. But whenever I'd return for a visit to the States, when I was about to take leave of her again she would begin to weep. I'd lean over to kiss her good-bye, seated in her lace-embroidered chair, and she'd shout, "Hurry – *go!*" for she didn't want me to see her burst into tears.

* * *

A couple of years after I returned to the States, Sophie called one day and left a long, rambling message on my machine. It was nothing less than a eulogy of thanks: of how much she'd appreciated my support, and how she cherished the time that we'd spent together. "It meant so much to be with someone who cared," she said, "especially during those difficult days."

Puzzling over why she might leave such a laudatory greeting, I immediately returned her call.

"I've been diagnosed with non-Hodgkin's lymphoma. I had a test last year. That's when they discovered that the lymphoma entered my spine. The doctor said that I have about ten years to live. I probably shouldn't say this, because I don't know for sure, but I did some research on my own, and I think that I have only half that time. ..."

What unnerved me almost as much as this awful news was the equanimity with which she faced it. Sophie's courage was truly astounding.

She added that although her daughter had recently returned to Kentucky, her son was thriving in Paris. Which was rather fortunate, because at least she had someone to look after her.

"Do you have any plans to travel to the States, to visit your daughter? I could buy you a plane ticket, and we could see each other."

"Oh, no; my health would never allow for me to fly. I wish I could come to visit you. But because of the way I am right now ... If I get better, I will. But if not, well ..."

Since it was approaching December, Sophie had decided to postpone the next round of chemo until after the holidays, so she could visit her mother.

"Perhaps you could stay with her while you receive the treatment."

"Yes. And I want to be with her when I die. But while I'm healthy, I want to remain here with my son. So that he can get to know me and spend some time with me. So that, when I won't be here anymore, at least he won't say, 'I never got to know my mother.'"

She would recommence her chemotherapy in January, she said, and she promised to call when it was finished. But the budding leaves of spring never arrived for Sophie. Midway through the treatment, she fell into a coma and perished.

The news of her passing came as a shock, and for the longest time I couldn't grasp it. Yet there it was, taunting me like a stiff grinning mask.

As I wept, I realized just how much she'd meant to me. Thus does the spirit of death bring life itself into such sharp, frightening clarity.

Through Sophie, I learned that it's far more important to be appreciated than to be understood. It was also thanks to Sophie that Lutèce – that great love of my life – revealed her kindest face. And for that, I would always be grateful.

Coda

Shortly after I repatriated at the end of the year 2000, I stopped by Arthur's house to collect some belongings. Seated in the living room, he was simultaneously watching TV and scanning his beloved *New York Times* – a daily ritual that he still followed with a religious devotion.

Gathering some dusty tomes and old manuscripts, I chanced upon a memento that I'd nearly forgotten about, stashed away in a closet.

In the early Seventies, Arthur had worked for the Department of Social Services in the newly opened "Twin Towers" or World Trade Center – then the tallest building in the world. One day he came home with a paper bag containing a pair of cement cylinders: cores that had been drilled from the Trade Center floors, he said, in order to install telephone cables.

They'd been removed from a brand new office in the South Tower, and their tops were still covered with beige linoleum. Five-inches high and four-inches wide, for many years they served as bookends at my desk in the Gravesend basement, where I'd launched my first half-baked literary efforts.

Removing the cores from the closet, I inspected them more carefully. The cement was reinforced with a mixture of dark pebbles. Along the smooth sides of the cylinders, the stones had been sliced in half, resulting in a surface dappled with flecks of gray. The building's engineers had informed Arthur that this ferroconcrete was estimated to last over a thousand years.

* * *

When I pack my bags and bid Arthur goodbye, he asks if I have everything. Then his gaze wanders to a book cradled under my arm: a tome about comparative religion, left over from my university days.

"Remember," he grins wickedly, "politics and religion are the two great poisons of the world."

On the train back to Manhattan, with the cores nestled on my lap, I gaze out a graffiti-splattered window. The skyline, packed with skyscrapers, is dominated by the looming hulks of the Towers. Their aluminum alloy facades shimmer with iridescence, catching the blazing the rays of sunset and glowing with a molten-red splendor.

But for me, the view represents nothing more than a bleak horizon. Where were the medieval cathedrals? Or the centuries-old museums? Or the well-worn cobblestones that never led me astray as I wandered beside the serpentine Seine?

At that moment my only remaining desire was to walk once again upon ancient streets … and to be laid to rest in a foreign soil.

For the homeland isn't only where we choose to live. It's also where we choose to die, surrendering every last souvenir until we come to the end of our wondrous tale.

Afterword by Christopher Sawyer-Lauçanno:

It's a *Wonder*ful Life

What is it ye would see? If aught of woe or wonder, cease your search.
– Horatio to Fortinbras, *Hamlet*

Merriam-Webster's defines "Wonder" as 1: a cause of astonishment or admiration; 2: the quality of exciting amazed admiration; 3a: rapt attention or astonishment at something awesomely mysterious or new to one's experience; 3b: a feeling of doubt or uncertainty. All of these definitions come into play both for the author and for the reader in Rob Couteau's new book.

What Couteau has created is far more than a coming-of-age chronicle "with all the David Copperfield kind of crap." Like the best authors who have chosen to write about becoming their own person, Couteau focuses his sharp eye on the world that formed his being. From the first pages we get a sense of who the author is and what events – from the sublime to the difficult to the ludicrous – formed his sense of identity. This is an account of how consciousness is acquired, how ideas become forces, how the individual reacts and responds to those forces bearing down on his very being.

This is not to suggest that Couteau has written a philosophy tome. While philosophical musings do crop up with regularity, this book is also a rollicking ride through Brooklyn in the 60s to Venezuela in the 80s, Paris in the 90s and back to the States. The book is not episodic in the conventional sense of one anecdote or event following another. Couteau is not afraid to flash forward to put the past in perspective, to flash back from the writer he is now to the young artist struggling to make sense of his own time and place in what was often a chaotic milieu. Purposeful digression serves as a talismanic touchstone which adds to and enriches his very compelling and strong narrative.

Unlike many memoirs, Couteau frames scenes so that the reader can see what the young author was looking at and experiencing rather than being told explicitly what was happening for him at any given time. In other words, Couteau shows us his life, his friends, his complex family, his intimate relationships, his doubts and misgivings, his certainties and uncertainties, his adventures – large and small – his experimentations with art, writing, and sex. Along the way he reflects on historical events that occurred often before he was born, on writers and writing, on painters and painting.

None of these details are gratuitous. Rather, what Couteau is striving to do, and admirably succeeding at doing, is to remind us that our lives do not exist in a vacuum. We are a part of our time and time is part of us. What Couteau demonstrates so ably is that being engaged in the life of one's own time – whether journeying across the ocean or around our room, playing pranks, making love, reading books, painting canvases, having some good laughs – all help determine who we are. *Being* is complex, as Couteau continually reminds us.

This is a rich book. It is also a long book, but it needs to be. Couteau's brilliant narrative style of limning events from the inside out, of working assiduously to understand the frame that holds it all together and helping us see it, too, could not and certainly would not work in a short book. Vignettes are connected to other vignettes; thought to practice; reflection to enlightenment. For all of the "action," there are equal measures of musing on what and why those actions happened. The effect is rather kaleidoscopic, or perhaps more aptly Picassoesque, in that each segment interconnects to both the inner and outer realities he is attempting to encompass.

His mission is not so unlike that of Proust who word-painted an entire panorama of his life that included in-depth examinations of his relationships to acquaintances, family, and above all to passing time. Genet, and that other Brooklyn boy, Henry Miller, also come to mind, for Couteau is always willing to engage us, in remarkably beautiful prose, in his more graphic corporeal encounters. Above all, this book is a "song of himself." Like Whitman, Couteau is attempting to embrace the full spectrum of what constitutes the human comedy while also embracing the person he is and how that individual is a contributor to this vast human comedy. All the while he is unfolding a belief system that he develops to steer his course on life's way.

What Whitman wrote in his Preface to the 1855 edition of *Leaves of Grass* sums up quite well the immensity of living that Couteau has absorbed into his consciousness and very being: "This is what you shall do; Love the earth and sun and the animals, despise riches, give alms to everyone that asks, stand up for the stupid and crazy, devote your income and labor to others, hate tyrants, argue not concerning God, have patience and indulgence toward the people, take off your hat to nothing known or unknown or to any man or number of men, go freely with powerful uneducated persons and with the young and with the mothers of families, read these leaves in the open air every season of every year of your life, reexamine all you have been told at school or church or in any book, dismiss whatever insults your own soul, and your very flesh shall be a great poem and have the richest fluency not only in its words but in the silent lines of its lips and face and between the lashes of your eyes and in every motion and joint of your body."

A former creative-writing teacher at MIT, Christopher Sawyer-Lauçanno is the author of *The Continual Pilgrimage: American Writers in Paris*, *E. E. Cummings*, and *An Invisible Spectator, A Biography of Paul Bowles*.

www.ingramcontent.com/pod-product-compliance
Lightning Source LLC
Chambersburg PA
CBHW051307190726
48290CB00001B/47